The Women of Donnybrooke:
Jane Promised Not to Tell

Avrie Kaufman

All rights reserved under International and Pan-American Copyright Conventions. No part of this book may be reproduced in any form or by any electronic or mechanical means, including information storage and retrieval systems, without permission in writing from the author.

This book is a work of fiction. Names, characters, places and incidents either are the product of the author's imagination or are used fictionally. Any resemblance to actual persons, living or dead, events or locales is entirely coincidental.

Book cover photography copyright © 2013 Avrie Kaufman

Copyright © 2013 Avrie Kaufman
All rights reserved.
ISBN-10: 148951208x
ISBN-13: 9781489512086
F.L.O. Publications

To My Children:
Brandon, My Anchor to Reality, My Saving Grace
And Jaydaline, My Miracle Child, My Sounding Board.
To My Family and to My Friends
For their Unconditional Love.

Dedicated In Loving Memory of
My Parents, Stanley and Ruth Kaufman,
My Sister, Patricia Maluskie, My Friend, John MacNeill,
My Godmother, Elizabeth "Betty" Gabert,
And My Grandson, Darien Kaufman,
Whom I Miss Every Moment that I Breathe.

ACKNOWLEDGEMENTS

I want to take a moment and thank my sister, Patricia Maluskie, and my friend, John MacNeill. Although they are not here to read the finished version of my novel, I felt their presence around me as I toiled over my manuscript. Thank you, Patricia, for your constant encouragement, for believing in my ability to tell a story and for surviving through so many of our reckless, youthful escapades while being constantly by my side. Thank you, John, for being strong enough and for caring enough to stay my friend after our romantic relationship ended. I still see your smiling, surprised expression after reading the first draft of my novel and hear your words, "This is really good!" That moment kept me going through times of writer's block and self-doubt.

Thank you, Mom, for your suggestions and for verbally berating my grade seven teacher who had informed my classmates that I had written the worst speech she'd ever read. Mom, you turned my tears into the stubborn determination that helped me to win prizes the following year.

Thank you to my godmother, Elizabeth "Betty" Gabert, who told me, years ago, that I should write about my life. Although this story is fiction, there are moments of truth throughout. Thank you, as well, to my niece, Lisa, for your enthusiasm and for your encouragement. If you could write all of my reviews, I'd be a very happy person. Thank you to my cousin, Donna, my little sister, who was the best playmate a child could have unless we were arguing over who got to play with the Barbies. You have been a wonderful and true friend over the span of years.

I want to acknowledge the contributions of my daughter, Jaydaline, who was my constant sounding board, who was my technical, computer whiz when I drowning in the midst of coding compatibility issues and who is a gifted writer in her own right. You are an inspiration to me always, and some of my favourite elements of this story are ones that we worked through together. For better or for worse, the acorn didn't fall far from the nut. Love you to the moon and beyond.

I also want to thank my friend and soul-sister, Adrienne Jones McLeod, for gently goading me to start writing again after

Patricia died. I was safe in my shell of sorrow, but you were right. I couldn't stay there forever. Thank you as well, for all of the hours that you spent proofreading my work, for being honest enough to point out any inconsistencies and for offering objective suggestions.

A special thanks, as well, to Heather Renshaw who graciously agreed to do the final review of my manuscript.

I seriously could not have done this without all of you.

This poem mulled around in my mind for two years after my sister's death. I knew what I wanted to write, but I wasn't quite sure how to make it work until the concept finally came together one evening while I was watching the movie, *Thick as Thieves*. Weird that but true.

For my sister, Patricia Ruth Kaufman-Maluskie. Born: March 12, 1954 Deceased: May 16, 2007.

Sisters Before Sisters Again

The cave, protective fortress, dark, dank, shadowy,
A small fire crackling,
Smoke rising, searching for escape.

Bearskin shrouds, encompassing,
Prepared by tribal hands,
Staving off winter's biting cold
From gnawing through youthful flesh.

Sisters huddling.

The younger watching embers dying,
Mesmerized, eyelids drooping, snuggling
Closer to her sister's side, safe and warm.

The elder lovingly watching, waiting for
The child's eyes to flutter a final time,
Sleep prevailing, another day done.

Sisters before. Sisters again.

White-headed daisies, bobbing in unison,
Inspired by a wafting breeze and
Basking under the late spring sun.

Clouds of butterflies, flittering,
Disturbed from floral perches

By long skirts covering petticoats,
Schoolbooks swinging through the air.

Sisters swooshing.

The younger, lost in the clouds, dreaming
The purity into her soul, lags behind.
Spying a purple hairstreak and, with a
Whoop of delight, giving chase.

The elder scolding ruefully, reminding
Her adolescent sibling of chores waiting.
They need to get home.

Sisters before. Sisters again.

The bar, well-oiled, towels hanging, glasses
Sliding, customers leaning, whiskey vanishing.
Dry summer heat, parched throats, parched souls.

Tickets tallying hopeful suitors
Roused by gartered calves and creamy shoulders,
Never pondering hidden Derringers.
Doves cooing in the night.

Sisters laughing.

The younger singing, her voice enchanting,
Warily watching her sister's partner,
Unconsciously readying for any trouble that may ensue.

The elder flirting, her dance card filling,
Winking at familiar features assuring,
Sing on my lovely sparrow. Do not worry, all is well.

Sisters Before. Sisters Again.

The teapot loudly whistling over children's
Constant arguing, television programs changing,
Fall lineup breaking boredom, e-mails left unread.

Tears softly falling, serotonin levels plummeting,
Heart painfully aching over another lover gone.
Cigarettes burning, deeply inhaling.
Tissue box emptying, eyes swollen and red.

Sisters sharing.

The younger whispering words of comfort,
"We'll grow old together", and
Questions the wisdom of mixing rye and Paroxetine.

The elder laughing despite her loss,
Picturing them venerable in an old farmhouse,
A hundred cats weaving around their feet.

Sisters Before. We'll be sisters again.

March 19, 2009

And now on with the story…..

FREEDOM BOUND

We, who are freedom bound,
Must pay the price of
Broken hearts and loneliness.

We, who have set our sights high,
Must now lower our aim.

And, I, my dear friend,
Shall survive because
You and I are survivors.

We may take our falls
And grind our teeth
In disillusionment;
But, we are determined
In our empirical pursuit
Of idealistic happiness.

Our mere existence is a triumph
To the abandoned world
Of the mortally insane.

Life in 3-D

THE END

CHAPTER ONE

She had been set up by two men in her life--both were named Nick, (she hated that name) and both had gotten her pregnant. Her son had been the result of the first incident. It had taken three months and two doctors to determine what was wrong with her the second time; the result being a rather nasty, sexually transmitted infection called Trichomonas (the male often does not exhibit any symptoms, but it can cause exceeding discomfort to any unfortunate female) and a miscarriage that had left her emotionally and physically exhausted.

God, how men frustrated her. She had not been looking for any kind of relationship either time and yet fate, or some cruel coincidence, had brought them together. She preferred to believe in fate. Everything happened for a reason, whatever that was; and we, as mere mortals, were not supposed to know why but learn from the experience. It did not matter how cruel the lesson was, how much we felt that it was undeserved to begin with, or how much we believed that we could have existed quite nicely for the rest of our lives without the first-hand knowledge. We were here to learn. Case closed.

Her name was Jane, a simple, easy-to-remember name that she abhorred for those very reasons. Names had always intrigued her. By the time she was twelve, she had already named her would-be, future children--three girls and three boys, with three names each. Her favourite was Jasmine Josephine Julie-Anne.

As she grew older, she was determined to change her own name to something more exotic like Alexia Covell or Eden Reed. Jane had never actually gone through with her plan, but she did manage to annoy her parents for several years with the possibility of one day showing up on their doorstep with the announcement that their youngest daughter's name was now Devina and would they please refer to her as such from now on.

The thought made her laugh now, but back then she had been quite serious about changing her name, bearing six children and becoming a world-famous psychologist, all at the same time. At that age, the sky was the limit.

She was going to own a monstrous, two-storey, red-brick

house complete with six large, airy bedrooms, a picturesque playroom full of toys all tidily lined up on painted, wooden shelves, a distinguished den walled by leather-bound reference books and all of the other comforts that a six-digit income could provide. Money was an amorphous commodity. The estate would be situated in the country and surrounded by tall, stately oak trees and rolling hills, away from the hustle and bustle of urban or big city life where you did not know your neighbour, did not care to know your neighbour and were always running somewhere or doing something. The beehive city routine made her dizzy. Hers was to be an altruistic existence, totally dedicated towards raising her abundant family and helping others less fortunate than herself.

Of course, she would have the world's greatest nanny to assist with the children and a gorgeous, perfect husband who also earned a six-digit income to match her own. Jane spent numerous, lazy hours fantasizing about the day when she could help reconstruct her patients' lives so that they could solve all of their varied emotional problems and lead normal, fulfilling existences of their own. Ah yes, it was too bad that reality was not that simple. She had begun her life with such well-meaning and honourable intentions.

By grade ten, it had become painfully apparent that her above-average aptitude in arts and English was not transferrable to advanced mathematics which was also a prerequisite for a degree in Psychology. Leaving her daydreams behind, Jane had decided to follow her strengths and see where she landed.

Jane glanced casually out of the tinted side-window of her burgundy, packed-to-the brim, Toyota Matrix as it progressed smoothly along the highway, all six cylinders purring. She peered down at the speedometer and noted, with a sigh of border-line irritation, an even-paced ninety kilometers per hour. It was going to be an extremely long trip at this speed.

Her very first car had been a 1972 Gremlin, lovingly dubbed "The Poof" by a close friend. When she had enquired as to the rationale behind the name, her friend had merely laughed and replied, "You get in and, Poof, you're gone!" Jane had purchased the deteriorating, vintage vehicle from her uncle and, with the aid of an older cousin, had spent the majority of one summer's earnings reconstructing the body and replacing whatever needed to be replaced (seemed like half of the car at the time) to pass certification.

With an enormous amount of tender loving care, the unkempt automobile had metamorphosed from a body-filler brown to burgundy, complete with a silver sports stripe. The interior's torn vinyl was hidden by imitation sheepskin seat covers. The defunct radio was succeeded by a stereo system with enough volume to completely annihilate any extraneous sounds. Over-sized, Rally Sports had replaced the splitting tires. Jane liked the idea of the sport tires even if they did conjure the occasional odd look or odd comment by those who noticed.

During the two years that she had driven the car, the vehicle had consistently supported her cousin's garage and had been a major strain on her already over-taxed budget; but, all in all, the Gremlin had been a good friend. Jane would rev the little automobile up to one hundred and fifty kilometers per hour and reach her parents' farm, a usual three-and-a-half hour drive, in two hours flat.

Nine points later, Jane had slowed down, basically because she could neither afford to purchase another car nor to lose her license. Besides which, cops weren't generally all that gullible anyway. One rather disgruntled, highway patrolman had pulled her over asking if she was aware of exactly at what speed she was travelling. Jane had only smiled sheepishly and stuttered an off-handed excuse about the speedometer not working properly due to the over-sized tires (which she later discovered were illegal to have on her car in the first place) and gave an I'm only a female and don't really understand why shrug. The constable just shook his head impatiently and marked the ticket down to one hundred and ten kilometers per hour, grumbling that no one in his or her right mind would ever believe him that the Gremlin could travel the actual speed that he had clocked. I think you need to re-calibrate your gun there, Fred. Hee, hee, ho, ho.

When Jane's luck eventually did run out (one ticket too many), she was faced with the rather embarrassing situation of explaining to a large, matronly woman at the License Bureau why this nice lady should not take her license away for a while just to emphasize why the nice constables handed out tickets in the first place. Jane had practiced her speech to flawless perfection and had managed to slip through, but she never forgot how close she had been to two-footed transportation.

    She had almost cried the day The Poof had been sold to a collector, feeling as if she was abandoning a well-known companion, betraying her best friend. To her, the little automobile cried out like a small child, twice abandoned, Don't leave me here! Don't you love me anymore?

    Sometimes, Jane felt almost certain that her fate had really been to become a race car driver, and she had just missed the appropriate turn in life. She smiled dreamily, mentally visualizing herself in a cart, red and white trimmed with gold. Very classy. The critics would laugh, of course. Who had ever heard of a little country girl who lived a half-kilometre from nowhere competing against top-name drivers?

    The day was scorching, thirty-two degrees Celcius in the shade, heat waves rippling up from the stark, black pavement. The grounds and bleachers were packed to capacity with a hundred and thirty thousand sweaty fans, some of whom had a month's hard-earned wages bet on their favourite car, some of whom had travelled hundreds of kilometers just to be there for this event.

    Jane tensed her aching muscles as the pacer car led the way. Her starting position was too far back, fourteen on the grid. Damned engine trouble during the qualifying rounds. Work on it, Jack! Sure thing, Jane.

    Jack, the Chief Mechanic, was tall, angular, in his early fifties and turning gray. There were days when he honestly believed that his hair would turn completely white before Jane had finished the race; but, he would look in the mirror afterwards and note, with astonishment, that he still looked the same, give or take the deepening furrows of worry lines.

    He loved Jane like a daughter and often wondered why she wasn't married to a nice chap, bouncing babies on her knee, like his own daughter. But then, Jane wasn't like his daughter. Anything but. He would watch Jane and, if he looked carefully enough, he could sometimes glimpse a restlessness under her well-constructed facade as if she was almost certain that, at any given moment, someone or something, would jump out from within the shadows to grab her and drag her, screaming all of the way, down into the black lagoon from where she would never be seen or heard from again.

Yup, she was a moody one all right. Sometimes, she would sit on a trolley by her car for hours just thinking about god-knows-what, and other times no one would see her for a day or so until she knew that her presence was necessary. She would come back smiling then, all hyped up to run a good race, to beat all odds.

Some of the other mechanics would make jokes about Jane finding herself a good piece of tail placating her feminine wiles, but Jack wasn't sure. There were even rumours about her playing tag with one of the other drivers maybe even her team-mate-- but nothing she would ever admit to. She was a difficult one to piece together, and she never talked about where she had been.

Jack had asked her once, during one of her gloomy days, what was troubling her? She had looked up at him, her eyes distant as if her soul was galaxies away, as she sat drinking black coffee while perched on a metal stool in the auto shop.

"Jack," she began, her jade green eyes still clouded over, "do you think Gilles Villeneuve misses racing?"

Jack had answered her off-handedly knowing that Gilles was her all-time idol, saying that he probably won all of the car races in heaven; but, he had resisted any temptation to ask for her inner thoughts since then. There was a bigger part of him that was afraid to hear the answer.

Jane's breath felt hot inside of her close-fitting, white and red (trimmed with gold) helmet. There was definitely no room for claustrophobia in this business. The helmet was snug and so was the chassis which had been built to fit her body. The compartment was so small that she had to attach the steering wheel after wriggling her way in. Once inside, she became a part of the car, the brain center that sent signals back and forth from the central nervous system to the peripheral extremities. If the car laughed, she laughed. If the car cried, she cried. If the car felt pain, she felt pain. An hour in the Memorial Chapel before the race had done little to ease the butterflies in her stomach. Steady. Steady. Steady.

Jane had grown up spending hot, dusty, summer Sunday afternoons watching two of her older, male cousins race stock cars. When she was in her late teens, she had convinced a local auto body shop to sponsor a car of her own. Jane was definitely good, cat-like reflexes and extraordinary spatial capabilities getting her out of tough spots and tight squeezes. From Powder Puff races to main events, she had won the hearts of the fans and of the media.

Ambitious, Jane wasn't satisfied with the local, back-woods circuit. Stock cars just were not fast enough. When she decided to try her luck with Go-carts at Mosport, she instinctively knew that she had found her niche in life. The progression from Go-carts to Indy Lights had been a major breakthrough. Again, she had become a media sweetheart, this time on a much larger scale. They called her a Contender, a Force to be Reckoned with, a Natural Born Thriller. And, trying not to let her ego become too large, Jane felt confident that it would only be a couple of years before she headlined the male-dominated cart races.

The Honda Indy, Toronto's claim to auto fame, was her dream. She had studied the course meticulously, and watched years' worth of videos, trying to pick out the critical errors that eliminated the pros. It would take a studious personality, the experience of a pro and a lot of just plain guts to beat Michael Andretti's record, but she was young and time was on her side.

And now, she was here with one of the best pit crews that money could buy and a service crew worthy of their combined weight in gold. More than once that season, the boys had saved her ass when she had miscalculated the necessary speed for a turn. Thankfully, she was a fast learner and gained enough points to finally be taken seriously. In fact, the only request that she could not get anyone to fulfill was that for an indwelling catheter to be inserted just before the race to empty into a well-hidden leg bag. For some unknown reason, she was the only one who thought this was a scathingly brilliant idea. The guys suggested she wear an adult brief instead.

Turn Three was her worst nightmare (besides Tracy riding her ass) a quick turn to the right with no slope to round on. Too often, she had witnessed experienced drivers lock wheels and pile into the tire wall. Too often, she had witnessed crashes and spinouts that caused major damage to the vehicle and left the driver cursing and swearing his or her way back to the pits. (Yup, a catheter would come in really handy at those moments… so much better than pissing into a brief…)

Just as Turn Three was her worst fear, Thunder Alley was her heaven. In the straight- a- way, she could top out at three hundred and sixty-eight kilometers an hour. That was officially more than twice as fast as the Poof on her best days. If only the cop could see her now. Yes, Officer, I do know how fast I was driving. Yes, Officer, the speedometer works quite well with over-sized sports tires. If you want to come back to the Paddock area later, I'm sure that we can arrange a tour.

The green flag lowered abruptly, the pacer car veering out of the way. Jane caught her breath and pressed harder on the accelerator, feeling certain, feeling good.

A powder-blue convertible, packed full of laughing teenagers suddenly cut in front of the Toyota causing Jane to automatically jam on her brakes and curse at the lousy drivers on the Q.E.W. Aw yes, the Q.E.W. Fucking reality. Her fans would have to get by without her for the time being.

Jane casually reached down, tuning her FM radio into a nearby rock station. Unlike her mother, who totally refused to listen to music of any kind while driving, claiming that she could not concentrate with the added noise, the music relaxed Jane, unknotted her brow and helped to pass away the tedious hours.

Poor Mom, Jane thought. She knew that her parents would never understand. How could they? They had been raised to accept their responsibilities and live by them. You just did not pick up and run away from home. It just was not done, no matter how unhappy you were or how confined and totally frustrated you felt. Life was like that. No one ever got everything he or she wanted. We were not meant to. But you had to cope, day by day, with what needed to be done, with reality. Get married, have children, and wish for the rest of your life that your soulmate looked like Charlie Hunnam, Garrett Hedlund, Ryan Gosling, Bradley Cooper, or Gerard Butler instead of a bad imitation of Oscar Madison. Watch your favourite daytime soaps, mentally patting yourself on the back that, at least in your small town, there had not been a murder in twenty years. The worst you could come up with was the time the Amison twins both became pregnant by that no-account Hessler boy, and you'll be damned if he didn't refuse to marry either one of them.

Dye your hair blonde one year and green the next, but don't smoke cigars in public or light up a cigarette while walking down the street. Have another baby and make good and sure that you have a proper, three-course meal waiting for your husband when he comes home from work, then smile and wave good-bye as he leaves to go have a few beers with the boys, never once dreaming that you are about to murder the four screaming, snot-nosed brats whom he fathered, burn down the three-bedroom house that desperately needs renovating and drive that thing that he lovingly insists is a car into the nearest river, all the while with a large, lopsided grin on your face because you have just swallowed the largest quantity of benzodiazepine that you could lay your pudgy, dishpan hands on.

Well, at least her friend, Gertie, had wished her good luck; but then, Jane felt positive that she and Gertie had originally been one spirit that had somehow miraculously been split in half to make two people. They were just so much alike.

The two had met after Jane had graduated from high school and, eager to taste independence, had moved to a not-so-nearby, small city. Jane had landed a job as a telephone marketer, selling coupon booklets for a charity organization. Not much, but a beginning and she'd been good at it. Many people declined, but if a man answered the other end, she would convince him to buy even if he neither wanted nor needed the booklet.

Gertie had worked for the marketing company as well. They had been introduced by a mutual acquaintance and, although the other girl was long gone, Gertie and Jane had become soul-friends.

Jane had studied Gertie fondly once while getting primped for an evening out and said, "Stick with me and I promise that you'll never have a boring time."

She had kept her word. They had never actually gone out looking for trouble. Trouble found them.

CHAPTER TWO

"Honey, let's have a baby." Jane's voice lilted as she quietly crept up behind her husband who was reclining comfortably in his all-time favourite (THIS IS MY CHAIR), black leather Barcalounger, while glancing through the local newspaper and drinking white rum and Coke from a tall, powder-blue Tupperware tumbler that had been a bridal shower present.

"Anything you want, Sweetheart," Elliot agreed nonchalantly, not turning around. He could mentally envision his wife of three years wearing her thread-worn, gray jogging pants and an old, seen-better-days-but-refuse-to-throw-out sweatshirt, having just completed her daily thirty-minute workout.

After the couple had purchased the two-and-a-half storey, red-bricked bungalow, Jane had insisted on setting up a good portion of the cemented basement for exercising—free weights, floor mats, benches, a rowing machine, a treadmill, a weight machine, a recumbent bike, a stepmaster, plus a stereo for mood music. Her favourite inspirational piece was the theme from *Rocky*. She said that it wasn't just the rhythm of the music, but the You can Do it! theme that inspired her. Personally, he very rarely ventured into his wife's domain for the purpose of exercising. That was Jane's thing, not his. He was way too exhausted after managing the store all day to be bothered walking five extra kilometers on the treadmill or bicycling to nowhere. Besides, Jane was always teasing him that she liked her men to be a bit on the heavy side so she had something to snuggle up to during the long, cold, Canadian winter nights. Regardless of his lack of extra regulated exercise, he had inadvertently lost twenty-five pounds since their marriage just by going from his mother's 2,000-calorie-per-meal, grease laden, home cooking to Jane's version.

Sure, at 195 pounds, he did feel better, but it had been rough going. Jane absolutely refused to bake anything more fattening than peanut butter cookies and muffins; both made with a sugar substitute. Cakes were only for birthdays, and pies and donut-shop pastries were strictly prohibited from entering the front door. Red meat was taboo. Jane ate nothing hoofed.

She could, occasionally, be persuaded to cook a roast of beef if he bought one. The roast would be perfect, just the way he liked it--rare and loaded with onions. Then they would all sit down in the dining room for the evening meal. Jane would watch him eat, not saying a word, except to scold Brydon for playing with his mashed potatoes. Her solemn disposition always unnerved Elliot. Quiet Jane was an oxymoron at best. Eventually, he had given in and almost grew to like Jane's infamous tofu and spinach casserole. Emphasis heavily on the *almost*. The task of masticating would have been much easier if the dark green glop on his plate had not reminded him of the cattle dung found in the back pasture of Jane's parents' farm after the beasts had wandered into a patch of fresh clover.

    Once in a while for lunch, Elliot would saunter off to a nearby bar and grill called, "The Pig Pen". (The Pig Pen was located four doors down from his store, two doors down from "Martha's Sit and Sip", where a person could curl up with a good book, a raisin scone and a cappuccino while taking a break from reality, and right beside "Tony's Stop and Gawk" gift boutique.) The owner was a retired cop who was rather grizzled looking in a "I may be getting older but don't think you can fuck with me" kind of way and whose amazing sense of humour drew a loyal patronage that consisted of most of the area's local police force from the nearby city cops to the marauding O.P.P.s. Rumour had it that the bar was especially popular after hours when the men and women desperately needed some down time to debrief and let go of the day's events before heading home to spouses or to children, who could not truly understand the daily stress they faced, or before heading home to lonely apartments or to ramble around houses where they were met only by silence and TV dinners. Local rumour also claimed that any police officer who arrived in uniform ate and drank for half-price.

    When the mood demanded, Elliot would order a rare T-bone steak, a large, baked potato with extra sour cream and hot apple pie a la mode for dessert. The pretty young waitress would smile as he always ordered the same thing while most of her luncheon crowd preferred a hamburger and fries or the "Soup de jour après hier" and a tossed salad. After the meal, Elliot would feel so guilty that he would skip lunch completely the next day, dreading Jane's

Friday morning weigh-ins, dreading the appearance of her furrowed brow as she waited for the bathroom scale's digital readout--guaranteed one hundred percent accurate up to three hundred and fifty pounds.

    Every Friday morning was the same. After his shower, Jane would smile and gesture for him to weigh himself. He would step on and instinctively hold his breath, feeling like a small child who was waiting to be reprimanded for the crime of insolence. He had spent three years complying, not knowing exactly why except that for some reason Jane had taken on the responsibility for his health and it was easier to get on the god damned scale than to argue with his trim (never call her thin or willowy), five foot seven, hundred and twenty-five pound wife.

    Elliot had to admit that there were good reasons behind Jane's attitude concerning their diet, but he definitely did not have to like it. He had been suffering from liver and kidney problems off and on for two years before their marriage, and with his blood pressure also being a bit too high, for safety's sake, Jane had decided to take control. She claimed that a proper diet, vitamins, the proper herbal supplements and exercise could cure almost any ailment giving the example that she had been in and out of the hospital since childhood with gastric ulcers and other various stomach and bowel maladies. After five years of completely shirking red meat, her ulcers were completely healed. And yet, she still smoked a pack of those stupid cigarettes a day, which Elliot could not fathom. It was an absolute dichotomy. She would just smile her smug little smile and casually comment, "Elliot, I have given up everything else. In a couple of years, I'll give up smoking too."

    "I want to have your baby, Elly," Jane's voice cooed softly.

    Elliot hated being called Elly and had informed his wife of that fact on at least a dozen occasions. The last guy who had called him Elly was in high school and had suffered a severely broken nose and a couple of cracked ribs for his articulations. Elliot would never dream of hitting Jane, but...He began to turn his head to, once again, remind her, but quickly discovered that he could not move. "Jane?" he whimpered hoarsely. What the fuck was going on? He knew he was paralyzed but why?

Her voice soothed sardonically, "Elly.... Sweetheart..." Elliot could hear her move closer behind him, her running shoes scuffing along on the polished, hardwood floor.

"Jane, I don't understand what's wrong with me, but I can't seem to move. I was fine a moment ago...what the fuck?!" The terror was unmistakable now, panic settling in. Something was restraining every ounce of his frantic body, something cold and unyielding, like the piercing talons of a screeching hawk enclosed unmercifully around its tortured prey, prey that screams in vain for freedom.

Her soft voice lulled, "I know, Elly, Darling, I know..."

Her warm, minty breath caressed his ear. He watched as she slowly moved into his line of vision, a brilliant smile playing on her full, red lips, her sensitive eyes exuding genuine affection. "Jane," Elliot's voice edged on hysteria, "what the hell's wrong with me?" Panic rose from the bowels of his being spewing bitter bile. As hard as he tried, he could not will one digit, one small toe, one strained muscle to respond to his conscious commands. His right hand remained clutching the tumbler; his left hand framed the newsprint headline, "Jays Win Five in a Row!" Elliott began to tremble like an unsheltered leaf about to weather a harsh, summer storm.

"Nothing, Love. It's okay. Sssh now," Jane consoled. She drew a long, slender finger to her dry lips to hush him. Her long, pointed fingernails were painted cranberry red, a startling colour she rarely wore. Whore-Red her sister called it. "Everything will be fine. You'll see." She soothed as if he was a small child wakening from a frightening nightmare. "Just relax, Darling," she instructed, her calmness placating his shattered awareness. "Trust me. Everything will be just fine."

Elliot watched, still petrified, as she knelt down before him and unzipped his fly. He almost smiled as she worked his navy-blue work pants and smiley face boxer shorts down around his hips, exposing him to the cool, living room air. An erection. At least something still worked.

Jane looked up at him from her kneeling position, grinning. Her teeth sparkled in their surreal whiteness. "I just want to have your baby, Honey, Elly. To do that, I need your sperm. Don't I?" Her exaggerated grin distorted, as if he was looking at her image in a fun-house mirror.

Opening his mouth to speak, only a gasp escaped. From somewhere, Jane had produced their sharpest butcher knife--a large, heavy knife that she generally hated to wash for fear of cutting herself. The blade gleamed brutally. My sperm, he thought. "Oh god, Jane, no. Please, Jane...NO!" He screamed in vain as the sharp utensil severed its target.

Elliot's eyes sprang wide open as he pulled himself forcibly back to reality. He awoke in a sitting position, beads of perspiration trickling down his forehead. "SHIT!" he swore as he wiped the sweat away with the back of his thick hand. He consciously relaxed his tense muscles, lying back down on the bed, waiting for the waves of panic to subside. "Shit," he repeated aimlessly to no one.

He glanced beside him, half expecting to see Jane curled up in a fetal position on her left side. She either slept on her stomach or facing away from him. Elliot had often wondered at her unwillingness to snuggle; but, like everything else about his wife, he had grown accustomed to the lack of physical closeness. Jane was not there.

Their cream-coloured clock-radio that adorned the natural pine nightstand read only eight a.m. Sunday morning. "Probably out on an all-nighter," he groaned to himself. But then, she had said something about going to visit a friend for the weekend.

Elliot had left on Friday evening to play softball in a weekend tournament and, since his team had lost out early, had decided to come home. The house had been empty--no note, no Brydon, no Jane. Just silence and the stupid cat. Elliot hated cats and Barclay knew it. Every time he went past Jane's twenty-pound, orange Tom, the cat would arch its back and hiss ominously. And yet, when Jane and Brydon were around, the animal was the all-time perfectly mannered pet. He would purr and clean himself, quite content. Doctor Jekyll and Mr. Hyde that cat, only no one would believe him.

Swinging his tired legs out of the sweat-soaked bed, Elliot pulled himself back into a sitting position. He slowly rubbed his tanned hands over his stubbly face, working the sleep out of his bloodshot eyes. A belch began working its way up through his irritated system. One too many beers yesterday--drowning the defeat, beating the heat, whatever.

    Elliot shook off a sudden impulse to check below to see if all of his parts were still there and in working order. Still, the dream had been so damned realistic. Jane held firm in her belief that there were hidden meanings in dreams. Elliot had passed the conviction off as yet another one of his wife's mysterious quirks; but, he could not remember ever having a dream that was so vivid. So intense. So real. So sickening. Did Jane really want to have another baby? She did say once, when Brydon was tiny, that she wanted a big family.

    They were not married then. In fact, they were barely on speaking terms. One hot, muggy Monday afternoon, he had decided to hang out at the local garage for the lack of anything more interesting to do with his vacation time. Jane traipsed in, accompanied by her young niece and nephew and a small bundle of Brydon. After spending a fun-filled afternoon at a nearby swimming hole, the group was in search of cold refreshments. The garage's original owner, Jane's uncle, had carried snacks just for the local youngsters and the tradition had been maintained thereafter. At first, Jane had looked startled, not expecting to see him there; but, she had soon regained her usual composure. She purchased ice cream bars and cream soda for the two older children and a pack of cigarettes for herself.

    Elliot had some difficulty mentally adding up all of the various prices, mentally damning the present owner, Jane's cousin, for not having an electronic cash register, and ended up writing the prices down on a note pad, embarrassed as he carried the two and added five. Jane had waited patiently, her eyes gleaming mischievously, and casually commented that she had always wanted a large family. Her niece had tugged at her arm reminding Jane that she only had Brydon. Jane, her smile never fading, said yes, but she was paying for a large family. Wasn't she?

    Elliot grinned to himself, thinking of how she looked similar to a wet cat that day--her long, wet, sandy-blonde hair slicked back harshly exposing a small, well-shaped face and emphasizing her high cheekbones and jade green eyes. She was pretty, even wet, and he supposed that had always been one of her problems. Regardless, back then, all he thought of was that she could be a royal bitch when she wanted to be. The part that irritated him most was that she knew it and enjoyed playing the part, as if she could sense how she could torment him even when she was being outwardly pleasant.

    Rising slowly from the warm bed, Elliot stretched out his post-softball aches and pains and strolled towards the upstairs washroom. He concluded that he would talk to Jane again about having more children--that was, whenever she returned from wherever she was presently hiding. The thought actually appealed to him. With another baby, maybe Jane would settle down a bit more instead of always seeming so restless...a restless spirit looking for a place to land.

    As Elliot strolled down the cream-coloured hallway, he decided to double-check Brydon's room to make sure that the six-year-old was not snuggled up in the bottom bunk of his bed, covers pulled tightly around him. Opening the wooden door, Elliot surveyed the usual collection of paraphernalia. There must have been twenty stuffed animals of all shapes and sizes from the Cookie Monster to teddy bears scattered amongst toy trucks, educational toys, picture books and whatever else Jane or their families had purchased for the child. Jane was raising Brydon to be "well-rounded", which meant anything from a small computer system, plastic dolls and playhouse dishes, to Tonka bulldozers, Lego sets, a Fisher Price farm set and video games could be discovered amongst the menagerie of his child's world. It was seriously time to sort through Brydon's belongings and give away anything he had outgrown instead of encouraging his present hoarding. The kid is spoiled, Elliot thought. Spoiled.

    Jane, herself, had made the bedspread and matching curtains that adorned the blue room. The set was sky blue with darker blue and white hockey and baseball players appliqued to the show side. The woman had spent literally hours sewing, practically ignoring both him and Brydon until the set was completed. The whole world could have vanished and Elliot would have bet his next week's wages that Jane would not have noticed until she went to hang up the curtains and the window was gone.

    The feat had totally amazed Elliot. He would admit to that. He had known Jane for most of his life and would have never dreamed that she could sew. She just did not seem the type to sit and work with her hands. That was for the local, dowdy farm women.

And yet, Jane had knitted heavy, patterned ski sweaters for all of them (his had a winter scene on the front), made stuffed teddy bears and monogrammed bed pillows for his nieces and nephews, pieced and quilted the silver and baltic blue comforter for their bed and a matching wall-hanging. Jane was in constant motion, claiming that the crafts were relaxing--a creative outlet--but, personally, Elliot thought that she seemed much more relaxed after each article was completed. Jane was indeed a creature of obsession during these periods of time and finishing the present project finally broke the spell--like a hypnotist counting down, Three, two, one, awake.

"What are you making now?" Elliot questioned as he studied his wife's knit one, pearl one.

"A sweater for Brydon." Jane continued, trying to ignore her husband's presence.

"Where did you learn how to do this stuff, anyway?" Elliot enquired, genuinely interested in knowing every element of his wife's multiple layer personality.

Jane made her usual, don't bother me now, I'm trying to concentrate expression, then abruptly changed her mind. After scrawling down a few numbers on a nearby scrap of paper, she placed her knitting down beside her in order to talk more sensibly to her husband. "My mom was always making something when I was young. I can barely remember a winter going by when she wasn't piecing a quilt out of scrap material, sewing clothes for us, or knitting one of us a sweater. I guess living out in the country in the winter had a lot to do with why I followed her example.

When I was growing up, there wasn't much to do on the farm in the winter that didn't involve freezing to death or feeding barn animals, so you learned how to entertain yourself. Besides which, we didn't have a great deal of money. If I wanted anything new, it was cheaper to make it myself. That and I hated going to school to discover I was wearing the exact same shirt from Walmart that five other girls were wearing the same day."

Elliot was intrigued by the many facets of Jane's character, but it was her temper that made him cringe. Not that he was a saint himself, but, with Jane, you seldom saw her rage coming, lightning splitting clear blue skies followed by Thor-like thunder. No warning. Just bam!

Brydon had proudly displayed one of his home-knit sweaters to a couple of young playmates. One of the mothers had innocently asked the boy if his grandmother had knit the garment for him. Jane had been infuriated past all reasonable explanation.

"Sometimes," Jane snarled as she had bitterly reiterated the event to him, "I feel like taking out a full-page ad in the Sun Times saying, I MAKE THINGS! Then, maybe, just maybe, people would finally figure out that the way I look has absolutely nothing to do with the person I am." She stomped off in a pout.

Brydon was not in his room.

Brydon was a cute kid, Elliot had to admit that. Jane had done a pretty good job raising the boy by herself those first couple of years; but, the kid could be a handful. He was an awful lot like his mother--sandy-haired, hazel-eyed, tall, slender, intelligent and aggravatingly stubborn.

Closing Brydon's door, Elliot smiled, his mind parading through fond memories. An insistent meowing interrupted his private trip down nostalgia lane, even though Elliot tried his utmost best to ignore the cat's plaintive cries for immediate nourishment. Instead of acknowledging the animal's wishes, Elliot went into the tidy washroom to relieve himself.

Being married to Jane and becoming a father to Brydon had been difficult at first. Brydon was extremely possessive of his mother, never before having to share her affection. From what Elliot could gather, there had only been one other steady man in Jane's life since Brydon was born. There must have been offers, but Jane would not say much, just that she did not like to put herself into a position that she could not walk away from. What did that mean anyway? He made his second mental note of the morning, this time to ask his wife to expand on that specific comment.

In the beginning, there had been temper tantrums and

arguments over disciplining. Jane did not believe in spanking, and he had been raised that the occasional cuff never hurt anyone.

Eventually though, life had quieted down. He and Brydon had settled into being father and son. He and Jane, husband and wife.

Brydon sat, staring aimlessly out of the window. He saw nothing in particular, nor did he care. He missed Daddy Elliot and Barclay, and hoped that they would get along okay while he was gone. Would Daddy Elliot remember that Barclay got a raw egg mixed in with his morning Meow Mix, and that he liked his cat-milk room temperature not cold straight from the fridge? Would Daddy Elliot remember to let Barclay in before going to sleep so he wouldn't have to roam the streets all night, all alone?

Brydon hugged his baseball glove fondly to his small chest. The glove had belonged to his mom, even though he had confiscated it before he was three-years-old. Her name was written in black magic marker across the thumb. The "Jane" was now crossed out and "Brydon" was neatly written above. Brydon was proud of his glove and loved it even more than his talking Cowboy Woody doll that had been his constant companion until he had discovered the world of sports and video games. Now he wanted to play softball, just like Daddy Elliot. Frowning and narrowing his eyes menacingly, Brydon took the glove and, in a fit of six-year-old's anger, heaved it as hard as he could across the room. Softly pounding the window with closed fists, he cried, his heart feeling like lead. "Mommy, come back. Mommy, I want to go home! I want to go HOME NOW!!!"

After turning off the jet of steaming, hot water, Elliot stepped carefully out of the shower stall and wrapped a large, soft, blue bath towel around his thick waistline. He had installed a clothesline in their ample backyard at Jane's insistence--spent hours digging two holes deep enough for posts and cementing the posts in, then running the plastic-coated clothesline and tightening it with an appropriate metal tightener guaranteed to be simple enough that a child could use it--but she never hung the towels out to dry, always insisted on using the dryer. That way, Jane claimed, they would never step out of the shower to stiff, scratchy towels. He wondered if that was true. Would the towels come off the clothesline stiff and scratchy? Didn't his mom always put vinegar or something like that in the rinse water to soften the towels?

Feeling utterly ancient, Elliot wondered how he had possibly managed to end up settled into married life when he had spent his first thirty years answering to no one and having as few personal responsibilities as possible. To make matters worse, he was actually contemplating how or how not to dry towels. Holy shit.

Dripping over the white-tiled floor to the wooden vanity, he gazed into the pine-framed mirror of the three-door medicine cabinet, one of Jane's first purchases for the house. His chestnut brown hair was mussed from shampooing. Reaching beside him to the white wicker towel-holder for another towel to rub his hair dry, Elliot noticed more gray strands than he had before. God, he thought, I'm going to be totally gray before I'm forty. Totally gray and experimenting with freshly washed bath towels to see if they dry stiffer on the line with or without being rinsed with vinegar water compared to being tossed in the dryer, gobbling up precious kilowatts. Senility was surely next. Forty, totally gray and fighting early onset dementia. He was not enthused.

What had happened to his youth? What happened to the days when he and his twin brother were in high school? They had scammed their way through so much back then, and even though they were mirror twins--he was right-handed, while Nick was a south-paw--they were enough alike in appearance and mannerisms that the teachers could be fooled.

"Nick," Elliot cuffed his brother affectionately across the arm as Nick desperately tried to remember the combination for his twin's locker, "I'll write your math exam, if you write my geography."

"Think the teachers will notice?" Nick asked, not totally convinced.

"Did Sharon and Lynda notice when we switched dates Saturday night?" Elliot's eyes gleamed with a playful wickedness.

Nick shook his dark head, returning the gleam. He hated math.

Elliot studied his reflection more closely in the mirror. Jane had been one of the few people he knew who had never gotten the twins mixed up. He had asked her why once. She had just looked at him as if he was quite insane.

"But Elly," she whispered as she toyed with the dark hairs on his chest, "you and Nick don't look anything alike."

"I mean when we were younger, before I grew the moustache and gained forty pounds," Elliot emphasized, remaining curious. He was allowing a combination of sensations to float through his body as he lay on their queen-sized bed with Jane curled up beside him: the cool, silky feeling of the baltic blue, satin sheets against his skin; the fresh smell of the warm, spring breeze as it wafted through the partially opened window; the rapture accompanied by the soft glow of candlelight as designs danced across the room; the smug feeling of total relaxation and intimacy after making love; and, most of all, the closeness of the soft, warm body of the woman whom he had loved for the last nine years. If this wasn't heaven, it was close enough for him.

Jane remained silent for a while, contemplating. She leaned up on her left elbow so that she could look directly into Elliot's face. Grinning, she exhibited a certain fondness for him that she kept hidden away for private moments. "It was simple really." She smoothed back his dark, chestnut brown hair from his forehead and tenderly kissed his warm flesh. "You were always in the lead."

CHAPTER THREE

Reaching down beside her, Jane rooted through her brown leather purse and produced a package of King light cigarettes and a red, disposable lighter. She lit the cigarette automatically, her eyes never leaving the highway stretching out to infinity before her. Taking a deep drag, she readjusted her sitting position. It had been a while since she had driven this far without stopping, and her body ached for a change.

Rolling her throbbing shoulders in a backward motion, she tried to work out the beginnings of the unwanted kink in her long, slender neck. Damned neck had never been the same since high school when, after celebrating a football victory, she had crashed.

There had been three of them in the station wagon — Jane and two female friends. After closing down a small town tavern (the kind that does not ask for I.D. as long as you pay as you play) and managing to make the usual fool of herself, the threesome had staggered off to traverse the fifty kilometres home to soft beds and morning hangovers.

With all of them in the front — Jane in the middle (her dad referred to the middle as the 'suicide seat') — the excursion had commenced uneventfully. That particular fall had been a wet, miserable one and when they had met an on-coming car, their chauffeur — who had little driving experience on country roads — inadvertently ran onto the soft, gravel shoulder. When the tires rutted in the soggy gravel, she lost control. The station wagon's bumper caught, causing them to flip rather ungracefully, end-over-end into a farmer's freshly plowed field, totally missing the wire mesh fence and a number of very old, very large maple trees. Pretty nifty driving when seen performed in a movie by well-paid stunt drivers, but one hell of a way to travel in real life.

Jane did not remember much after the initial swerve, except waking up harbouring the most excruciating pain — like sharp, hot daggers — in the back of her neck. After crunching her forehead on the rear-view mirror (should have worn her seatbelt as the blow knocked her out), she had flown backward on impact. When the automobile finally somersaulted to a stop, Jane's body was still inside of the station wagon. Her head, however, was outside. The heavy hatch had literally bounced off the back of her head, leaving a five-centimetre gash but miraculously not cracking her skull. The hatch had then bounced down onto her left shoulder, miraculously not paralyzing the nerve (although years later enough scar tissue would build up to block the nerve thus causing temporary, partial paralysis of her left arm) before coming to rest neatly on the back of her agonized neck. Just as surprisingly, hitting the back hatch from the inside did not crack her skull or break her neck. No one could explain why.

After spending several long, shock-filled days in the local hospital--that included passing out in the bathroom because she never could use a bedpan--what the ambulance driver thought was a possible broken neck was diagnosed as a severe whiplash. Besides accumulating stitches on her forehead, a traumatized nerve in her left shoulder, a gash on the back of her head, a few loose teeth and a broken nose, she was informed that she had fared pretty well, all things considered. If the hatch had not hit her exceedingly hard head first, her spinal cord could have been severed, leaving her dead, or severely damaged, leaving her paralyzed from the neck down.

If she had flipped heads up in the great coin toss of life, the hatch could have very quickly crushed her windpipe. Lights out.

Yes, Jane considered herself lucky to be alive. Opening the back hatch with her head had compressed C-5 and C-6, which left her in some chronic pain and a half of a centimetre shorter, but the occasional muscular knot was far more tolerable than the other potential alternatives. Still, years later, the memories had not grown vague and distant like memories sometimes will. It was one experience she never wanted to go through again.

The first night had not been so bad really. She was far too inebriated to feel much of anything other than semi-detachment. Jane remembered telling the two, burly ambulance attendants that if she was too heavy, she could walk. Honest. She even asked one of them how he liked working the graveyard shift, wondering why he saw it necessary to apply pressure to her forehead but not bothering to make an enquiry. Her eyes shut slowly as she drifted in and out of reality—too difficult to keep them open, too difficult to focus, too difficult to really care about what was going on. Better to let the nice men worry...their job, not hers.

When the attendants wheeled her into Emergency, she was exceedingly polite. The nice doctor informed her that the stitches would hurt. She assured him that the pain could not possibly get much worse anyway. Go for it. Eventually, she even remembered to ask how many stitches would be required to close (that would explain why the attendant was pressing down on her forehead) the wound. Seven, he had responded. Seven, she said was a nice number although she really did prefer six. Six was her all-time favourite number, but seven was fine. Just fine.

Alone, sometime later, she had finally recaptured the use of her eyelids. The faceless doctor had asked the faceless nurse to 'clean her up a bit'. Curious as to what the fuss was all about, Jane commanded her eyelids to rise, allowed the room's brightness to settle in, then raised her left hand to see what 'clean her up a bit' actually entailed. Blood. Everywhere. From the tips of her fingers, she traced the redness to her upper arm then quit. Enough. Starting to shake, Jane had closed her eyes again. Best to let the faceless nurse worry about the mess...her job, not Jane's.

Jane shivered involuntarily. If God had wanted me dead, she thought, that would have been the night. He or she certainly had his or her chance.

After recuperating, Jane had become obsessed with wanting to do everything, to try everything and to live life to its extremes.

Jane glanced down at her quartz watch. Ten a.m. and she needed coffee badly — double cream, double sweetener — and maybe a piece of whole-wheat toast with butter, no jam.

She wondered how Elliot was doing at the tournament. She had grown up watching softball, spending many warm summers and chilly late falls cheering for the local men's and women's teams. The team her father had coached consisted of young men just a few years older than Jane herself. Her father may have taught them the game, but Jane taught them how to play.

"Gertie, do you feel as bad as I do?" Jane glanced over at her friend. The Saturday's stifling heat definitely did not make for a good combination with the previous night's partying with one of the team members, Brian, who also happened to be the only decent first-base player

they had.

"Worse," Gertie concluded as she choked down a bite of a ketchup-laden hot dog followed by a swig of cola. "One thing's for sure though, I do not envy Brian." Gertie motioned towards first base as he missed an easy catch. Safe on first.

Jane nodded in agreement. "He's definitely not the shiniest coat in the closet this morning." Brian seriously looked green around the gills. All during the evening before, he had threatened her that if he could not play ball the next day, he was going to tell her father that it was all her fault.

Although a definite babe, wavy, chestnut brown hair with luminescent blue eyes, he was pretty naïve. Could she help it if Brian had never tried Ecstasy before? Even so, he should have known that mixing the drug with a bottle of tequila was enough to keep anyone up overnight, and coming down the next day was not a trip worth taking.

"Absolutely threadbare with no sheen left whatsoever." Gertie chuckled, smiling her gorgeous smile. "If you can't handle the pace, stay out of the race." When you're nineteen and single with no responsibilities who really gave a damn anyway?

"Well, I'm out of this race," Jane notified the red Chevy Malibu ahead of her as she signaled at the exit and headed her sport wagon towards an inviting truck stop. "Fortification time."

Most of the players on her father's team had grown up, married, settled into full-time jobs, quit playing softball and had moved onto other pastimes (like fishing) but not Elliot.

"Elly, do you ever plan on quitting softball? You're getting too old for this." Jane massaged her husband's tight shoulder muscles as he complained about being out of shape.

"I'm not that old," Elliot grumbled. "Babe Ruth and Yogi Berra both played Major League baseball until they were forty, Reggie Jackson played until he was forty-one, Ted Williams and Hank Aaron both played until they were forty-two, Mickey Mantle didn't retire until he was forty-three and Rickey Henderson lasted until he was forty-five."

"Okay, you've made your point," Jane conceded, "however; they were all professional athletes who played baseball for a living and not in the majority by any means. There are a zillion more players out there who *didn't play that long and you know it. Joe DiMaggio retired when he was thirty-six, Dizzy Dean retired when he was 37 just to name two. Give me a few minutes on a computer and I can print out a list of the rest.*

Elly, I didn't mean that you should stop playing altogether, but you know what the doctor said. At this rate, you'll be lucky if your knee lasts another two years without surgery...or maybe you just really like the cortisone shots."

"My knee is fine, Jane. I wear a sports brace when I play. And the cortisone shots are shit, you know that."

"Right and all I'm saying is one wrong twist and the cartilage is history. Nick, Brian and a few of the other guys are playing slow-pitch in an Owen Sound league now. They seem to like it. Think about it. You'd still get to play but at a slower pace."

"Someday, I might," he agreed, teeth clenching suddenly as Jane encountered a tender area, a large knot that she pushed hard with her thumbs in the attempt to force the muscle into submission. "Geez, Jane, that freakin' hurts!"

"Yeah, and babying it won't help so quit your whining. You're worse than Brydon." After a few more minutes of inducing semi-welcomed torture, she slapped him gently, signaling that she was finished and wiped the excess baby oil from her hands with a paper towel. "Put heat on your shoulders for a bit tonight...twenty minutes tops...and you should feel half human by tomorrow." After crawling off his buttocks, she plopped down beside him on their bed. "What do you mean, someday?"

Elliot rolled onto his right side to face her. "I'm not ready for a walker yet thank you very much." His fingers began to caress her side, very slowly, very gently, playing with her ectomorph nerve endings like a tightly strung harp.

Jane glared at her mate. "No, and I would like to keep it that way."

End of conversation. Nothing was more important to Elliot than sports, drinking and being a big shot around town. He was thirty-three and still wanted to act eighteen. But then who was she to talk? She was twenty-seven and running away from home.

I shouldn't have married Elly, Jane thought earnestly. It had been a mistake. She did not love him when he had asked her to be his wife, had not been in love with him through their three years of marriage (although she was sure that she did love him as a person she had never felt the "I'll die without you in my life" intensity of emotion that she classified as true, romantic love) and was not in love with him now. She had married him as a matter of principle.

She had been twenty-four with a small son who needed a father and, after spending the previous two years living on next to nothing (washing cloth diapers in the sink by hand, rolling her tobacco addiction and eating Brydon's leftovers for her supper on way too many occasions) then moving back with her parents because she was exhausted from shouldering all of the responsibilities by herself, Elliot had ridden back into her life like a knight-in-shining-armour.

She had thought, why not? Marrying Elliot meant a home of her own and not having to live with the ultimate guilt of sponging off of her parents anymore. She had lived a fairly exciting, carefree existence up until that point. Maybe it was time to settle down. Since fate had dictated that she could not have the only man whom she had ever truly loved, she had readily agreed to Elliot's proposal. It just had seemed like the right thing to do at that time. How could she have been so wrong?

CHAPTER FOUR

Elliot sat peacefully at the large, rectangular, oak harvest table (an antique that Jane had purchased at an auction), listening to the local, classic rock radio station—the kind of station that followed a music format he could tolerate, but that Jane detested as she claimed that way too many boomers were mentally stuck in the 60's, 70's and 80's and thought it a dire, sociological atrocity that this demographic was pandered too instead of being forced to move on and deal with the facts that poofy bangs and mullets were no longer in fashion, that they were indeed getting older, that their golden days were over and that eight track tapes were now extinct—and hungrily consumed his breakfast of a three-egg-mushroom omelet and four slices of whole wheat toast laced with peach marmalade.

Jane had made the marmalade herself, saying that the less unnatural preservatives her family consumed, the better it would be—reciting the example that her cousin, a large, Grizzly Adams type of man, who had spent ten years of his life repairing lumber equipment in the great white north, went absolutely insane every time he consumed canned sandwich meats or store bought cookies. And, since "the men" in her life insisted on having jam and peanut butter on their toast, she might as well make sure the jam would not eventually turn them both into vile, raving, uncontrollable lunatics. Besides, they would save money in the long run.

Elliot had even helped, feeling a sense of weirdly innate pride as he and his wife filled dozens of small, sterilized mason jars with the gloppy orange gelatin and, after the marmalade had cooled, placed the jars in the freezer chest. 'Winter Stock' Jane had called it as if they were still back in the time of hunting and gathering.

Elliot frowned as he munched on his toast and drank black coffee. Why hadn't Jane left a note? She was the one who had always insisted on everyone's whereabouts being posted on the refrigerator door. Even if she just went down the street to the store, he would find a piece of paper plastered onto the refrigerator by one of those stupid magnetic fruit things that were scattered haphazardly across the surface.

He thought that maybe she might have stayed overnight at her sister Pam's house. Jane and Pam sometimes went out for a drink or two, triple that if Gertie was up visiting, and Jane, too inebriated to drive, would have ended up spending the night on Pam's sofa. That would solve the mystery of the missing note as Jane wouldn't be expecting him home until tonight, and she would have planned to be at home sleeping off a hangover by then. Elliot made a mental note to call Pam later.

Deep in thought, Elliot suddenly felt something soft and furry rub against the sensitive skin of his bare foot. Instinctively, he kicked the foreign object sending an annoyed Barclay, meowing in his pain and indignation, sprawling from underneath the table.

"Barclay, you stupid cat," Elliot growled, his eyes narrowing with hatred. He had forgotten all about the animal during his shower, had, in fact, blissfully put the cat right out of his mind.

Barclay regained his composure and settled into a sitting position beside the table, glaring at Elliot and twitching his long tail from one side to another in summation of their mutual disdain.

Unwilling to be pushed around by a cat, Elliot finished his meal slowly, trying his best to ignore the creature's insistent stare. Those green eyes unnerved him, almost as much as Jane's could.

"Look Daddy E.! Look what Mommy got!" Brydon jumped up on Elliot's lap with an unquenchable expression of enthusiasm, his small hands clasped together in joy.

Elliot, who had been watching the Dodgers play the Yankees on television — a close game at that — was not too sure that he really wanted to know what Brydon was referring to. With a laudable sigh, Elliot hesitantly enquired, "What did she get this time, Bry?"

Jane sauntered into the living room carrying a tiny bundle of orange fur tucked close against her body. She looked happier than he had seen her since they had unpacked a month before.

Brydon pointed at his mother and began to bounce up and down, causing Elliot to groan in male discomfort. "A kitty, Daddy E. A kitty. Oh, he so pwetty!"

Jane smiled lovingly at her son, then at her new husband. She gently stroked the tiny, frightened animal as it tried desperately to disappear into her armpit. "I want to call him Barclay," she announced.

Any would-be beginnings of a smile died on Elliot's lips as he groaned, picked Brydon off of his lap, set him down on the floor and walked over to inspect the new intruder. "Jane, you get that thing out of here," he ordered. "You know I can't stand cats!"

Jane returned his glare with an air of complete astonishment, as if horrifically shocked by the mere thought of not keeping the kitten. "But Elly, it's just a kitten." She bent down and placed the small bundle on the hardwood floor. The kitten stumbled, shook out its tiny body, then skittered off to inspect the nooks and crannies of his new surroundings and, if possible, out run the little boy who was busily scurrying behind yelling, "Pwetty kitty, Barcy!"

Rising from her squatting position, Jane strolled into the adjoining kitchen to make a cup of hot, mint, herbal tea. Elliot followed, exceedingly annoyed that she was ignoring him.

He leaned up against the refrigerator and crossed his arms. "Kittens grow into cats," he informed her haughtily.

"And little mice grow into big mice, especially in old houses like this one." Jane faced away from him, preparing her drink.

Pushing himself away from the refrigerator, Elliot stood erect, his 6' frame postured for battle. "I said no cats."

Jane stopped playing with her white porcelain mug, the one that had World's Best Mom inscribed on the side in large blue letters, a Mother's Day gift from Brydon, and turned to face her husband. Her eyes had darkened, the jade green clouded over almost black. "Wow, Elly, and just who are you to tell me what to do? You don't get to make all of the decisions around here."

"And you do? I don't think so. This house is half mine. I should at least get a vote."

"I absolutely agree. The house is half yours...emphasis on the half. So I would suggest that you figure out just which half of the house is yours, and we'll keep the kitten on my side. The side without the mice."

"Jane, I freakin' hate cats. They are soulless, evil creatures that don't belong in a house." Elliot placed his hands on his hips, broadening his stance.

Jane stared at her husband, with a look that said she was in the process of biting back what she truly wanted to say. "I'm going to ignore that comment. Trust me, you really want me to pretend that you didn't say that."

"Not only did I mean what I said, but I'd be more than happy to

repeat it if you didn't catch it the first time."

Jane took a deep breath then exhaled. She turned back towards the cupboard and put the teabag into a plastic container they kept under the kitchen sink for compost scraps. When she spoke again, her tone had softened, "Are you allergic to cats?"

Elliot shook his head. "No."

"Then deal. Brydon and I both wanted a cat. That's two votes against one." She turned around and looked up into her husband's face. "Look Elly, I really don't want to fight about this. Pets are good for kids. They teach them responsibility. End of discussion. If you don't like it, feel free to leave."

Elliot threw up his arms over his head in frustration, stormed out of the kitchen, turned off the colour television, made a very noticeable exit from the house and walked the three blocks to a nearby tavern for a beer, and whatever conversation he could conjure up.

The tavern had been a home-away-from home ever since he had reached legal drinking age. The place was small, the entertainment consisting of a pool table and a juke box, but most of the town's populace went there at one time or another.

There he could have a cold beer, a game or two of pool, listen to the latest in local news as told by the various regulars and not feel threatened by Jane's insistence that he was not 'the King of the Castle' or 'the Head of the Household'. Of course, there was the usual good-natured teasing. Was the honeymoon over already? He didn't mind. It was all in fun, and he had been on the other end as often as not. After all, how could the honeymoon be over when they never had one? Most of all, he, Elliot Fallis, was a big man there, doing well for his thirty years, and the respect he received at the tavern made him feel good. Why not? He deserved it. He'd worked hard to get where he was at RND Sporting Goods, and he was proud of himself.

By the time he returned home, dusk had fallen. Supper had been vanquished from all sight. Jane, who claimed to be busy writing an e-mail to one of her distant, college chums, was also conspicuously ignoring him. Elliot decided to watch television and lay down on their brown, faux suede couch to doze through the remainder of a very boring movie. When he awoke, it was almost midnight. His first conscious thought was that he had an ominous case of the dries. His second conscious thought was that the orange thing was curled up on his chest, purring and staring at him curiously.

"Why Barclay?" Elliot asked, curious as to the name chosen. His temper had cooled, basically because one beer had turned into six, and he had almost forgotten what he had previously been upset about. It was just that he wanted a puppy and knew that having both would be financially impossible right now. Every boy needed a dog, and Elliot did not see why Brydon should be the exception. Even if their back yard was not overly huge, it would have been big enough for a small dog – a Terrier or a Pug. But then, dogs don't catch mice.

With the laptop put away, Jane was curled up in a rocking chair reading a supernatural thriller by Stephen King...practically the only author she ever read. "Because Brydon has a difficult time pronouncing the 'cl' sound, and I thought it would be good practice for him."

"Oh," Elliot replied, carefully set the kitten on the floor, rolled over and fell asleep again.

Barclay stayed.

With a final gulp of black coffee, Elliot rose, wary of Barclay's rather annoying habit of pouncing when upset. Although the cat generally preferred to wait until Elliot was coming through a doorway before ambushing him — sneak attacks that had often sent Elliot cursing that one of them had to go or else--Elliot had occasionally endured claws scraping his bare legs for no other reason other than his just being alive. And, although Jane had agreed to keep Barclay's dagger sharp nails trimmed, actual declawing, according to Jane, was quite inhumane.

Regardless, Barclay was a seriously stupid name. The cat was evil incarnate and deserved a name like Lucifer or Hades...or maybe Mephisto. Mephisto, Elliot thought, just like the 1980's German, subtitled movie that Jane had insisted he watch to bring some culture into his life...not that he managed to actually follow much of the movie anyway while trying to keep up to the subtitles. (*Die Hard with a Vengeance* or *The Fast and The Furious* were more his speed) Yes, Mephisto would work. Mephisto...the devil.

Elliot rinsed off his breakfast dishes in the immaculate, stainless steel sink and placed them into the portable dishwasher.

Barclay followed, meowing all of the way (actually, the noise sounded more like a Merrow) and finally positioned himself in front of the white, side-by-side refrigerator.

Elliot bent down and extracted a box of dry cat food from the bottom shelf of the tidy cupboard. He walked over to the matching white stove and poured some of the mixture into the cat's brown, plastic dish that sat on a catmat beside.

Barclay didn't move.

Deciding that the animal must be thirsty and remembering that Jane occasionally gave Barclay a bit of cat-milk as a treat, Elliot grunted, opened the refrigerator, took out the small carton of cat-milk and poured some into a shallow bowl beside the cat's food and water dishes.

This time, Barclay quickly followed, sniffed the food, rejected it, took a lick of the cold milk and sat down on his haunches to, once again, commence his plaintive cries.

Irritated and frustrated, Elliot could feel a headache beginning to pulsate just behind his left eye. I should have never allowed Jane to keep the cat, Elliot mentally chastised himself, regretting the precedent ever since. Without hesitation, he scooped the feline up by his mid-section, stomped to the back door, opened it and tossed the confused creature outside, causing Barclay to sprawl ungracefully onto the well-kept lawn—totally disproving the theory that cats always land on their feet. "If you don't like what I give you, feel free to go get your own," Elliot brusquely informed the startled animal. With a feeling of ultimate satisfaction, Elliot slammed the wooden screen door behind him as he re-entered the house, as if punctuating his superiority. So there. He was the King of the Castle after all.

The sound of the front door opening and closing startled Elliot out of his reverie. He half expected Barclay to reappear, demanding an apology. "Jane?" Elliot called, walking briskly back through the small laundry room and into the bright kitchen.

"Elliot. It's me." A voice, all-too-similar to his own floated back. "Don't you ever lock your doors?"

Elliot met his brother in the front entrance-way. "Don't you ever knock?" he snarled in response. He had unlocked the door first thing coming down that morning, just in case Jane had forgotten her key.

"I didn't know that I had to," Nick retorted. Ignoring the innuendo, Nick walked past his brother, sat down on the plush, brown couch and rested his feet on the pinewood coffee table.

"Where's Jane? I didn't see her car parked outside."

Elliot shrugged as he sat down in his Barcalounger. A scene from his dream flashed momentarily through his mind. Unconsciously, he repositioned himself, mentally noting that he should secure the culprit knife for a while. Just in case. "Don't know. She wasn't home when I got back yesterday."

Looking relieved, Nick asked, "Did she take Brydon with her?"

"I guess. What's up?"

"Mary's knocked-up. She's at mom's talking about baby stuff." Nick lit a cigarette and inhaled deeply. He had taken up smoking two years before, claiming that it relaxed his nerves.

"So, my little brother's going to be a daddy is he? Congratulations, Nick," Elliot offered without enthusiasm. He often wondered why Nick had married that ugly sleaze bag of a wench. Personally, he could not tolerate the sight of her. Slightly taller than Nick's 6' 1", large-boned, broad-shouldered, with masculine facial features and a deep, husky, nasal voice that grated on his nerves, Mary could easily pass for a cross-dresser in heat. Elliot wondered who really wore the pants in that household; but then, what the hell, he wasn't the one who had to wake up and look at that every morning. Nick was.

"Aw come on, Elliot. Be happy for me. You're just sore 'cause Jane wouldn't let you adopt Brydon."

Elliot frowned. "For your information, little brother, Jane doesn't have a problem with me adopting Bry. She just doesn't know where the kid's father is and needs to contact him first so he can sign off parental rights. She was going to claim that the father was unknown until we saw a lawyer who said that it was a bad idea. It would be better to contact the jerk than to claim the father was unknown in case the guy does show up out of the blue someday."

Nick took a long drag on his cigarette and exhaled a perfectly formed smoke ring. "And just who is Brydon's dad anyway?"

In one final sweep, Elliot had enough for one weekend and, although he loved his brother more than any other living being, he was not in the mood to chat about anything right now. "Why the fuck do you care? For the last three years, you haven't said three fucking words about the kid and now you've got questions? Why does it matter who the kid's father is? He's probably the guy she dated in college. He's not around. That's all that fucking matters."

"So she hasn't told you who the father is? Man, have you even asked her?"

"What makes you think that I didn't fucking ask? Do I look stupid to you? Of course, I've asked. What kind of question is that? I asked before we went to see the lawyer."

Nick leaned forward. "What'd she say?"

"She said she'd handle it." Elliot jumped up from his recliner. "It's time for you to go, Nick. I was just about to head out for a run. By the way, we don't like anyone smoking in the house. It's bad for Brydon."

Nick stubbed the cigarette out in a nearby pottery ashtray. "Noted. You might think about getting rid of the ashtray then."

"Jane uses it when she goes outside for a puff."

Nick sighed and rose from the couch to exit, stage right, and only glanced back once on his way out. "I'll call you later."

"Yeah," Elliot grunted a response as he watched his brother leave.

Deciding that he did actually need to get out for a while, maybe go for a jog to stretch out the stiffness, Elliot entered his bedroom and began to rummage around, looking for his black sports watch — the one with the odometer on it.

His blue eyes skimmed over the surface of their antique bureau. Brydon's school picture was gone. Elliot's mahogany valet with his wallet, spare change and odd and sods was there. Jane's wooden jewellery box — the one that played the show tune that neither of them could remember the name of — was there. Three small, brass-framed family portraits were there. Yes, ladies and gents, there was no doubt about it, Brydon's picture was definitely missing.

Elliot spun around to scan the rest of the bedroom. Normal. Everything else in the room was just as it had been since they moved in. Elliot progressed to the closet. At the count of three, he held his breath and pulled back the wooden, bi-fold doors expecting to see Jane's half empty. Nope. Hangers full of clothes. Jane had so many clothes that Elliot wasn't quite sure just how to determine if an article was missing anyway. Shirts, blouses, dress pants, skirts, dress jackets all neatly hung where they always did. Sweatshirts, sweaters and blue-jeans, folded and piled neatly in the closet organizer. Shoes and boots lined up on the closet floor.

Elliot swallowed hard. The house was suddenly too quiet.

Leaving the closet door askew and chastising himself for being worried for no tangible reason other than the knot that clenched the base of his stomach, Elliot walked over to the black, portable telephone, sat abruptly down on the firm bed and dialed the number for Jane's cell phone. No answer, just her voice mail asking the caller to please leave a message after the sound of the beep. He left a brief, hi it's me, call me when you get this, I'm home, message and hung up.

Taking the handset with him, he returned to the closet and casually started moving hangers back and forth as if seeing what was there would somehow magically conjure up visions of what may have been packed. Where did Jane keep the suitcases anyway? The storage room maybe? He shook his head and closed the closet doors. She'd disappeared before, but she'd always come back after a few days. The knot tightened.

He dialed again. This time the connection made good. "Hello?" a groggy voice answered.

Elliot glanced at his wristwatch. Only ten but it felt so much later. "Hi, Pam. It's Elliot. Is Jane there? She's not answering her cell phone, and I promised Bry that we'd toss the ball around for a while this aft if we got beat out early…"

CHAPTER FIVE

Feeling better, her aches and pains momentarily relieved, hunger satiated, Jane, once again, merged into the heavy traffic. Having changed from her faded blue-jeans and favourite red sweatshirt into khaki-coloured, walking shorts and white t-shirt, she felt cool and refreshed. Breakfast had proven to be edible, although what had passed for coffee was the most horrendous brew that she had tasted since her days of college vending machines. At least the little restaurant had whole-wheat toast and the pretty, young waitress did not try to encourage her to order the stomach buster complete with five slices of crispy bacon and home fries. Jane thoroughly disliked pushy waitresses or waiters.

God, it's going to be a scorcher, Jane thought glancing up at the cloudless, blue sky. Jane loved the heat and could barely wait to get settled in a climate where 20 degrees Celsius was considered cold. Not that New Jersey was a tropical state by any means, but it was definitely a step in the right direction.

Jane hated the cold, abhorred winter, and felt absolutely positive that she had just miscalculated when she, or some greater power, had decided that it was her time to "live again". Everyone was blindfolded, placed in front of a world map and instructed to point to a continent. She was certain that she had been aiming for somewhere in the United States like California or Florida and had just missed. Jane could picture herself groaning and requesting a do-over when she looked to see where her finger had touched down. Canada? Oh shit. The summers were great, mind you, — quite often hot and sunny — but way too short. The funniest part was watching the American tourists traipsing around in the middle of July, looking for snow, as if the Georgian Bay area where she lived was a smaller version of Baffin Island or the North Pole. Snow. Yup, you bet. We have snow. Just keep going north say, sixteen hundred kilometres or so and see what you find....

Regardless, Jane froze all winter. The winter that she had moved back to her parents' farm had been no exception. If she hated winter in the city, the season seemed twice as grueling in the country where she had hibernated for three months, living on Unemployment Insurance, and only going out to seek supplies or to catch an occasional movie with a friend.

    Even Todd's phone call to make a skiing date had not budged her from her parents' warm abode where she could stoke the wood furnace and, at least, pretend that there was not over a metre of brilliantly frigid snow outside waiting to either torture her 2005 Matrix and/or to send endlessly radiating shivers through every centimetre of her slim body.

    Todd. A small, dark cloud formed in the recesses of her mind. She had almost forgotten how devastated she had been when their relationship had crashed and burned, had stashed the events away with the rest of her bittersweet memories.

CHAPTER SIX

"Good morning, Elliot," Pam responded. "Jane's not here."

Elliot felt anger rising, reality edging its nasty way inward bit by bit. The emotion worked its way up from his pounding heart and settled heavily in his throbbing temples. He felt positive that Pam was hiding something—trying to stall him, to give Jane time to get a little bit further away. Did she take Brydon? Where was the boy? He was going to start grade one in the fall. Surely, she wouldn't tear him from a familiar environment and take him someplace where he wouldn't know the area or any of the kids, where he would get lost on his way home from school or possibly get picked up by some sordid stranger with even more sordid pedophile intentions. Surely, she wouldn't be that cruel.

And what about the league finals? How could he concentrate on playing well if Brydon wasn't there to cheer on his Daddy Elliot? He had played hard all season to make the finals. It didn't come as easily as it used to. He was stiffer at the end of the tournaments and his breath was short after running after a hard hit ball, home plate seemed further away now when he was running the bases. Jane didn't care. It was Brydon who was his biggest fan. It was Brydon whose face shone with pride after Daddy Elliot made a good play or hit a good ball. It was Brydon. Brydon.

Elliot inhaled deeply and pressed his forefinger to his left temple to control the throbbing. Suddenly, it was very important to him to sound casual, matter-of-fact, as if he was just innocently trying to locate his wife. His wife...

"Yeah?" he managed to reply in an almost casual tone. "Jane didn't leave a note, and I just thought she might be there. I wasn't supposed to come back until later on this evening."

"You lost then?" Pam half-asked, half-stated.

Elliot felt his temperature rise again and fought to control it. "Yeah, got beat out yesterday two to one. Shitty umps." He hated losing due to unfair calls. The game had been so damned close.

"Too bad," Pam said quietly, then added, "I haven't seen Jane since Friday afternoon. She came over for a coffee after work."

Elliot's heart sank. The emotion was the same feeling he used to get when he did poorly on a school exam that he was positive he had aced, a feeling of disappointment and confusion rather than of anger. "Did she mention anything about going down to visit Gertie this weekend?"

Pam hesitated, thinking back. "No, I don't think so. She mentioned something about spending a quiet weekend sunbathing and taking Brydon swimming. I wouldn't worry too much Elliot. You know Jane. She probably decided to go somewhere on the spur of the moment. She'll probably be back this evening before she's expecting you to get home."

Elliot pondered the idea for a moment and realized that Pam was probably right. Jane was notorious for spur-of-the-moment decisions. It was summer, the weather was gorgeous, he was supposed to be away, so why not? Jane had many friends who were always telling her to come and visit, so why not? He was being totally irrational. Of course he was. Jane loved him as much as he loved her. Didn't she? This was their home. Jane had spent many long hours fixing up and redecorating the house until it had suited her tastes—sort of a cross between modern and old, with antiques coinciding happily with the portable dishwasher, the microwave and the flat screen TV. This was Brydon's home. He, Elliot, was the only father Brydon had ever known. Brydon loved him. He loved Brydon. Simple. Of course, a spur-of-the-moment trip. Jane hated staying at home in the summer when she had her weekends off. It all made sense now. He was being irrational, a worry-wart. Silly.

"Okay, thanks Pam." He smiled suddenly, feeling relieved and a little bit embarrassed. "If she calls, tell her to phone home." He knew that he wouldn't really relax until he heard from her.

"Will do, Elliot," Pam signed off. Her children were yelling in the background for their breakfast.

Elliot replaced the telephone receiver and lay back down on the bed. He placed his sturdy hands over his eyes, trying to figure out which friend Jane would visit. She had college chums in Toronto who were constantly calling to tell her to come back to civilization, at least for the weekend. And Gertie lived out-of-town but still remained in close contact. She hadn't been feeling well the past while so maybe Jane had traversed the 300 kilometres to St. Catharines to cheer her up. After all, Gertie and Brydon were like aunt and nephew. It would lift her spirits just having him around for a couple of days.

Elliot and Gertie hadn't gotten along well for the past few years. He realized that it was partially his fault, but he had tried often to make amends. Blonde and energetic, she was always delving into something—making freelance films, taking university courses, writing romance novels. He just thought that maybe she should get a real job somewhere, and his advice had not gone over well.

Or maybe, Jane had gone to see Dylan. That was another alternative. Elliot had gone once with Jane to visit her brother and had vowed it would be the last time. Not that Elliot was entirely homophobic, but seeing Dylan with his latest love definitely made Elliot feel uncomfortable, diffident. The two men were just so openly gay. Behind closed doors was one thing, but when Dylan kissed his partner in front of him and Jane, Elliot had desperately wanted to be someplace else, anyplace else.

Elliot glanced at the digital clock-radio. Ten-thirty. He wondered when Jane would show up—maybe seven o'clock that night, maybe earlier. She had to be in for work at eight-thirty a.m., so she probably wouldn't leave it too late. She liked her sleep too much.

With a supreme effort, Elliot heaved himself off of the bed. He felt old and worn out like last year's wool socks. He wished that he had slept in, then rejected the idea of going back to bed. He wouldn't sleep anyway; the house was too quiet, almost spooky.

"Brydon, what's wrong honey?" Gertie hugged her favourite little boy.

He returned the hug with fervour. "I'm scared," he whimpered softly, crying on her familiar shoulder.

Gertie drew back from him and wiped away one of his tears with a soft tissue. She studied his small, puckered face. "Scared of what, Sweetie?"

Brydon sniffled, trying to regain his composure. He was going to be a big man like Daddy Elliot. Big men didn't cry. Daddy Elliot didn't cry when he got hit by a fast ball the pitcher threw last week. He wouldn't cry either. Brydon stared into Gertie's clear, blue eyes.

Mommy always said she could tell if he was fibbing by the look in his eyes. "Is Mommy ever coming back for me?" he asked, feeling certain deep down in his little soul that she wasn't.

Gertie hugged him close to her, feeling a part of her heart tear open, leaving a gaping wound of sympathy and concern for her little friend. "Of course she is. Your mom has a job interview at a television station, remember? Then if she gets the job, she'll come back to get you." She kissed his soft, damp cheek and continued to hold him, to reassure him.

Brydon sniffed. "And if she doesn't get the job?

Gertie smoothed the unruly hair back from his brow. "Then she'll spend a few days to see if she can get a lead on another position, but your mom's so good at what she does that they'd be stupid not to hire her on the spot.

Brydon, your mom loves you more than anything. I bet she calls tonight to check in and see how you're doing. You'll see. Everything will be just fine. I promise."

Elliot strolled around slowly and, for the first time in a long while, surveyed the bedroom. The room was comfortable — family pictures, serene colour schemes, offset by the blue trimmings, his clothes tossed in a small heap in the corner waiting patiently to be gathered up for laundry.

He could mentally picture the day that Jane had wallpapered. She had been decked out in old, faded blue jeans and her grandfather's plaid work shirt, looking quite at home with wallpaper and glue. She had used flour, water and salt to make the extra paste. "Old houses need old remedies," she had announced brightly, "otherwise, the damned stuff won't stick to these rough walls."

Pam had helped, laughing at her sister's insistence on hanging up old, flea-market pictures of people — the tin-plate kind with their decorative, wooden frames. They had absolutely no idea who the people were, so the two had made up names — a tiny, prim, Great-Aunt Martha accompanied by a very stern, unsmiling man, Uncle Harry. Uncle Sid, his wife Lydia and their twelve poised children all duded up in their Sunday best for a two-minute exposure.

Elliot had felt a pang of jealousy that day. Pam was seven years older than Jane; however, the family resemblance was unmistakable. Pam was shorter and heavier set, but their colouring was the same. They both harboured the same sparkle in two sets of cat's eyes. He had been the outsider, an intruder, an unwanted and unneeded third party. He was on the outside looking in.

True, the room had turned out beautifully, like something out of an early nineteenth century story book, but it had been entirely under Jane's control. He had stood briefly in the doorway and watched and had, eventually, ended up retiring to the tavern for a cool one. In a way, it was Jane's room, not his. Even now, he could feel her presence.

His eyes fell on the well-polished bureau. The missing picture of Brydon stood out defiantly, a total anomaly. Where had it gone? Had the picture accidentally been broken? Had Brydon decided to look at it and accidentally dropped it, smashing the glass frame?

Elliot rubbed his eyes, tired of the questions. The tavern didn't open until two p.m. on Sundays. It was going to be a very long three and a half hours.

CHAPTER SEVEN

With another hundred kilometres behind her, Jane found a turn-off that led to a small, family restaurant beside an almost abandoned tourist rest area. Grateful for the almost quiet, she sprawled underneath a mature Dogwood tree, wishing she could have seen the vibrant pink, springtime foliage, and tried her best to recompose herself before continuing her quest for the Holy Grail.

There was a handful of young children of various ages in the well-kept park, giggling incessantly and playing on the wooden Swing-n-Slide as they stretched out 200 kilometre cramps from well-tanned legs. Parents sat, chatting, eating ketchup-laden hotdogs, drinking cold soft drinks or ice tea, keeping vigil at nearby wooden picnic tables. Occasionally, the children squabbled over a favourite, stolen toy, a momentarily empty, yellow plastic-seated swing, a spilt, vanilla ice-cream waffle cone or just because it seemed like the thing to do to pass the time.

Jane could never totally comprehend parents forcing their offspring to endure long car trips. The journeys were boring, tedious, tiring and by the time the family arrived at their destination, everyone was bickering—unless, of course, you could afford to buy or lease one of those really cool min-vans that were complete with everything from climate controlled air-conditioning and individual DVD players to robotic nannies. Of course, portable DVD players and hand-held video games were always an option; but, how many movies could a child watch before the distraction lost its effect? Before little Tommy or little Sally, bored to the point of irrational behavior, decided that hitting his or her sibling over the head with the player was a better option than one more movie? If she and Dylan had been put into a similar situation when they were children, they would have lasted two movies maximum. Two movies, four hours, before all hell would have broken loose. And forget about Dylan sharing his hand-held video game. She could have beaten him into unconsciousness and his fingers still would have been gripped tightly, as if the game was actually a part of him, an extension to his hands. Jane smiled at the thought.

At least at home, the energy-driven youth could hang out with their various neighbourhood playmates, do their best to avoid the local ruffians, scheme, swim, join a local soccer league, make a bit of money cutting grass for their neighbours, catch a matinee, go on picnics, walks, pretend to be the X-men, Wonder Woman, Batman… whatever. She supposed that living in a small town like Donnybrooke, where you practically knew everyone and didn't live in constant fear that your child would be abducted before dinner, was an entirely different world than having growing children trapped in a small apartment, battling the sweltering, mid-day heat on the fourth floor of an overcrowded apartment building during summer vacation.

One of Jane's all-time paranoias was that if she lived, as she had, with a third-floor balcony and a patio door screen that forever fell off, no matter how careful she was (dozens of complaints to the apartment complex's manager yielded nothing more than dozens of promises to have the dysfunctional door repaired and the waiting list for a first-floor apartment was extensive), her small, adventurous son would eventually find some way of clambering over the metal railing and would end up crashing to the brutally unforgiving pavement below. She had often witnessed children in their ultimate naiveté sitting haphazardly on the edges of balconies, casually swinging legs to and fro, completely oblivious of what may happen if their balance should fail, should big brother Billy tease that one time too often…The thought sent chills up Jane's spine. Her imagination had always been too vivid for comfort's sake.

Jane yawned, tired from the seemingly endless car ride (only 314 kilometres left to go) and the intense heat. She was, however, thankful for the reliable air-conditioning and the GPS unit that Elliot had given to her for Christmas with the "to help you find your way out of any brown paper bag, love always, Elliot" note attached to the festive, kittens wearing Santa hats wrapping paper. Her mind wandered aimlessly, relaxing its attentions, drifting on white puffy clouds of what could have been.

Where had she gone wrong? She couldn't blame it on Brydon. He hadn't asked to be conceived into the situation. She probably hadn't been assertive enough. She had always been too busy dealing with the reality of survival to push herself towards her dreams. Images of a slightly overweight, but exceedingly energetic casting director, floated into view.

"Jane, you have an absolutely perfect face for day-time soaps." The broad smile lit up the dullness of a Toronto Day – sky scrapers blocking out the sun by three o'clock that afternoon.

Jane only grinned good-naturedly, weighing the fact that being a single parent who could barely survive in Toronto would only be exaggerated beyond proportion if she uprooted Brydon and herself to move to someplace like New York where she was not only just one more unknown face but an uncultured actress as well.

The images faded, becoming, once again, a random piece of her jigsaw past.

In many ways, Jane abhorred small town life. Donnybrooke with its 5,000 people had been named after Captain Donnybrooke in 1884. The area consisted mainly of German and Polish settlers — farmers most of them trying to find a better way of life for their children. Now, generations later, their descendants wouldn't understand the initial hardships that they had overcome settling in the area. Sad, but true. Regardless, Jane was really no different. Her maternal great-great-great grandmother, a widow with four children, had emigrated from Germany to keep her sons out of conscription. A few generations later, Jane knew absolutely no German except for her great-grandmother's occasional exclamation like "Ach mein leben!" (Oh my life!). Her great-grandfather had spoken only German until he was eleven, then was forced to be assimilated into the English schools. How much had they lost? How much had they gained? Jane couldn't really say. All she knew was that it annoyed her that everyone in town always knew when she blew her nose or pulled up her socks. If they didn't know, they made up something of interest, and it was always taken as the gospel truth until the rumour Rockwelled back to the victim.

Jane managed to avoid gossip only by ignoring what was being said about any individual in particular at any given time. And yet, there was always someone who hadn't been taught the fundamentals of finesse who would ask you straight-out about something they damned well knew was none of their business. Fucking nosiness was all. No more. No less.

Jane's television teacher had once told her he could ask her a hundred questions and be lucky if she answered two — doubly lucky if one answer was the truth. Of course, he had been exaggerating. She was usually very honest and a bit blunt by nature; but, if a person asked a question about a subject that she would rather not talk about or if the subject was destined for the proverbial water cooler clique, it seemed logical to make up a good story. That way, their nosiness (and the men were just as bad as the women) was satisfied and her privacy was left intact. Jane was always careful to make the tales as juicy as humanly possible just to appease their warped little minds.

There was only one slight problem with this. When the locals got together to compare notes, they often discovered that they had all been told different stories. Either they got the hint and didn't ask any more questions, or they would find a way to indirectly crosscheck, hoping that she would have forgotten which version she had told them. Jane never forgot. It was her game. Besides, her sharp mind had been trained for details no matter how insignificant that detail seemed — continuity was everything.

Jane's good, trusted friends always knew the truth, and she had a varied selection of allies who accepted her, and, on numerous occasions, had defended her eccentricities, claiming that was just the way she was. Why they were so loyal, she never did actually understand.

Although Jane had a sharp, writer's memory for detail and a keen, logical instinct, she was not organized by choice in either her personal or in her business life but by necessity. She duly hated rigid, structured, nine-to-five jobs which was one of the better reasons she had studied broadcasting in college. In actual fact, after leaving her dreams of being a psychologist behind, she had wanted to become an actress or a singer; her parents, being practical, had insisted on a skill. With Audio/Visual Arts being the closest-related major she could find, she had often volunteered to be the talent in her classmates' productions--such epics as a spoof on birth control when she was seven months pregnant with Brydon.

Her friends were slightly surprised when she agreed to do the public service commercial; but, it suited her sense of humour — humour that often delved into the macabre of the idiosyncrasies of nature. Amongst her acquaintances were Wiccans, psychics, or experts on whatever realm of the unknown that fascinated her at that particular time in her life. Jane's open mind demanded information on every aspect of life, sorted through the data, filed and catalogued the megabytes for future reference. Life intrigued her immensely, like a prowling feline searching for the perfect mouse, unafraid to stalk through thick, dark shrubs, thorns awaiting their next innocent victim. The thorns were meant for others, more careless. Not for her. Never for her. Or so she had believed. The spoof, was both a means of entertainment and supposedly, might make just one young, naïve female think twice about her next date. Maybe then, one less thorn would hit home, puncturing and destroying youth's idealism.

Impractical and a dreamer at heart, Jane had spent a greater part of her existence rebelling against everything that her parents stood for — security, marriage, religion and what they lovingly insisted was a "normal life". Better to drift off on the clouds and explore the outer limits of the cosmos…

Relaxing in her camper, sipping ice-cold tonic water with a large twist of lime, Jane casually rehearsed her lines, running through them until perfection prevailed. She, of course, knew every line in the entire scene. It was just a matter of proper inflection on her part. The correct intonation for the character at the right time, the proper nuance.

An impatient knock sounded at the trailer door, echoed off the wall and bounced back. Jane rose, stretching her long, shapely legs and greeted Harvey, the Unit Manager.

"Hi ya, Jane." He climbed into the trailer and plopped himself down at the white kitchenette table. Jane, he noted, had the nicest trailer of all. But then, why wouldn't she? She was, after all, the star. Movies didn't make her; she made the movies.

"Hi Harvey." Jane smiled, an easy smile of authentic fondness. She offered him a tonic and he accepted gratefully. She gave him a glass of the cold liquid, the condensation already dense on the outside, and sat down across from him. "So, how's it going on the set?" she inquired earnestly.

"We're taking a quick break, and then we're ready for your scene." He pulled a blue, leather notebook from his cotton shirt's breast pocket for reference and flipped determinedly though the numerous, scribbled pages.

Harvey was old-school and refused to switch to any number of electronic gadgets that would have quickly organized the information with one click. "Scene number 300."

He liked Jane. She wasn't as stuck-up or as demanding as some of the pretty stars he had worked with. In fact, she almost seemed shy. Until, of course, the director yelled, "Action!", then she was just simply amazing. There was no other word for it. She had a way of making the audience, and even sometimes the crew, believe. There was nothing glamorous about her, not really. She was pretty, but not what he would consider drop-dead gorgeous, and she was intelligent as well. She didn't try to impress or out-do anyone, which was unusual for the very competitive profession. There were no rumours of casting-couch aerobics, cocaine party parades or any hint of scandal. It was just the simple fact that she put so much heart and soul into every performance that made her a director's delight.

He remembered the daytime soap that she had been on. Even his wife had cried when the character had died of cancer, leaving behind two small, helpless, sobbing children who would be raised by an uncaring aunt. Edith had said that she couldn't help but cry. It was just so touching, so real.

Jane's eyes had overflowed with tears as she whispered her final, pitiful goodbyes to little Jeremy and Melissa. Edith had said she just looked so brave and so helpless at the same time that a person would have had to be made of stone not to cry along with her. The empathy of motherhood shed hot, plentiful tears.

Harvey had actually commented to Jane about it once, near the beginning of the filming. Jane was sitting at a wooden picnic table, near the canteen, drinking a cup of bad coffee from her ceramic mug. He had felt as if he had known her for a long time as it was his wife's favourite soap, and Edith talked about the program incessantly, recalling even the tiniest of details.

When he had asked Jane if he could join her, she had smiled her compliance. He had gotten a coffee and sat down to chat. Usually, except when filming, he preferred to stay clear of the actors, but she seemed harmless enough. She was easy enough to talk to, although she didn't offer much about herself. He had eventually asked her how she had ended up working stateside in soaps. Edith would love the trivia. It would make her the envy of her bridge friends – inside information, not from a super market rag or from an unauthorized autobiography but actualities from the person herself.

"I met a casting director for the CBC once who said that I had a perfect face for soaps." Jane grinned sheepishly. "I thought that I'd give it a whirl. To be honest though, I never really expected to actually get a part."

They had chatted about various plot lines during her two-year stint on the show, until they worked their way through to the character's tragic demise.

"How come they had you die of cancer?" he had asked. He knew she had been good for the program's ratings and had always wondered if there had been some seamy controversy involved that not even the gossip magazines had discovered.

Jane had suddenly grown quiet, vague. She stared off into the distance as if visualizing something familiar but definitely unpleasant. A brief look of faraway pain encased her pretty features. She looked at him again, sadness in her eyes that he had never witnessed before. "Everyone has to die," she had whispered, "sometime."

Harvey gulped the tonic water and stood up. "Well, Jane... ready?"

Jane nodded, taking a deep breath and slowly exhaling. She had already spent two hours in makeup and wardrobe in preparation for this scene. As long as there were no last minute re-writes, she knew that she would do okay. The usual butterflies crept into her stomach, fluttering their ever-present wings to annoy her.

She nodded again and rose to follow Harvey. Jane never actually felt like an actor until she was in front of the camera, director and crew. Sometimes, the crew members aggravated her with their blatant remarks – the off-scene come-ons of men away from their families for just a little too long – but the director was an old friend and that made up for some of the little inconveniences.

Scene 300 was set by a meandering stream. She and her husband were having a romantic picnic. The scene was a flashback. Yesterday, he had been killed in a mining accident, and she was left widowed with a small son. Today, Tyrus' final day on the set, they were newlyweds, in love and blissfully unaware of the fate that quietly waited.

Tyrus was already in his place. She sat down beside him on the cool, plush grass. A tacky, red-checkered tablecloth and a picnic lunch were spread out before them.

Tyrus was her idea of gorgeous – well-tanned and fair with chiseled features. They had already made one love scene that had ended in

an actual late-night rendezvous. Sometimes, acting was the difficult part.
　　　He smiled as she sat down, the genuine fondness would have been quickly apparent to anyone who really took the time to notice, but everyone was too busy with the preparations. The two sat solemnly as the last minute checks were made – lights, sound, camera angle, continuity. The set grew quiet as the moment grew closer. Finally, every detail was acceptable to the director's stringent approval.
　　　"Lights!" he roared, making his control clear to everyone.
　　　The powerful light board flicked on to drive away any menacing facial shadows that might dare to disrupt the perfect shot.
　　　"Camera!" he roared.
　　　The camera began to run, obtaining focus and speed.
　　　"Slate it!" he roared.
　　　A woman sprang in front of the camera with electronic clapboard, "Scene 300, Take 1", then quickly moved out of the way.
　　　"And…Action!" The director cued them to begin.
　　　Jane took the cue. She stared deeply into Tyrus' grey eyes and bit her lip nervously to keep it from trembling. "Do you think we'll always love each other as much as I love you today?" Her eyes searched those of her husband for the answer that she needed to hear.
　　　Tyrus smiled lovingly, reassuringly. "No matter what happens, I promise that I'll always, always love you." He bent forward to kiss her.
　　　Jane studied his eyes as they came closer and closer. She knew, deep down in the bottom chambers of her soul, that what he said was true. She prepared herself for the soft touch of his full mouth on hers and, for a brief second, closed her eyes.

　　　An excruciating pain seared her forehead as she felt a thump. Startled, Jane opened her tired eyes and, with effort, focused on her surroundings. The cause of her pain had been a Frisbee – a bright, red, round, Frisbee. She looked up. There, standing above her were four munchkins of varying ages all looking as startled as she felt and a little bit frightened as well.
　　　"You okay lady?" one inquired nervously as another one grabbed the Frisbee and sped away to face a screeching mother.
　　　Jane grinned and rubbed her anguished forehead. "Yes, fine. It's okay. Really."
　　　"Sorry," another one managed to spit out before they all took off in one gigantic flight of awkward, tanned legs.

Jane gingerly stood up, testing out her limbs for numbness. There was no crew, no camera, no gorgeous Tyrus—just a bunch of parents with bored, hot, obnoxious children. "So much for Hollywood," she murmured to no one in general as she brushed herself off.

CHAPTER EIGHT

The living room wall-clock chimed eight p.m. before Elliot grudgingly started to prepare his evening meal. Somehow, he could not motivate himself into beginning their usual Sunday feast, the only meal of the week when Jane actually relaxed her strict dietary guidelines. Sundays were supposed to be special—summer barbecues with marinated chicken pieces (dark meat for Jane, white meat for him and Bry), thick, Porterhouse steaks medium rare, creamy potato salad, crisp vegetables fresh from the garden, juicy, ripe, pink watermelon or winter gluttonies with oven-roasted chickens, whipped potatoes smothered in steaming spiced gravy, surrounded by buttered baby carrots--accompanied by smiling faces, spontaneous laughter and too-full tummies then television until bedtime. Sunday evenings were for the family. Together.

Elliot noticed that the Winchester chimes were beginning to drag. Must be time to wind the damned thing, he mentally noted. Sometimes, he fervently wished that Jane wasn't so adamant about her eclectic assortment of antiques.

He remembered the farm auction where she had purchased the antiquated timepiece--three generations of proud, hard-working, cattle farmers coming to a brusque halt when the lineage ended with no heir who desired to take up the reigns. So much easier to make a living working at a local factory or moving to the city to find employment that was not based on the fickle meat market.

The day was hot and sultry. Elliot had groaned and grumbled endlessly, bored to proverbial tears. He had wanted to leave but could not convince Jane. He had felt claustrophobic in the milling crowd with the constant nudging of elbows as people edged closer wanting to see the next item up for bid. At times, he could barely breathe due to the scent of perspiration, cheap cologne and even cheaper perfume. He had a dire, and growing desperate, urge for one breath of fresh, untainted air.

He had waited through four hours of mind-numbing tedium to get to the wall clock, had lost Brydon twice as the boy went in search of new treasures, had waded his way through a series of asinine, small-talk conversations with everyone from his mother's favorite euchre partner, Irma (lovely lady that one, always took the time to inquire about his mother's whereabouts and her general health as if the two women didn't talk on the telephone every other day), to complete strangers (his brain hurt from the constant attempt to smile and at least appear somewhat interested, could be bad for potential business otherwise) and the only other item Jane had bid on was a large box of old, blue willow dishes that were mostly in good condition, minus the two cups missing handles.

He watched as Jane surveyed the crowd to eye-out her upcoming competition. She could peg who would bid against her and who would drop out. She whispered conspiratorially, "It's an authentic H & B, Edwardian Westminster, made around 1920 in Germany. Mahogany wood. The listing says that the clock is in excellent working condition so it's worth at least $150.00."

"Jane," he asked her out of curiosity, "how do you do it?"

"Do what?"

"Know all of this stuff." He was honestly amazed that the woman who couldn't remember birthdays unless she wrote them all down on the kitchen calendar could randomly recite the name of the manufacturer, the year of manufacture and the estimated value of almost any antique they chanced upon.

"It's simple. You like baseball, especially the golden oldies like Babe Ruth. As a result, you've read a lot about them and can recite almost any statistic about any player. Antiques are my equivalent of baseball. When I read about an auction, I check out the listings and do my research. There's nothing magical about it. It's not like I have an eidetic memory or something. I just retain what interests me, same as you."

Elliot made a mental note to google the word "eidetic", not wanting to give Jane the satisfaction of knowing that he didn't have a clue what she was talking about. "So, if you know, doesn't that mean that everyone else does too? Why wait for four hours when everyone else has access to the same information?"

"Elly, I started bidding at auctions when I was ten-years-old. You get to learn how to read the crowd. If there are antique dealers around who are also waiting for the same item, you might as well forget it and go home. Most will have a potential buyer in mind before they even begin to bid. Otherwise, a person has a fighting chance. Most people are here looking for a cheap deal. They're here to buy a twenty-dollar dresser or

whatever because they can't afford to spend four or five hundred for a really nice one at Leon's or at The Brick."

True, the vintage clock was exquisite, but electric or battery-operated were so much simpler. If they had purchased a battery-operated clock, it would have taken a half-hour to walk into a local department store, pick out a clock, which came complete with a one-year warranty, and check out. Why Jane insisted on surrounding herself with another era he would never understand.

"It has character," Jane insisted as Elliot struggled to hang the clock on the living room wall. It had to be level, he'd been lectured, or the clock would run too fast or too slow.
"It has what?" he mumbled, straining to see what he was doing. He knew if the clock dropped there would be more than hell to pay.
"Character," she repeated and stood back to get a better look.
Elliot had to admit that it was true. The damned thing was nearly a metre long with a pendulum chime, and, at this point, he was positive that it weighed 150 pounds easy. Once the clock was tightly fastened in place (nothing less than a tornado or an earthquake, 6.5 on the Richter Scale, would shake it loose), he climbed off of the wooden stepladder and stood beside his wife, not exactly to admire the grand new addition, as to get accustomed to the time-piece being there.
He looked at Jane questioningly, "Who is going to remember to wind it once a week?"
She laughed and hugged him. "I will." She kissed him quickly on the cheek. "You won't have to do a thing. Promise." She crossed her heart, imitating a child's oath.

Well, it was her clock, so she could wind it when she came home. He wrote a hasty note on a scrap piece of paper to put on the refrigerator as a reminder, "Jane: wind clock".
Opening the refrigerator door, Elliot gazed inside at the well-stocked contents and selected beef cold cuts for a quick sandwich. There was no use starting anything major. If Jane had gone to visit Gertie or Dylan, which he presumed she had, the trip back took a minimum of three hours. Jane always stopped halfway to let Brydon stretch his legs and pig out on a hamburger and

french-fries (a bribe for being a well-behaved travelling companion).

The house was conspicuously quiet. Even Barclay hadn't returned. Damned cat, Elliot inwardly growled as he constructed a triple-decker, complete with mustard and dill pickle slices. Jane wasn't there to scold him about his cholesterol count, and what she didn't know, wouldn't hurt him.

Relaxing in front of the television with a cold beer and his mouth full, Elliot found that he could not concentrate on the Sunday evening movie, a slow-paced drama that seemed destined to lull rather than to inspire. Instead, his mind wandered back to the spring that he had finally asked Jane to marry him.

He had caught glimpses of her all that seemingly endless, bitterly cold winter trudging down the snow-packed sidewalks dressed in a long, bulky, down-filled, black winter coat and Artic Sorells. Rumour had it that she was hiding at her parents' farm; however, sunny, crisp days found her shopping, taking Brydon to a children's Saturday Matinee in Owen Sound, or for a Sunday skate at the local arena—bob skates at this point, single blade would probably wait until the next year. Elliot would stop by the arena mid-afternoon just in case she was there and watch intently from the much warmer viewing area. Jane always looked pale, rather disheveled and exhausted. She wore little to no discernible makeup to cover the dark circles under her eyes. Her long, blonde hair was constantly pulled back in a loose braid that stuck out like an afterthought from the bottom of a warm, multi-coloured, hand-knitted and very unbecoming toque. The local gossip was that a close friend of hers had died, but no one knew the exact details or even if it was true.

Brydon was always with Jane--her constant and only companion--decked out in his grey-blue snowsuit, sapphire blue, knitted toque, matching scarf and warm, nylon mittens, nose running from the cold, cheeks healthy, flushed, large, round, hazel eyes determined to see everything at once. When the snow was too deep, Jane hoisted her son onto her left hip. Otherwise, he seemed content to walk along at her side, safely hand-in-hand.

Jane had looked as if her spirit had finally been broken, like a wild colt that had bucked a saddle until all instinct to kick was vanquished. The spark was gone from her eyes. He couldn't remember the last time he had actually seen her really, truly, sincerely smile.

Slowly and unconsciously, Elliot's curiosity metamorphosed into near obsession. Thoughts of Jane haunted his every waking moment. Yes, Mrs. James, we have a very large selection of CCM hockey sticks. I'm sure that you'll find the perfect stick for Gerard. Let me show you a few, and we can figure out which one would work best for him. He's how old now, ten? Didn't Jane Kirkland babysit Gerard on weekends when he was little? Crazy how fast kids grow up! Good day, Mr. Henderson, great to see you. In fact, I was just about to call and let you know that the figure skates you ordered for Emily arrived this morning. How does she like her lessons this year? Wow, her first axel! That must have been great to watch. Lots of natural talent that one. Seems like only yesterday that I saw Jane Kirkland teach Emily how to skate backwards for the very first time.

Dozens of times, he had reached for the telephone to ask Jane if she would consider meeting him for a coffee; but, since she had rather blatantly rejected him in the past, he would always pull back. Surely, he had learned his lesson. Or had he?

When his curiosity--turned obsession--began to border on stalking, Elliot decided it was time to call Pam before Jane noticed that he was constantly and quite obviously (no lurking in the shadows for this boy) watching her from the distance and called the local Ontario Provincial Police (O.P.P) to request a restraining order. No Officer, he hasn't made direct contact yet, but he's like always there in the background… it's really starting to creep me out. Can't you just please make him go away?

Over a glass of rye and water (heavy on the rye, light on the water, no ice), Pam had enlightened Elliot. According to the elder sister, Jane was in the midst of a major winter depression, refused to look for employment, rebuffed any well-meaning suggestion of seeing a medical doctor, scoffed at any well-intentioned mention of anti-depressants or counselling and had basically informed anyone who cared, to fuck off and mind his or her own business. The entire family was just patiently, or rather impatiently, waiting for Jane to pull herself out of her maudlin mood, to get through this theorized episode of Seasonal Affective Disorder, to get a grip and to get on with her life. By the time Elliot had left, he was determined that all Jane really needed was for him to sweep her off her size seven feet, paint her toenails the brightest shade of cherry red that he could find, make love to her in ways she never dreamt possible and provide a much-needed relief from her family's constant, well-meaning if not well-intentioned badgering.

After a great deal of soul-searching, that included Elliot's supreme wonderment at his own obviously masochistic predisposition for embracing emotional torment, he tentatively decided to ask Jane to marry him though he'd wait for a month first to see if he could come to his senses. If a month had passed and he still felt the same way…that strange, bizarre feeling of being possessed by a desire so intense that it destroyed all sane, rational thought…he would ask her. If Jane said no, that was fine. Perhaps then, the spell would be broken. Elliot had a fairly steady broad on the side anyway. Diana wasn't really much to look at--a bit on the heavy side in a these-hips-were-made for-popping-out –babies-way and not nearly as pretty as Jane—but she was an easy lay when he needed or wanted one, could cook a four-course, gourmet meal with her eyes closed and would marry him tomorrow if he asked. Of that, he was positive.

With a stiff swig of rye in his system for courage, Elliot climbed into his jet-black, two-seater, Mazda Miata convertible and headed over to Jane's parents' farm. He was a knight-in-shining-armour with his trusted steed (over 130 horsepower at the wheels) about to rescue his fair damsel-in-distress. He felt carefree with the top down, letting the cool wind tousle his dark hair. Another winter was over at last. Almost like being twenty again, full of vim and vigor with a thousand plans for the future.

As he drove up the gravel lane-way, Elliot noticed Jane walking on the spacious, two-acre lawn. Dressed in jeans, black and white runners, a heavy, red plaid work-shirt and work gloves, her hair pulled back in the trademark braid, he assumed she was more focused on spring clean-up rather than on enjoying the kiss of rebirth in the welcomed warmth of the early spring sun. His heart skipped a beat – a cliché he had often heard but never actually understood until that precise moment.

Jane stopped briefly to watch him gear down and bring his car to a halt. Emanating neither curiosity nor confusion, she hesitated only for a moment before she removed the beige work gloves and turned to go inside the red-brick farmhouse.

  Elliot eased into park and quickly jumped out of his car, determined to get this potential fiasco over with before his waning courage completely vanished. What the hell had he been thinking? Seriously. Not too late to make up some lame excuse about wanting to talk to her dad. "Jane," he called. "Can I to speak to you?" Oh, hell, too late now. He waited, hoping that she would listen.

  Jane stopped at the sound of his voice and slowly turned around to face him. She eyed him curiously now, a slight frown creasing her smooth brow, and started walking towards him. Elliot could see Mrs. Kirkland peer through the kitchen window, probably wondering who was there, then the window was empty again.

  Jane spoke softly, almost inaudibly, "What do you want, Elly?" She did not smile or look at all interested that he was there or that he even existed. She stopped at least two metres away from where he stood leaning on his freshly washed and waxed car trying desperately to appear calm and debonair, like Robert Redford in the Great Gatsby. Could she tell that his heart was pounding so fast that he could barely breathe?

  "Come here," he bade her, smiling, and motioning with his right hand for her to advance. Willing her to advance. Inwardly, pleading with the fates, the cosmos, and any god or demi-god out there who would listen to make her advance. Something so personal should be done within a personal range, not yelled so that the neighbours the next farm over could hear.

  Reluctantly, she moved closer and positioned herself in front of him. Edging closer, she remained well outside of his comfort zone, her eyes noticeably mistrusting – as if she was preparing for a hasty retreat if necessary.

  "Jane," he cleared this throat and lowered his voice hoping to sound sincere, "you and I have known each other all of our lives. I know that we've had a few misunderstandings in the past. I'm sorry if I seemed possessive, but it was because I cared for you so much that the thought of you with anyone else drove me absolutely crazy. I also know that I have said and done some pretty nasty things that I can never erase. I want to make it up to you."

  Jane looked at him, still not smiling. "Elly, get to the punch line." She did not look impressed by his well-rehearsed speech.

  Elliot inhaled deeply and, with all of the courage he could muster, threw a lifetime of insecurities and his battered heart to the wind. In response, in the distance, he could hear the ritual, springtime mating chorus of male frogs, establishing their territory and hoping to attract mates. Rock on, my brethren and good luck, he thought. If they could do it, so could he. "Jane, I love you. I want to marry you." He stared at her, awaiting the words, awaiting her suddenly breaking out in uncontrollable fits of laughter, waiting for his heart to be finally destroyed forever. She could torture him with her silence, mutilate him with a whisper.

She studied him, dark green eyes narrowing, and folded her arms over her small chest. "Really?" she asked, her head tilting slightly to the right.

Elliot fought to control his breathing, fought to regain a normal heart rhythm. "Really." He reached his left hand into the pocket of his black leather jacket, his fingers enclosing the small, pink velveteen ring box.

Jane straightened her head, her eyes never leaving his. "You do realize that Brydon and I are a package deal, right?"

"Of course, I realize that. He's your son. He's a part of you. I want to watch Brydon grow up and be a part of his life. I want to be a part of your life. I want you both to be a part of my life. I want to be a family." When Jane grinned, Elliot felt positive that his heart would explode.

"So is that why you spent the entire winter following us?" She chuckled and shook her head.

Deflated, Elliot released the ring box. Shit. Busted. He hoped that the frogs were doing better than he was. "Guilty as charged, but I can explain..."

Jane shook her head and moved to stand beside him, leaning on his car. "No need." She caressed the spotless, grey leather upholstery. "Nice ride. It's only a two-seater so I guess if you ever want to see a movie with Bry and me, we'll have to take my car."

Not the answer he was hoping for but maybe one very small step in the right direction. He felt like such a fool to think that she would just fall into his arms. "I can always sell the car, Jane. It's just a car."

"Not yet. It's a very nice car." For the first time in months, Jane really, truly, sincerely smiled. "Do you want to come inside for a coffee? Bry is napping, but he should be up soon. I'll warn you though, he plays a very mean game of Go Fish."

Three months later, not only had Jane procured employment in the Audio Visual Department at the local hospital, written, recorded, edited, and burned to DVD her first thirty-minute training program on Sterilization Procedures for SPD (Sterilization and Processing Department), but Elliot had managed to painstakingly polish her perfectly pedicured toenails three various shades of pink--magenta and fuchsia being his favourite--cherry red, periwinkle, lavender and sparkled silver.

By Jane's birthday, Elliot had decided to propose again, this time stepping up his game plan and adding a touch of romance. In preparation, he'd spent the better part of two vacation days scouring his spacious apartment (the bottom floor of an older house, character included with its high ceilings, multi-paned, casement windows and original wainscoting) and made sure every nook and cranny could pass a white glove inspection. Two weeks of dirty laundry, bath towels and dishes were washed and neatly put away. Fresh, white cotton sheets, wrinkle-free and ready to caress bare skin, hugged the newly flipped double mattress. Any moldy food item or plastic container filled with an unclassified, unrecognizable substance had been removed from the refrigerator and disposed of. He had even remembered to make sure that the roll of soft, two-ply toilet paper was hanging so that it rolled-out over and not under.

Furniture and electronic equipment were freed from multiple layers of dust. The random assortment of bargain basement and flea market finds were arranged so that the oak-veneered coffee table became the main focus. On the coffee table were a white porcelain budvase with a single red rose, a bottle of Chardonnay, two long-stemmed wine glasses, two unscented, red, pillar candles and his gift to Jane--a vintage emerald and 14K yellow gold bracelet that he had purchased on eBay and then taken to a jewellery store to have appraised to make sure that he hadn't been ripped off—boxed and wrapped in pink wrapping paper with a white bow.

Dinner, cake and ice cream with Jane's parents and Brydon were mandatory. Thankfully, Mrs. Kirkland had readily agreed to watch Brydon afterwards so that he and Jane could spend some time alone.

Nick had adamantly tried to talk Elliot out of proposing to

Jane, had, in fact, informed his brother that the very idea was absolutely ludicrous when Elliot had no idea who the kid's father was. Not that it was any of Nick's business, but Elliot had asked Jane to which she made it absolutely clear that the topic was not presently open for discussion. Brydon's father was just a guy, a sperm donor, who she'd been briefly involved with who didn't want children. Elliot assumed that said sperm donor was Jane's college ex-boyfriend, Todd, who, again, was a topic that was presently not open for discussion. Clear? Absolutely.

Jane smiled in genuine delight when Elliot guided her into his living room. "Wow, your place looks great! What did you do, hire a maid?"

Elliot returned the smile, inwardly pleased that she had noticed the difference. It wasn't that he was an irreversible slob; he just didn't normally take the time to really notice his surroundings until he occasionally woke up knee-deep in filth and thought, how the fuck did that happen? "Nope, I had a few days off this week, so I thought I'd do some cleaning. Why don't you sit down, and I'll pour us some wine?"

Jane curled up on the couch with her back against the padded arm. She accepted the glass of wine and watched as Elliot lit the candles then sat down beside her. "A man who cleans is very sexy. Do you cook too?"

"Nope. Pretty much live on TV dinners and take-out when I'm not with you, but I've never turned down a dish towel to help clean up after a meal someone else has cooked. That should count for something." *Elliot raised his glass as if to toast.* "Happy Birthday, Jane."

Jane clinked her glass against Elliot's. "Thank you." *Jane sipped her wine then grinned.* "Wow, Elly, this is really nice. Candles, wine, a rose. Are you, by any chance, trying to seduce me?"

"Always," *Elliot replied. He tried to sound casual, hoping that his growing nervousness would not betray him.* "That goes without saying. But first, I have a present for you." *He picked up the wrapped bracelet and handed the box to Jane.* "I hope you like it."

Jane searched for a coaster and placed her wine glass on the coffee table. "Thank you, again." *She smiled as she carefully unwrapped her present. Her eyes grew wide when she opened the box.* "Oh My God, Elly. It's beautiful! I won't say you shouldn't have because it's absolutely gorgeous!" *Jane laughed, her eyes exuding pleasurable amazement.*

"Genuine emeralds to match your green eyes." *He reached for the* bracelet. "Here, let me help you put it on." As Jane held out her wrist, he continued, "Each emerald is connected by a tiny, 14 karate gold butterfly with pinpoint diamonds set in the wings." The appraiser had assured Elliot that the oval-shaped emeralds and the tiny diamonds were both real and of good quality. A professional cleaning had made the bracelet sparkle like new. "Emeralds symbolize loyalty and faithfulness. Butterflies symbolize transformation, our journeys in life, and life itself." Elliot could feel his hands begin to shake as he closed the clasp on the bracelet.

Jane readjusted herself on the sofa so she could kiss Elliot on the cheek. "Wow. I love the fact that you put so much thought into the gift. That makes it all the more special. I will treasure the bracelet always."

Elliot cleared his throat trying to fight off a sudden constriction. Nerves. "I have something else for you. Wait here and I'll be right back." He gulped down half a glass of wine then rose to walk to his nearby bedroom to retrieve the same small, pink velveteen box that he had clutched in his hand just a few months before. A part of him felt like he was about to die. The sex was good. He and Brydon got along like gangbusters. Still, maybe it was too soon. Not for him but for Jane. Maybe he should wait until Thanksgiving or Christmas…or New Year's Eve…Elliot pulled open his dresser drawer before he could lose his nerve and extracted the box.

He walked back into the living room. Jane had shifted on the sofa so that her feet were planted firmly on the floor… getting ready to run maybe… She had her head tilted slightly to the side with a look that screamed curiosity. He knelt down beside her, held up the box and opened it so she could see the ring – a brilliant cut diamond set in yellow gold with two small emeralds in heart settings on either side.

Elliot took a deep breath to steady his nerves. "Jane, I love you. I love Brydon. I want us to be a family. Will you marry me?"

Jane straightened her head and swallowed. "Can I teach you how to cook?" she enquired earnestly, humour playing around her eyes.

"Jane, you can teach me anything you want." Elliot extracted the ring from the box and held it up to her. "If I learn how to cook, will you marry me?"

Jane, after motioning for Elliot to rise, held out her hand for him to place the ring on her finger. "Elly, I'd marry you even if all you ever do is burn water."

The wedding was a small, intimate Partnership in Life Ceremony at a non-denominational wedding chapel in Kitchener with immediate family and close friends only in attendance. Nick was his Best Man; Pam was Jane's Maid of Honour. As Elliot and Jane spoke the vows to cherish each other in honesty, tenderness, and faithfulness, he knew that his life was being transformed forever. With the utterance of two simple words he would instantly transition from being a self-possessed bachelor to being a husband and to being a father both. Jane looked so elegant, so beautiful in her simple, cream-coloured dress that Elliot knew, deep down in his very soul, that he would never regret this moment. "I do."

With Brydon safely tucked away at Pam's for the night, Jane and Elliot returned to his apartment choosing to wait and save for a real honeymoon later on. Elliot studied his new bride as she slowly strolled into the bedroom towards him. Jane had donned a long, black silk negligee that gently clung to her curves. The high side-slit revealed her long, slender legs, exposing black stockings fastened onto a garter belt. Very sexy. Elliot caught his breath, mentally capturing the vision to store it forever. He had wanted this woman for an eternity and now he could barely believe the day's events.

Jane lit a long, tapered candle, placed it on the nightstand and turned off the light. She looked so breathtakingly beautiful. Elliot had bought champagne and handed Jane a long-stemmed glass as she sat down on the bed beside him. Jane accepted then waited. He held up his glass and announced, "I would like to make a toast. To Mr. and Mrs. Elliot Fallis. May our marriage be a long and happy one."

Jane took a sip then held up her glass in a return gesture. "I, too, would like to make a toast – to new beginnings." She set down her glass, stood up, and, never once taking her eyes away from his face casually dropped the gown to the floor exposing her tanned, naked flesh in the soft, glowing light.

Elliot folded back the blankets to allow her access to their marital bed. He placed his own glass on the nightstand and snuggled down beside his new bride. He began to caress and stroke her, his mouth searching for hers. God, she felt so good.

Her hands were skillful in their maneuvers unlike any other lover he had known before. By the time he entered her, he was almost at the peak of his own ecstasy. If he had maintained any doubts in the beginning, they quickly faded away.

Afterwards, Elliot reluctantly blew out the dwindled candle. Jane had quietly rolled over to her side of the bed and was either sleeping or trying to make him believe that she was. Totally satiated, he curled up close to her, spooning himself around her, not wanting to lose the moment he had so often dreamed of.

Yes, everything was finally falling into place. Elliot had even put a down payment on a house as his wedding gift to his new wife. A surprise for tomorrow. The 1950's bungalow, originally built by a local farmer as a retirement dwelling, boasted a picturesque front porch with white trim and a carefully maintained, fenced-in backyard that was perfect for Brydon. Initially, Elliot's heart had shuddered when he heard the asking price; however, he quickly decided that his family would have a proper home even if it meant spending his entire life savings. They could take possession in three weeks then everything would be fine. He knew it would be. It had to be.

Elliot finished his beer, totally ignoring the remainder of his sandwich. Nine o'clock had chimed and still no familiar sound of crunching gravel in the driveway.

Beginning to really worry, he walked over to their large, oak roll-top desk that harboured everything needed to organize their household, and extracted Jane's personal directory. Elliot riffled through the pages until he came to Gertie's name and telephone number. A sealed envelope tucked inside Jane's smaller, matching address book caught his attention. The envelope was addressed to him in Jane's writing.

Elliot grabbed the letter and sat down in front of the television. The Sunday night movie was playing, but he did not notice.

Oh god, he thought. Two things ran through his mind—a suicide note or a Dear John letter. He mentally rejected both possibilities. A person doesn't generally tuck away a suicide note, and Jane had vowed to love and cherish him forever. Goodbye was not an option.

Five minutes later, after opening another beer, Elliot gained enough courage to open the envelope. He pulled out Jane's rose-coloured stationery—very feminine. She saved it for special occasions only.

Dear Elly,

By the time you read this, I'll be far away.

I don't know how to explain this, but there's so much of life I want to try yet, so many things I want to do, so much left to explore.

Brydon is fine. He's staying with a friend until I can get him. Thanks for being so good to both of us.

I'll call once I get settled to make arrangements to pick up Barclay and our stuff.

I'm really sorry.

Love,
Jane

Elliot read the note three times before the words began to sink in, hammering at his wall of denial. Three times before, she'd dropped Brydon off at her parents and had disappeared for a few days, no explanation, no warning. Three times before, he'd tracked down the boy and brought him home before finally locating Jane. How many fucking times did he have to go through this? He wanted to scream but found no voice.

Instead, he walked over to the desk and took out the leather bound directory. He dialed Gertie's telephone number and tried desperately to compose himself.

"Hello?"

"Gertie?" he inquired, his breath shallow, his heart pounding.

The voice hesitated. "Yes. Elliot, is that you?"

A tear formed in Elliot's left eye and he blinked it back angrily. "Yeah, it's me. Is Jane there?" He could hear his voice shake and struggled to regain control.

"No, she's not," Gertie replied softly.

Elliot swallowed, an acrid taste in his mouth, and continued. "Do you know where she is? She's not answering her cell phone. Look, I know she's gone again. All she left was this freakin' vague note about leaving to find herself. I just want to know that she's okay."

"Jane's okay. She has a job interview tomorrow at a small TV station in New Jersey. A guy she went to college with tracked her down on Facebook and asked her if she'd be interested. Elliot, I can't believe that she didn't tell you. I'm so sorry. Other than that, I seriously don't know what to say."

So much for vowing to be honest. This was just fucking ludicrous. "This is the first I'm hearing about it." Elliot breathed in deeply. "Is Brydon there?" he asked, hoping for a positive reply.

Again the voice hesitated. "Would you like to speak to him?"

Elliot sighed in partial relief. "Yes, thank you," Elliot responded mechanically, trying not to take his emotions out on Gertie. After all, it wasn't her fault. She was just helping out an old friend. God knew what Jane had told her.

After a moment of silence, an eternity of silence, Elliot heard whispering, then a small, "Hello?"

"Brydon," he managed, "are you okay, Buddy?"

"Daddy Elliot," Brydon sobbed ruefully, "I want to come home." The child's voice was full of indignation. "I want to come home now!"

"Ssh Brydon, it's okay." A rebel tear coursed a path down Elliot's cheek.

"Daddy Elliot, I love you. Please come and get me," the little voice begged urgently.

"Okay, Bry. Let me speak to Gertie again." Below the tears, below the unexpected hurt and the sense of betrayal, below the pain, Elliot felt anger starting to form like a storm brewing out of the west waiting to spew lightning and drench all who were caught within the range of its downpour.

"Hello," came Gertie's familiar voice. "Elliot, are you okay?"

"No, I'm not okay," he snapped, no longer caring. How could he possibly be okay? In one weekend, he had lost a ball tournament, his wife and his family. It was like asking if he was enjoying the weather when it was forty below and he was standing outside buck-naked and penniless. He was definitely not okay. Not even close. He retorted defiantly, "Turn on the porch light. I'm coming to get my son."

CHAPTER NINE

The motel room was small but neatly kept; the air-conditioning, miraculously enough, worked. The bright, burnt orange, polyester bedspread matched the bright, burnt orange, polyester curtains. The immaculate bathroom came complete with soft, white towels, a paper-wrapped drinking glass, travel size shampoos and soaps. On top of the long, wooden dresser sat a television, two plastic cups, two plastic spoons, a small coffee maker along with a plastic basket full of tea and instant coffee pouches. On the wooden nightstand lay a brochure: "Welcome to the Chiften—50 Fully-Equipped Rooms, Air Conditioning, Cable T.V., Direct Dialing and a Heated Swimming Pool all for your Overnight Pleasure".

Jane wondered about the term "fully-equipped". As compared to what? She surveyed the room, mentally envisioning what it would look like with only a bed, naked mattress and nothing else. Would she still pay seventy dollars per night if the room was only "partially equipped"? Her idea of "fully equipped" included a tall, blonde male with a body paralleling a Greek god, a bottle of very expensive brandy, soft music and a queen-size bed with satin sheets.

She reclined, quite relaxed, on the hard bed and scanned through the television channels. A Cosby show re-run—one of Brydon's favourites. She wondered if he was watching it too. Was Elliot?

Elliot was definitely not like the tall blondes she'd always had a soft spot for. Nowhere close. Jane had met her "ideal" man once though and it had proved to be a mistake grandiose. Sometimes, it was better to have fantasies than having a fantasy become reality. At least a fantasy wouldn't let you down and you could make up your own ending.

Her cousin, Dana, had convinced her to try Toronto. "You're wasting your time living in Welland," Dana had often scolded after Jane had graduated from Broadcasting: Radio and Television. "There's nothing there for you."

Jane had hesitated; however, it was true that Welland was beginning to get to her. She loved its sprawling, small town atmosphere, but she had spent February and March with no heat in her apartment except for the radiant space heaters she had scrounged to purchase. Numerous calls to her local MPP had led nowhere, and the landlord refused to believe that there was anything wrong. By mid-April, Jane gave her notice. Enough was enough.

Leaving Brydon with her parents until she could get established, Jane moved into the tiny, Briar Hill attic apartment with her cousin. There were exactly 46 steps from the outside of the house to the top of their stairwell which left her exhausted on moving day. Thankfully, Jane had decided to put most of her belongings in storage until she could get a place of her own.

The part that Jane could not get used to was the fact that, in order to get to their apartment door, they had to literally walk through the hallway of second-floor apartment. Talk about an intrusion of privacy.

"The guy who lives on the second floor," Dana confided, *"is a male model."* She grinned mischievously over her Caesar salad while taking a lunch break at an exceedingly busy cafeteria near her Bloor Street office.

Intrigued, Jane's face lit up. *"Yeah? What does he look like?"* Jane had yet to meet the other tenants and had assumed that whoever lived there was not the type to make first moves when meeting new neighbours. Neither was she.

Dana smiled, knowing her cousin well. *"He's tall,--6' 1" maybe-- has short, blonde hair, great body. His name is Nick. I think he's gorgeous, but then we always did have different tastes in men so you can decide for yourself."*

Jane could feel herself grimace, her stomach knotting. *"His name is Nick? You have to be kidding me."* She hated that name.

Dana shrugged. *"Sorry, that's his name all right."*

"So, what's he like?" Jane pressed for further details, her curiosity slowly mounting again. She had never lived above a male model before — a would-be rock star who only knew one cord of any given song, yes, but a real, bona fide, certified, write- home-to-mom, male model, no. It was the type of situation that sparked the imagination and would be super material for a short story in an erotica section of a provocative, women's magazine. Almost as good as the male, exotic dancer she had briefly dated while in college. Someday, she decided, she should seriously think about taking up

a career in writing sexually explicit love scenes, but this part of her life was definitely all about research.
    "Okay, I guess. I've only met him a couple of times. Seems nice enough. He said that he was discovered at the age of sixteen while walking down Yonge Street, then rushed off to New York for photo sessions and life in the fast lane. Now he travels all over the world but keeps his home base here in good ole Toronna." Dana grew serious as she changed topics, the time for lunch break almost over. "Are you going to work this afternoon?"
    "No, I'm off until tomorrow at one." Finding work in a nearby camera store had provided Jane with a basic income until she could find a way to break into broadcasting. Major market, major tough she had discovered.
    "Have you talked to Todd yet?"
    Jane sighed as she gathered up her empty paper plate and cup. "He won't return my calls." She stood up to leave. "Look Dana, I have to run. I want to check out a few things this afternoon. I'll see you at home. Movie and strippers tonight?"
    "You've got it." Dana laughed. "Catcha later."
    Todd had been a thorn in Jane's side all spring. She must have apologized three thousand times to no avail. He wouldn't return her calls, or reply to her texts and if she did manage to reach him on his land-line, he was always cold and brief. She tried to convince herself that he would gradually come around, but after all of the continuous rejections, she had her doubts.
    These days, the closest she usually managed to talk to Todd was his roommate, Quin – a saxophone playing street musician who was constantly on uppers or whatever else he could find. Quin was interesting, Jane had to admit, although she quickly grew tired of his constant sexual innuendoes and stories of how his last lover had been addicted to Meth and alcohol. "Deadly combo, Jane. Deadly." She had no inclination of filling the part-time lover position Quin offered – he only dated green-eyed blondes--and had informed him bluntly that she was not interested.
    After trudging up Yonge Street, uphill all the way, Jane sighed with relief on seeing their house. The weather was hot and sticky. The city smelt foul. Her legs ached, not used to footing it everywhere. All Jane could think about was soaking in a tub of cool water and Epsom salts before going out.
    Finally finding her key in the very bottom of her purse, she attempted to unlock the outside door. Up to this point, the door was either

already open or Dana had been there. "Damn it," she growled after several unsuccessful attempts. "What's wrong with this stupid lock?!" She could get the key in, but it would not turn.

Paranoia and frustration set in. The landlady, a large, Swedish woman, lived on the first floor and had not been exactly thrilled when she had discovered that Jane was staying with Dana. The apartment was tiny and Dana was already sharing it with a mutual, male friend. Jane kept expecting the lady to come out any moment and commence her lecture one more time.

True, the arrangement wasn't great, (Jane had no space of her own) but, thankfully, it wasn't permanent. She would be getting an apartment soon. Jane just had to find something suitable and had discovered, much to her chagrin, that potential landlords were not overly thrilled to rent to a single mother. It didn't matter that she had a job and references, the combination of her and Brydon was a risk. At least Dana's apartment had a good-sized bathroom with a comfortable tub. She hated those little pretend tubs where she had to fold her long legs up when she sat down in order to fit in. It reminded her of the days of washing her feet in the kitchen sink when she was a child.

Finally losing patience, Jane rang the buzzer for the second-floor apartment, hoping there would be someone home to rescue her from her embarrassing plight. On hearing footsteps approach from inside, Jane silently gave thanks for small mercies.

The door opened, exposing the most gorgeous specimen of male flesh she had ever encountered. He looked as surprised to see her as she was to see him. Regaining her composure, Jane introduced herself.

"Hi. I'm Jane. I'm staying upstairs with Dana. I was hoping that you could let me in as I can't seem to get the key to work in the lock." She smiled, trying desperately not to drool. Certainly, he was more than just a mere illusion.

The illusion smiled and assured her that she wasn't the first person to have trouble with the pesky lock. It had taken him days to perfect opening it. He took Jane's key and demonstrated the correct approach. "See, it's not so tough if you know how."

"Thanks," Jane managed to force out. She could feel heat rise to her cheeks. Odd, she thought. Why am I blushing over a key?

She followed Nick as he led the way to her landing, waiting for him to suddenly disappear, to find herself back outside struggling to get in.

He stopped as they reached her door. "So, you're Dana's cousin." He smiled, exposing perfect, white teeth.

Porcelain veneers, maybe, Jane thought. "Hard to tell, I suppose," Jane offered, thinking that she and Dana were almost opposites in appearance. Dana was a petite brunette with wide-set, blue eyes and a lovely, open, confident smile that automatically set her customers at ease. A great asset when working for a stockbroker.

"Not really," his voice was smooth and low, "you're both very attractive." He held out his hand. "By the way, my name is Nick." His dark blue eyes sparkled with self-confidence.

Jane shook his hand, thinking naughty thoughts.

All during her long, relaxing bath, Jane's mind kept drifting back to the semi-demi god who lived just below her. All of her life, she had kept a mental image of the perfect man in the back of her mind. Nick was everything and more. They just did not make them like that back home. Dana had also informed her that he lived there with his fiancée, but she was in New York shopping for a few days.

On their way out for the evening, Dana asked Nick if he cared to join them. He declined, saying that if he wanted to see a naked man, he could take his clothes off and look into a mirror.

The movie was super, an epic thriller, and the exotic dancers were entertaining. Regardless, Jane could not concentrate. All she could think of was that her ideal man was at home and all alone for the weekend.

"Is Nick's fiancée as gorgeous as he is?" Jane asked Dana, unable to keep thoughts of Nick from roaming through her very vivid imagination.

Dana shook her head. "Surprisingly enough, she's actually fairly average looking. From the way she talks, I think her family has money though. Her father is paying for the apartment, and she receives an allowance of some sort so she doesn't have to work full-time."

"Wow, nice." Jane groaned in envy.

"Why?"

"No reason really. I was just wondering what Nick would be like in bed, but if he had an absolutely stunning fiancée, I was going to quit dreaming before I end up with a massive crush on the guy." Jane laughed good-naturedly. Crush or all out obsession. Whichever came first.

"Personally, I'd be afraid to find out," Dana confided. "Someone who looks that good has got to be bad at something!"

When the two young women returned home, they giggled quietly as they began to sneak up the stairwell, hoping to not disturb the second-

floor inhabitant with their late night antics. Brief thoughts of trying to reach her bedroom at her parents' house after a night of barhopping without waking her father flitted through Jane's mind. At least back home, she knew every step, every possible creak. This house was foreign territory. Once they reached the hallway that connected the open, second-floor apartment to Dana's, Jane realized their well-meaning efforts were totally unnecessary. Nick was still awake and eager to play.

The living room archway of the second-floor apartment was directly across from Dana's apartment door. It reminded Jane of living in a boarding- room house rather than being two, self-contained apartments. Soft glowing lights drew the girls' attention, an instinct so innate that no conscious thought was involved. They gaped in unison as Nick reclined on his black, leather couch wearing nothing but a black, satin G-string as he innocently watched a movie on his flat-screen TV. Jane's first inclination was to cover her eyes, but she couldn't resist spreading her fingers to peak. When Dana decided to call it an early night, Jane decided to get to know her new neighbour a little better.

For the next two hours, Nick and Jane discussed life and their experiences while drinking herbal tea. She told him about growing up in the country, about school, about looking for work in her field, about her son. He listened intently, saying how strong and how brave she was to keep going forward despite the difficulties that she must face. When he asked about the father of her son, Jane just shook her head and said the guy was gone like a bad dream. Nick sighed, saying he couldn't understand men like that. It was obviously the guy's loss, not hers.

Nick's life was no less complicated. His father was a Lead Foreman for a commercial construction company and thought being a model wasn't a job for real men. There had been many arguments over the years with his mom always mediating, trying to keep the peace. There had also been many times when Nick had thought about quitting. Being a model was not as glamorous as it seemed. At the age of 25, he was almost a recluse, for once he stepped outside, he became public property.

"Once," he emphasized, "I missed my subway stop by five places because an old lady wouldn't leave me alone. I don't go out much anymore. I don't drink, or smoke, or do drugs because it affects my skin. I have to be careful who I'm seen with as it could affect my career. If I'm not working, I'm working to stay in shape. It's a meat market out there and no one wants to pay for less than perfection."

The two talked easily, exchanging stories, until the conversation, by following the random pathways that conversations can traverse when there is no concrete destination in mind, turned to waterbeds and how uncommon they had become except in specialty stores. Jane admitted that she had originally gotten hers in order to appease old injuries. The bed had been a graduation present from her parents. She had saved for half and they had paid for the remainder.

"Where are you sleeping now?" Nick asked nonchalantly. "Dana's apartment is so tiny."

"Dana has a bed in the window dormer, Justin has the bedroom and I sleep on the couch. It's not the greatest arrangement in the world, but it's only temporary so we make do." Jane stifled a yawn. It was getting way past her bed-time. "And it's definitely better than sleeping in a homeless shelter downtown. I'm looking for an apartment, but I'm discovering that finding one is easier said than done."

"Sleeping on a couch night after night can't be comfortable though. What size is your actual bed?" Nick inquired, innocently enough.

"A queen size," Jane shared, beginning to intensely miss her bed, her sheets and her snuggly warm, down-filled comforter.

Nick jumped up gracefully, his leg muscles flexing in the effort. "I'm not sure what size mine is. It's either a double or a super single." He strolled past her and into the bedroom. "Come here," he called, "and tell me what you think."

Every centimetre of Jane suddenly tensed. She knew what was happening but was not sure if she was ready yet. Taking a deep breath, she rose from her sitting position and followed.

Reclining on the bed, propped up on his elbow, Nick grinned boyishly. "Well," he asked, "what do you think?" The sweeping gesture of his free hand only emphasized his true intentions--'look at me and try to resist'. So much for the art of subtle seduction.

Jane was petrified. A part of her wanted to say good night and then crawl back to the safety of Dana's couch. Another part urged her forward. Trying to act casual, Jane studied the bed. It looked so inviting, adorned in red satin from sheets to comforter and pillow shams – utopia.

She sat down gingerly on the edge and tried to smile. She did not want him to know how nervous she really was. "I'd say it's a double," she commented. Jane wished desperately that she was built like a playboy bunny. She felt like hamburger next to a T-bone steak.

When Nick motioned for her to join him in closer proximity, Jane hesitated then thought, okay kiddo, he's only another human being, nothing to be afraid of. She studied his warm, friendly, blue eyes and asked him if he would care for a massage. Nick agreed without hesitation.

Jane excused herself momentarily to pee and to wash her hands. When she returned, the bedside lamp had been turned off and candles had been lit instead providing a soft, intimate atmosphere. Nick was under the covers from his waist down, waiting patiently. After he rolled onto his stomach, Jane took off her shoes and climbed on top of his comforter-clad buttocks to let her fingers work their magic along his taunt, smooth, blemish-free skin.

"I found a small bottle of baby oil on the vanity in the bathroom. Is it okay if I use it on you?" The last thing she wanted to do was cause a skin eruption of any kind. Yikes. He made his living with this skin.

"Sure. Sounds good." Nick smiled as he adjusted the pillow under his head.

Jane squirted a small amount of the oil onto his skin then began manipulating the well-defined bicep and triceps muscles of his right arm. She could feel his sexual energy vibrate through her hands. I could really use another drink, she thought. A drink and a joint. That would be so sweet.

"So how often do you have to work out to maintain the muscle definition?" she asked as she worked her way up to his deltoid…broad, strong shoulders…mmm…

"I actually started out working in construction with my dad before I went into modeling full-time, so I built the base muscles the old fashioned way. When I started modeling, the agency set me up with a trainer to make sure I didn't bulk up too much. Right now, I generally work out for an hour or so a day unless I'm on a shoot." Nick purred his appreciation as Jane moved to his left arm. "You wouldn't believe how good that feels. I may have to take you on the road with me."

Jane smiled. "Kind of tough to travel with a kid in tow. Nice thought though."

When she had finished his left arm and shoulder, she dribbled baby oil onto his back, careful with the amount as she didn't want to stain his sheets. Good thing, she thought, that I'm not massaging his front or I'd totally lose it. Concentrate girl. "You have some major knots in your trapezius muscles. This may hurt for a second." Nick winced in pain as she pressed down on the knots to try and release them. "Don't hold your breath," she scolded. "It'll only make it worse."

"Seriously, Jane, where did you learn how to do this? I pay a lot of money for massages half this good."

Once the knots had forfeited their grip, Jane moved onto a deep muscle technique, pressing down hard and working her way up in long, smooth strokes to lengthen and relax the deeper muscle tissue. "My friends and I used to give each other massages in school, especially around exam time. I got curious one day and decided to do a bit of research on the different muscles and on the different massage techniques. Nothing major. I just like doing things the right way. For example, there are 700 muscles in the body. The back, alone, has three different layers of muscles-- superficial, intermediate and deep. So if you want a gentle, relaxing massage, you work on the outer layers only. However, if you want a really good massage, you need to work hard enough to reach the muscles of the vertebral column."

"Wow, I'm impressed. You must have been very popular in school." Nick grinned.

Jane laughed. "I certainly didn't lack for volunteers to practice on." A naked, smiling Todd flashed through her mind. Todd, who never relaxed long enough for Jane to complete the massage. Todd, who once she hit the sensitive spots halfway down his back, would twist around and catch her before she lost her balance and fell.

When she arrived at the small of his back, Nick quickly motioned for Jane to lift her hips so that he could pull down the comforter. Jane was not surprised to see that the black G-string had magically disappeared, his round, very firm buttocks left exposed. "Then there's the buttocks muscles," she continued. "This muscle is your gluteus medius and this one is your gluteus maximus." She gently traced his lines with the tip of her index finger. "They are two of my favourite muscles."

Nick moaned softly then swallowed hard. "Can I ask what your favourite muscle is?"

"That would definitely be the pectoral muscles," Jane admitted. "I have a huge male nipple fetish. When I see a guy with nice pecs, I absolutely melt."

Nick sighed audibly. "I must be doing something wrong then. My pecs didn't make you melt."

"Are you serious?" Jane cajoled. "Your everything makes me melt. I have to keep thinking about the ugliest guy I know or I'd end up dissolving into a complete puddle of goo, oozing off the bed and onto the floor."

"Jane," Nick smiled and murmured half into his pillow. He shifted his position slightly so he could reach back and touch her leg. "If you want, you can spend the night with me. There's no use being uncomfortable on Dana's couch when this bed's big enough for both of us."

Jane was glad that Nick couldn't see her face. She felt like Bambi going off into the woods for the very first time, curious, in awe, and just a little bit frightened of the unknown elements that may lay ahead in the shadows. "Okay," was the only word she managed. Lame, she thought, and I was doing so well.

When the massage was over, Jane carefully maneuvered her way off of Nick and crawled in under the covers beside him. She kissed him on the cheek, faked a yawn, rolled over to face away from this god of temptation. "Good night." She could feel her heart pounding in her chest.

From behind her came a very soft, slightly amused voice. Nick had finally gotten past the point of hinting. "Jane," he whispered into her ear, "do you always sleep with your clothes on?"

"Nope," she replied, "but I'd have to go upstairs to get my p.j.s and I don't feel that ambitious at this exact moment."

"I would lend you a pair of mine," he teased as he played with her hair, "but I always sleep in the nude."

Jane rolled over to face him. When would she ever get the chance again to have sex with a man who looked like this? Every ounce of him was sheer perfection. It wasn't like she was being unfaithful to anyone. Todd had made that abundantly clear. So maybe, just maybe, this was the universe's way of helping her to douse the torch and finally extinguish the flame. Jane's stomach knotted at the thought. Or maybe not. When Nick reached forward to caress her cheek, Jane knew that stopping now would not be an easy option. Every atom of her body wanted to feel this man inside of her, wanted to feel his energy pound through her in waves of passion. "What about your fiancée?"

Nick leaned forward and gently kissed the corner of her mouth. His hand moved to stroke the length of her arm. "We have an understanding. I travel so much that she doesn't expect me to be totally faithful, just careful." His softly inquisitive lips touched Jane's. As his hand moved away from her arm, his long fingers caressed the side of her breast. "You are so beautiful," he murmured. "I'm so hard right now, it hurts."

"Must have been the massage," Jane offered as Nick pressed himself into her so she could feel his very large erection. Oh my god, she thought, he's huge. Turn my belly button from an inny to an outy type of huge. She reached beneath the covers out of curiosity and gently stroked him. Yup, past the belly button and doing a reverse deep throat kind of huge. Before having Brydon it would have been physically impossible for her to accommodate him. Even now she was not so sure.

"You definitely have magic fingers, Jane, but that's not exactly what I had in mind." Nick reached down and grasped her hand in his to stop the motion. "I was thinking more along the lines of reciprocation. Just say the word and I'll give you an internal massage that you won't soon forget."

Jane closed her eyes momentarily to try to regain her bearings. It's not like she wanted an on-going, romantic relationship with Nick. It was just one night. Right? It was just one life experience that she could look back on with fond memories when she was old and gray. Todd would never have to know. There were millions of people living in Toronto. The chances of Todd meeting Nick were slim to nil. The odds of Todd meeting Nick and discovering she'd had sex with Nick had to be at least a zillion to one. The feel of Nick's warm lips and his moist tongue on her neck sealed the deal. He was stimulating nerve endings she didn't realize existed.

Jane opened her eyes and gulped. "To be honest, I don't know if I can handle all of that."

Nick drew back, his face serious. "All you need to do is to shout stop and I'll stop."

"It's not like I haven't been with well-endowed men before, but you're kind of beyond well-endowed bordering on stallion status. I totally understand that the vagina elongates when the penis enters. It's something like, what, seven centimetres long until arousal and then it can stretch up to something like 20 centimetres. We kind of covered that in health class. Problem is that, when I was pregnant with Brydon, I was told that my vagina is only two-thirds the normal length. So, if I don't stretch for the extra length, you'll hit my cervix." Way to kill the mood, Jane, she chastised herself. Still, all she could think of was this really bad horror movie from the 70's that she watched with her sister. It was about the Salem witch hunts and the one means of torture was to drop a woman onto a point-sharpened post, impaling her from the opening of her vagina up. Not that Nick was as big as the post, but the man obviously had an extra litre of blood somewhere in his body to make that baby stand to attention.

Nick smoothed back her hair. "Jane, you're not the first woman I've been with whose had reservations about my size. Trust me, I know from experience what to do. You're not the only one who has done your research," he assured her. "As long as you're fully aroused, your vagina should elongate and your cervix should lift up and out of the way. The best position for both of us, the first time, is doggy style. And, if at any time, you want me to stop, I will. I won't do anything to hurt you, Jane. I promise."

Jane let out a breath that she didn't realize she'd been holding. "Okay then. Do you have any protection? It's been so long since I've had sex, I'm not on anything. That and I'm totally clean and I want to stay that way."

"Not to worry, I'm perfectly safe." Nick leaned forward and sighed in relief as if he'd just cleared the highest hurtle in an obstacle race and was eager to continue. "There are condoms in the top drawer of the bedside stand. They're kind of old because I haven't had to use condoms in a while, but I'm sure they'll be okay." Reaching over Jane, Nick opened the drawer and placed the box of condoms on top. "So, Jane, is that a 'yes' then to an internal massage? I promise I'll only go in as deep as you feel comfortable with. All you need to do is to shout whoa and I'll stop. Okay?"

Jane grinned back. "Absolutely, but can we skip the foreplay? I've been wet ever since I walked in and saw you lying on the couch wearing nothing but the G-string."

With a sincere laugh, Nick shook his head. "No way. You're nowhere close to full arousal yet." Nick bent forward and kissed her, this time not so gently but with a building desire. His tongue probed and danced, easily matching Jane's rhythm. He stopped only long enough to help Jane undress. "My turn," he whispered, his voice hoarse with lust. As he removed Jane's slinky, red, nightclub top and her red-lace bra, his mouth travelled down her breast, tongue and teeth, stopping at her nipples to suck, to caress, to nibble. Jane lay back, stroking Nick's hair, letting each sensation fill her. Small shivers rippled through her torso as nerve endings sent shockwaves of pleasure coursing along pathways previously unknown. "I can feel that all the way down to my toes, Baby," she cooed. "All the way down."

With her breasts naked against his hot flesh, his insistent mouth once more on hers, his tongue, demanding, exhilarating, Jane inhaled him deeply. His scent, his musk, his sweat. Everything forgotten but this moment. This stranger, yet not a stranger. This lover. This man. The ache inside of her grew.

"Oh my god, Nick," Jane reached down suddenly to unzip her jeans "just so you know, if you don't plug the hole soon, I'm going to *drench your bed."*

He momentarily broke free from her pulsating flesh. "Here, let me help you." He pulled the pants free, removed Jane's socks and tossed the unwanted garments onto the floor. "I've been thinking about this ever since you and Dana went out this evening. I don't plan on rushing so feel free to come as often as you want." He toyed with her red lace underpants, spread her legs and moved aside the skimpy material so could insert two long fingers deep inside of her. His eyes grew smoky with heat as he made sure that she was ready to take his entire length, his entire girth.

Jane gripped the bed sheets in desperation as she felt his fingers enter. "You don't understand. The women in my family are ejaculators. We're not like normal, have an orgasm and create tidy little wet spot types. If I come hard enough, I can literally soak the whole bed. So, I would suggest that you either grab a towel or place that wonderful penis of yours inside of me before I ruin your satin sheets."

He gently pulled his fingers free and sucked her juices. "Like I said, feel free to come as often as you want. Satin or not, sheets wash."

As Nick slid her panties down and off, Jane prepared for the next wave to wash over her. *This is so not fair,* she thought. Then thought no more.

When Nick's face disappeared between her legs, Jane was ready to scream. She gasped, trying to catch her breath, trying to slow down her heart rate, "Oh fucking hell," she moaned as his tongue and teeth teased her clitoris, his fingers back inside of her, applied upward pressure to double the sensation. No longer able to maintain control, the final wave embraced her. As her vagina constricted, pulsated, trembled, she felt his fingers leave replaced by the warm pressure of his lips sucking her juices as she expelled them from her body.

Before she was able to recuperate, before she was able to remember her own name, he was hovering above her. "Jane, it's time to turn over and hold on." She let him help her change positions, feeling like clay in the hands of a master sculpture. With her buttocks towards him, she opened her stance to make entrance easier. Nick plunged inside, slowly at first, but long and deep. She moaned softly.

"Are you okay?" he enquired, intent on determining if he should continue, true concern in his voice.

"Yes, I'm okay," she assured him. "There is a fine line between pain and pleasure, but please don't stop. I think my G-spot has just fallen in love with you."

With a brilliant smile, he kissed the side of her mouth. And as she tasted herself, salty and sweet, Nick plunged deeper inside with an intensity matching his fathers before him. Jane clung to Nick like a lifeline, lost in the sensations, lost in the excitement of the moment, lost in the rapture that would sail both of their spirits over the edge and into the cosmos.

It was only after their bodies had climaxed and their juices had meshed, when they were cuddled together, satiated and relaxed, that Jane realized they hadn't used a condom. Fuck. She mentally slapped herself on the side of the head as she nestled into Nick's side, his arm around her holding her close. Jane wiped the sweat from his brow with the back of her hand.

Nick's breathing was slowing back down to a regular rate. He stroked her hair as he spoke. "I think I just had an out-of-body experience. I've been having sex since I was fifteen. I've never had that happen before."

Jane turned her head and kissed him on the cheek. "Don't panic. It happens when the sexual experience becomes heightened and includes the spirit as well as the body…same thing happens in tantric sex. It doesn't happen with every partner. Just with people who have very compatible energies. That's probably why the massage felt so good. Our energies meld well."

"I don't know anything about energies melding, but I definitely think I just spoke to God himself so thank you for that."

Jane grinned, hoping that Nick was just teasing. "You are very welcome, I guess. What did God have to say?"

Nick stared up at the ceiling. "God said, 'son, this is the closest you'll get to heaven without being dead so take full advantage of the gifts that you've just been given'."

Jane giggled. "Guess Nietzsche was wrong after all. God is not dead. He's alive and well and hovering above Toronto watching people have sex. Kinda creepy don't you think?" *She patted Nick on his chest.* "I have to get up." *After disentangling herself, she sat up in bed and began to rub her temples. She desperately needed a cigarette.*

Nick rolled over onto his side and propped himself up on his elbow. "Where are you going?" *he enquired.*

Jane clenched and unclenched her jaw as she swung her legs out of the bed to get dressed. "Nowhere, just need to go outside for a smoke." *She glanced at the box of untouched condoms.* "I can't believe we forgot to use a condom, so I'm also a bit annoyed with myself right now. You wouldn't happen to have a cola in the fridge by any chance?"

"Cola, no. I can get you a glass of water though if you're thirsty," Nick offered as he sat up cross-legged and stretched lazily.

Jane sighed. "Water would be great. Thanks." She'd read an article online once that cola could be used as a spermicide after sex. She couldn't think of any drugstores in their area that were open all night where she could buy actual spermicide, but there might be a convenience store somewhere nearby where she could grab a pop. Except, of course, Jane didn't exactly feel safe walking around Toronto at 3:00 a.m. so it was a moot point at best.

As she watched Nick stride past her, headed towards the kitchen, she was totally astounded by his exquisite body. His personal trainer was obviously worth every penny. Deciding to be prepared in case Nick was up to seconds, Jane picked up the box of condoms and looked inside. The box was empty. Her stomach clenched. Did he know that the box was empty when he took it out of the drawer?

"Are you hungry?" Nick called from the kitchen.

"No, I'm fine," she called back.

"I'm not much of a cook, but I can manage an omelet," he offered as he arrived back in the bedroom with two, crystal glasses in his hands. He handed one glass to Jane and, after taking a drink, set his glass down on the night stand.

"Sounds great." She smiled up at him, her mind racing. "Maybe later. Right now I'm nic-fitting like crazy." When Jane had also taken a drink, he relieved her of her glass as well.

"I bet I can make you forget about the cigarette," Nick jested as he sat down beside her. "Smoking is really bad for you." He brushed back her hair and kissed her shoulder.

"So is having unprotected sex. I already have one child. I can't have another one right now." She picked up the condom box and handed it to Nick. "And since your box of condoms seems to be empty, I'm thinking that my only option is to grab a morning after pill tomorrow and hope for the best."

"Empty? Seriously?" Nick looked inside, genuinely confused. Frowning, he crumpled the box and threw it into a nearby garbage can. "What do you mean, hope for the best?" Nick's eyes held no humour.

Jane pulled away, wanting to clear her head and afraid that her hormones would take over again. Besides which, another go-round like the *last one* and she'd be walking bow legged for a week. "The morning after pill is only 95% effective, and I'm one of those weird people who always fall into the medication minority for some insane reason." Jane reached down to retrieve her clothing and began to get dressed. Nick caught her hand and turned her towards him.

Nick's features relaxed as he put his arms around Jane's shoulders, pulled her close to him and leaned his forehead against hers. "Jane, I know we didn't plan this, but it's not often that I come across a beautiful woman who can handle the whole package. I should have pulled out. I guess I just got caught up in the moment. I'm sorry. I really didn't mean to put you in this position.

Look, I really like you. You're smart, you're funny, you're real. Lily and I are having serious problems. That's why she's away. She said she needed a break to think things over. With Lily, that means intense retail therapy. Bottom line is that Lily doesn't want children and I do. So if you do end up pregnant, you've got to know that I don't believe in abortion. What are the chances that I can convince you to forget the morning after pill and let fate decide? If you're not pregnant, then no harm's done. If you are, then we'll have a really cute kid. I'll take care of you, our baby and your son."

Jane smiled in spite of herself. Men, she thought. They really have no clue. Here was this breathtaking hunk, this Adonis, asking her to carry his child and all it did was infuriate her because, not only did she barely know him, but she was no one's fucking broodmare. She chose her words carefully. "Meeting you and making love with you has been amazing. While I appreciate the offer and your good intentions, and agree that, if we had a child, he or she may very well be modelesque, the only thing I really want right now is nicotine. If you will please excuse me, I need to get dressed, go outside, inhale at least two cigarettes and then get some sleep." She kissed Nick lightly on the cheek, removed his arms from her shoulders and continued to reclaim her clothing.

He leaned back on the bed to watch her. "If you do end up pregnant, you'll quit smoking though, right? Smoking would be really bad for the baby."

"Of course," Jane agreed. She would have agreed to anything at that particular moment. She would have gladly sold her soul to the devil if it meant that she could go outside and smoke her brains out. Only six hours before the drugstores opened.

In the days to come, Jane met Nick's fiancée, Lily, who introduced her to Nick, then his other roommate who repeated the procedure. She would just smile and say that they had already met in passing.

At first, Nick had a way of looking at her that made her uncomfortable, as if she was being appraised--even more awkward when the look in his eyes categorized her as possible dessert. Finally, she smiled at him and simply said, "No harm. No foul." Nick sadly nodded his understanding.

The last time she saw him, Nick was moving out of the apartment. It was late at night and, if it hadn't been for a last cigarette before bed, she would have missed him. He and Lily were officially over.

"I'm leaving for Spain next week on a two-month contract. The offer's still open," he suggested as he placed several large suitcases into the trunk of a taxi.

"If only life was that simple." She smiled wistfully, knowing that she would sincerely miss seeing him around.

Jane gave Nick a hug, wished him well and waved one last time as he drove away.

So much for my ideal man, Jane frowned as she changed channels on the television. Her friend had been more of a romanticist about the situation.

"How many women ever get to meet their ideal man, let alone sleep with him?" Gertie commented over a cup of tea.

Jane had agreed for the sake of conversation. "Yeah, but how many 'ideal men' turn out to be both slightly crazy and contagious?"

Gertie disagreed. "I don't think he was crazy. Lonely, maybe, but not crazy."

"Really? The man is gorgeous beyond all rational thought and yet he was ready to impregnate a perfect stranger. How does that not make him a little crazy?"

"That's it exactly. To him, you were this perfect female, or at least what he thought of as being a perfect female for him. He was unhappy in his relationship, but he didn't want to be alone. Women get pregnant all the time to entrap a man. What makes you think it doesn't happen the other way around? It makes him human, not crazy.

You know, Jane, you really should quit your bitchin'. Men like that are so far out of my league, I can't even fantasize that. You, on the other hand, have them just drop into your lap like manna from the sky."

In retrospect, Jane was eternally grateful. The results of her irresponsible behaviour could have been far worse. Compared to AIDS, the miscarriage had been painfully brutal and the Trichomonas had been uncomfortable and embarrassing, but neither had been fatal.

CHAPTER TEN

The somber darkness of the muggy evening unfolded before him as Elliot sped down the many kilometres of winding highway. He knew that he was driving too fast, but the ultimate urgency of the situation far exceeded his common sense. He had to get to Brydon before Jane did. He had to get his son home safe and sound before Jane could whisk him away to some faraway, unknown dwelling place in New Jersey — a place where he would not be able to find the lad nor lay claim to a son he had never officially adopted. He had to get Brydon. He had to take him home where he, Elliot, could personally tuck him safely in his own bed in familiar surroundings. He had to get Brydon. He had to get his son.

Jane, he thought, how could you do this to me, to us, to our family?

Jane's letter was safely tucked away in his shirt pocket. Elliot wanted to show the note to Gertie. Maybe she could help him to understand what he had done wrong...why this was happening to him. Maybe Gertie could explain why Jane would do this. God knew, he could not.

He had been a good husband. Hadn't he? He knew that sometimes he drank too much, but it had never interfered with his work or with their home life. Had it? Maybe he didn't look like Johnny Depp, but he wasn't altogether ugly. Was he? Maybe he wasn't good enough in bed? Maybe he was too short-tempered, didn't compromise enough? Maybe he had laughed once too often at her idiosyncrasies? Maybe he had over-reacted when she had said that she didn't want any more children but to concentrate on her career instead? Maybe there was another man? Another woman? Did she run off to be with someone else? Maybe...maybe...maybe...

Elliot tried desperately to turn off the multitude of questions that flew ephemerally through his conscious thoughts. He could not. No matter which dark avenue his mind turned down, he could not find a logical explanation for what was happening. The mouse in the maze could not find the cheese. How could Jane possibly rationalize splitting them apart like this? One spouse did not simply disappear for the sake of "exploring life". Absurd. Fucking crazy.

Rubbing his left temple, Elliot moaned at the pain he felt. His soul was ripping apart. He had thought that she was ready to settle down and spend her life with him. If not, why had she agreed to marry him in the first place? It just did not make sense. It was not fair. A part of him was dying, and he wasn't sure how to keep that part alive.

There were too many memories now, too many things they had shared together, too many remember whens, to just forget everything and to pretend that they had never happened. How was he supposed to pick up the pieces and carry on when he needed both of them so much? How? How?

"Damn you, Jane!" he screamed furiously at the vague distance. "What gives you the fucking right?!"

For an instant, he hated her. What was he supposed to do, just say fine, okay, go and get this out of your system? I'll wait. I'll keep a candle burning in the window just in case you decide someday to come home? What the hell was she trying to prove? Who the hell did she think she was to do this to them? Didn't she know how much she was hurting all of them—not only him but Brydon as well? What gave her the right to play God with their lives, as if her mere existence and curiosity were more important than the family structure they had so carefully constructed? How could she just toss him aside as if he was an old sweater with too many frays and holes to mend and wear? What made her so fucking special? What? What?

Elliot realized that, under the circumstances, their marriage had not been an easy one at times. He knew that, deep down, Jane would always harbour bitterness towards certain members of his large family; but, it was he who she had married, not them.

"Come on, Jane! We're going to be late," Elliot called up the hallway stairs. His mother had her usual multi-course, Christmas dinner planned, and he did not want to miss the before meal conversations. It was the only time of year that his entire family got together. Brydon was patiently waiting by his side, decked out in a bulky, hand-knit sweater and new, pre-faded blue jeans. "Dinner's scheduled for 6 o'clock and it's 5 o'clock now!" In the winter, the usual twenty-minute drive to his ma's

new condo in Owen Sound could take twice that long if the country roads were bad and, by the looks of the blowing weather outside, it might take a while to reach their destination.

"Daddy E," Brydon tugged impatiently on Elliot's pant leg, "is Mommy coming?" He, too, was getting anxious to leave.

Elliot bent over to help Brydon on with his blue, two-piece snowsuit; his irritation with Jane was briefly forgotten. "I sure hope so, Bry."

They had spent the day before at Jane's parents. Everyone was laid back and sociable. He liked that. Her family had always made him feel like a part of them. Her parents had blessed the marriage.

Then, Christmas morning had been just for the three of them. The week before, Jane had helped Brydon make bright decorations for their tree, saying that they were more special than store bought ones — snowflakes, gingerbread characters, Rudolph in all of his glory, snowmen, stars and tinfoil balls. Watching Brydon as he sat in front of his treasure tree and opened his presents had been the ultimate experience. He and Jane had just sat back, with coffees, to watch. Elliot had felt as if he had finally found his place in life. Christmas had never really meant anything to him before, other than having to buy too many presents and, at least, appear to be cheerful. There had always been an unexpressed void in his life and, now, that void had been filled. For the first time in a long while, he was truly happy and optimistic about the future.

"Jane!" Elliot called again, losing patience. "I've got Brydon ready, so hurry up before he gets too hot in this damned get up!" Elliot glanced at his gold watch to clock the passing minutes. Women! Jane appeared at the top of the stairway, startling him.

"I'm ready already," she retorted, hurrying downwards to meet them.

Elliot gasped but caught his initial reaction and inhaled it, determined not to make a big scene. His brothers' wives always dressed up for the occasion wearing their fancy dresses or dress clothes and gloating that they had received them from their loving spouses and families, showing off new gold watches, sparkling rings, glittering necklaces accompanied by the appropriate oohs and awes. "Look at what Bill and the kids gave me! Isn't it lovely?!" How carefully he and Brydon had picked out and purchased a golden pendant to adorn her long, slender neck — a gold heart with inlaid diamonds encircling a smaller duplicate to represent their family unit.

Jane, racing towards him, wore faded blue jeans and a sweatshirt that she must have had for years. He glared at her impudence. "Are you actually going dressed like that?" he demanded brusquely. He knew instinctively that the pendant lay untouched in its red-velour gift box on top of her pine bureau. The only jewellery she wore was a plain gold, wedding band that she had purchased for herself only a few weeks after their wedding claiming that she was afraid that the original one, with its three small, embedded diamonds, would get ruined at work.

She studied him intently, as if surprised by his annoyance, and abruptly stopped in front of him. She challenged his query. "Is there something wrong with the way that I'm dressed, Elly?" Their eyes locked.

Elliot bit back the remark that tried to push past his gritted teeth. Countering the remark would have been like spitting into the wind. It had taken him weeks to convince her to go in the first place. If she was looking for an excuse to argue, she would not get it from him. Jane was just apt to go off pouting to her room for the evening and, of course, have the reason she needed to stay at home. The incident would be labeled his fault for picking on her. Instead, Elliot unclenched his jaw and held out her beige parka. "Let's go," he growled in a low sotto voce.

The evening went badly. Jane sat in a dimly lit corner for most of it, consuming mass quantities of Johnny Walker Scotch and water while the other wives chatted easily about their children, their jobs and various other by-the-way topics. Jane made little to no effort to join in on the pleasantries or to even offer to help with the meal. Elliot thought that she was acting like a spoiled adolescent until…

It was one of those moments that should have been saved for an on-the-floor scene in a bad, daytime soap opera. Jane excused herself past the group of women and sauntered into the small den where the bar was set up. When she did not return promptly, Elliot went searching for her, half-expecting to find his wife passed out on the brown leather sofa. He could not for the life of him comprehend how she could ingest so much scotch and still walk straight. It certainly was not very ladylike.

He strode into the small den to find his sister-in-law, Tabitha, and Jane arguing. Tabitha was renowned for being overly-blessed with drunken opinions, and Jane's temper was about ready to explode. Her face was flushed with anger, her right eyelid twitching slightly in response to internalized emotions.

"You know you're nothing but a fucking slut," Tabitha snarled at Jane. "You and your bastard will never belong in this family. God, you make me sick. What gives you the fucking nerve to think that by marrying Elliot, we'll accept your brat as a Fallis?" Tabitha gulped her drink and poured herself another one.

Jane studied Tabitha, jaw clenched in a gridlock. Elliot could tell that she was trying to formulate the perfect retort. Her eyes shone with the fury of a thousand venomous daggers. Elliot knew those daggers well and how they aimed to kill, never to just maim.

Tabitha continued, unabated, "How you managed to seduce Elliot is beyond me. All I can say is that you must be a wonderful fuck because you're definitely not much to look at." Tabitha turned to look straight at Jane and suddenly spat into her face. "You whore!"

Elliot rushed forward, wanting to divert the inevitable. "Jane, NO!" He was too late. Jane had studied karate and it took her no more than fifteen seconds to leave Tabitha lying on the floor, writhing in pain – one neat hand to the base of the diaphragm and one swift kick that connected with the side of Tabitha's knee. Jane literally stepped over the groaning bulk of Tabitha and strode coldly past Elliot who was left standing silently only an arm's reach away, staring in total disbelief.

"Elly, take me home...NOW!" It wasn't a question but a demand.

He complied, not wanting any further scenes that evening. Not really knowing what to say to anyone or what to do. How was he supposed to react anyway? Tabitha was obviously being a bitch, but still she was his brother's wife. Elliot decided to definitely talk to Troy about keeping Tabitha under control next year. If there was a next year.

The ride home was quiet except for Brydon's numerous questions about why. Why did they have to leave? Why couldn't he stay and play with the rest of the kids? Why couldn't he at least have opened his presents there? Why did Mommy look so upset? Why? Why? Why? When the child finally dozed off, Jane remained silent, peering out of the window into the darkness as if the answers were out there somewhere, and if she looked long enough, hard enough, she would be able to find the solution to all of their problems.

Elliot could not find the words to express what he felt. He was angry with Tabitha; however, he was angry with Jane as well for spoiling the evening for him and Brydon. It was supposed to have been a special evening – their first Christmas as a family--not a demonstration on how to destroy 'peace, love and joy all over the world'. If Tabitha didn't charge Jane with assault, he would be very surprised. On the other hand, Tabitha had spit on Jane first so that had to count as physical provocation or as *minor assault in its own right. Elliot decided to let Troy know that he had witnessed the spitting and that Jane could counter-charge Tabitha. Better to just call it even than to bother the courts with their family problems.*

Elliot couldn't help but to smirk. Deep down, he knew that he was pretty impressed by his wife's ability to defend herself. And maybe now, Tabitha's ten-year reign of terror would be over. God knows, Troy could never keep that woman in her place. The astonished look on Tabitha's face when she hit the floor had been priceless. Still, it was Christmas and Jane should have just walked away. Didn't Jane say that she'd signed up for kick-boxing lessons? God help them all.

The next morning, Jane remained distant. She seemed calm but had that "I don't want to talk about it" expression on her pretty face. When he finally cornered her into a conversation, Jane made her feelings perfectly clear. "Next year, Elly, you can take Brydon and spend a perfectly wonderful evening at your mom's. I, however, want nothing more to do with Tabitha or anyone else in your so-called, Loving family."

Elliot began to respond, saying that next year things would be different, that everyone would realize that the past no longer mattered, that they were a family now and had to be accepted as one…but Jane's eyes were so cold that they chilled him instantly, a deep freeze, dry ice. There would be no discussing the matter any further. As far as Jane was concerned, the case was closed.

CHAPTER ELEVEN

Television, Jane decided, was basically geared to average individuals—people who sat around in their cozy living rooms or in their paneled family rooms, relaxed in their comfortable bedrooms or cooked in their bright, cheery kitchens. Most of television was just white noise, a friendly background murmur for those who would rather not be alone but who were, regardless of their efforts. Television replaced what was truly missing in people's lives, filled the void, passed the time, entertained and, with any luck at all, informed. It was a diversion, an escape from reality where people were not forced to think about their own lives, their financial or their personal problems, the arguments they had with their children, their spouses, their ex-spouses, their lovers, their ex-lovers, their bosses or their parents, or to miss the loved ones they had just lost. Television helped people to unwind after a hectic, stressful day, provided a commonality where families could spend a few hours sharing popcorn and a few laughs, catching up with their favourite plot-lines as characters became friends.

Jane needed that white noise right now. She did not want to think about how Brydon had felt after she had dropped him off at Gertie's for a 'short vacation'. Had he sensed there was something wrong? In the past, he had gone there numerous times for a week or so. This time he had looked so distrusting, so wary, as if she wasn't telling him the whole truth and nothing but the truth so help her God—cross your heart and hope to die. Had he overheard Gertie and her talking? Had her smile seemed too forced or too phony as she hugged and kissed her little trouper goodbye, making him promise to be a good boy for Auntie Gertie until she picked him up again? Or was it her own paranoia, her own sense of guilt that made her insides feel all tied up in proverbial knots?

She did not want to think about Elliot arriving home from another blasted ball tournament to find an empty house. If his team had won he would stroll in, sunburned and half-drunk, more from the post-tournament celebration than from the sweet exhilaration of victory. He would make it to the living room couch before collapsing to snore the weekend off, fully expecting her to wake him up the next morning in time to take three ibuprofen, to inhale two cups of very strong coffee, to grab a hot shower and to make it to work on time Monday morning where he could gloat about the home run that he had hit or the amazing plays he had made. If they had lost, he would stagger in, totally drunk from watching the final games and gulping back too many beers. He would crawl up the wooden stairs to the second floor, expecting to find her snuggled up in their bed. She would automatically fight off his insistent, slobbery advances. If they lost, he always wanted sex, as if to re-establish his manhood after one defeat. She hated the smell of the stale beer on his wretched breath and had always turned away, listening impatiently for his exalted snoring to commence. The entire process took less than five minutes. Occasionally, she would move to the couch downstairs, but usually, she would just curl up on her side and will herself to sleep.

  Jane ran a cool bath and stepped in, relieving herself of the day's constant heat and driving. She had traversed many kilometres, but her destination still seemed so far away. When Chad had originally contacted her about the research position, Jane had been skeptical at best. His insistence that he could arrange a Fast Track Working Visa under the NAFTA agreement had finally convinced her that it was worth checking out. She loved her job at the hospital but longed for a chance to prove herself within the industry.

  In the background, MTV drowned out the ever-present hum of the air-conditioner. Sinking lower, she let the water engulf her lean, stiff body. It was so rarely that she had the time to truly enjoy the sensations that were merely a part of simple, ordinary existence.

"Jane! Jane! Jane!" the screaming fans chanted, anxiously awaiting the appearance of their favourite rock star. "Jane! Jane! Jane!" they continued, some already waiting for hours in cramped lineups for general admission seating, hoping to get a good view of the show – a front row seat where they could see their goddess in her full, ultimate glory.

  "Jane, you've got exactly five minutes to show time." The frustrated Stage Manager called through her dressing room door. "The band is already warming up, and the audience is getting restless."

  "Yeah, yeah," Jane retorted abrasively, knowing too well the

routine. "I'll be out in a minute. Don't get your shit in a knot. I'll be ready."

Jane sat at her dressing table, putting on the final cosmetic touches. She had to look perfect for her fans. They didn't care if she was exhausted and still hung over from last night's bash at Rod's. They didn't care if she had been on the road for the last six months and couldn't remember what town she was going to next or where she had played a week ago. All the crowd cared about was getting their money's worth. All her manager cared about was getting his money's worth. All she cared about was giving them their money's worth, needing good reviews to ensure the next stop would be sold-out.

One thing that she knew well was the longevity of her career depended totally on her music and on her concert sales. Too many talented artists had been lost in the rush, burned out, or just simply chose to drop out of the madness, the rat race, the constant bombardment of road tours, album cuts, parties, gala social events. Too many talented artists had been forgotten or abandoned after one hit, never again creating another perfect combination to enchant the masses. Disbanded, they were now either tinkering in local bands or selling shoes to supplement the band that they would surely get back together one day.

Studying the reflection in the mirror, Jane noticed that, regardless of regular Botox injections, faint lines around her eyes were already beginning to appear. Thankfully, the lines were still undetectable under heavy stage lighting or under the air-brushing skills of a reliable photographer...not to mention the amazing things professionals could do with computers these days. Photography was a marvelous craft. If the photographer concentrated on her eyes and her pouty mouth, air brushing the lines and diminishing her nose, she ended up appearing a quaint imp instead of the aging rock star she knew that she was in reality.

She applied another layer of lip gloss to make her mouth look fuller and caked on blush to give her cheek bones greater height. She had back-combed her streaky blonde hair, using mousse and spray to keep the wayward strands spiky, seemingly unmanageable.

A soft knock sounded at the door. "Come in," she called, not really caring who was there. Probably one of the band members wondering what the hell was keeping her for so long.

The mirror reflected another face – that of her friend and close confident, Rod. Jane quickly turned around and stood up to give him her biggest hug.

He grinned wryly. "Just stopped off to tell you to break a leg." He kissed her cheek lightly so as not to smudge her fabricated face.

"Thanks a million." She laughed, knowing his true intentions. "I've got to be on in a minute. How do I look?" She drew back from him and pirouetted.

He clapped his hands, applauding her outfit – the scathingly short, black leather skirt and bomber jacket, mounds of gold jewellery and black running shoes. (better for on-stage antics) She had become a fashion idol, any number of young women strutting around imitating her latest fashion indulgence. Her costume could be anything from beat-up blue jeans and a tube top to total adornment – whatever hit her fancy at that particular moment.

"Leather really suits you. I love simple seduction."

"What better way to show off the $25,000 I paid for a butt tuck and liposuction?" She smiled good-naturedly. "Are you sticking around for the show?" Jane inquired as she grabbed her energy supply from the table and gulped down the tiny pills with a glass of white wine.

"Wouldn't miss it for the world, Darling. You know that," he scolded her with a laugh. "Meet you back here afterwards for a night cap and unwind session?"

"Sure thing," Jane agreed. She had no place else to go anyway and gearing down after the performance took time.

The five minutes had passed and the fans could wait no more. As Jane strolled down the narrow walkway to the brightly-lit stage, she could hear the band playing, their music radiating loudly. She could feel the pills beginning to work. She strutted to the rhythm, preparing herself for the perfect entrance. She would bounce on from stage right, grab the microphone and curtsy for the audience, smiling her sweetest smile to enchant her fans, and tell them how much she loved each and every one of them.

Stepping out onto the stage, adrenaline suddenly rushed through every artery and vein in her slender body, pushing her forward. She waved gaily to the band and grabbed the microphone from its silver stand. Blowing kisses to the screaming crowd, she curtsied as planned.

"Good evening, Toronto!" she spoke lovingly into the microphone, eyes gleaming as the audience roared its approval. Suddenly, she began to shiver, a chill passing swiftly through her body.

Jane's eyes popped open wide, a thought haunting her mind, like a wry ghost who can only be caught in peripheral vision. All day, she had dealt with a constant, nagging feeling that she had forgotten something. Something important.

Clambering out of her bathtub retreat, Jane hastily folded a monogrammed towel around her sodden body and ran back into the bedroom. She tossed her suitcases onto the bed, opening them one by one, and rummaging through the contents. Nothing. She grabbed her large tote purse and sat down with it on her lap, once again searching, carefully spreading the contents beside her on the bed—cheque book, wallet, date book, a dozen tissues, old receipts, brush, makeup....

"Fuck shit," she growled at her own negligence. "I must have left it in the desk." She tossed the contents back into her purse with a fury that the inanimate objects did not deserve. "Damn... damn...damn," she scolded herself heedlessly. Now she would have to call Elliot.

She'd stuffed the envelope into her address book so she wouldn't forget to leave the note out for Elliot before she left then had, inadvertently, left her address book behind. He would never look in the desk. The desk was hers, full of her belongings, not his.

Deciding that tomorrow morning would be soon enough to call and leave a message on their voicemail--before Elliot would think to file a missing person's report with the local O.P.P.--Jane extracted a short, t-shirt nightgown from one of the suitcases before placing them in a nearby closet. Tomorrow, she would be in New Jersey—safely out of his reach. She cringed at the thought of Elliot's voice grating through the telephone line; perhaps, he would scream or just demand her return. He definitely would want to know the whereabouts of Brydon. Their closeness sometimes sent pangs of jealousy searing through her being. She was the one who originally wanted the child. She was the one who fought to bring him into the world. She was the one who had sacrificed, who had cried over his hurts, who had lulled him through teething pains, through croup, through surgery. It was her. Not Elliot. Her.

"A woman can only raise a son so far, and then he'll naturally turn to a man as an example for his own upcoming manhood." Elliot's

words reverberated in her skull. "The woman has to let go."

Life would have been so much simpler if she had given birth to a daughter. Jane had wanted a daughter since she was five.

With a headache skulking around the perimeter of her brain, Jane crawled into bed, pulling the sheets snugly around her. A good night's sleep would make tomorrow easier, if that was at all possible. The note, she knew, had been a cop out anyway — so much simpler than facing Elliot in person. So much easier than a possible scene or the look that would crease his brow. So much easier than trying to find the right words, knowing full well the implications.

"Sorry, Darling, but I don't want to be married after all. It seemed like a good idea at the time, but it's just not working out." Sleep crept in slowly, graciously obliterating the emotions that Jane refused to face.

She was sitting in a brown plaid recliner in the basement family room at Gertie's parents. The large room was the family gathering spot where they could watch television or visit with friends. Gertie sat close by on a matching plaid couch, chatting on and on about her latest lover, her latest adventure, her latest quest in life. Jane was listening intently, absorbing every syllable.

"Janeee..." She heard a familiar voice calling softly, as if from a great distance away. Where had she heard that voice before?

She glanced over at the staircase, eyes transfixed on the long, jean-clad legs slowly finding their way downward. Gertie chattered on as if not seeing that someone was about to make his or her presence.

"Janeee..." the voice called again, the legs reaching the bottom of the staircase.

Jane caught her breath suddenly, almost afraid to exhale. Todd. It was Todd. She glared at Gertie, who prattled on, not noticing Todd's entrance.

Looking once again at Todd, Jane's expression transformed from one of pleasure to absolute horror. Her beautiful Todd looked ill — deathly ill. His face, white and gaunt, harboured dark, sunken eyes. He was emaciated, as if he had been starving for a very long time. Extending his long arms towards her, Todd softly repeated his call, "Janeee...I've missed you." He smiled, showing off badly rotting teeth, dark and putrid.

Jane immediately jumped up from her chair, leaving the insistent chatter of Gertie behind, and dashed into the arms of her young lover. He's sick, she thought. He needs me to take care of him. His body felt cold in her arms causing her to shiver involuntarily.

"Janee," he whispered in her ear. "I always knew you'd come back to me."

CHAPTER TWELVE

For their first anniversary, Elliot had wanted to do something really special to mark the occasion. He was a romanticist at heart but not by nature. He had read once that left-brained people tended to be more logical — they thought first and felt later. This was his plight.

Jane was definitely right-brained, creative and intuitive, feeling first then thinking afterwards, more often somewhere down the road once she had a chance to take a step back and gain some distance from the situation. She was more apt to cry during sad movies, would leave the room entirely if someone was about to embarrass his or herself, stating that she couldn't bear to watch public humiliation, more apt to burst out laughing while dancing with Brydon to a favourite song on the radio, more apt to spontaneously combust over issues Elliot personally thought trivial. At one point, Elliot had seriously wondered if his wife was bi-polar. After talking to a very knowledgeable friend, Elliot had decided that, instead, Jane was just slightly hyperemotional.

Understanding this, Elliot knew that whatever he decided to do for their anniversary would need to trigger a positive emotion and to provide the correct symbolism. Jane was an ogre about symbolism. For reasons that Elliot could not understand, someone somewhere somehow had decided that red roses equalled passionate love, that yellow roses equalled friendship, that the traditional gift for a first year anniversary was paper (from a love poem to life insurance), that the modern gift was plastic (from Tupperware to yoga mats), that a heart symbolized love, that an apple symbolized ecstasy. Thank god for the internet and the thousands of websites devoted to the supposedly true meanings of everything imaginable.

After a couple of hours at work searching various websites between customers, Elliot decided on a simple strand of white pearls. Supposedly, pearls symbolized purity and honesty but, more importantly, were reported to lift the spirits and make the wearer feel beautiful. Sold.

That evening had been like a scene from a one of the many chick flicks that he had endured throughout his dating career —

expensive restaurant, gourmet meal, fine wine, soft music and candlelight. Looking back, he wasn't sure if all the extra effort was for Jane's sake or if it had been more for his own.

The two had chatted easily over the delectable meal, comparing notes about their busy days. Jane's career had always intrigued him. He thought that there must be a great deal of satisfaction in taking an idea, visualizing it and then transforming that first glimmering moment of conception into a reality. She was the one who made the ultimate decisions on how the piece would be written, how it would be edited and on how it would turn out. She had the control over its fate. Almost like playing God.

Elliot had felt so gallant when he had handed his wife the long, narrow, gift-wrapped box and wished her a Happy Anniversary--the charismatic, handsome, male lead sweeping his beautiful counterpart off of her dainty feet with his love and adoration; she, swooning in his strong arms...

Jane accepted the gift and opened the card. On the front of the card was a young couple on a beach walking and holding hands. Not claiming to be a poet, Elliot had written, "Roses are red, violets are blue. Jane, you are my every dream come true. Love Elliot."

Jane smiled warmly as she read the card. "Awww, that's so sweet," she cooed. She stood the card up on the table then gingerly unwrapped and opened the gift, her green eyes growing wide with delight at the contents. "Oh, Elly, they're beautiful. I love pearls!" Her smile dimmed, eyes narrowed. "Please tell me they're fake. We can't afford them if they're real."

Elliot laughed. "They are real, but freshwater so they won't break our budget, I promise. I thought they'd look perfect with your black dress."

Jane's smile regained its former brilliance. "Yes, they will. Thank you. If I'd known, I would have worn the dress tonight." Jane paused for a moment in thought. She reached across the table to take his hand in hers. "I'll tell you what. I'll wear them later when I give you your present."

"And what did you buy for me?" Elliot grinned.

Jane motioned with her index finger for Elliot to lean towards her for a private tête-à-tête. Her voice was low and sultry. "It's not so much what I bought but what I can do for you. I have a confession to make. I had no idea what to buy you for our anniversary so I did a bit of research online and the modern, first-year anniversary gift is plastic. The one example was adult sex toys which definitely got me thinking. Men love tools, right? Vibrators are kind of like tools. From there I found a great Cosmo article on little known, male erogenous zones, and I'm dying to experiment. So, I was thinking of trying out a couple of different speeds with your new tool, starting off very low and eventually working my way up to the Indrani position."

Elliot swallowed. He could feel the sexual energy from her eyes as it spread across his body. She had a certain look that said, I want you now and I want you naked. It was a look that he could never resist. Elliot had absolutely no idea what the 'Indrani position' was, but, as long as he didn't put his back out, he was game to find out. He motioned for the waitress to bring their bill. "We are definitely skipping dessert."

He had felt on top of the world back then. King of the castle. Now he had been abruptly pushed off and she was out there somewhere chiding, "And you're the dirty rascal". She was laughing at him. He could see her face, humour illuminating her eyes. Ha, ha, gotcha. Thought you had me, didn't you, Sweetheart? Thought you could buy me with your pretty baubles, didn't you? After all that you did to me, you thought that you could buy my forgiveness, didn't you?

Elliot glanced down at his dashboard clock. Soon he would be at Gertie's. Soon he would greet his son with a warm smile and a loving hug. Soon he would have his son back. Soon.

The memories tore at him, vultures hovering over a dying man, picking haphazardly at his torn flesh, hoping to speed up the process of death and decay.

Jane's note reverberated through his mind, bouncing, and echoing relentlessly. "I'm sorry," she had said. "I'm sorry."

"Well, Jane, Sweetheart," he chastised her memory as Gertie's bungalow came into view, "you may be a great deal sorrier that you ever imagined possible."

CHAPTER THIRTEEN

After checking out of the sprawling motel, Jane felt absolutely melancholy. The dream...nightmare...whatever... was still too close, too real. Goosebumps appeared immediately on her slender arms whenever her mind even partially allowed even a tiny segment of the dream to enter into her conscious state, as if an alarm system was sounding the warning of an intruder. Get back! It's not safe! Get back!

Nevertheless, she knew where she had to go. Todd was calling to her. Her Todd. Her first true love. Her lover. Her friend. Her soulmate. She considered telephoning him but knew that she needed to see him in person, with her own two eyes, to make sure that he was truly okay. Alive. Safe. Happy. Healthy. She also knew the jaunt back up north would throw off the travelling schedule she had set for herself. Regardless, New Jersey would have to wait. When she'd explained to Chad that she'd be a day or so late due to a family emergency, he had agreed to reschedule but was very honest that he could not hold the job forever.

Before getting back into her car, Jane decided to walk and think (she could always think better while in motion). She turned on her cell phone and activated Gertie's number. "Hey Gert. You're not going to believe this, but I'm on my way to Toronto to see Todd." Jane felt drained, as if a thousand tiny punctures had left her system emotionally empty.

"Jane," Gertie interrupted, the urgency in her voice caught Jane by surprise, demanding her total attention.

"What?" Jane halted and unconsciously held her breath.

Gertie continued, "Elliot was here last night. He showed me your note. I know that you don't like having your cell phone on when you drive, but you really need to start checking your messages occasionally. I tried calling you at least a dozen times before he got here."

"Oh fuck," Jane gasped, mentally berating herself for not turning her cell phone back on as soon as she'd gotten to the motel, then visualizing the possible sequence of events. Elliot finding the note...Elliot breaking down Gertie's door...Elliot storming in... Elliot pulling a gun... "Tell me details." This was not the way it was supposed to happen. This was not the way she had planned it.

Gertie's voice grew calm. "Jane, relax. It's okay. Elliot's upset, but I don't think that he's homicidal. We had a long talk, and he's confused is all. Jane, he's really hurting. He loves you, loves Brydon, and just wants to know why you left."

Jane's mind spun circles and landed on Brydon. "Gertie, where's Brydon? Tell me that Elliot didn't take him?" Panic rose like a tidal wave drowning out the traffic noise of the nearby roadway.

Gertie's voice remained calm, placating. "Yes, but Jane, it was Brydon who wanted to go. Elliot's his dad now. It would have been cruel to make him stay when he was so unhappy here."

Jane swallowed back her fear. "It's okay Gertie…It's fine. I totally understand. I have to go." Jane ended the call and raced back to her car.

Threateningly dark clouds looked determined to drench the humidity-weary race of beings below the overcast sky. Jane cringed as lightning coursed a jagged pathway through the air, unconsciously counting the seconds in between the lightning and the impending clash of thunder. The nadir of despair became her best friend.

She knew that, somehow, she would have to pick up the pieces of her life. Elliot had Brydon. Fuck. Her plan had been a dismal failure. Now that Elliot knew, he would fight her taking Brydon across the border. If necessary, he would find a sympathetic lawyer who would search through every known court case to find a precedent. While it was true that Elliot had not officially adopted Brydon, he had taken on the father-role and that would surely have some weight in court. Jane groaned. Her window of opportunity had slammed shut on her fingers leaving her wanting to scream in agony. She would never be a racecar driver, or a movie star, or a rock star. She would be damned lucky if she had a son when she got home. She wept then. She wept for Brydon, sorry for uprooting him one more time, for constantly denting his innocence when the child only wanted a stabile life. She wept for herself and for a lifetime of shattered dreams.

When the tears subsided, Jane blew her nose, started her car, reset her GPS to retrace her route home and maneuvered the vehicle out of the parking lot. Brydon was all she really had in this world, and she was not going to let Elliot have him. Jane turned on the car's wipers just as the clouds began to unleash their heavy burden.

"Look Mommy, the wipers are dancing across the windshield to the beat of the Moody Blues!" Brydon giggled as they drove home from a rained-out T-ball game.
Jane laughed and nodded. "You're right, Sweetie. They do look like they're dancing." She ruffled her son's hair affectionately, impressed that, not only was he not pouting about the game being cancelled, but that he actually knew who the Moody Blues were.

Jane's lower jaw set in determination. There would be no time for an overnight pit stop. Her beautiful Todd would have to wait. She would drive all night and reclaim her son before the Fallises could arrange a retainer.

CHAPTER FOURTEEN

Elliot squatted down as he tucked Brydon in bed, pulling the bright covers up to the boy's tiny shoulders. Tucking Brydon in bed had always been Jane's nightly ritual. Now he wondered why he had just accepted being a bystander. He had learned more about the child in one day alone at home with him than in the three years that he and Jane had been married. Elliot bent over to kiss Brydon's tanned forehead and to brush back the strands of unruly hair.

Brydon looked up at him, his round, hazel eyes full of the usual million questions and more. "Daddy Elliot, can I call you just plain 'Daddy'? I know that you're not my real dad, but I love you like you are."

Elliot swallowed back the tears that had threatened to surface all day. "Sure thing, Buddy," he soothed. "I'd be very proud if you called me just plain 'Daddy'." A mixture of pride and sadness overwhelmed him. Elliot knew the simple request was an acceptance on both of their parts. It should have been a moment of rejoicing instead of one of doubts. He had his son for now. A part of him had almost died when he thought Brydon was gone. The thought of losing him again was more than he could endure.

"Daddy," Brydon studied him, eyes drooping with the onset of sleep, "is Mommy coming home tomorrow after the interview?"

Wanting to be strong in front of the lad, Elliot bit back the comments that edged at his mind. "We'll see, Bry," was all he could truthfully say. "You get some sleep now." He kissed Brydon's forehead again, eased himself back into a standing position and walked out of the bedroom. *I could raise him by myself,* Elliot thought. *I could even learn to tolerate that stupid cat if it made Bry happy. It'd be tough, but I know that I could do it.*

Damn you, Jane, Elliot chastised for the thousandth time that day. *Where are you? Why won't you answer your phone? Why are you doing this?* He strolled slowly down the cream-coloured hallway.

Gertie had been super. He had expected a confrontation or an argument from her. Instead, she had made him a coffee and quietly listened as he blew off some steam. He had wanted black and white answers but had learned nothing concrete. It didn't make sense. Nothing made sense anymore.

Why had the job interview been so covert? It should have been something that they sat down and discussed as a couple, he and Jane as man and wife. He would have understood her wanting to work in an industry she spent three years preparing for in college...or at least, he wanted to believe that he would have been supportive.

Elliot sauntered downstairs, deep in thought, and into the kitchen to retrieve a cold beer from the refrigerator. The kitchen was a definite disaster zone—scads of dirty dishes were tossed haphazardly into the stainless steel sink, dried-on food stained the cream-coloured counter. Later, he decided. He would worry about cleaning up later. Elliot opened the refrigerator and took out a beer. Jane just up and leaving did not coincide with the image he had of his sparky wife. She had always met everything head-on. If she needed to try new things, wanted to expand her career, why hadn't she sat down and discussed it with him? He had known her since they were kids, but now he felt like she was a total stranger.

CHAPTER FIFTEEN

Jane tried to stifle a yawn as the minutes had turned into hours and the grey skies had metamorphosed into night. The torrential rains had eased up enough to make the driving a bit more tolerable, but Jane growled at her bad luck anyway. Whenever she met another vehicle, everything looked blurry as the oncoming lights temporarily blinded her while her wipers tried to keep up with the insistent rain. Twice already, she had lost sight of the road while tracing a curve and held her breath until the cars finally met and her vision was slowly restored.

Another yawn broke loose before she had a chance to catch it. Unconsciously, she glanced down at her watch and wondered what time the face read. Difficult to read in the dark, dummy, she thought. She shook her head in annoyance.

Rolling her shoulders, Jane decided to stop at the next town for an extra-large coffee, double double. Glad to be off the major highways, with their major idiots, Jane had relaxed a bit. A few more hours and she would be home. She could not think any further than that. Tomorrow was another day that would unfold on its own accord, without her worrying about it now.

The music emanating from the radio had been slowly fading for the past ten kilometres, losing broadcast-range. Jane looked down and pressed the scan button. Music, once again, filled the automobile. A country and western station. Not really her taste in tunes, but better than dead air, and she didn't feel like rooting around through the several emergency CDs she had tossed onto the seat beside her.

As her car sailed over the next knoll, Jane's headlights caught two, bone-thin coyotes on the road ahead feeding on road kill (odd that)…aw yes, the trickster, one her favourite native symbols….refines the art of self-sabotage to perfection….

She braked gently not wanting to spin out as the asphalt was slick and greasy and honked her horn. She expected the animals to run. Instead, frozen by her headlights, they remained motionless. Once the information registered, finding its way through the proper channel of synapses, Jane slammed on her brakes with both feet hoping to avoid a collision. Her tires, not finding traction on the watery pavement, merely skidded forward.

As the animals drew closer at what seemed like an incredibly surreal speed, Jane panicked. With eyes locked on the stunned animals, Jane grabbed her steering wheel, knuckles white and cranked it to the left hoping to swerve around them. Instead, her car began to fishtail. Oh god, she thought, the baby....

A woman's voice sang out from the radio, "When darkness descends and the flowers all die, with the last glimpse of sunlight, so will I...."

CHAPTER SIXTEEN

Elliot supposed that life was much like softball. If there were no rules, no tampered plays, no close calls, there would be no need for umpires. Sometimes, the distraught players yelled in their annoyance or in their anger as the calls seemed unfair or downright wrong. In the end, someone had to decide. Some umpires were fair. Some umpires definitely played favourites. Some umpires were just plainly unsure of the rules and made bad calls. But, at the end of the game, the scores would be tallied. Someone would walk away the winner and someone would always come in second. Jane had not been playing fair, not even close, and Elliot was determined not to lose.

Taking a vacation on short-notice from work had created only minimal problems and confusion. Elliot had informed his assistant manager that he was in the midst of a family crisis and could be reached at home in case of emergency only.

Surveying his immediate surroundings, Elliot did his best to tidy up the disheveled kitchen while Brydon sat, spell-bound by a videogame on their gaming system. At least the child was occupied and had, for the time being, shelved his overly abundant questions regarding what was going on and where his mom was. If Jane had been there, the brightly-painted kitchen would have been spotless by now. Instead, Elliot felt awkward at best, wondering if every item was in its proper, allotted space.

When the telephone rang, Elliot was not prepared for the sudden intrusion on his thoughts. Startled, he dropped a rose-coloured, ceramic mug (Jane's favourite) that he had been taking out of the dishwasher. Instinctively jumping back so that the large mug would not hit his bare feet, he watched, transfixed, as the object shattered, numerous pieces scurrying across the white tile floor in a frenzy of uncontrolled motion. "Damn it," he scolded as he stepped between the pieces and headed towards the incessant ringing.

Brydon jumped up in a six-year-old's anxiousness to make it to the telephone first. "I'll get it, Daddy!!"

"Bry, wait..." Elliot began, knowing that he was already too late. The boy was quick. Elliot's insides tightened. He had already reported Jane's disappearance to the police to establish abandonment. The constable had politely informed him that if it was simply a case of marital dispute, they would rather not get involved. After all, whether Elliot liked it or not, Jane was an adult, free to come and go as she pleased. After explaining Jane's potential emotional state (Jane would freak when she discovered that he'd taken Brydon from Gertie's) and asking to speak to Constable Jeff Thornton personally, the attending officer had agreed to take a message for Constable Thornton who was presently out on a call and also reluctantly agreed to check with a few hospital emergency departments. That was the best he could do unless charges were being laid. Elliot should, the constable recommended, seek the counsel of a good lawyer. Elliot had thanked him and hung up. He didn't want a fucking lawyer. He wanted his wife back.

"Hello?" Brydon spoke half into the receiver, listening intently and wanting to sound as polite as possible. His mommy had shown him how to talk on the phone. Look at me, Mommy, he thought. Am I doing good?

"Elliot, you have to let Brydon answer the telephone occasionally," Jane insisted stubbornly. "How else will he ever learn?"

Half-heartedly, Elliot agreed. They had been discussing Brydon's recent telephone antics. "Fine but what about Saturday when your mom called and Bry told her that he was here all alone? I was in the basement working on the furnace and, five minutes later, I had your mom storming in here to see what the hell was going on. I felt lower than a slug."

Jane began to chuckle, her eyes sparkling with good humour as she visualized her mother enroute to rescue whoever needed rescuing.

"Elliot, we discussed that incident with Brydon already. Remember? We told him how worried Nana had been and that he was to tell her the truth from now on. What if you had been hurt and couldn't make it to the telephone? What if Brydon was the only other person here? He's old enough to learn how to use the phone. It's just a matter of practice," she tried to stifle a giggle, "and working out a few of the bugs."

Crossing the remainder of the kitchen floor carefully so that no small, unnoticed daggers could pierce his soft, exposed flesh,

Elliot sought to hear the conversation that had lit up his son's face.

"Who is it?" Elliot inquired, mentally keeping his fingers crossed that it was not Pam or Gertie or Nana or Santa Claus.

Brydon heaved a sigh. "Just a minute," he spoke into the receiver, then looked up. "Daddy, please. I'm talking."

"Yes, Bry, but who are you talking to?" Elliot discovered that he had inadvertently picked up a red-checkered tea towel and tossed it towards the counter.

Brydon, very dramatically rolled his eyes towards the ceiling. "Uncle Jeff."

Panic swept through Elliot's emotions coincided by a brief flight of anger. Concern fought through—a desperate need to know—as he raced towards the telephone. "Let me speak to him, Bry." He abruptly grabbed the telephone away from the boy, trying to ignore Brydon's indignation. Brydon stood glaring, his small hands planted firmly on his tiny hips in defiance.

Trying to steady himself and feeling like he was teetering on the edge of a bottomless pit, the abyss of all abysses (it's a long way down if you lose your balance), Elliot returned his attention to the telephone.

"Jeff, it's Elliot. What did you find out?" Elliot squatted down and drew the child close to him. He could feel his own equilibrium tottering. Don't lose it now, damn it. For god's sake, don't lose your balance now.

THE MIDDLE

"Then you came into my life. You taught me new things. I learned how to cry in fear. I learned how to hide in shame and guilt. I learned how to not talk. I learned how my body was not just mine anymore. I learned how to hate and how to distrust.

You forced me into a prison, leaving me to wither and die on Emotional Death Row. I heard you laugh as you locked the door and walked away because my screams for help were not successful. No one wanted to listen."

> Emotional Death Row
> Life in 3-D

You know that you are truly alone
When you cry out and there is no echo.

7 years earlier…

.

CHAPTER SEVENTEEN

Jane could scarcely believe that she had actually survived her first year of college. Between the initial finally-away-from-home bouts of college parties where beer was bought by the keg and joints of marijuana and cubes of hash were handed out like candy at some kid's birthday party, various boyfriends whom she would have not dared take home to meet her parents and studying for way too many exams, Jane was exhausted.

Initially, she had planned on spending the summer vacation travelling to British Columbia to meet up with a high school friend who had gotten drunk after a very ugly split up with her latest Mr. Wrong and who had, a week later, found herself in Vancouver. She still wasn't exactly sure how she managed to get there but had liked the city enough to stay.

However, Jane's parents were not quite as enthused as she was. They had, very bluntly, given her the choice between going home and getting a summer job, whereby they would pay her tuition the next fall, or her going to Vancouver and no tuition. Grudgingly, and with the internalized malice of the very young who do not understand that money does not pop out of thin air on demand, Jane chose the tuition.

Then there was the problem of what to do about Todd. She had grown very fond of her classmate, but would their blossoming relationship survive four months of summer vacation, especially with 320 kilometers between them and no easy access to a vehicle safe enough to occasionally close the gap? He did not understand what it would take for her to survive through those months, and she did not quite know how to explain what life in Donnybrooke was really like for her. It wasn't that she was going home to reacquaint herself with everything she loved. It would be more like visiting hell and doing everything and anything physically and emotionally possible to get back out again.

If someone had told her on the first day of school that she would eventually hook up with Todd on a romantic basis, she would have laughed. With fifty of her classmates being male in a class size of sixty-five, the male/female ratio was wonderfully staggering. Jane felt like a little girl in the world's largest Toys-R-

Us. And, since a rather gorgeous blonde who could not understand her desire to continue her education versus staying in the area and spending the next forty years of her life working in a factory had just dumped her, Jane was looking for fun, not commitment.

Todd had started off as a friend, someone to fight over the remote with on a boring Saturday night. Todd, with the girlfriend back home. Todd, who mumbled through radio lab. Todd, who did not fit any description of the men she was usually attracted to-- too clean cut, definitely not blonde, played hockey instead of getting stoned. Todd, whose voice sounded so astonishingly close to Garfield that, if she shut her eyes, she could actually picture him as that unscrupulous, orange feline, minus his very misunderstood counterpart, Odie. Todd.

"Todd." Jane shook the strong shoulder of the man who lay beside her, the man who had, only recently, become her lover. With an increasingly stronger feeling of melancholy, she visually traced the curve of his shoulder. She studied the way his long, brown hair covered part of his face while he slept, fighting an urge to brush back the locks so that she could see his face clearly. She had been awake for two hours already trying to sort everything out in her mind and finding no resolution.

Todd only moaned and rolled over onto his back. The covers, slipping down from around his arms, exposed his swimmers build, strong but slim.

Jane, with her finger-tips, began to trace small circles on his smooth chest, starting at his left nipple. Around and around, bigger and bigger. Reverse. Smaller and smaller until she was back to the nipple. She bent forward and gently, ever so lightly, began the pattern again, this time with her tongue. Manna for the orally fixated. Her long hair swept down beside her face, brushing Todd's bare skin as she continued her voyage. Down from the nipple, continuing in small circles. Down to his belly button where she stopped briefly, nibbling and taunting his sensitive skin, before continuing her quest.

"Jane," a sleepy voice finally spoke as Todd began to fight his way to the reality of what was happening to his body.

Jane, who had travelled a remarkable way down before her lover had awakened, grinned and snuggled up to Todd, her head on his shoulder. "Did I wake you?" she teased.

"Uh huh." Todd's eyes opened as he turned his head towards her, a smile caressing his lips. "What time is it?"

"Ten o'clock. I leave for Donnybrooke in three hours." Jane's left hand began to work its way below the folds of covers. Her touch was gentle but insistent. Her need great. The feeling of his skin beneath hers, ecstasy.

Todd's hand grasped hers, stopping her in mid-motion. "Wait."

Jane moaned. "Todd, I'm leaving in THREE hours. I probably won't see you all summer."

Slowly, Todd extricated himself. "This isn't the movies, Jane. Just give me a couple of minutes to wake up, brush my teeth and take a piss. Okay?"

Jane sighed and relinquished. She watched as Todd strolled away from her, completely nude, his butt muscles flexing as he walked. There was something so totally unfair about life that men should naturally have beautiful, muscular butts while women had to sweat buckets as they endured hours of painful aerobics and then pray that cellulite wouldn't take over before they reached thirty. She grabbed a package of cigarettes off of the floor and lit one. She inhaled deeply in the attempt to temporarily placate her rampant hormones.

Five minutes later, Todd's face peaked into the bedroom. "Jane, do you want a cup of tea?" His hair was still tussled from sleep.

"No," Jane pouted, "I want to fuck like mad dogs. But, yeah, you might as well make a pot." She reached beside her and stubbed out the cigarette in a nearby ashtray. She rose from the mattress that acted as a bed and joined Todd in the tiny kitchenette.

The apartment was Todd's and sparsely furnished. Unlike Jane, Todd was working his way through college. His budget did not include room for anything that was not a necessity for survival. She sat down at the tiny table, watching Todd make the tea and wondering where he had found jeans to throw on. Probably in the bathroom. Todd definitely had his own method for sorting his clothes. He had his dirty pile in the hallway, waiting for a trip to the Laundromat, his clean pile in his bedroom, waiting to be worn, and his in between pile in the bathroom, clothes that could be worn once more before joining the pile in the hallway.

He handed her a ceramic mug of steaming tea. "Sorry, I'm out of milk."

"No prob," she assured him.

"You know, Jane. When we first started school, I thought of asking you out a dozen times, except I didn't think that I was enough man for you." He joined her at the arborite topped table. "I still don't know if I really am, but I like what we have. I was thinking that maybe we could share an apartment next fall. What do you think?"

Jane blew on the hot, dark liquid, took a small sip then set the cup down. "First of all, you had a girlfriend at the beginning of the year so I wouldn't have gone out with you even if you had asked. Secondly, you are lots man enough, so get any notions that you aren't out of that cute head of yours. And last but not least, I think that in a few hours, I have to load up everything I own in my mom's car and head back up north." She stood up and placed herself behind him, stroking his long hair. "I think," she bent over and kissed the top of his head, "that I want to fuck you so much it hurts." Walking around him, never taking her hand off his shoulder, she straddled him, her face close to his. Her short nightgown exposed long, well-shaped legs.

"Jane, I'm trying to be serious here. Whenever I try to talk to you about anything serious, you change the subject. There's more to life than sex you know." He reached up and brushed the hair back from her face.

"I know but humour me anyway." She kissed one cheek, then the other, then his forehead and his nose. "We can talk afterwards." She kissed him deeply and finally felt the stirring beneath her that she longed for.

Todd pulled away from her, holding Jane's face gently in his hands. "Promise me."

"Promise you what?" Jane's hands slid between her legs to unfasten his zipper.

"Promise me that you'll at least consider what I said." His brown eyes smouldered with a harnessed passion.

"Okay, I promise. I'll call you in June and if you still feel the same way, we'll discuss it further. Okay?" Her breathing quickened as her fingers played rhapsody on his stiffening organ.

Todd smiled, breathing deeply. "Okay." He released her face, let his hands slide down to the bottom of her nightgown, grasped the ends and pulled the unwanted article over her head. After twirling it once in mid-air like a lasso, the nightgown spun through the air and landed ungracefully in the corner of the room.

"You know, we've never had sex in your kitchen," Jane teased as she leaned forward to smooth his hair back so she could kiss the side of Todd's neck, searching for the sensitive spot that she knew would make him quiver. She loved that spot. "In the bedroom, yes. In the bathroom, yes. In the living room, absolutely." As her tongue and lips worked their magic, she could feel Todd's energy shift, his sexual desire on the rise. A slow burn increasing in heat. "And for some reason, Mr. Linwood," she continued, "we've never had sex in the kitchen."

"I think we can fix that, but you'll have to stand up long enough for me to take my pants off."

Jane rose, still straddling Todd, and watched, enrapt, as he slouched his hips forward, pushed his jeans down and kicked them off in great haste. Then, holding the sides of her wanting hips in his strong hands, he guided her onto his very firm erection.

As they moved together, creating a rhythm unique only to them, Jane memorized every sensation, every part of Todd. The way he moved, the way he felt, the way he smelled, the way he breathed. They came together in a spiritual melding of the souls, an energy so intense that, for a moment, they were one.

And as she sat curled around him, physically satiated, Jane felt an intense urge to forget about college, her career, her dreams, her aspirations and become a waitress. Anything, just as long as she could stay.

CHAPTER EIGHTEEN

Elliot surveyed the shipment of softball equipment--Rawlings wooden bats, retail starting at $29.99, brown and black leather, fielding gloves, starting at $44.99 and softballs, starting at $2.99 each. As the new Assistant Manager, it was now his responsibility to check all incoming shipments to ensure that the proper amount of each item ordered had been received without any defects. Any defective product was immediately returned to the wholesaler for replacement or for credit. Wholesalers were also contacted with any shipping discrepancies. Once the shipment had been checked and inputted into the store's inventory, the product was either stockpiled in the backroom of the store or placed out on the shelves for display and purchase.

Basically, Elliot liked his job and felt a tremendous amount of pride in his advancement from part-time (during high school) to full-time sales (after graduation) to his recent promotion. He was twenty-six and doing just fine. The store was 2,000 square feet, with large, deep-set windows perfect for seasonal displays, privately owned, not some small link in a major corporation chain, and most of the customers were people he had known all of his life. Some of whom had said that he would never amount to anything during his earlier years of heavy drinking and bar-room brawls. Now these same people were coming in to purchase, from him, sports equipment for themselves or for their children. Elliot had miraculously transformed from the town's likable ruffian to the town's utmost authority on anything from lacrosse sticks to jockstraps. He had even incorporated a large corkboard behind the cash register where customers could post snapshots of their children decked out in their uniforms. The moms loved that.

He was bright, business-oriented and had a talent for sales. Elliot did not believe in selling people more than what they needed or at a higher price than they could afford. This ideology had taken him far with the local residents. No gimmicks. No car salesman's smooth talk. Just basic good sense and an excellent knowledge of the products that he sold. Eventually, it was his dream to open his own store; but for now, he was content with learning the business from the bottom to the top.

A bell sounded the arrival of a potential customer. Elliot did not look up from his task, expecting one of the salespeople to wait on the person.

"Hey, Elliot. Got a minute, man?"

Elliot glanced up at the mention of his name. He ticked six junior fielding gloves off of the invoice, then placed the clipboard on top of a carton of 11-inch softballs (he always thought it a bit odd that softball sizes were still better known in inches, probably just easier to remember than 27.94 centimetres). "What can I do for you, Nick?" He greeted his twin with fond affection, glad for the momentary interruption of his task.

"Have you heard the news, man? Jane's back from college." With his hands stuck in the front pockets of his dirty jeans, Nick restlessly shifted his weight from one foot to the other.

Elliot felt his stomach knot. "So?" Elliot hated when his brother fidgeted, a bad habit that Nick had picked up as a child. The guy could just never stand still.

"What do you mean `so'. Shit, we haven't seen her for eight months, man. Aren't you at least a little bit curious?"

Elliot shook his head, moved the clipboard then took a silver utility knife out of his pocket to slit open the carton of softballs. "Not really."

Nick shrugged. "'Kay, fine, man. Have it your way. If you're not interested, no big deal. Means the territory's open then, right?" He grabbed a brand-new ball from the carton and began to toss the ball in the air with his left hand and catch it with his right.

Elliot locked eyes with his brother, his good humour quickly dissipating. "What do you mean by that?" He snagged the ball in midair and returned it to the box.

"You know what I mean, man. I must know at least ten guys who would give their left nut for the nerve to ask her out--except that they're all afraid of you--and you're going to stand there pretending like you don't care. Since when?"

Elliot shrugged and began to sort through the softballs, finding enough room on the shelf for a dozen and leaving the rest in the carton for storage. With the season quickly approaching, the minor sports leagues would be buying them in bulk anyway. "What Jane does is her business."

"I don't know. Rumour has it that she looks good, man. College must have agreed with her."

"Nick," Elliot felt his patience about to end, "enough. I'm too busy right now for this bullshit."

"Fine, man. I'm outa here, but I'll see you later at the dance, right?" Nick smiled good-naturedly and turned to leave.

"Yeah. Later." Elliot hoisted the cartons of surplus supplies and headed to the back room.

What had originally started off as a rather pleasant afternoon had definitely taken a plummet. There wasn't one guy around who did not understand that Jane was off limits. The only person he could never seem to convince was Jane.

It had taken him three years to establish his territory. Three years of Nick telling him if he had seen her with another guy and then Elliot following up with a surreptitious chat. The meeting would be planned so that he would happen upon the planned target with the air of complete coincidence. Wow, you exit out the back way from the bar too! Imagine that. He would begin chatting, being very well known locally for his gregarious mannerisms. And, eventually, he would route the conversation to his desired destiny. Jane. If the so-called suitor was just a passing acquaintance, Elliot would let the matter slide with a casual cut down. He would explain to his fellow man just what a stupendous bitch and slut the woman really was as if it was common knowledge. If the target had romantic intentions and did not really care what anyone else said about Jane, Elliot would bluntly tell the guy to stay out of her life or suffer the consequences.

Occasionally, he and Jane had locked horns over the matter but that hadn't stopped him. He was certain that, eventually, she would come around and agree that they were meant for each other. If not, he would do his best to make sure that she grew old alone.

Then, of all things, she'd had enough nerve to trot off to college. She'd always been such a bitch about that. No local guy was ever good enough for her. Oh no, she had a five-year plan to get rich she said--three years in college and then two years to find a man with enough money.

Even then he had never thought that she would actually leave but she had. For the past eight months, she had been entirely out of his life, out of his control. He had accepted that, taken up with a fairly steady girl and focused his energies on the business. Now she was back. Jane was back. Elliot did not have the slightest clue what he was going to do.

The hours between work and the spring dance dragged ominously. When the time finally arrived, Elliot could not believe just how nervous he felt. He, Elliot Fallis, nervous, right down to sweating palms. Fucking ridiculous.

He watched, drinking beer, as local couples began to congregate in the Community Centre, all decked out in Saturday night duds, wonderfully glad that winter was over and that they had an excuse to get out of the house for the evening.

The lights dimmed and the disc jockey commenced the evening's frolickings with a lively country and western piece. Elliot hated country and western music. He took another swig of beer. His eyes travelled over the undulating crowd, searching for one face only.

"Elliot, do you want to dance?" his date leaned towards him and enquired. He had chosen a table at the back of the hall, the best strategic location to get a full view of anyone coming in or leaving.

He replied tersely, "Not to this shit."

His date frowned, marking her disappointment, and took a long swig from her beer.

Nick rescued him. "I'll dance with you, Glenda."

"Thanks, Nick. At least someone's in the mood to have fun."

Nick took Glenda's hand in his to lead her out onto the dance floor. "Didn't anyone ever tell you that I'm really the fun one of the twins?" Their voices were swept away.

Elliot stood up from the table. Time for another beer. Nick was pacifying his date. Everything was under control. No problem. Weaving his way through the gyrating dancers, Elliot managed to make it to the bar without bumping into anyone for a change and ordered another beer. The evening was still early. Maybe Jane would come later. Maybe. Maybe not. He paid for the beer and began to turn around to survey the crowd.

"Rum and gingerale, please."

Elliot stopped in mid-motion, the beer halfway up to his lips. Jane. What the hell? How had he missed her? He turned around slowly to face her. His could feel his heart pound softly in his chest.

"Hi, Jane." Elliot smiled his most radiant smile. He could see the curiosity in her eyes, an untrusting curiosity at best. A `why are you being so friendly' type of curiosity.

"Hi, Elliot." Jane reached past him to retrieve and pay for her drink.

"I heard you were back. So, how was school?" Small talk. That's always a good way to start like nice weather or I heard little Johnny got straight A's this semester...

"Fine. Tough. Interesting." She shrugged non-committedly. "See you on the dance floor." She held up her drink in a `cheers' type fashion and began to walk away.

Elliot quickly reached out and caught her arm. He felt her muscles tense under his grasp. "Are you here by yourself or did you bring a date?" He tried to keep his voice calm but the sharp edge of his tone was undeniable.

Jane's laughter startled him. She jerked her arm out of his hold. "That's really none of your business. Bye, Elly."

He watched as she managed to hazard her way through the thickening crowd. He watched as she placed her drink on a table at the opposite side of the hall. He watched as she leaned down to talk to a sandy-haired man whom they both knew. He watched as the sandy-haired man stood up and took Jane's hand. He watched as they maneuvered their way out onto the dance floor. He watched as they began to dance.

Elliot knew exactly what he had to do. Making his way back through the crowd, Elliot could not control the force that drove him. It was totally irrational, he knew, but he was beyond all reason, all caring.

Elliot made his way to his date. "Nick," Elliot tapped his brother's shoulder as he interrupted the dancing couple, "take my beer back to the table and let me dance with my lady."

"Whatever, man." Nick mimicked a bow towards Glenda, grabbed Elliot's beer and sauntered off nonchalantly.

"Glenda," Elliot took the hand of his waiting date, "let's dance."

"Well, it's about time." Glenda smiled.

Elliot carefully led her to the middle of the dance floor and held her closely so that she would follow his lead with the ease of those who have the rhythm of the music embedded in their souls.

"I was beginning to think that Nick was right," Glenda commented into his ear.

Elliot, who was surveying the dance floor and slowly maneuvering his way towards his destination, did not respond. The air was getting thick with the smell of perfume, aftershave cologne, sweat and alcohol but that was the least of his concern.

"Elliot?"

Elliot looked at Glenda, almost surprised that she was still there. "Yeah?"

She spoke a bit louder this time. "I said that I was beginning to think that Nick was right."

Seeing Jane and her dance partner near the front of the hall closer to the stage where the DJ was busily spinning tunes, Elliot moved gradually towards them trying not to be too noticeable. "Right about what?"

"That he was the fun one of the two of you." Glenda dodged the elbow of the man on her left who suddenly decided that it would be a brilliant idea to twirl his partner.

Elliot's face remained emotionless. "He is," Elliot complied.

"He's what?" Glenda asked.

They were close now. A couple more steps and he would be within reach. "Nick is the fun one."

Glenda sighed audibly over the music. "Oh."

The song ended. The next song was more to his liking, a good old-fashioned Rock and Roll classic. Lots of rhythm and motion.

"One more dance?" Elliot smiled broadly as if he had been having the ultimate time of his life.

Glenda nodded. "Sure."

Elliot watched as Jane stood with her partner, chatting and laughing easily. Would they have one more dance? Fingers crossed. He was so close now. He liked the way that she looked in her blue jeans and shirt. Comfortable. Casual. A bit too thin but nothing that three good meals per day wouldn't fix. Didn't she eat in college?

The music began. Elliot grabbed Glenda roughly and twirled her towards Jane. Jane and her partner had just begun to dance. Her back was turned. One more twirl but better make it quick. He barely noticed the frown on Glenda's face as she tried to keep up.

Closer. Closer. Closer. Elliot's face broke into a wide, sardonic smile. His turn. With the grace of a good dancer, Elliot took two more steps backwards and swung to his right. His right elbow found its mark--right between Jane's shoulder blades. Bull's-eye.

The impact sent Jane sprawling ungracefully into the arms of her dance partner who caught her fall. "Ouch," she cried in pain. She turned around in surprise to see what had happened.

"Oh crap, Jane. I didn't see you. You okay?" Elliot let Glenda's hands drop and gently grabbed Jane by her narrow shoulders as if making sure that she was unhurt. He bent close to whisper into her ear, "Sorry, Darlin'. From now on, if I were you, I'd watch your back."

CHAPTER NINETEEN

It had taken almost three weeks of constant searching before Jane had finally talked her way into adequate summer employment. The pay was good for a student, and the hours were 8:00 a.m. to 4:00 p.m., Monday through Friday, with the occasional Saturday to be spread out over the summer. She had purchased a used car, with the better part of her first two paycheques promised to her uncle. Yes, indeed. Life was looking up.

Two, long telephone conversations with Todd and a thousand text messages had established that he had not changed his mind about sharing an apartment. In fact, he had even offered to borrow a car and drive up for her birthday so that they could plan everything together--how much they could afford with their combined savings and student loans, who would bring what furniture, what they needed to purchase and so on. Eventually, she had been persuaded, although the thought of Todd discovering all of her personal "its", those little things that not even her best friend was aware of, still made Jane nervous. And now she had his visit to look forward to as well. Todd. Her Todd. Her grounding source, her reality, her sanity in the midst of chaos and confusion.

He wanted to see where she was from. He wanted to meet her parents, whom she still had not found the nerve to tell that there was a remote chance that their youngest daughter might be living with a male come September. Better to let her parents meet Todd first and then tell them about the living arrangements after she had moved back--a long distance call where she was on her own territory again. Or better yet, an e-mail. A long letter explaining the economic standards of student living being well-below the poverty line and how, this year, many students had decided to pool their meager resources in whatever fashion they could so that they did not have to live on one meal of macaroni and cheese per day in total squalor.

Jane took a deep breath and exhaled slowly. She was getting herself all hyped up about something that had not happened yet and admonished herself accordingly. Todd's visit was still more than a month away, and she would survive until then. She had her day job, her car, her sense of freedom and Gertie to party with.

Gertie, who not only had her own apartment but who also had access to a constant supply of Northern Lights, Pink Ladies and Ecstasy--Jane's three favourite brain cell killers. She would don her conservative mask, work all day, then as soon as four o'clock arrived, she would tuck the mask safely away, meet up with friends, party until she was about to drop, catch a couple of hours of sleep, pop a couple of bennies, grab an extra-large, double double and then start all over again. Life was good.

Then there was the problem of what to do about Elliot. One dance with a mutual friend had provided all of the information that she had needed to know. Elliot had not changed. Eight months away from Donnybrooke had not changed the dynamics at all. It was as if he was stuck in some surreal time warp and wanted to suck her in with him, so that they could spin around and around forever and an eternity.

She had even tried talking to Nick about it. Jane felt sorry for Nick. He always seemed to live in Elliot's shadow somehow. Elliot was loud and outspoken. Nick was quiet and a bit backwards. Nick gracefully accepted a 'no' when he occasionally propositioned her. Elliot growled ruefully and covertly unleashed his Thor-like qualities. Nick was her friend; Elliot was her nemesis.

Nothing had been resolved. Elliot's behaviour had gone downhill drastically since the dance. Nasty was the catchword of the day. That man could be just plain nasty. The part that Jane did not understand was just how he seemed to know her every move, who she had been out with the night before, or where she was going two hours from now. Three more months of his bullshit then she would be gone again. This time for good. The problem was, how to survive until then.

Jane reached her friend's apartment and pulled her car up close to the curb. Tonight was girls' night out.

Gertie's apartment was the second floor of a house. Jane liked that. Large apartment buildings generally had such little character. Everyone lived in identical beige boxes neatly stacked on top of each other. And, if the guy three floors below you decided that tonight would be a really perfect night to fall asleep with a lit cigarette in bed and a bottle of tequila, then you would be damned lucky to get your sorry butt outside, or on the balcony to be rescued.

Jane shuddered at the thought. She would definitely tell Todd to stay away from any buildings over three storeys.

"Hey, Gertie. Aren't you ready yet?" Jane wandered around the living room, waiting for her friend to emerge from her bathroom. Yes, the apartment definitely had a character of its own. Posters of pot leaves adorned the walls right alongside the oak trim, wainscoting and crown moulding that were a part of the original architecture. At least someone had the common sense to either strip the trim back to the original wood, or to have not painted it at all.

"Give me a minute," a voice called back from the great beyond. "Hey, Bud, light up a joint while you're waiting. The power toker is in the top drawer of the end table."

Jane fetched the red, plastic bottle, sat down on a plush blue chair and expertly rolled a joint on the coffee table to put inside. She inhaled deeply and waited for the day's stress to slowly subside. She could feel a calm encompassing her, a calm where nothing really mattered. Life was good indeed. "Have you talked to your parents lately?" Jane handed the paraphernalia to Gertie as she entered the living room.

Gertie plunked herself down on a blue loveseat, across from Jane's chair, inhaled deeply from the toker then handed it back to Jane. After holding her breath for a few seconds, she exhaled a stream of smoke. "Yup. I checked in with them a couple of nights ago."

"How are they?" Jane had met Gertie's parents on several occasions and genuinely liked the somewhat unorthodox couple.

"Just as crazy as ever. The last time I was there, Dad said that Mom had finally gotten out of her Paul Gross phase and has now moved on to an actor named Tommy Flanagan." Gertie stood up from the loveseat and went to the kitchenette to fix drinks. "Want a drink before we go?"

"Sure. Wow, I thought Paul Gross was the lust of her life?" After taking another long drag, Jane set the toker down on the wooden coffee table. Jane turned to watch Gertie.

"I guess a ten-year crush was enough, though I have to admit he's still pretty hot for his age." Gertie walked back into the tiny living room, handed Jane a glass of rum and ginger ale and sat back down. "Anyway, according to Dad, they had a local 'Movie in the Park' night that showed *Braveheart*. Tommy Flanagan is this Scottish dude who plays a supporting character named Morrison. I looked it up online. After watching the movie, Mom went home with a new fantasy man so Dad let his hair grow out a bit, grew a goatee and walks around the house trying to imitate a Scottish accent."

Jane chuckled and took a drink, savouring the taste. "I'm surprised it didn't turn into a Mel Gibson fest. Can't beat a gorgeous man who looks amazing in a kilt."

Gertie sighed. "I'm pretty sure that Mel Gibson is the real reason that I was conceived. Mom has copies of all his *Mad Max* and *Lethal Weapon* movies. After Mel was dethroned, Richard Gere took over for a while then Johnny Depp, then Viggo Mortensen. She collects every movie her man of the hour has been in so you can tell the chronological order. If nothing else, she does pick drop-dead, gorgeous men."

Jane shook her head. "Your poor dad."

"He's actually a pretty good sport about it, says it adds spice to their relationship." Gertie sipped her drink.

Jane tried to picture her parents being that open-minded and involuntarily shuddered. Nope. She definitely didn't want to picture her parents fantasizing about anyone let alone having sex. Best not to go there.

"I'm surprised that Patrick Swayze didn't make the list. I'm pretty sure that *Dirty Dancing* was directly responsible for the baby boom of 1988." Jane played with her ice cubes.

"Actually," Gertie thought for a moment, "now that you mention it, Mom was never that big on Patrick Swayze. I'm not sure why, but it's probably a good thing because Dad has two left feet. He can't dance to save his life."

Jane smiled. "Aha. Then maybe there's more method to your mom's madness than meets the eye."

Sudden understanding lit up Gertie's eyes. "Gotcha. Give Dad a role to play that's within his comfort zone. That way, he'll keep playing along." Gertie nodded. "Smart." She took another draw from the bottle and offered it to Jane.

Jane shook her head. "What about your dad? Does he have a fantasy woman?"

"Nope. He says that Mom is the sexiest woman he's ever seen so he doesn't need anyone else."

Jane smiled at her friend. "I have to admire your mom. Most of us just covertly fantasize. She puts it out there and says, 'deal with it' and your dad does. Not too many people I know have that kind of openness and acceptance in a relationship. What about you? Who's your fantasy man?'

"Me? That would have to be Went Milner. Soft spoken. Intense, smouldering blue eyes. Sexy. I read on a fan blog that he likes to play Scrabble. Gets my motor running every time."

"Scrabble gets your motor running?" Jane chuckled. "That's a new one."

"Well, maybe not the game exactly, but that and the way Went talks. He has this soft, sexy voice. All he'd need to do was put his letters on the board, look at me with those eyes and say, 'that's a triple word score for 30 points' and I'd be dragging him off to the bedroom." Gertie sighed.

"Kind of tough to make it through a game that way," Jane commented. She adored Gertie.

"Could take years," Gertie agreed, "but it would definitely be a game worth playing."

"I didn't think you were into nice guys. I've seen him on television interviews and he comes across as nice, smart, funny, down-to-earth. Kind of normal, really. He hasn't put himself up on a movie star pedestal yet." Jane retrieved a cigarette from a package in her purse, then rooted around for her favourite green lighter. She lit the cigarette and inhaled. Any more drugs and she'd be sleeping instead of dancing.

"I'd make an exception for Went. Besides which, he's an actor so he could pretend that he's tough, and, you know, put on an occasional temporary tattoo and then take on his badass save-the-world persona."

"You might as well not even start that game of Scrabble if he does that," Jane teased.

"Wouldn't make it to the bedroom either. All he'd have to do is walk through my front door and say, 'Hi, Gertie', and I'd have him naked before the door closed." Gertie put the cap on the toker bottle to extinguish the contents.

"That might be a bit awkward for the neighbours."

Gertie nodded. "Point. Okay, note to self, close the door before nailing Went." She smiled, a radiant beam lighting up her pretty face.

Jane giggled. "Too bad that your chances of actually meeting this guy are like one in six billion."

Gertie sighed as she conceded. "Better odds at getting hit by lightning."

"Exactly."

"It's always good, though, to have a game plan, just in case. Weirder things have happened. I've seen a couple of semi-famous rockers, who have property on Manitoulin Island, shopping at the mall in Owen Sound. So one never knows what the fates have in store." Gertie took another drink. "What about you? Do you have a fantasy man?"

"Just Todd. I'm like 98 percent sure that I'm falling in love with him."

"What about the other two percent?"

"The other two percent is waiting to see if we actually make it through the summer or if he meets some chick who sweeps him off his feet and leaves me choking in the dust." Jane's stomach softly clenched. The thought of that happening, of Todd and her not being together in the fall was unthinkable.

"That two percent may be very wise to wait. Men can be such fickle creatures."

"Agreed."

Gertie raised her glass ready to inhale the remaining contents. "Drink up, my friend, I want to get to Buck's while there's still open tables."

The night club was full of people milling around in search of the perfect drunken stupor, the perfect one-night stand or both. Commonly referred to as the "Meat Market", there was an unwritten understanding that whatever happened after the club closed was only temporary. Prince Charming played elsewhere.

With the music loud, and Jane's worries on-hold, the twosome eventually found a table and sat down.

"Can I get you ladies a drink?" enquired a friendly young waitress.

"Sure." Jane smiled. "Rum and ginger ale, no ice."

"Make mine a lager," Gertie chimed in.

Both tipped the waitress well when she returned with their drinks.

"Bar waitressing," Jane began, "has to be one of the toughest jobs I've ever tried. I only lasted six weeks before quitting. I don't know what it is, but men instantly assume that the waitress is an easy pick up. The one night at the end of my shift, I had this guy come up to me with a piece of paper and tell me to write down my phone number for him. I mean this guy wasn't even in my section. He just came up to me from nowhere."

Gertie grinned. "And just what did you do?" She tipped her beer up and took a drink.

"I informed him that he was seven propositions too late and left him standing." Jane shook her head in a punctuating manner.

Gertie laughed, then stopped, her face growing serious. She motioned towards the back door with her beer bottle. "Look."

Jane turned around casually to see what her friend was pointing at. Elliot, with an entourage of three of his best buddies.

"Damn it." Jane turned back to face her friend.

Gertie looked at her with a note of sincere concern. "It's going that well, is it?"

"And even better." Jane quickly glanced around once more to see where the group had seated themselves.

Gertie leaned over close to be heard above the opening song of the on-stage band, which was quite a bit louder than the disc jockey had been two minutes before. "Why don't you just tell Elliot that you're not interested? Tell him that you've got a man waiting for you when you go back to school."

Jane shook her head in exasperation. "It doesn't work. I've tried everything and nothing works. The only thing that does work is moving out of town and that, my friend, is that."

"You've tried everything?"

Jane nodded. "Short of sleeping with the guy."

Gertie smiled mischievously. "Then I have an idea. Let's buy those guys a drink and have it sent over to their table."

"What?" Jane could not quite follow her friend's line of rationalizing. It would be like sending Hitler a care package.

"Why?"

Gertie gave Jane a "trust me" look and summoned the waitress. "You see those guys over there?" She pointed to the foursome.

The young waitress nodded.

"Buy them each a drink on us. Okay?" She dug out her wallet to pay the correct amount plus a tip.

The waitress nodded. "If they ask who it's from, do I tell them?"

"Definitely." Gertie smiled brilliantly.

Jane grabbed her friend's wrist to get her attention. She could feel an anxiety attack hovering close by. "I don't understand. What's the point behind all of this."

"The point is that you still have three months before going back to college, right?"

"Right."

"As far as I can see, you have two choices. You can either continue to antagonize Elliot and put up with the wrath of his demi-godness or you can play it cool and enjoy the summer." Gertie watched as the waitress gathered the drinks and gave them to the foursome. The waitress bent over closer to Elliot so she could hear him speak then motioned in their direction.

Jane thought for a moment and sipped on her drink. "You mean, let him think he's winning?"

"Exactly. Think you can handle that?" Gertie tipped her beer back for a long draw.

A smile slowly emerged. A smile of hope. A brief glimmer of light at the end of a very long, dark, dank tunnel. "Like Ichpuchtli. " Jane finished her drink in one long tip of the wrist then stood up.

"Where are you going?" Gertie asked.

"I have a little errand to take care of. I'll be right back." Jane winked at her friend. "Like you implied, don't be sorry, get even."

Slowly, but efficiently, Jane began to squeeze her way through the crowd of steamy bodies. As she advanced to Elliot's table, she took in a deep breath to steady her nerves.

She placed her slim hand on Elliot's wide shoulder. He looked up at her from his sitting position but did not smile.

"Enjoying your drink, Elliot? I bought it just for you."

"Yeah, thanks," he complied without sincerety. "Jane, what do you want?"

His brusqueness sent a chill through Jane, but she maintained her composure. She squeezed his shoulder gently. "Something that only you can give me, Elliot." She smiled obsequiously and let go of her hold.

Without looking back, she casually sauntered over to her own table and sat down. "You can see Elliot from where you're sitting, right?" she asked Gertie.

"Yup."

"What's he doing?" Jane wanted a play-by-play.

"He's looking this way." Gertie summoned the waitress to bring another round of drinks. "I don't know what you said to him, but he just polished off his drink and ordered another one."

Jane smiled, satisfied. "Good." Instinctively, Jane knew that she was playing with fire. But then, she was not planning on being the one who got burned.

CHAPTER TWENTY

Elliot laid awake, slumber evading him as he tossed and turned in rumpled, cotton sheets. The night was warm, muggy, the air conditioner set on low to provide only enough comfort to sleep. The floor fan hummed rhythmically as the oscillating motion moved the still air. The house was quiet.

The evening had definitely not turned out the way that he had expected. His buds had been keeping eyes open for Jane for the past three weeks. Quick text messages and Elliot had developed a fairly good idea of Jane's usual routine. Work, then Gertie, then one of the nearby bars in either Donnybrooke or in Owen Sound. No man so far. She went to the bars with Gertie and left the same way. When his friend, Ryan, messaged this time, Elliot decided to see for himself. He had planned on going to the loud, crowded bar hoping to blend into the background, just a night out with the guys and watch Jane from a comfortable distance. Now this. What was Jane up to? What game was she playing? Why the sudden change?

With a heave of the light covers, Elliot disentangled himself and sat up in bed. His head pounded softly. Too much beer.

"Nick," he whispered into the darkness, "are you awake?"

No reply.

Elliot rose from his bed and carefully made his way across the large bedroom to the side where his brother lay sleeping. The twins had shared this room since birth, and Elliot figured that they probably would until either one or both of them could afford to move out on his own. Identical twin beds, identical, gray tubular metal headboards, identical, shamrock green bedspreads, two identical pine, four-drawer dressers showing the wear and tear of two rambunctious boys, two matching pine nightstands. On Elliot's side, melamine shelves had been attached to a pale-green painted wall to display his numerous high school and softball league trophies. Nick's only trophy sat on his dresser. There was no need for shelves. Instead, a poster of James Dean and Marilyn Monroe, forever immortalized in their youth, kept vigil over Nick's belongings.

Elliot could hear the sound of Nick's steady breathing interrupted occasionally by a soft snore. With the streetlight providing only enough illumination to show a silhouette, he shook Nick's bare shoulder. "Nick. Wake up."

Nick moaned and opened his eyes as he reached consciousness. "Wha...What..." He rolled over and looked at the black, digital alarm clock sitting on his wooden night stand. "Elliot, there better be a fire. It's 4:00 a.m. I was sound asleep, man." He yawned and rubbed his eyes trying to focus in the dark. Sitting up, he turned on his bedside lamp.

"I know what time it is," Elliot growled. "I need to talk to you for a minute then you can go back to sleep. Okay?" Elliot sat down on the firm bed beside his brother.

"Yeah, right man." Nick yawned before his voice drifted off. "Whatever." His eyelids fluttered then closed, his head began to droop.

Elliot shook his brother's shoulder once more, determined to get his full attention. "Wake up!"

Nick's eyes reopened as he turned to face his sibling. "I'm awake already. Keep your voice down, man, before you wake up Ma. This better be important, man, I was right in the middle of this great dream about Charlie's Angels. We were on a yacht off the coast of the Caribbean and…"

Annoyed, Elliot interjected, "Yeah, okay. I get the basic idea. I just needed to ask you something."

"And it just couldn't wait until morning? Okay, but like I said, this had better be good, man." Nick stared at his brother, waiting.

Elliot briefly mulled over the summer's multiplicitous moments trying to get a clear focus on the situation. How could he explain this to Nick? How could he explain that one random moment, one random, unforeseeable action had totally annihilated any chance of sleep? He had to figure this out or he wouldn't be able to rest. "Jane was at Buck's tonight with her friend, Gertie."

"Is Gertie the blonde chick I always see her with?"

"Yeah. Anyway, the guys and I were just kind of hanging out at the other side of the bar, totally minding our own business, watching the band..."

Nick interrupted, "Elliot, can you make this quick, man? I know you've had Jane on chick watch since she got back. I get it, but I have a long day tomorrow and I seriously need some shut-eye." Nick ran his long, tanned fingers through his short, dark hair.

Elliot frowned. "Sorry, I keep forgetting how many brain cells you actually need for construction work. Two, maybe, three?"

"Okay, okay. Don't get your shit in a knot, man. Just get to the good stuff."

"I would have by now but you interrupted me." Elliot suddenly grew too annoyed to continue. "Forget it. Go back to sleep." He rose from his brother's bed and walked back to his side of the room. He stood in front of the bedroom window, looking outside. The street appeared tranquil, no traffic at this time of the morning, the houses dark, nothing on but the streetlights.

"Elliot," Nick's voice summoned his attention. "I'm sorry, man. Look, I'm awake now. What's up?"

"Never mind. It's probably nothing anyway. Jane was being nice tonight. That's all." Elliot watched as a short-haired, black cat scavenged through the garbage left out by his neighbour for morning pick-up. The black, plastic bag had been split open at the seam--possibly by a stray dog or by a raccoon also in search of nutrition--its contents strewn across the well-tended lawn. The cat looked old, malnourished, sections of its fur were missing. The animal was definitely sick. Mange maybe.

"Yeah?" Nick's voice sparked with interest. "What'd she do?"

Elliot turned his attention away from the stray and went back to his bed. "Nothing, really. She just bought me a drink, had it sent over to our table and smiled. That's it." He felt tired now, stupid to obsess over nothing. He lay down on his bed and fluffed his feather pillow into shape. "Go back to sleep, Nick."

"Jane, nice. Yup, I can definitely understand how that could make the local news. You just never know with that bitch. Don't sweat it, man. You should have given up on her years ago. You're way too good for her. She doesn't deserve you, man. Hey though, maybe if you and Jane are getting along now, you can get Gertie's number for me. She's hot." Nick turned off his bedside lamp and lay back down on his bed. "Good night."

"Good night," Elliot echoed as he decided to try counting backwards from a hundred to see if that would still his overactive mind.

    Propped up on his elbow, Nick stared across the darkness in his brother's direction and frowned.

CHAPTER TWENTY-ONE

She woke, screams shredding her dreams, startling her into reality. The screams were real, not the nightmare that she had hoped for. As she crept from her soft, warm bed and made her way through the darkness of her bedroom, her heart began to beat rapidly like a bird testing its wings then preparing for lift off.

A dim light, a bedside lamp, illuminated her parents' bedroom, emanating just enough light into the night-filled hallway to cast eerie shadows of awaiting monsters--monsters that, if they so desired, could spring out at any time to grab wary ankles.

She walked, as if in a trance, towards that light, the screams grating on her courage like fingernails on a chalkboard.

With the doorway before her, she froze as still as a statue. If she looked in, there would be no point of return. The stairwell to the main level was on her left, close by, nearby, the security of escape. The continuing screams drew her. She did not want to see, but like a moth to a flame, she was drawn by some innate instinct that was beyond her thirteen-year-old level of understanding.

Her parents were on their double-bed in intimate nakedness. Her mother was on her back with her father straddling above. As his large fist came down, pummeling the well-loved face, her mother turned her head preparing for the onslaught of brutal pain.

Seeing her daughter, she pleaded, "Get help. For God's sake, call someone!" Tears ran down the already swollen cheeks in desperate helplessness.

The girl, transfixed by the horror that she witnessed, hesitated. Eyes widening in fear, she willed her shaking legs to move towards the stairwell.

Anger so deep, so violent, so totally irrational, oozed from every pore in her father's face. "You do and you'll be next!" The words stunned, hitting harder and deeper than any physical punishment ever would, creating wounds that would never heal, sparking the fire of an internal rage fuelled by a bottomless well of atrocities endured in the hope of seeing one more day of sun.

The girl, in fear, sought the comfort and solace of her familiar bed, pulling her pillows over her head to silence the screams. Through acidic tears of guilt and shame at her own weakness, she cried herself to sleep.

Jane forced herself to surface out of the dream, pinching the skin on her cheek to make sure that she was really awake this time, not just dreaming that she was awake. She wiped away hot tears.

It was coming home that had brought back the dream. She had been free of her nightmares for months. She listened intently for extraneous noises and heard only the soft snoring of her father in the next room. She rose slowly, preparing to go downstairs and make herself a cup of herbal tea, knowing that she would not be able to sleep again until the strong talons of the nightmare eased their grip.

She loved and hated this house. Good memories. Bad memories. Too many secrets. Secrets that, in an unspoken oath, she had promised not to tell.

CHAPTER TWENTY-TWO

Elliot had spent most of the day wandering around the store, feeling like his brain was covered by a dense fog, unable to concentrate on any one task for any extended length of time. He would start straightening the contents of a shelf, replenishing popular items or retrieving ones that had travelled to different locations within the premises by unknown hands and then remember that he had planned on reordering stock that morning and had totally forgotten to do so. He would decide to leave the shelves until later making a mental note to ask a part-time employee, Jill, to refill the bins when she came in, walk into the back room to do the reordering only to find himself in the storage area, not remembering what he had gone to retrieve. He became increasingly annoyed with his lack of concentration. Even so, he could not manage, regardless of how much caffeine he ingested, to shake himself out of the ozone layer that his brain had picked that day to inhabit.

By six o'clock, Elliot was ready to go home and soak his head in a couple pints of beer. He sat in the small, windowless office at the manager's desk to start the day's bank deposit. The front door bell startled Elliot as he was almost positive that he had locked the door before beginning the daily closing procedures-- another misadventure to add to his rapidly accumulating list. Thank God the manager was on holidays and not witness to his embarrassing ineptness.

"Hello," a female voice called from the next room. "Is anyone here?"

Jane. He would know that voice anywhere, the even, pleasant, medium pitch, the soft lilt of her words. Elliot jumped up from the metal desk, not quite sure what to do. What the hell was she doing here? His first impulse was to run, to hide. He was not in fighting condition. Instead, he took a deep breath, exhaled, and sauntered into the store's main area trying to look as nonchalant as humanly possible. "Can I help you?"

Jane greeted him with a brilliant smile. She stood just inside the door as if ready to make a hasty exit if necessary. "Hi. I'm glad that you're still here. I meant to call first, but then I got too busy at work and I decided to take my chances and just drop by after I was finished."

Elliot studied Jane as she spoke. There was definitely something different about her, a certain nervousness that was highly unusual when compared to her normally composed, self-assured personality. Jane stood solidly on both feet as she played incessantly with a ruby, birthstone ring on the second finger of her right hand, twisting the band around and around without seeming to notice that she was doing so.

Elliot walked over to a nearby, electronic cash register and rang out the till tape. "Actually, Jane, I was just in the process of closing the store. It's been a very long day, and I would like to go home."

Jane's smile faded from brilliant to half-mast. She moved slowly towards him, picking items off a center-aisle display rack, studying each one for a second, and then returning them to their original position. "I can relate. Then I guess I'll get to the point."

Elliot counted the float in the cash register, put the excess money and sales slips into a banker's envelope, and shut the drawer with a calculated bang. He looked up at her. "Well, I'm waiting."

By now Jane had advanced to within a metre of him. She had quit playing with her ring. The smile, more subdued, was still toying at the edges of her mouth. "I was hoping that you and I could call a truce for the summer."

"A truce to what?" Elliot decided that this time there would be no misunderstandings. He was tired of mixed messages and reading between the lines. He was tired of always trying to be one step ahead of Jane. He was tired of the whole thing; however, for some unknown reason, he just could not stop himself. Jane was like an addiction without an available 12-step program. Jane with her long, naturally blonde hair that waved around her lovely face. Jane with eyes that emanated intelligence and spirit. Jane with her small, pert mouth, with her full, naturally red, pouty lips. Jane with her always trim figure, her round, heart-shaped bottom. Jane with her long, slender legs that looked heavenly in heels. Jane.

"Well, here's the plan as I see it. You and I have been fighting for what seems like an eternity. I was hoping that we could just kind of put that all behind us and start over as friends."

Jane moved up to the check-out counter and began to drum lightly on the surface. He thought it sounded like the theme song for the Lone Ranger, but the rhythmic tapping was so soft that he couldn't quite be sure. Her hands were slender, her fingers long and graceful, her nails, extended like cats' claws, looked dangerous.

"Define friends." Elliot moved closer to her, closing the gap to see if she would back away. Jane did not move.

Jane stopped drumming her fingers. "Well, I was hoping that we could, you know, maybe go out for dinner sometime or catch a movie." She shrugged her shoulders in a non-committal manner. "Or just hang out, take a walk, talk, grab a drink. Whatever, just, you know get to know each other as adults and leave the whole name calling and hair pulling kid stuff behind."

Elliot studied her open, pretty face, searching for clues. If she was not being sincere, it would show in her eyes. Her eyes gave everything away. Jade green when she was happy. Almost black when she was angry. There were no storm clouds today, only a continued slight nervousness in the way her eyes quickly darted from his face to her hands and back to his face again. Elliot nodded. "I suppose that could be arranged," he acquiesced. He felt like a lottery winner who would not totally believe in his own good fortune until the money was safely in his bank.

"Great!" Jane's smile returned. "Are you busy this evening?" she enquired.

Elliot stared at her, unprepared, not quite sure what to make of the situation, of this sudden change in dynamics. First of all, he was exhausted from lack of sleep, and his brain still felt like it was lagging three steps behind the real world; but, if he let Jane know that, she could possibly figure out that her actions the night before were the reason for his present affliction. That would never do. Never show vulnerability behind enemy lines.

Second, he had just survived through a very long day. With the local, minor softball league gearing up for another season, cleats or sturdy running shoes needed to be fitted, batters' gloves and lost or worn-out ball gloves needed to be replaced, additional uniforms, helmets, wooden bats and boxes of softballs needed to be ordered. The Donnybrookers took softball very seriously. From T-ball up, the youth were taught by adamant parents and volunteer coaches the importance of being part of a team. Each team was sponsored by a local business who felt an ultimate sense of pride and personal accomplishment when their team did well. With the entire community involved, this week's steady influx of customers would be paralleled only by the also very serious hockey players come fall.

Third, regardless of Jane's temptation, all Elliot really wanted to do was to go home, take a warm shower, drink a couple of cold beers, put his aching feet up in front of the big screen television for a couple of hours with a triple-layer, cold-cut sandwich, mustard, no mayonnaise--belch or fart if need be—watch a game and then collapse into bed. "Sorry, but I really can't tonight. I've already made other plans. Don't you and Gertie hang out every evening anyway? I see you out together a lot lately."

Jane's smile faded once more. "We're not exactly attached at the hip. Gertie's actually out with her boyfriend tonight. Ted usually works afternoons, but he's on holidays right now so I'm free. Hey, if you don't want to go out this evening, we can do it some other time. No big deal. It was just a thought." Jane looked down at her hands again, played with her ring, and then looked back at him, disappointment exuding from her like the last rays of sunlight seconds before sunset. "Okay then, I'll let you get back to closing up. I'll give you my cell phone number." Jane opened her purse and pulled out a small notepad and pen. After she had written the number down, she tore out the sheet of paper and handed it to Elliot. "Call me sometime if you want, and we'll try for another evening." She turned to leave.

The front door bell sounded again, signaling the entrance of yet another person. Elliot chastised himself for the second time for not locking the damned door.

Nick sauntered in, his blue jeans and white cotton, short-sleeved t-shirt covered in dirt and grime from work. "How come you're still open, man?" he enquired good-naturedly.

Elliot strode past both people and walked directly to the door. With one quick motion, he turned the lock. "We're not," he said as he passed Nick on his way back to the counter. "I just forgot to lock the door."

Nick grinned. "Okay, man. Whatever you say." His smile broadened as he joined them. "Hi, Jane."

Jane turned to face Nick. "Hi, Nick. I haven't seen you in a while. How's work going?"

"Fine. Hot. Dirty. Otherwise okay. Can't complain, man. It pays the bills. What are you doing here, anyway?" Nick asked with obvious curiosity.

Jane ignored his question. "Rumour has it that the mini-mall is going to be open for Christmas. Is that true?"

"Should be, man, as long as we stay on schedule. So, to what do we owe your fine presence?" Nick glanced from Jane to his brother then back again as if one of them truly owed him an explanation.

Elliot interjected before Jane had the opportunity to respond. "Jane and I were just about to leave and get a bite to eat. We'd ask you to join us, but you're filthy," he gestured towards Nick's attire, "and you seriously stink."

Nick glared at his sibling. "Some of us actually work for a living, man. Nothing a shower can't fix. But, yeah, no problem. I'll just catch you later at home." Nick's eyes roamed between Elliot and Jane as if unable to decide on whom to focus.

Elliot smiled wryly. "Don't bother to wait up little brother. Jane and I are planning to pop over to Owen Sound to catch a movie later." He knew that Nick had a million questions on the tip of his tongue and gave his brother his best 'not now, I'll explain everything later' look.

"Little brother?" Jane interrupted.

"Yeah, I'm a half an hour older than Nick. I was born first and then Nick came out backwards. He's been like that ever since." Elliot smiled fondly at his twin.

"Ha ha. Very funny, man." Nick who had caught the message, grinned, and gestured towards the door. "Look man, just let me out, okay? I'd really like to go home and grab a shower. I've been sweating like a pig all day and the summer is just starting."

"Big plans for tonight?" Jane asked.

"Nope. Just me and a couple of beers. Think I'll catch a ballgame on the tube and call it a night. Take care of my brother." Nick winked at Jane, turned, and walked towards the front door followed by Elliot.

Once out of hearing range, Nick caught Elliot by his arm and whispered, "What's going on, man? What's up with you and Jane?"

Elliot unlocked the door and held it open. "I'll explain later. Just tell Ma not to hold dinner for me. Okay?"

"Okay, man." Nick nodded and left.

Elliot finished calculating the bank deposit with Jane patiently waiting beside him. She sat silently paging through a well-used sports magazine and didn't utter a sound until his task was completed.

With the money ready to deposit and with the door locked and double-checked, Elliot asked Jane if she would like to walk the two blocks to the Pig Pen so that they could enjoy the early evening sunshine. June was turning out to be warm and sunny, foreshadowing the summer to come. Elliot made a quick stop at the TD bank machine along the way to rid himself of the cash. It always made him nervous to carry large amounts of money he knew that he could not afford to replace. Thank the gods for debit.

They walked quietly for a while until Jane stopped to look into the large front window of a clothing store. The display case held several mannequins--a man, a woman and a child--clad in brightly coloured swimming suits, enjoying an artificial picnic on an artificial beach. "One thing that I don't like about working in an office," Jane offered, "is the fact that I'm going to miss most of the summer."

"Yeah." Elliot could empathize. Selling customers swimming goggles and snorkels wasn't quite the same as actually spending an entire afternoon lazing around Sauble Beach. "Are you a secretary or something?"

Jane turned away from the mannequins and resumed her journey. "Something. I'm spending the summer working at the hospital microfilming medical records from before everything became computerized."

Elliot noted the slight bounce in Jane's walk, like a little girl trying not to hop, skip, and jump all the way down the street. For the first time that day, he genuinely smiled, his previous weariness beginning to evaporate. "Sounds interesting."

"If you call spending the summer in a dark room taking endless pictures of paper interesting then I suppose it is. Personally, I find it monotonous. The women in the outer office are great though. That makes a big difference. They let me listen to my iPod so I don't fall asleep or die a slow, painful death of boredom. As is, I've microfilmed my head twice and my hand once."

Elliot chuckled. He was beginning to believe that this wasn't some kind of extremely perverse joke after all--that he and Jane could actually have fun.

"Do you know what is really interesting about it though?"

"No. What?" Elliot decided it was easier to let Jane talk about her work rather than to think of something intelligent of his own to counter with. At least they hadn't resorted to the weather. That was a good sign.

"The case files. I keep finding myself reading people's case histories instead of just pulling the sheets from the files and recording the information."

"You actually have access to everyone's medical history?" Elliot momentarily panicked, scanned his memory banks in search of any humiliating medical incidents from his past. Coming up with nothing more interesting than a couple of broken bones, a tonsillectomy and chicken pox, he relaxed.

"Yup, on paper and in the computer, but it's all strictly confidential. Anyway, remember the car accident I was in a few years ago?"

Elliot nodded. "Of course. You looked like hell for weeks."

Jane laughed. "Yes, yes I did. I felt like hell for weeks afterwards too. Anyway, while I was in the hospital, I had to go to the bathroom like crazy. I buzzed for a nurse for about fifteen minutes. When no one came I finally gave up, got out of bed and went to the bathroom by myself. It was an adjoining bathroom between two hospital rooms. I'd just finished and opened the door to the other room when I promptly passed out. The woman in the next room ended up getting help for me. I guess I hit my head on a bedpan as I was falling and had re-opened the cut on my forehead, so I was quite the mess."

"Ouch."

"That's not all. When I looked up my own history, the nurse had documented that I fell while she was in my attendance and that it happened so quickly she didn't have time to catch me."

"In other words, she was covering her ass," Elliot mused.

"You've got it. So far, my favourite case study is this pregnant psychiatric patient who absolutely denied that she was pregnant."

Elliot glanced at Jane to see if she was joking. "Are you serious?"

"Absolutely. Her file is huge. It starts off with her around five months pregnant being admitted by her family doctor. She refused pre-natal care, wouldn't take her vitamins or anything, all because she very firmly BELIEVED that she was not pregnant."

"Wouldn't the baby be kicking and stuff by then?" He wasn't the world's leading expert on pregnancy but had to admit that it was difficult to fathom anyone not knowing that she was pregnant by five months.

"Well, you'd think so wouldn't you?"

Elliot was so focused on Jane that he barely noticed the world around him. Extraneous sounds blurred into an inaudible hum. Vehicles passed by invisibly. Buildings melded into one. Nothing existed except Jane. Jane, who had lost all signs of nervousness. Jane, who was comfortably chatting about her work like they were the best of friends. Jane, who had, within minutes, put him so at ease that any hint of prior animosity was eradicated, forgotten. The two slowed down as they reached the entrance to the bar and grill. "So, what happened?"

"Well, to make a long story short, they kept her in the psychiatric unit, forced her to take her vitamins etc, until the baby was born and then Children's Services took the baby away. The woman didn't care because, even after everything was said and done, she still firmly believed that she was never pregnant in the first place."

Elliot was dutifully impressed. "Some nut case."

"Agreed, but the thing that I can't understand is how this woman's mind could block out the realities of pregnancy and childbirth. I can kind of understand how some woman aren't aware enough of their bodies to realize that they are pregnant but childbirth? Come on! Man, that's gotta hurt. The woman was definitely not sailing on a full ship."

Elliot settled into a good mood, leaving the day's worries behind. The Pig Pen Bar and Grill, busiest at the dinner hour, offered several available booths—the kind with the high-backed, wooden benches visually obliterating the customers sitting directly behind you and offering the illusion of dinner conversation privacy. Elliot glanced around to see if there was anyone he knew, anyone who would later spread the gossip that he and Jane were together, smiled and chatted briefly with several of his loyal, store customers as he meandered his way through the menagerie of square, wooden tables that provided daytime seating in the main area and could later be shoved to one side if anyone cared to dance, then chose the booth closest to the back of the large room. He slid in with Jane taking the bench directly across from him.

Jane accepted a multiple-paged, plastic-coated menu from their evening's waiter and began browsing through the selections and the specialties. "Do you see those two women sitting at the bar?" Jane, keeping her voice low, motioned with her head towards two pretty women in their mid-twenties, one a bottle-blonde and the other a brunette, scantily dressed in short, form-fitting, faded denim skirts and low-cut, cleavage-oozing tank tops, sipping from glasses of draft beer and tenaciously trying to strike up a casual conversation with two nearby, well-built pool players.

"Yeah. So?" The last thing Elliot was interested in was anyone other than himself trying to get laid.

"They're badge bunnies." Jane grinned as the off duty constables finally offered to play doubles, making both women giggle in anticipation. "Cop groupies. If Jeff and Ron play their cards right, those babes will fuck them silly and then some before the night's over."

Elliot frowned, wondering if Jane was trying to pull a fast one on him. "I didn't know that cops had groupies. Maybe I should apply to the Police Academy."

Jane grinned and nodded. "Maybe you should."

"So, I take it that you know those guys, but how do you know that the girls are groupies? Maybe, they just want a game of pool." Elliot casually flipped through a menu, trying to remain calm, trying to fight his irritation at the unusually slow service, and motioned for their waiter to take his order. The waiter should have asked him right off the top if he wanted a drink. Wasn't that proper waiter protocol or something? A drink while you decide what you want to eat.

The waiter brought Elliot back to reality. "Are you ready to order?"

Elliot cleared this throat and looked up from his menu at the young man before him, a college student probably, just old enough to serve drinks and in need of summer employment, money for school. "Just a drink for now, rye and Coke. I'll need a minute to decide what I want to eat. Jane?"

"A glass of white house wine for me thanks," Jane included.

"So, you didn't answer my question."

Jane looked at him quizzically. "What question?"

"How do you know that those women are groupies, and how do you know those guys are cops?" Elliot watched as the blonde began to caress the bare, tanned, well-muscled arm of the shorter man, very gently teasing his nerve endings, while the brunette chatted with the taller man as he racked the Boston balls. The shorter man grinned impishly as he sat back against the pool table, his fingers tracing the curve of the blonde's hip then leaned close to whisper something into the blonde's ear. When she grinned and nodded in agreement, he summoned a pretty, young waitress to order another round of drinks. The taller man flipped a coin to see who would break then motioned for the blonde to begin. When the waiter arrived with Elliot's drink, Elliot sighed audibly, inhaled the liquid in one long, greedy swallow and ordered another.

"Oh, right. It's easy. Jeff and Ron are brothers. Ron, the taller of the two, is a few years older than Jeff. My sister, Pam, used to date Jeff when they were in their teens. Jeff was a bit on the wild side back then, always like one step away from getting caught doing something illegal, so when Ron decided to become a cop, he told Jeff that he'd better straighten up his act or he would personally have him arrested, brother or no brother. Jeff must have taken Ron seriously because he managed to stay out of trouble and followed in Ron's footsteps a couple of years later. Remind me to go over and say hi before we leave. Jeff's single, but Ron's married with a couple of little girls so it will be interesting to see if he takes the bait or if he goes home. He married his high school sweetheart so my money's on him going home to his wife."

"You can definitely tell they're brothers. They look a lot

alike," Elliot noted. Both men were tall with Ron's 6'3" frame slightly exceeding Jeff's 6'1" stature. Both were wide-shouldered, slim hipped, workout muscular marking hours spent sweating in the gym. Probably even spotted for each other. Elliot couldn't imagine him and Nick doing that. Way too much work. Both men wore their straight, sandy-brown hair cop short.

As the blonde bent over to break, her ample, youthfully firm cleavage well-exposed, the short skirt riding high and skimming the bottom of her round, firm buttocks, Jeff glanced over at his brother and winked. Ron frowned back and took a long pull from his bottle of beer. The brunette had closed the gap and looked to be trying her best to spark the interest of the older brother with little success.

Annoyed with himself, Elliot felt stirrings below. Forget about just wanting another drink. He needed another drink. At least. His entire being, every molecule, yearned, ached to see Jane naked. A yearning, an aching so intensely more than he had ever dreamt humanly possible and watching the badge bunny flaunt her wares over the pool table wasn't helping. No. Not at all. In fact, if he had to get up from the booth at that very moment, it could prove to be highly embarrassing…not that he was overly attracted to the badge bunnies, but his imagination had magically transported Jane into a similar scenario, similar attire and that was a whole different story. A crimson, racerback, low-cut, mid-riff tank accentuated the gentle swell of her small, firm breasts. A scandalously miniscule, black leather skirt outlined the delicious curves of her model slim hips. Torturous, teasing promises of treasures awaiting release from their binds. Her long, slender yet muscular legs spread slightly as she bent over to sink the 8 ball. Throw in a pair of black mesh stockings for good measure. Black stiletto heels. Fucking hell. Literally.

"Other than that," Jane continued, totally oblivious to the inner workings of Elliot's mind and thankfully unaware of the outer workings of his hormone deluged anatomy, "my friend, Gertie waitressed here for a bit. I'd come and hang out occasionally and those two lovely ladies, Mandy and Sandy, were always here looking for a boy in blue out of uniform. Sometimes they get lucky; sometimes they don't. Depends on the night and on whether or not the boys are willing to play."

As the blonde, Mandy, tried her best to break, leaving most of the balls untouched, Jeff stood up and summoned the brunette to his side. He leaned over, tucked the brunette's long, dark hair behind her ear and whispered secrets. She too nodded, grinned, and clinked her glass against his bottle for good measure.

Fascinated now, Elliot just shook his head. "Kind of like sports groupies or women wanting to get laid by band members? You'd think they would have a bit more respect for themselves." Elliot nearly choked as he forcibly swallowed his desire, physically pulling himself back from the edge. Think… Think… Think middle-aged Mrs. MacIntyre from next door, curlers rolled tightly against her scalp, breasts sagging to her waist, strutting around her backyard last summer in a skimpy, bikini bathing suit that no one over twenty-five should wear. Large sacks of cellulite rounding out her hair-mottled thighs. Rolls of loose skin hanging over the hot pink bikini bottoms. Can't get much worse than that. Okay not working. Not sure why. How about Mr. MacIntyre? Fuck. Can't focus. Double fuck.

Jane just smiled. "Who the girls or the guys?"
"Both."
"Oh I don't know. Mandy and Sandy have their fun and then they go home." Jane nodded her head towards the pool table. "By the looks of it, I'd say Jeff's trying for a threesome. It wouldn't surprise me in the slightest if Jeff convinced both the girls to go home with him. That makes sense as Ron's pretty straight-laced. Besides, his wife, Nancy, is gorgeous and nice. Not an easy combination to find around here. It would be stupid to risk losing her, especially when they have kids.

Seriously, I don't think the girls are hurting anyone. The cops are just men like anyone else except they are literally willing to put their lives on the line every time they go on duty. The girls are well-known to them, that's for sure, but if they're ready and willing, why not take advantage of that and blow off some steam? Have some fun? I think it's a fairly symbiotic relationship when you look at it objectively. Both parties involved get what they want. The girls get off on sleeping with cops. The cops get off on screwing the girls. No harm. No foul."

Elliot nodded in agreement. "Kind of like supply and demand. Makes sense when you put it that way as long as the girls aren't hoping that some cop will fall in love with them. Then, it could get messy."

"Agreed and you never know. It could happen. Or one of the girls could end up pregnant. Only time will tell, I suppose."

"Are you saying then, if you were married to a cop, you'd have no problem with him screwing around with a badge bunny?"

Jane shook her head. "That's not what I meant. I think some cops, like Jeff, are kind of like adrenaline junkies. Ron's fairly easy-going but more serious by nature. Jeff has a good heart, but he's always hyped up or stressed out about something. It's like he has twice as much testosterone as a normal guy, right. He just can't relax. Walks around with a constant hard-on about everything. So, if I was married to a guy like Jeff, I'd become his own personal badge bunny…you know, like make sure he had sex at least twice a day to burn off the excess energy."

Elliot studied Jane's face. She wasn't joking. "Wow," he said, "if I become a cop, would you be my personal badge bunny?"

Jane sipped thoughtfully on her wine. "Is that a marriage proposal?"

The idea of marrying Jane caused a genuine smile to tug at the corners of Elliot's mouth. "Could be, but only if I get accepted into the Academy."

"Then I'll wait with bated breath before I give you a yes or a no."

When the waiter returned, Elliot ordered, "another rye and Coke and a Porterburger Platter for me." Elliot handed his menu to the waiter then looked at Jane who seemed fully engrossed in her task of determining what to eat. "Jane, are you ready to order?"

"Pretty much. Initially, I was thinking of getting the Ken-dog, but that's a foot-long which is a bit too much for me to handle so I think I'll stick with the Chicken Caesar salad and another glass of house white wine please." With a wry smile, she handed the menu to the waiter as well then turned back to face Elliot.

Odd, but for some inexplicable reason Elliot had never really pictured Jane as having a sense of humour. "So, if a foot is too long, what is your limit?" he enquired, wondering how far he could take this.

Jane smirked and leaned forward on the table. "Personally, I prefer a regular-sized dog. Add some relish and a bit of ketchup and that's enough to fill me."

Oh crap, Elliot moaned internally. Think of anything other than his penis filling Jane, of how it would feel to be inside of her, surrounded by her tightness, her moist warmth… think, what? Fuck! Think! Not working! Don't think! Count. Backwards. 100, 99, 98, 97, 96…

Jane reached over the table and touched his hand. "You look a bit pale. Are you okay?"

"Yup, fine. Long day." How one woman could have that much power over his penis was beyond him. Obviously, he needed to get laid more often. Either that or bars needed to start offering camp-ground-like, cold shower stalls ($2.00 for 10 minutes) right beside the washroom vending machines filled with condoms and cheap cologne.

"Hey, Little'un!" a husky male voice smashed through Elliot's reverie. "Thought that was you sitting here. Why didn't you come over and say hi?!" Jeff's dark blue eyes glimmered with humour. "Get up girl and give me a hug!"

"Hey yourself, Jeff. I was going to come over and say hi, but I didn't want to interrupt your fun." Jane rose from her side of the table and virtually disappeared in Jeff's embrace. "Mandy and Sandy are looking pretty hot tonight."

Elliot waited patiently for Jane to remember that he existed.

"That they are but there's always room for one more." With the flowing, graceful motion of a limber dancer, Jeff unfolded Jane from the embrace and held her at arm's length. "I swear, Little'un, if I wasn't still madly in love with your sister, I'd marry you." He leaned towards Jane and lightly kissed her cheek. "My god, you grew up sweet. A little thin maybe, but nothing that some good Jeff cooking wouldn't cure. Home for the summer then?"

"Yup, first year down and two more to go." Jane motioned towards Elliot. "I'm actually here having dinner with a friend. Would you care to join us for a minute, or do you need to get back to your game?"

As if noticing Elliot for the first time, Jeff relinquished his grasp on Jane and held out his right hand to shake Elliot's. "Oh hey. I'm Jeff. Old family friend." Jeff smiled wide, exposing perfect, Hollywood-white teeth.

"Elliot," Elliot returned as he felt every bone in his hand crunch. Absolutely no way in hell he would want to be taken down by either brother. A very good reason to stay on the right side of the law. Well, if nothing else, the interlude had relaxed his erection. He obviously was not attracted to cops. At least not of the male persuasion. Were there male badge bunnies who went after policewomen? There must be although they probably weren't called badge bunnies… something more masculine like badge bucks maybe or just plain cop groupies, stalkers. After an eternity of insanely painful seconds, Elliot felt Jeff's grasp loosen and pulled his own hand back to safety. "Good to meet you."

Jane motioned towards the table. "Do you want to sit down?"

Jeff shook his head then nodded towards the pool table and his glaring older brother.

"Better not. It's almost impossible to get Ron out for a beer these days. The man just doesn't know how to relax and have fun."

"You taking both girls home with you then?" Jane poked Jeff good-naturedly in the stomach.

"A man's gotta do, what a man's gotta do. Never was one to disappoint the ladies. Speaking of ladies, rumour has it that Pam's single again. Is that true?"

"Yup. She finally left the asshole. Why? You still interested?"

Jeff covered his heart with his large, tanned, right hand. "Oh, Little'un, your sister is the love of my life. Pretty much destroyed my heart when she married that jerk." Jeff's tone grew serious. "Neighbours called in a domestic one night. Went out and when I saw Pam all black and blue, eight-months pregnant, I nearly lost it. Tossed the asshole in a holding cell for the night, then signed myself out so I wouldn't seriously hurt the prick. Couldn't believe she didn't leave him. Tried to talk to her, but she wouldn't listen. Happens more oft than not. Glad to hear that she finally came to her senses though."

Jane nodded. "It took a while, but I'm glad that she's out of it too. She took out a restraining order on him, then rented a small apartment for her and the two kids over on 5th Street. She's starting over and holding her own. I'm sure she'd love to hear from you."

Jeff brightened. "Yeah?"

"Yeah."

"It's not too soon?"

"Not if you take it slow. Maybe suggest meeting for a coffee first. Give her some time to heal. Show her and her kids that not all men are abusive bastards."

Jeff nodded. "Cool. Just might do that. Think my heart could stand one more round, and kids are no problem. The more the merrier." The seriousness passed as quickly as a storm cloud blown free from the sun. He winked at Elliot. "And if it doesn't work out, I hear she has one smoking hot, little sister." He laughed and bent over to kiss Jane's cheek again. "Good to see you, Little'un. Gotta a cell phone with you?"

Jane nodded, dug her black, basic cell phone out of her purse and handed it to Jeff.

Jeff added his name and telephone numbers to Jane's contact list then handed the cell phone back to Jane. "Put in my cell phone number and my land-line. Call me if you ever need me. Sex-text me anytime. " He winked. "Until then, this man's going to get lucky tonight times two." As Jeff swaggered back towards the pool table, he turned once, smiled, winked again, and added, "Don't tell Pam…"

Once Jeff was at a safe distance, Elliot flexed his fingers to make sure all digits were still in functioning order. "All those two need are a couple of Uzis and an attitude and they could make a hit TV show."

Jane grinned and nodded. "That may be true. Jeff would be perfect for Reality TV — 'When Good Cops Go Wild'--but I don't think Ron would go for it."

"Little'un?"

"As in little sister."

When their food arrived, Elliot began to relax, and allowed himself to enjoy his meal of a Porterburger--a huge, area-renown patty of freshly ground beef, topped with fried mushrooms, a slice of ripe tomato that was grown in the restaurant's greenhouse and crisp, green lettuce—and freshly cut fries. He listened intently to Jane's stories about work and about what she had learned at college. She was majoring in television but had to study film, radio, and photography in her first year as well. Elliot hadn't realized that the course was so in-depth. He was slowly beginning to understand that there was much more to Jane that he had ever imagined.

After dinner they decided to see a comedy, as they both agreed that they could use a good laugh. Although Jane had grudgingly accepted his offer to drive them both into town so she wouldn't need to waste her gas, in his mind, it had made the date official. Elliot bought two, medium-sized root beers, a large bag of buttered popcorn and a bag of red licorice. He wasn't hungry, but watching a movie without massive amounts of junk food seemed unthinkable, almost like blasphemy.

Elliot handed Jane her paper cup of pop and the bag of licorice as he struggled to unfold the seat next to her. After quickly juggling her drink, she came to his rescue laughing at their combined awkwardness.

Once Elliot had settled, Jane leaned towards him. "Elliot, I have to tell you something before the movie starts."

"Yeah. What?" Elliot placed his drink in the armrest's cup holder.

"I've had a really nice time this evening." She reached over and touched his arm. "Thank you."

Elliot beamed. His winnings may not be in the bank yet, but, for the first time ever, he could feel the prize within his reach. "You're welcome. By the way, thanks for the drink last night."

Jane smiled, her eyes warm and friendly. "No prob."

The two quieted as the coming events paved the way for the feature attraction. Neither of them noticed as Nick slid into a seat six rows behind them. He wasn't watching the movie.

CHAPTER TWENTY-THREE

Today was Jane's twentieth birthday. She could barely believe that the teen years were behind her now--years filled with emotional turbulence and the omnipresent sense of being trapped into an existence from which there was no escape. Her whole life was ahead of her. College. Career. Independence. Todd. Eventually, she would leave Donnybrooke and never, ever look back.

Two more months. Less than 61 days. If she could get everything wrapped up at work early, she could leave before Labour Day to get the apartment organized for her and Todd. Jane wondered if this was how an incarcerated prisoner felt, mentally counting down a jail sentence to look freedom in the face once more. Sentence reduced for good behaviour. The light at the end of the proverbial tunnel growing stronger. Fighting the adrenaline that made you want to escape early. Knowing that any attempt to escape now could bring dire consequences. Two more months. Less than 61 days. Breathe deep. Patience. She could do it. She had to.

The plan with Elliot was working wonderfully, almost too well. After years of bickering and surviving Elliot's covert, guerrilla warfare tactics, she was actually beginning to honestly, truly like the man who she was getting to know. He could be funny, sweet, thoughtful, kind--personality traits that she would have never, in a million zillion years, attributed to him.

Today, she needed to focus. She needed to wipe any thoughts of Elliot clean from her mind, put them in a box and stick them on the back of a mental shelf. Today, was all about Todd. Todd was due to arrive any minute now. Todd. Her Todd. The man who she would be living with soon. The man who would share her living expenses and who would help her with her college courses. The man who she would go to bed with every night and wake up beside every morning. The man she would make love with as often as humanly possible. The man who she was meant to be with. Todd. Her soulmate. Todd. Her Todd. Not Elliot. Todd.

And, with any luck, if the gods were kind, if the gods were genuinely on her side, Elliot would not find out that Todd had been there. With her parents' farm being five kilometres outside of town and not on one of the main roads, Jane felt safe enough as long as she could convince Todd that walking around on the hundred acres would be just as much fun as going into Donnybrooke or spending time in Owen Sound. Despite her best efforts to convince herself otherwise, Jane knew that the cognitive dissonance she felt was due to guilt. Plain, simple guilt. She pushed the annoying thought aside.

"Jane," her mother called upstairs, rousing Jane from her thoughts. "Todd's here!"

Jane quickly glanced into her dresser mirror to make sure that she was more than just presentable in her pink tank top and faded jean cut-offs--she wanted to look spectacular, drop dead gorgeous, drool-worthy--then raced downstairs wishing she'd had more time to work on her tan. "Thanks, Mom." Jane ran outside to greet Todd at his car, a blue Chev that he had borrowed from a friend to make the trip.

Todd extracted himself from the vehicle and stretched his arms above him. Wearing a black, Nirvana t-shirt and faded jeans, he looked stiff and tired from the journey but glad to be there all the same.

"Todd!" Jane reached her man and hugged him. She kissed him on his stubbled cheek, then swiftly on his lips. She grasped his hands in hers and stood back so that she could take a good look at him. "Man, I can't believe how much I've missed you." Her eager eyes travelled up and down from head to toe in lustful appreciation of his boy-next-door good looks and dark construction worker tan. "You look absolutely yummy!" she exclaimed in delight. The physical labour had already started to show, adding muscular shoulders and a more pronounced chest to his otherwise sleek swimmer's build.

Todd smiled in return, his face lit up in true affection. "I've missed you too. Happy Birthday, Jane." Todd hugged Jane close to his body.

Jane felt the warmth of him against her, the hardness of his muscles, the softness of his touch, inhaled the faint scent of his aftershave and knew beyond any doubt, beyond any previous reservation or fear, knew with every fibre of her being that she was doing the right thing. She loved this man. Todd. Her body yearned for this man. Ached for him. Burned for him. Two months away from him had changed nothing. Two months, two years, two lifetimes would not change the way she felt. He was her soulmate, her saviour.

"Well, come on in." Jane disentangled herself and took Todd by his left hand. "My mom is dying to meet you. One warning though, I haven't mentioned anything to my parents about us living together yet."

"How come?" Todd asked as they sauntered slowly on the stone walkway that cut through a perfectly groomed lawn towards the back of the large, brick farmhouse. As they approached, six or seven cats, wary of the new intruder, sprang from the side porch and zoomed towards the presumed safety of the nearby barn.

"Mom and Dad are very set in their ways, so I think it's better that they get to know you first and then we'll take it from there. Okay?" She studied his light brown eyes, loving how the flecks of gold caught in the sunlight. Jane did not bother telling him that waiting to tell her parents would also save her two months' worth of lectures on the immoralities of living common-law — a practice that was strongly opposed to for religious reasons in this neck of the woods.

"Sure," Todd agreed amiably. "I can understand that. You're their daughter. I'm just some guy you met at school. For all they know, I could be a serial killer."

Jane stopped briefly and glanced at Todd. "But you're not right? You're not a closet psychopath, student by day, predator by night…or a serial rapist who preys on young girls…"

"If I was, why would I admit to it?" Todd teased. "Why would I blow the perfect cover?"

"Good point," Jane conceded. Her mind quickly sifted through a list of sociopathic/psychopathic characteristics-- superficial, manipulative, callous, pathological liars, lacking in empathy or in guilt, delusions of grandeur….problem was most people she knew could definitely fit into there somewhere. Did Todd? That would be just her luck. Fall desperately in love only to discover that the man of her dreams was a modern day version of Ted Bundy, albeit a very cute one with a butt second to none.

As Jane began to walk again, Todd pulled her back towards him. "I do have to ask you something before we go in."

"If you're looking for an alibi for the night of the murder of your latest victim, it will cost you. Big time."

Todd chuckled and drew Jane close to him so that he could whisper into her ear. "Is there any chance of us getting in a bit of quality time before I have to leave tomorrow?"

Jane moaned softly, her body responding to the innuendo. The energy he exuded strummed through her like electric fingers. She had almost forgotten just how good he felt. How perfectly they fit together, two parts of a single entity, complete, absolute, only when they were united. "How do you feel about nature?"

"Meaning?"

"Well, these farms are strip farms — two fields wide and straight back. At the back of the farm there's ten acres of bush. My parents expect that I'll want to show you around anyway after lunch. So how do you feel about having sex amongst tall maple trees with only the birds providing the background music?" Jane's tongue gently caressed Todd's ear in a slow, outward motion. The weather was sunny and warm with only a slight breeze. Perfect for an outdoor picnic with Todd as the main course.

Todd closed his eyes and inhaled deeply through his mouth. "I think that if we don't go inside now, I may not make it to lunch."

Jane giggled despite her best efforts to stifle the reaction. She stepped back. "Come on then, before I drag you out into the barn and rape you in the haymow."

Todd opened his eyes, sighed deeply and followed.

Jane managed to get her laughing under control before they entered the large, country kitchen. Her mother stood at the kitchen's stainless steel sink washing ripe, rain-plump strawberries for strawberry shortcake. She wiped her hands on her white cotton apron. Jane loved the kitchen with its warm, earthy tones and its multitude of green and flowering plants. In her household, this room had always been the centre of family conversations and get-togethers. Friends or relatives would come over and sit around the large wooden table for hours, talking or playing cards. Good times. Good memories.

"Mom, this is Todd. Todd, this is my mother, Marie." Jane

made the formal introductions.

"It's nice to meet you, Mrs. Kirkland." Todd held out his hand to shake hers.

Mrs. Kirkland accepted the greeting. "Marie's fine. Mrs. Kirkland sounds so formal somehow. It makes me feel old. Please, relax and make yourself comfortable. Lunch is almost ready. Jane's father is at a job in town today so we're going to wait until dinner for the cake and ice cream. Todd, can I get you something cold to drink?"

"Sure. A glass of water would be just fine, thanks."

Mrs. Kirkland smiled, took a pitcher of cold water from the white, side-by-side refrigerator and filled a glass. She handed the drink to Todd then looked at Jane. "Jane, why don't you take Todd's things upstairs and put them in the guest room?"

Todd took a drink and placed the glass on top of the beige counter. He gestured towards his car. "I left my duffel bag in the car. I'll just go and get it. Be right back."

"Jane, while Todd's outside, can you get a loaf of bread up from the freezer for me, please?" Mrs. Kirkland smiled and nodded towards the basement door.

Jane glanced at Todd who shrugged and nodded. "Sure, Mom," she replied. She didn't want to let Todd out of her sight for a second, but she also didn't want to make a big deal over a simple request. After all, as her mother constantly pointed out, Jane's legs were younger.

As Todd headed back out to his car and Jane headed towards the basement door, Mrs. Kirkland caught hold of her daughter's arm. Damn, Jane thought, caught.

"Jane," Mrs. Kirkland half-whispered, "Elliot just called."

Jane turned back towards her mother. "Elliot? What did he want?" Jane felt the colour drain from her face. Friggin' hell. Not today. She couldn't deal with Elliot today.

"He said that he was wondering when your birthday was so that he could plan something special. He thought it was some time in the summer but couldn't remember the exact date. Would you mind telling me what's going on?" Mrs. Kirkland stood with her other hand on her hip in her common 'don't-lie-to-me-child' stance.

Jane swallowed hard. "Nothing's going on. Elliot and I have

just been spending some time together. We're friends. That's all. What did you tell him?" Jane watched through the window as Todd rummaged through the trunk of the car. Todd. Her Todd. Nothing or no one was going to spoil this for her.

"I told him that it was today and that you'd already made plans." Mrs. Kirkland looked concerned, her forehead furrowed. "You obviously like this Todd guy?"

Jane smiled sheepishly. "You know I do."

"And he obviously cares about you or he wouldn't have driven all this way to be here for your birthday. Does Todd know about Elliot?"

"No, there's nothing really to know."

"Does Elliot know about Todd?"

"No, it's none of Elliot's business. Elliot and I are just friends."

Mrs. Kirkland let go of her daughter's arm. "Jane, you know what Elliot's like. He's had a crush on you for years. If I were you, I'd do a lot a hard thinking before someone gets hurt. If you're just leading him on, it's not going to end well."

Jane nodded. "Mom, you worry way too much. No one is going to get hurt. Trust me, I have it under control." Jane went to open the basement door.

Mrs. Kirkland shook her head. "I don't need any bread." She walked back to the kitchen sink to finish washing the strawberries.

Jane stood, momentarily transfixed and confused. How did Elliot know that her birthday was in the summer? She didn't remember mentioning anything about it.

"So, what do I say if he calls again?" Mrs. Kirkland asked as she placed the berries in a plastic calendar in the sink to drain.

"Tell him that we have relatives visiting from out of town, and that I'll call him back tomorrow," Jane responded as Todd entered the house once again.

"I'm back," he noted cheerfully, swinging his black duffel bag at his side.

"Come on, I'll show you where you're sleeping tonight." Jane motioned for him to follow her as she made her way towards the second-floor stairwell.

Once upstairs, Todd placed his duffel bag on the carpeted floor beside the very ornate spool bed in the pale blue, guest bedroom—a medium-sized room that had, at one point, been Jane's until Pam had moved out and, being the youngest, Jane had finally been able to upgrade into one of the larger bedrooms . He sat down on the blue and white, daisy chain quilt and motioned for Jane to join him. "Nice bed."

Jane sat down gingerly, her mind still on Elliot. "Thanks. It's a family heirloom. My great-great-grandfather's parents brought it over from Germany with them. My great-grandmother on my mother's side made the quilt. In fact, the whole house is full of antiques passed down through the generations. You'd have to ask my mom what came from whom because I can never remember." Jane stopped in mid-thought to study Todd. "Are you tired? I know it's a long drive. You can take a nap after lunch if you want."

Todd laughed and circled his arms around Jane's waist. "Believe me, I did not drive for almost four hours to sleep." He kissed her neck. "In fact, sleep is the last thing on my mind."

Jane smiled, pulled away, and stood up, extending her right hand to Todd. "Come on. Save it for later. Lunch will be ready in a few minutes, and then we'll go for a walk. Okay?"

With a good-natured groan, Todd rose off of the bed and took Jane's hand. "So, what do you want to do tonight, a hayride or a corn roast?"

Jane could feel butterflies invade her stomach. "Very funny city boy. Unless we do a second cut, the hay season is already over and the sweet corn's not ready until mid-August. I know, how about we just hang out here? We could play a game of Canasta. Sit on the porch. Enjoy the stars. Whatever." She headed towards the stairwell.

"Actually, I was hoping that you could show me around. Do some sightseeing. Check out Buck's Hot Spot. Meet your 'back home' friends."

The butterflies doubled in number. Monarch butterflies. Large, adult, Monarch butterflies all deciding at once that it was time to take flight and make the long, multi-generational journey back to Mexico. "Okay, but we have to do the cake and ice cream thing after dinner or mom will be upset. Why don't we just wait until later to decide?" She smiled wryly. "We'll see how energetic you feel then. Okay?" Jane turned around and kissed Todd. She kissed him slowly and deeply. Her fingers lightly caressed his hair, his shoulders, traced their way down to his waist. Suddenly, Todd pulled away. Jane smiled knowingly, mischievously.

"Jane, you are going to get me into trouble," Todd teased. "The last thing I need is to go downstairs with a boner. But yeah, I get the message, so let's go do lunch."

The lunch consisted of ice tea, salads, cold meats and strawberry shortcake for dessert. July food. Food designed to not over-tax an already too hot body.

"Mom," Jane began to clear the table after the meal. "I'm going to show Todd around the farm this afternoon. Did you and Dad have anything specific planned for after dinner?" She hoped.

"Here, I'll finish clearing," Mrs. Kirkland offered as she took the plates from Jane. "You and Todd go for your walk. And no, I guess we figured that the two of you would want to go out for the evening."

"Lunch was great Mrs. K...Marie," Todd interjected as he assisted with clearing the food. "I was kind of hoping that Jane would show me around. All she ever did in college was tell stories about how great it was growing up in the country and hanging out in a small town."

Jane locked eyes with her mother. Help, she pleaded. Oh, please help me, Mom. If Elliot sees Todd and I together, he'll go ballistic.

"Well," Mrs. Kirkland began, "maybe, she just wants to spend some time alone with you, Todd. Maybe, the two of you can go for a drive this afternoon and then spend the evening here," she suggested.

Thanks Mom, Jane thought loudly hoping that her mother would catch her brain waves. Elliot should be working until six...that should give them time for a quick tour before the eyes came out.

"Sure," Todd agreed. "Whatever you want to do, Jane. It's your birthday." He shrugged and grinned. "But first, you promised to show me around the farm." His brown eyes brightened in anticipation.

"Right." Jane nodded. "Mom, do you know where the bug spray is?" Jane began to rummage through the tidy kitchen cupboards. Her mother was the ultimate of organization. Everything in its place and a place for everything if only one knew where that place was.

Mrs. Kirkland looked confused. "Why do you want the bug spray?"

"I want to show Todd the pond and you know what it's like back there. The black flies will eat us alive if we don't take something." Not finding what she was searching for, Jane closed the cupboard door.

"I think the bug spray is on the top shelf in the bathroom cabinet behind the sunscreen," Mrs. Kirkland said as she ran the sink full of hot, soapy water to do the dishes.

"But, of course." Jane tapped herself on her forehead. "Why didn't I think of that? Where else would bug spray be other than with the sunscreen? Mom, you should have been a Prime Minister. The country would be a lot more organized!"

"I'll take that as a compliment and not as sarcasm," Mrs. Kirkland remarked good-naturedly as she watched her child bounce off towards the washroom.

Todd waited patiently by the kitchen door as Jane went to look.

Jane returned, holding up the bottle of bug spray to show them that the lost was found. "Well bud," she looked at Todd, "let's go."

As the two walked, following a tractor trail through the softly rolling fields and open gaps, Jane felt a sense of peace, the way she always did when she wandered through the fields of green pasture. Her father was what her friends called a hobby farmer. He was a residential building contractor, primarily constructing houses, who raised a small herd of cattle on the side. When she was little, they had raised meat roosters and laying hens as well. Now that her parents basically lived by themselves, the chickens were no longer needed to feed a hungry, growing family.

The butterflies had flown away, safely on their journey. Her stomach was hers once more. The day continued to be hot and sunny with a few clouds to give them an occasional break of coolness. A perfect summer day. A perfect birthday. Her first official birthday with Todd. Todd, the love of her life. Todd.

"Did I ever tell you that when I was a little girl, I used to think that the sun followed me?" Jane smiled at the recollection.

"No. How come?"

"When I was little, I'd take the dogs and go for walks through the fields. Every time I looked up at the sky, the sun would still be with me so I thought it was following me. Silly really, but I never felt alone that way." Jane stopped and pointed to her left at a large, rounded, igneous rock, veins of crystals glinting in the sun. A rock collared by June's remnants of wild, white daisies, in the middle of a pasture field. "Do you see that rock over there?"

Todd turned to see what Jane was pointing at. More like a small boulder than just a rock. "Yeah."

"My sister, Pam, my brother, Dylan, and I all used to come back and sit on that rock whenever we had a problem that we wanted to work through."

"Sounds like a good idea. Your own private getaway spot."

"Exactly. I used to call it the `thinking rock'. The really weird thing is so did my brother and my sister."

"What's weird about that?" Todd enquired.

"The weird part is," Jane continued, "that we all did the same thing and we all called the rock the same thing, but we never told each other about it until we were adults." Jane smiled at Todd and tugged on his hand to signal the continuance of their journey. She loved the way that Todd's hand felt in hers, so much bigger than her own, protective, reassuring and intimate. The connection that said we are a couple. I care about this person. She is with me. I am with her. Jane wanted this day to last forever. Just her and Todd on the farm. Too bad Todd would never agree in a million years to live in the country. He was a city boy through and through.

"That's really cool. Maybe it has something to do with the unspoken, intuitive connection between siblings," Todd offered.

"Could be, kind of like when one twin knows that the other one is in pain only not that direct of a link. More like universal knowledge shared between siblings."

"That works too."

"I'll have to run that one by Dylan. He's really into that kind of metaphysical, new age stuff, makes sure his chakras are always open and aligned, has crystals everywhere to balance out all of the universal energies." Jane turned right and walked through an open gap. "Pond's this way."

"So, how big is this pond of yours? Is it deep enough for skinny dipping?" Todd jested, hope lighting up his facial features.

"Small." Jane hated to burst Todd's bubble. "The pond is basically ground spring and spring runoff fed so the depth really varies depending on how much snow there was, how wet the spring weather was and on how dry the summer is. It's also fed by a small stream that runs through the neighbours' property. This year, the pond's about a metre and a half at the deepest point so it'd be more like skinny wading than skinny dipping. We can try it later if you want, but seeing us naked would probably shock the hell out of the neighbours if Chester or his wife, Beatrice, happened along the line fence." Jane laughed at the thought of Chester and Beatrice, middle-aged and pleasantly plump, wide-eyed and speechless in their attempt to act nonchalant as if nudity was common practice on the farms around these parts. Beatrie would eventually blush crimson then apologize profusely for the intrusion while scooting Chester back to the house and out of harm's way.

"Okay then," Todd conceded. "I'll leave my boxers on."

Jane nodded. "Good plan. Regardless of its lack of depth, I love the pond. My brother and I used to play there when we were kids. There was this old, fallen tree that was our ship and we'd pretend that we were either pirates or voyagers off exploring new worlds." Jane smiled fondly at the memory. "Dylan and I were huge movie buffs when we were kids. He's three-years-older than I am, so he was my playmate most of the time. Mom really disliked a lot of what was on television, but she loved the older classic movies so she'd buy DVDs and let us watch them. Dylan and I would take our characters from movies and let our imaginations run wild from there. Dylan preferred pirate movies so he'd be Long John Silver or Blackbeard and I'd be his first mate."

"Aw, Robert Newton classics." Todd nodded with an understanding smile.

"Robert Newton?"

"Robert Newton was the actor who played Long John Silver in the Treasure Island movies in the 1950's, and he also played Blackbeard in the 1952 movie, *Blackbeard the Pirate*."

"You know, you could be a gamer like normal guys your age instead of spending your weekends tracking down every old movie out there," Jane teased.

"Would you still love me if I spent every weekend obsessing over a videogame? There are gamers who play 24/7 for days on end, you know."

Jane thought for a second then responded, "I'd probably still love you, but I'd get bored after a couple of hours of staring at the screen so I'd leave to find someone else to have sex with." She smirked, smug in the knowledge that Todd was the only man in the world for her, and that she was the only woman in the world for him.

Todd shook his head. "Can't have you roaming the streets in search of unsuspecting prey. Jane, the night stalker. What do you call those things that suck out someone's life force when you have sex with them?"

"What?" Jane frowned. "Are you calling me a succubus? Seriously?" Jane stopped walking and stared questioningly at Todd.

He felt the tug as she stopped and turned to face her. "Not exactly."

"Exactly what then?"

He hesitated then continued, shooing a fly away from her hair. "When we have sex, it's like you're not happy until every ounce of energy I have is totally drained and there's no possible way in hell that I can get it up again."

Jane unconsciously tilted her head to the right as she tried to understand. Was Todd unhappy with their sex life? How could that be possible? "Are you complaining?"

"Fuck no. Just saying that I'd rather spend a Saturday night watching a movie and then fucking you rather than playing videogames and letting you loose on the rest of the world."

Jane straightened her head again, pouting. "It's not like I'm a menace to society."

"Unless a guy has a bad heart."

Jane laughed then, finally understanding what Todd was

alluding to. "Moss only grows on a sleeping stone, Todd."

"Even the hardest of rocks need sleep occasionally, Jane," he countered.

Jane nodded. "Is this your way of saying that, when we live together, I can't expect sex every night?" She tugged his hand, motioning for them to continue walking. Men, she thought. It would be so much simpler if they would just come right out and say what they were thinking instead of hinting.

"If you need sex every night to keep you happy, Jane, then I'm your man. You just need to remember that there are such things as quickies. I love you, Jane, but I need sleep too."

"I'll definitely keep that in mind," she agreed. "I wouldn't want you flunking out of school because you keep falling asleep in class."

"Thanks. Is Dylan coming for your birthday?" Todd asked, changing the subject. "I'd like to meet your whole family."

A frown creased Jane's pretty face. She shook her head. "Nope. Dylan is studying theatre in Toronto. When he's not in school, he goes to all of the auditions he can and gets quite a few parts in commercials or as an extra in movies. Let's just say that Dad doesn't quite agree on the lifestyle Dylan has chosen for himself."

"Why?" Todd's voice softened with curious concern. "Is Dylan gay or something?"

Jane nodded. "Pretty much. I told Dad a long time ago that not everyone can grow up to be a mechanic or a lumberjack, but I think Dad blames himself somehow instead of just accepting Dylan. To make a long, painful story short, Dylan and Dad have decided it's better to not spend too much time together right now." A smile replaced the frown. "Dylan did call this morning though to wish me a Happy Birthday, and that's the important thing I think. And my sister Pam should be here later with her kids. At least you'll get to meet them."

Todd nodded. "Cool. So, Dylan liked to be a pirate. What kind of movies did you like when you were a kid?"

"I preferred the Cowboy and Indian movies--can't remember the titles--but I always cheered for the Indians. I loved the whole wearing skins and feathers and living in a tepee vibe.

There's a Native burial ground on my uncle's farm and, when I was younger, I'd beg my uncle to let me walk through it. I was pretty young, and it always felt very sacred, like a church but better. Dylan found an arrowhead there once, and my uncle donated it to the museum. Me, I just liked to walk through the burial ground and feel the ghosts of the past. I think I must have been Native in a past life or something."

"I don't believe in ghosts. I think this is it. When we die, there's nothing else."

Jane stopped abruptly and looked at Todd in astonishment. "Todd, I can't believe that you said that. I didn't know you were an atheist."

Todd's eyebrows rose in question. "Is that a problem?"

Jane shook her head, her forehead furrowing. "Are you telling me that you've never had one experience ever that made you question if there was more to life than this one plane of existence? When we make love, do you not feel our spirits meld together?"

"Jane," Todd's voice was soft and smooth as if he wished to avoid an argument, "I think we should change the topic for now. I'm really not in the mood for a long, philosophical argument on life. I came here to be with you. This is the plane of existence I choose to live in right now. When you and I make love, there are no words to describe how I feel. When I'm inside you, there is nothing else."

"You're right. I'm sorry," she mumbled as they started walking again. The tension eased as Jane scolded herself for almost picking a fight. Not today. Not on her birthday. Not when Todd had driven all this way to be with her. Todd. Her Todd.

The pond came into view. "Are the bugs really that bad?" Todd asked. He hated bugs.

Jane smiled knowingly. "Not so bad at the pond, but they're hell on wheels in the bush."

CHAPTER TWENTY-FOUR

"Are you sure that Jane's birthday is in the summer?" Elliot asked Nick as they sat at the kitchen table eating double-decker sandwiches they'd made for a late lunch. Summer sausage, salami, thin slices of ham, crisp lettuce, cheddar cheese, mustard--no mayo--on rye. Elliot had slept in until almost noon, making up for a night out with the guys playing pool at the tavern for twenty bucks a game. He'd managed to break even which was fine by him.

Saturday and nothing better to do than hang out around the house for the afternoon, Elliot thought. Jane had said that she was working this weekend and would catch up with him early in the week. Maybe he could finally change the oil in his car — that was close to a thousand kilometres overdue--or check with his mom when she got home from shopping to see if she needed anything done around the house. Seemed like there was always something that needed repairing or replacing these days — shingles that needed patching, ceilings and walls that required a fresh coat of latex paint, pipes that clogged or leaked, eave troughs that longed to be purged of last fall's cornucopia of maple and ash leaves, flooring that had steadfastly withstood the constant abuse of a large family until the wear and tear finally began to take its toll. The joy of older homes.

Exchanging room and board for help around the house had benefited both the boys and their mom, but Elliot knew that the arrangement had to end eventually. He was seriously too old to live with his mother. Maybe he'd take a quick swim in the river afterwards to cool down. All he knew was that he wasn't in the mood to sit around doing nothing on his weekend off, especially when there were no ballgames scheduled on the tube for the afternoon.

Nick swallowed a mouthful of milk. "Yeah, man, I'm sure. I'm just not sure of the exact date. Man, for all I know, Jane's birthday could have been in June, but I don't think so."

Elliot chewed thoughtfully on a bite of his cold-cut sandwich and swallowed. "What makes you so sure?" He stood up and walked to the refrigerator to hunt for a jar of dill pickles. Sandwiches were not complete without pickles. Has to be dill. Any other kind was just wrong.

"Man, where have you been?" Nick shook his head in exasperation. "We've only known Jane forever. Remember two years ago, man, when we came in second in the ball tourney in Allenford?"

Elliot thought back. All he could remember was it had rained out all of the Friday night ballgames and they had to play very early Saturday morning and very late Sunday night to make up for it. "I remember that it rained a lot." He sat back down, opened the jar of pickles, extracted two, and then handed the large, glass jar to Nick.

Nick accepted the jar, took out a pickle and set the container on the table. "Yeah man, and what did we do all Friday night after they announced that the games had been postponed?" Nick picked up his sandwich again and pointed it towards Elliot.

"We stood in the beer gardens and got pissed. So?" Elliot was getting tired of this game and wished that Nick would just tell him where this trail was leading. Elliot's head throbbed, and his patience was limited as he waited for the ibuprofen to make a dent.

"Jane was there too, man. Remember?" Nick munched on the dill pickle.

Elliot thought hard, trying to visualize whom he had been talking to, whom he had been drinking with and who else had been standing around hoping that the rain would stop long enough to put sawdust down on the diamond to soak up the moisture. He honestly did not remember Jane. "Nope." He chased a mouthful of food down with a swig of beer. The best way to appease a hangover was to start a new one. Fuck five o'clock.

Nick shrugged. "Well, man, she was and I'm pretty sure someone said that it was just past her birthday 'cause seems like everyone was buying her birthday drinks even though she was underage. She got wasted, man. How could you forget that? You know what Jane's like when she's been drinking. She was hanging all over some dude from another team, and you were fuming."

Elliot mused at his brother's memory. Weird that Nick would remember something that he did not, especially since he was the one who had supposedly been doing the 'fuming'. Seeing Jane drunk on a weekend back then was not that unusual, so the memory probably just wasn't worth retaining. She was often under the influence of something, legal or otherwise, and one step away from being physically escorted into Detox. During one of her more affable benders, Jane had rather bluntly informed him that she didn't have a drinking problem, that when she drank, she was the problem and that was just fine with her. Regardless, it didn't surprise Elliot that he couldn't remember the specific incident in question. He also couldn't remember what he'd had for lunch two days ago and he wasn't about to obsess over that either. "So I'll call and ask her when her birthday is."

Nick frowned. "Don't you want to surprise her, man?"

"Kind of hard to surprise her when I don't know when her birthday is?" All in all, he did not like the way this was going. He was tired of being badgered by Nick on this completely inane topic. Then again, if Jane's birthday was in the summer, why hadn't she told him? As far as he was concerned, they were on their way to being a couple. Maybe not quite there yet but close. And part of being a couple included spending your birthdays together, even if that meant doing nothing other than just hanging out.

"So much for romance, man." Nick shrugged his shoulders. "Hey, I'm just trying to help you out, man. It's not like I'm the one who's had to listen to you bitch about her for the past two years." He paused as he took another bite of his sandwich. "I'll bet you ten bucks Jane's birthday is in July." Nick held out his right hand to make the bet official.

Elliot studied Nick's hand and then his face. There was something playing behind Nick's eyes, but he wasn't exactly sure what it was. Usually, he could read Nick's thoughts as easily as his own. Today was different. He took Nick's tanned hand and shook it. Why not? If Nick was wrong then he'd be up a few bucks. If Nick was right then he'd earn a few points with Jane. "Now what? Who are we going to ask if not Jane?" Elliot's face lit up with an idea, his headache temporarily forgotten. "I could call her mom."

Nick shook his head emphatically. "Better not, man. What if Jane overhears and asks what's up? Then you're screwed." Nick finished his sandwich in one large gulp.

Elliot nodded. "Yeah. Well, just how do you propose we settle the bet then?"

"We could call Pam," Nick suggested as he stood up,

gathered the plastic-wrapped packages of leftover meat and went to the white refrigerator to put the cold cuts in the meat drawer. He went back to the table to gather his dishes, rinsed them under the tap, then placed them in the built-in dishwasher.

Elliot nodded in agreement. "That'll work. Good idea." He shoved the last bite of his sandwich into his mouth, stood up, spun the bread bag shut and placed the remainder of the loaf in the wooden breadbox before heading towards the living room that looked as if it had been copied directly from a Homes and Garden magazine layout. Way too feminine for his tastes but it made his mother happy and it was, after all, her house.

"Have you seen Glenda lately?" Nick asked casually as he followed.

"Nope. Not lately."

"I didn't think so. Man, all you have these days is Jane on the brain. Does that mean that I can ask Glenda out? She's hot." Nick smiled good-naturedly.

Elliot flopped down on the green fabric sofa beside the cherry telephone stand. "Be my guest. It's about time you got laid and Glenda gives excellent head." He pulled a telephone book out of the one drawer in the stand and began to flip through the residential pages in search of Pam's telephone number. Jane had said Pam had moved. Considering the circumstances, there was a distinct possibility she would have an unlisted telephone number as well. Probably easier to call Information.

Nick sat down in a nearby matching green fabric chair. "Man, by the way your moods have been lately, my guess is that I'm not the only one around here who needs to get laid. So, tell me big brother, have you tapped that yet?" Nick poked between his teeth with a toothpick.

Elliot stopped flipping pages long enough to glare at his brother.

Nick dropped the toothpick into nearby ashtray. "Man, I'll take that as a 'no'."

"Take that as a 'it's none of your fucking business'." Not seeing a telephone number listed under Pam's married name or under her maiden name, Elliot dialed Directory Assistance and crossed his fingers.

"Don't get your shit in a knot, man. I was just curious. You've been out like five or six times and nothing? You must be doing something wrong, man. Local rumour has it that she's a first nighter."

Elliot growled, "Nick, go fuck yourself. It could be the most action you'll get for the next year." Sadly, the truth was that he and Jane hadn't come close to anything more than holding hands and a quick goodnight kiss. He hadn't pressed the matter either, figuring that it would happen when it was supposed to happen and had slowly, grudgingly resolved into the habit of self-serve until that time came. Rumours or no rumours, Jane wasn't putting out.

"Ouch. Just saying. No need to get angry, man."

The connection made good. To Elliot's surprise, Pam was listed on 5th. He wrote down the number and dialed.

"Hello?"

"Hi, is Pam there?" Elliot readjusted his sitting position to get more comfortable. He picked absently at the fray of his faded denim cut-off shorts.

"Speaking."

"Pam, this is Elliot Fallis. I don't know if Jane told you, but we've been out a few times and I was just wondering when her birthday is." Elliot glanced at Nick who looked awfully smug.

The voice on the other end was warm and friendly. "Hey Elliot. Actually, Jane did mention that the two of you were getting along better since she came home from college. It's good to hear that you two have called a truce. Oddly enough, today is Jane's birthday."

Elliot stared at Nick in annoyance. "Today?" He repeated in disbelief and sat up straighter.

"Yup. Today is Jane's twentieth birthday. My baby sister is all grown up now. We're going over to Mom and Dad's this evening for cake and ice cream. I'm surprised that she didn't mention it to you, but then Jane hates it when people make a fuss."

A small thundercloud formed in Elliot's mind. "Maybe she mentioned it and I wasn't paying attention or just forgot. Okay then. Thanks, Pam. Bye for now."

"You're welcome. Bye, Elliot." The line clicked off.

Elliot hung up the telephone, still staring at Nick. "How did you know?" Elliot replaced the telephone on its stand, heaved himself off the couch and strode over to his brother. Nick's eyes met Elliot's. There was laughter in those eyes--a taunting, I-told-you-so laughter. Elliot did not like it. He did not like it one little bit. He could feel his mercurial temper rise.

"I told you, man." Nick quickly rose from his chair. The brothers might look the same in many ways and, on occasion, sound the same; but, Nick was taller and heavier muscled after years of working in construction. He was not afraid to remind Elliot of that fact. "Like I said, man, I heard someone mention it at the ball tourney in Allenford. It's not my fault, man, that you didn't believe me. I still can't believe you don't remember that night. She was face fucking some dude right in front of you, and you got so pissed off you almost lost it."

Without a word, Elliot dug his leather wallet out of the back pocket of his jean cut-offs and handed Nick a ten-dollar bill. He stuffed his wallet back into his pocket, turned, walked towards the front door and grabbed his car keys out of a small bowl that sat on a narrow side-table in the entranceway.

"Hey, man. Where are you going?" Nick followed behind.

"I'm going to drive into Owen Sound to Flower Expressions so I can buy Jane a dozen roses. Then later, when she's home from work, I'm going down to her parents' house to give them to her." Elliot turned around to face his tailing sibling. "Do you have a problem with that, Nick?"

Nick grinned and held up his hands in an outward peace gesture. "No problem at all, man. Nope. No problem at all."

CHAPTER TWENTY-FIVE

Jane traced Todd's tan-line with her index finger, the smoothness of his taunt skin tantalizing the tips of her ultra-sensitive nerve endings. Nerve endings that, for some reason, held a direct connection to her Bartholin's gland. He was very brown for the beginning of July—obviously doing construction work shirtless at least part of the time. So many changes. Not only was he taller since she had last seen him; but, now that he was naked, she noticed his upper body and torso were both showing the marked beginnings of what would eventually become well-defined muscles. She loved the hair free smoothness of his chest, the luscious darker pigmentation of his nipples. Very sexy. Jane watched as he slept, wanting so badly to wake him for another round of pleasure, but she opted to occasionally swat at a mosquito that threatened to disturb his slumber instead. She hadn't realized just how much she missed curling up beside Todd…her Todd…how much she missed listening to the calm, rhythmic sound of his breathing.

A hawk screeched nearby as Jane lay quietly on the cool ground. Wanting to remember this place in time always, she greedily inhaled the orchestra that surrounded her—the harsh trill of blue jays warning the hawk as she passed their nest, the softer cacophonic chorus of swallows, the distinctive two-note whistle of the male chickadee, the familiar cawing of crows.

Todd stirred and slowly opened his soft, brown eyes, still more in dream than in reality. He rolled onto his side to face Jane and wrapped his arm instinctively, protectively, possessively around her slim waist. His eyes closed again as he travelled back to whatever plain of existence he had briefly visited from.

The sudden rustling noise of leaves from behind her caught Jane's attention. Her worst fear was the possibility of coyotes, bears, or cougars and more embarrassing would be a next-door neighbour searching for puff balls or morels. The best-case scenario would be a raccoon, a possum, or very large, black squirrels. She tried to turn around to see without waking up Todd who, obviously, needed more sleep. His arm held her. With the utmost of care, she rolled over onto her other side. Amongst the majestic maple trees that could easily be more than a hundred years old, half hidden by underbrush, a fawn stared back at her. "Todd, wake up," she whispered, hoping that she wouldn't startle the small creature before her. Mama was undoubtedly close by.

"Uhmm," Todd murmured as he surfaced one more time then closed the gap between them, spooning his long, muscular legs into the backs of hers, pressing the beginnings of another erection into her soft, warm flesh.

"Todd. Look," she urged him to see, to see the beauty of nature that she had always loved. "According to native beliefs, a deer symbolizes the gentleness of spirit." She felt his body rise behind hers, propped up on his elbow. His arm tightened around her waist.

"Do you think it was watching us?" he whispered into her ear and then kissed her cheek, his erection growing longer, harder, more demanding.

With her thoughts still on the Bambi-like fawn whose large, brown eyes had assessed them for danger, its nostrils flaring silently as it breathed, Jane rolled over onto her back so she could face her lover. "Isn't it beautiful?"

"You certainly are." He smoothed her long, tussled hair.

Jane brushed back a stray lock of golden brown hair from his face. "I'm so glad that you managed to come up. I've missed you."

"Me too. I get up, go to work and spend all day having conversations with you in my head. I go home, eat, grab a beer and spend all night thinking about how much I want to make love to you. It drives me crazy sometimes."

"Just how crazy?" Jane smiled impishly, tiny dimples framing her mouth, as she reached down to ever so gently massage his testicles with the heel of her hand while pressing up and massaging his perineum with the tips of her well-experienced fingers. He moaned softly in response to her touch.

She loved knowing what turned him on and what sent him over, right down to the one spot on his lower back that could make Todd totally lose focus and orgasm if pressed at just the right angle and with just the right amount of pressure. She called it the "now" button as in I'm almost there so let's come together NOW! Their energies colliding at the exact same moment in time felt fucking beyond amazing and was truly an experience beyond any known words in the English language to date. Could it get any better than that? Jane thought not.

"Certifiable," Todd replied, his voice husky with desire. In one smooth and surprisingly quick maneuver, Todd rolled over to straddle Jane, his elbows and forearms held his weight on either side of her head. His eyes, devil-darkened by heightened levels of testosterone, were the only answer Jane required. She knew that look, the brief insanity unleashed by the primal need to plunge deep within her, to claim her. There would be no foreplay, no gentle caresses, no tender kisses. Not this time. Jane repositioned herself to accommodate him, drawing her knees up to her chest for maximum penetration, wanting nothing less than all of him.

A guttural moan escaped from her throat as Todd's engorged penis impaled her, splitting open the virgin-like tightness of her vagina. "Show no mercy," she whispered hoarsely then closed her eyes. Nothing else existed. Only them. Only now. As Todd thrust deeper and deeper, Jane grasped the firm, lean muscles of his back, sharp nails rending welcoming flesh and, for an all too brief moment, escaped.

CHAPTER TWENTY-SIX

Confused that's what he was. Confused and frustrated with Nick. Not a great combination Elliot had to admit. He hated it when Nick was right. Hated it worse when Nick was right about something he should have known about. Hated it most when Nick shoved being right in his face.

Elliot was almost positive that there was a simple explanation. Maybe Jane thought their relationship was too new to include birthdays. After all, they hadn't really made any major commitments yet but the possibility of more was there. Wasn't it? He had worked too long and too hard for it not to be.

Seriously, just how many hours had he spent devoted to the thought of Jane? An occasional, passing interest when she was younger. Summers spent casually watching her develop from a long-legged, awkward youth with braces to a young woman full of self-confidence and mischief. Until it had suddenly hit him that she was no longer a child. The recognition, the knowledge had slammed into him like an unexpected punch to the gut. Jane was meant for him. She belonged to him. And in that exact moment, he also understood that, he, Elliot Fallis, would do whatever it took, no matter how long it took, to make Jane his wife.

CHAPTER TWENTY-SEVEN

Entirely satiated, Todd eased himself away from Jane's sweat-streaked body and sat down beside her. He looked around until he found his black cotton t-shirt and pulled it over his head. "Next month, I'm going to Welland to look for an apartment for us. That is, if you still haven't changed your mind."

Jane glanced over at the underbrush to see if the fawn was still there. Gone. Probably off to find its mother. She sat up, searched the pocket of her shorts for her cigarette package, lit a cigarette and inhaled deeply, enjoying the nicotine rush, a sensation that non-smokers could never relate to--the quieting of the nerves, the subduing of inner turmoil. "I haven't changed my mind, but is my smoking going to bother you if we live together?"

Todd's tone grew serious. "It wouldn't bother me so much if you only smoked a few cigarettes a day. You know that. It's the fact that you smoke a pack a day and those fucking things are going to kill you eventually, that bothers me. That and I really have no desire to die from second-hand smoke either." He raked his long fingers back through his straight brown hair for lack of a comb.

"Point taken." Jane whisked away another mosquito as she gathered her clothes. "If you like, I'll try to cut down--maybe not smoke in the apartment--but," she emphasized, "not around exam time or I'll turn into a stressed out bitch on wheels. Deal?"

"Deal." Todd surveyed the surrounding area as if seeing it for the first time. "It's really nice back here." He opened a plastic bottle of water they had brought with them, took a long drink then handed the bottle to Jane.

Jane sighed, accepted the bottle, swallowed a mouthful of spring bliss and thought about life in the city--cars, pollution, too many people, too much noise, too many buildings that blocked out the sun, too much asphalt. "Yeah, it's nice, but we'd better get back to the house before Mom sends out a search party to look for us."

After getting dressed, the two strolled through lofty trees of birch, maple, oak and walnut working their way back out of the bush towards fields of rolling knolls and flat lands. Jane loved the simple lay of the land, the earth divided into useable spaces by long rows of stone fencing; stones that had turned dark gray from years of exposure to the elements. She pictured generation after generation of farmers--from the early settlers with teams of horses to her parents with modern machinery--plowing the rich soil, unearthing endless amounts of fragmented metamorphic and sedimentary rock abandoned by the retreating glacier thousands of years before. Back breaking work as young and old alike, toiled to remove the unwanted stones before planting the fields and, having nowhere to put the cumbersome rock, turned them into fences, neatly stacked, high and wide, to avoid collapse.

    Some of the five-acre fields were fenced off for cattle corn, now waist high, long, lush, dark green leaves gently curling but the stalks still too young for tassels. Others were marked by a scattering of large, round bales. The smell of freshly cut hay wafted through the air like a woman's sweet perfume.

    "How many cows do your parents have?" Todd enquired as they crossed into the pasturelands. A small herd of cattle grazed lazily, made only slightly curious by their presence.

    "Thirty-five this year and they're steers, not cows," Jane corrected. "Dad buys the steers from somewhere out west when they're still pretty small--around 200 kilograms-- feeds them corn and hay in the barn for the winter then puts them out for pasture in the spring. He sells the steers in the fall for meat after they've doubled their weight. Some years he actually makes money. Some years not so much." She pointed towards one beige beast that had decided to greet his visitors. "See that charlet that's coming towards us?"

    "Yeah."

    "He's so tame that you can actually pet him. Watch." Jane moved very slowly and carefully towards the animal not wanting to spook him. His brown eyes never left her movements as they approached each other. When she was close enough, the steer stopped to let Jane stroke his head. He stood calmly chewing his cud like a child chews gum. "Do you want to try?" she called back to Todd.

    Todd, who looked as if the steer was a creature from an alien planet, did not move. "Pass."

    "Your loss." Relishing the feel of his coarse hair beneath her fingers, Jane patted the charlet between his wide-set eyes to say good-bye. "Good boy. Now go and join your friends." She waved her arms, startling the animal enough so that he would join his comrades instead of following her.

Jane retraced her footsteps back to Todd. On her way, she stopped to pick a straggling white daisy left over from June's wild crop. She began to pull off the white petals one by one. "He loves me. He loves me not. He loves me. He loves me not." She stopped beside Todd as she continued to free the stem of petals.

"No matter what that daisy decides," Todd interrupted, taking Jane's hand in his, "I do love you."

Jane smiled whimsically and tossed the daisy aside. "So you say, but do you love me warts and all?" she asked, staring up into the depths of his brown eyes, eyes now soulful and sweet, the devil once again receding.

"Warts? What warts?" Todd grimaced. "Are you telling me you have an STD? I don't remember seeing any warts. Jane, you really should have mentioned that before we started having sex without condoms."

Jane groaned and squeezed Todd's hand hard enough to make him stop talking. "Not literal warts, Todd. Warts and all means like the good, the bad, the downright ugly. That type of thing. And, just to be clear, I don't have genital warts. Geesh."

Todd sighed dramatically in relief as she eased the grip on his hand. "Just teasing. Yeah, of course I love you, the good, the bad, and the downright ugly, with or without genital warts." He grinned.

Jane shook her head and smiled. "Oh my god, Todd, you can be such a jerk sometimes." She believed that Todd did love her; however, a part of her couldn't help wonder if he would feel the same way if he knew the truth about her. Would he still profess his love? Or would he become totally disillusioned and leave her? There was so much about herself that she could not tell him.

Wondering what time it was, Jane glanced at her watch. Her eyes widened in disbelief. "Oh my god, do you realize how late it's gotten?"

Todd raised an eyebrow. "Is this another trick question?"

"Only if you are directly responsible for the rotation of the earth. Cripes, it's 4:30 in the afternoon. Just how am I going to explain to my mother why it took us over three hours to look around 100 acres?" She felt her pulse quicken in anticipation of her mother's impending disapproval. No words would be spoken, every thought clearly etched in the look on her mother's face, 'the look' that made all of her children silently shrink and wither in shame.

Todd shrugged, unconcerned. "She'll probably just figure that we were talking and lost track of time. Not a big deal. It happens."

Jane watched as a red-tailed hawk floated through the clear blue sky, stalking its next meal. She wished she could fly. It would be so cool if she and Todd were a mating pair of hawks, monogamous and mated for life. They would build a nest in a tree high above the ground then incubate their young together. Once their young were raised, she and Todd would fly south for the winter and just enjoy existing in each other's company, catch enough mice to keep them fed and spend their days soaring, carefree.

"Maybe, but maybe not. Mom's pretty smart, and she doesn't miss much." Jane dropped Todd's hand and stepped in front of him to scan his appearance. She brushed away a tiny twig that was caught in his layered, shoulder-length hair. "Turn around," she ordered.

Todd obediently turned around.

Jane fastidiously scanned his clothing for anything unusual--fresh grass stains, streaks of dirt, leaves sticking out of his back pockets, any clue. Nothing. "Okay. You pass."

Todd turned around to face her. "Inspection over?" His eyes sparkled.

"You wouldn't think it was so funny if you walked into my house and the first thing my dad noticed was leaves sticking out of the back of your pants." Jane loved her dad and knew his tolerance level was low when it came to his children misbehaving. She had found that out many times the hard way, once getting grounded indefinitely after staggering home totally intoxicated and under the influence of Ecstasy. Awkward when you can't figure out how to untie your own shoes and end up face down on the floor sucking vinyl tiles and dying from thirst...Twice she'd been threatened with

Rehab as if it would really fix her. Seriously whacked that. Her mom had intervened both times spouting some dribble about Jane going through female hormone changes, adolescent angst, and how it was just a phase Jane would grow out of. Problem was that the more her parents had tried to force her to behave, the harder Jane had looked for ways of not getting caught. But she was supposed to be an adult now. Right? Not some high school kid set on rebellious self-destruction. Oh god, what had she been thinking? It had been so easy when she and Todd had been in school. His place. Her place. Wherever. But this wasn't Welland. This was living under her parents' roof, following their rules. She was twenty not twelve and yet she was absolutely mortified that she was about to get caught after just having sex with the man she loved.

"Tough crowd?" Todd enquired good-naturedly, a grin tweaking the corners of his mouth.

"Very. He's a bit on the over protective side. No man is good enough for his daughters type of vibe. Okay, now it's my turn." Jane turned her back towards Todd. "Do you see anything that wasn't there when we left the house?" Jane tried to look over her shoulder to see for herself.

She felt Todd gently grasp her slim shoulders. "Relax, Jane. You look fine. Your ass is great as usual, and your shorts are definitely on the right way."

Inhaling deeply, Jane closed her eyes. She re-opened them as she exhaled through her mouth. Her heartbeat began to slow back down to a normal rate. Todd was right. After all, she hadn't seen him for almost two months. There was absolutely nothing bizarre about the concept of the two of them spending the afternoon talking and catching up on news.

In fact, it wasn't even far from the truth. They had talked. They had even compared present jobs and future aspirations. Todd was going to major in film; she had decided on television. Then there had been great sex, which, in her family, was a major sin against God unless, of course, you were married to your sex partner. She was to remain celibate until she was married or eighty-five--whichever came first.

Oh god, she thought, sex. She sniffed herself, smelled sweaty and a whole lot like a sperm storage tank. Friggin' hell.

The hawk suddenly swooped downward towards an unsuspecting field mouse. Once caught, the hawk lifted back up to the blue skies, its prey safely in the clutches of the long, sharp talons. The bird cried in exultation, thanking Mahanta for his bountiful gift of food.

Jane marveled at the graceful keenness of the bird. There was no second thought, no wondering about its next move. It just found its prey and, in one swift moment of complete acuity, the hawk held its future within its grasp. She envied that ability. Yup, next life she was definitely coming back as a hawk.

Todd wrapped his arms around her and kissed her on her long, slender neck. "I think you worry way too much. We went for a walk, we talked, maybe fooled around a bit. Why turn this into more than it needs to be?"

Jane turned around to face Todd and smiled. She had a plan. "We need to go for a quick dip in the pond before we go back to the house."

"Why? To cover up for us having sex?"

"Exactly. Right now, I smell like you, and I have at least a litre of come oozing out of me. Damn, I should have thought to bring condoms. I know I'm on the pill, but it's that fresh out of the oven sex smell that will give us away."

Todd grinned, mischief exuding from his eyes. "Personally, I really like that smell. Beats the hell out of freshly baked bread any day."

"Tell that to my parents. If we go for a dip, clothes on, it'll give me an excuse to grab a shower, douche and get changed. Capice?" Jane sighed in relief. The doorway out of their present predicament was just ahead. She'd be so glad once the summer was over. She would become an adult living on her own again, with her own thoughts, her own dreams, living by her own rules, instead of being just someone's daughter.

"Can we at least shower together if I promise your parents I won't try anything?"

"Funny guy. Come on. This is serious. My parents have absolutely no sense of humour when it comes to premarital sex."

"They can't possibly think that you're still a virgin. Can they?"

"I don't know what they think. They've never asked and I've never said. The point is, that this is your first time meeting them, and I really don't need another lecture about how the body is a temple and that my temple door should not be opened until marriage."

"How about if we were engaged? Would it be okay then?"

"No. Being engaged doesn't count."

"Gotcha. My parents are the total opposite. You could come to visit me and sleep with me in my room, no problem. Mom would even bring you a tea in the morning, no questions asked except to make sure you were comfortable and I hadn't spent the night hogging all the covers. Since your parents aren't like mine and since I really don't want to get you into trouble, it's off to the pond we go to rid you of my 'smell', which really is a shame, 'cause my boys worked very hard to produce those millions of sperm."

Jane heard the wasted seconds ticking loudly, mentally calculating how long she had to get ready before her family arrived for dinner, cake and ice cream. "My apologies to the boys." She kissed Todd on the cheek. "Please let them know that, under normal circumstances, I would be more than happy to accommodate them; however, today is not a good day to have their minions loitering around inside of me escaping at inopportune times."

"I think the boys can live with that."

"Good, now let's go. We just need to go in, splash around for a couple of minutes then get back out again." She took his hand in hers and quickly led the way.

CHAPTER TWENTY-EIGHT

"Can I get you something cold to drink?" Mrs. Kirkland asked.

Elliot declined as he slouched at the kitchen table facing the back door. "No thanks. I'm good." He had come to see Jane. Jane who, supposedly had been at work all day, had not been in her office when he had called earlier, was not answering his calls to her cell phone, was not responding to his texts. Not only that, but she wasn't at work period. In fact, she had the entire weekend off. Elliot was not pleased. Actually, that was a massive understatement. He was furious. He wanted to know exactly why Jane had lied to him. What better way to find out than by going directly to the source?

Mrs. Kirkland had graciously explained that a college friend of Jane's had driven up for the day. She had also explained that they were presently out walking somewhere on the farm. If he would like, she would give Jane a message to call him later. He did not like. He had thanked Mrs. Kirkland and said that he would wait. She had just gestured towards the kitchen table for him to sit there and then had commenced to putter around looking nervous. He wanted to see, for himself, why. Nope. He did not like at all.

Elliot unconsciously drummed his fingers on the wooden table. The storm cloud inside of his head was growing, rumbling with the sound of nearing thunder.

The back door opened. Mrs. Kirkland turned around to face the person who was about to enter. Elliot sat up straight and watched in curiosity.

"Beat you!" a male voice emanated from the porch.

"Todd! Wait!" A female voice called, not far behind. Jane.

Mrs. Kirkland blocked Elliot's view as she went to the door. Elliot remained seated at the table. His fingers stopped their drumming.

Elliot watched as the young man entered the kitchen and came to a quick halt on a brown scatter mat just inside the door. So this was Jane's friend. Yeah, right. A bit taller than him. In good shape. Looks like he works out some or does physical labour. Maybe he plays sports, but can he fight? Definitely not ugly and definitely closer to Jane's age. Very nice, Jane. Very nice indeed. The bitch seriously hadn't changed after all. His gut told him that he was being played, and, if it hadn't been for Nick, he would have never known. He'd make her regret this. Jane belonged to him, and it was about time she accepted that fact.

"Hey, Mrs. Kirkland…Marie. Sorry we took so long." Todd squatted down to remove his black and white running shoes then nodded at Elliot. "Hi." Once the shoes were off, Todd eased himself up with the fluid balance of a well-trained hind-catcher.

Elliot returned the nod. "Hi." He leaned back in the chair, laced his fingers behind his head and waited.

Jane followed, close behind.

"Jane, you have a visitor," Mrs. Kirkland announced as she took up position with her back resting on the cupboard in front of the stainless steel sink.

Jane breezed into the kitchen, tank top and jean shorts soaking wet, exposing every curve of her nubile body, a radiant smile beaming on her flushed face. "Hi, Elliot. I saw your car parked outside. What brings you here?" She pried off her running shoes with the toes of the opposite foot then went to the cupboard to retrieve an empty glass. She set a used, plastic water bottle and a crumpled package of cigarettes down on the beige countertop.

Elliot unlaced his fingers and rose slowly from the pine kitchen chair. After unconsciously wiping his large hands on the thighs of his blue jeans, he placed his hands on his hips, thrusting his elbows out to the side. "I came to wish you a happy birthday. I tried calling you at the office, but they said that you had the weekend off. I tried your cell and you didn't answer."

Jane's smile did not diminish. "Change of plans and my phone's upstairs in my bedroom. Elliot, I'd like to introduce you to a friend of mine from school. Elliot, this is Todd. Todd, this is Elliot."

"Hi again," Todd smiled and waved his hand in a friendly gesture. Elliot did not smile back.

Jane moved to the white refrigerator, took out a large, clear plastic pitcher of water, and filled the tall glass. "Todd, do you want some water?"

"Sure. Thanks," he said, accepted the glass, took a quick

drink and set the glass on the countertop. He took up position between Mrs. Kirkland and the door, resting his buttocks against the lower cupboards, his arms folded across his chest.

Jane poured another glass of water for herself and drank enthusiastically as if quenching an overpowering thirst.

Okay, enough of the pleasantries, Elliot thought. Lightning split through the mental storm cloud followed by a loud crash of thunder. Enough. He lowered his arms to his sides and crossed the kitchen. When he was close, he spoke directly to Jane. "Can I talk to you for a moment?" He glared at Todd. "In private?"

Jane placed her glass on the counter and nodded. "Sure, Elliot. Just let me grab a towel first. It was so hot out today that we decided to go for a quick dip in the pond." She turned towards Todd and placed her hand on his arm. "Todd, why don't you grab that shower you wanted? Don't forget you promised to show me some kick boxing moves later. Mom, did I ever tell you that Todd's his local league's champ? I've seen him knock out a guy in two moves. Scared the bejeezus out of me the first time I saw him do it. Pretty cool stuff though. Uber cool, just like Billy Jack." Jane left the room briefly then re-entered with a green bath towel slung over her shoulders.

So, okay, the boy can fight, Elliot thought. Still not impressed. No fucking way was this guy just a friend either. Or at least, if he was just a friend right now, it wouldn't stay that way for long. He knew a territorial stance when he saw one. In the minute that it had taken for Jane to retrieve the towel, Todd had repositioned himself closer to the door. With his legs spread for support and with his thumbs hooked in the front pockets of his worn jeans, Todd looked more like a street punk ready to protect his gang rather than a harmless college buddy. This guy wanted Jane. He wasn't about to scare off easily.

"Mom, can you show Todd where the towels and stuff are, please?" Jane smiled effortlessly at her mom. Jane's voice was soft and smooth, lithe fingers strumming a pedal harp, no hint of nervousness.

"Certainly," Mrs. Kirkland complied, took a step and patted Todd on his arm. "This way, Todd."

Todd did not move, his eyes still locked on Elliot. "Not yet thanks," he informed her briskly.

"Elliot, why don't we talk outside? I'm dripping on the floor." Jane wrapped the large towel around her torso as she exited the house barefoot.

Elliot followed Jane outside, brushing against Todd as he passed. He felt eyes follow him. No problem. He'd take care of Todd later if he needed to. Billy Jack or no Billy Jack. He'd dealt with bigger and tougher. Todd was just a city boy who was out of his league, another gnat that needed swatting away. This was Elliot's territory. His rules. And right now, Elliot wanted to talk to Jane. His Jane. Alone.

When Jane was halfway to the tree-shaded cars, she stopped, and turned around to face him. "So, what did you want to talk to me about?"

Elliot motioned with his head towards the farmhouse. "Who is he?"

Jane ran her fingers through her long, wet hair as she spoke. "I told you, he's a friend of mine from school. He called at the last minute to ask if he could come up for a visit."

"I thought you said that you were working this weekend." Moving in front of Jane, facing her, Elliot reached over and grasped her slender shoulders firmly so she couldn't move away. He desperately fought an internal, irrational desire to shake her. Shake her until she begged him to stop then drag her to his Camaro, toss her in the front seat and drive away. He clenched his jaw instead, willing the anger back to the dark recesses from whence it came.

She dropped her hand to her hip but did not attempt to break his grip. "I was but then Todd called so I switched weekends with Rose."

Elliot looked directly into Jane's eyes, searching. "Just like that?" His gut told him that she was lying.

"Oh my god. Yes, just like that." Jane nodded her head in punctuation. "It actually worked out really well. Rose was thrilled. She wanted next weekend off anyway. You can ask her if you don't believe me. Elliot, Todd's a good friend, and I haven't seen him since school ended. It's seriously no big deal. I don't know why you have to be so damned melodramatic about everything." She sighed dramatically in exasperation.

He released his grip on her shoulders and folded his arms across his chest. "Right. You're the one who flounced into the house, soaking wet with your nipples poking through looking like the runner up in some cheap wet t-shirt contest, and I'm the one who's being melodramatic." Elliot huffed sardonically.

Unconsciously, defensively, Jane crossed her arms over her breasts. "Runner up? What's wrong with my boobs?" she challenged.

Crap, Elliot thought. Women. "Nothing's wrong with your boobs. They're just too small to win first prize. You need to be at least a 36c to win."

Jane narrowed her eyes and grinned. "So, theoretically, if I was in a wet t-shirt contest with a bunch of flat-chested women, could I win first prize then?"

"Flat-chested women don't go in wet t-shirt contests," Elliot informed her as if he was an expert on the subject which he definitely was not. That was more Nick's department. Nick was the one who flipped through the cable channels late at night in search of any lurid programming previews...the channels that his ma refused to acknowledge let alone subscribe to.

Jane tilted her head to one side. "I said theoretically."

"Yeah, I suppose but quit changing the subject," Elliot growled. He needed to regain control. What a fucking lousy Saturday off this had turned into.

Jane smiled. "I didn't change the subject. You were the one who started talking about wet t-shirt contests..."

"Just one more question," Elliot brusquely interjected. Not this time Jane. You're not going to worm your way out of this by being cute or coy or clever, he thought. He'd seen her play this game before, deflect the attention or change the subject then just walk away. Unscathed.

She uncrossed her arms, her smile vanishing, and calmly clasped her hands in front of her. "What?"

"Why didn't you tell me that today was your birthday?" He was going to get his questions answered one way or another. He'd let his guard down, and now he was paying the price. It wouldn't happen again.

Jane unclasped her hands and touched his arm gently, her

voice calm. "To tell you the truth Elliot, I'm just not a birthday kind of person. I don't like a fuss being made. You know what I mean? People make such a big deal out of turning another year older. I prefer not to. I just usually have cake and ice cream with my parents, rent a movie," she shrugged her shoulders, "and call it a day. I'm sorry if I hurt your feelings. I really didn't mean to."

Todd appeared on the porch and leaned up against a wooden support post.

Elliot rolled his eyes. So much for privacy. "Are you fucking this guy?" Elliot asked bitterly, indicating Todd with a tilt of his head. That was the only reasonable explanation. Unless, of course, maybe Todd was just an absolute idiot. An idiot with a death wish.

Jane spoke just above a whisper, her voice harsh with its intensity. "Elliot, how many times do I have to tell you that Todd is just a friend from school? In fact, something like 75 percent of the students in my course are male. That is something that you'll just have to learn to live with. It's no FUCKING big deal. I do not go around screwing every guy in my class."

He still wasn't satisfied. "Yes or no, Jane. Are you fucking him?" Elliot inhaled deeply as the lightning seared his brain, the thunder so loud, so intense that he could barely hear himself think. The truth. That's all he wanted. The truth. "Yes or no."

Jane stood her ground, her dark green eyes never leaving his. A slight breeze ruffled her hair. She pushed the stray strands away from her eyes. "Elliot, you and I have made no commitments. Who I do or do not have sex with is none of your business."

Elliot spun around before he lost total control. It was his business. Damn it. He had every right to know. She belonged to him. If she was fucking this guy, it was going to stop, and it was going to stop now. Obviously, this approach wasn't getting him anywhere. "I have something for you in my car."

"Yeah?" Jane asked curiously.

"Yeah. Come here." Elliot motioned with his hand for Jane to follow him. He needed to get this over with, needed to get home before the migraine settled in, before he started to lose the vision in his left eye to the kaleidoscope of rainbow lights that no one else could see but him. Needed to take a migraine blocker and lie down in a dark room. Needed the truth before his fucking skull totally imploded.

Jane warily followed him to his black Camaro. When she spoke, her voice had magically reverted back to being calm and casual. "Elliot, if you want to come back this evening for cake and ice cream, you're more than welcome to. It would give you a chance to talk to Todd and get to know him. He's really a very nice guy."

Ignoring her invitation, Elliot took a long, white paper box from the passenger side of his car and handed the roses to Jane. "Here. Happy Birthday." This was so not the way he'd pictured this moment in his head.

Jane's face lit up in surprise as she opened the box. "Yellow roses. They're beautiful! Oh, Elliot, thank you. They're my favourite."

Elliot sat down in the passenger side of his car with the door still open. "You're welcome," he replied flatly. He opened the glove compartment and began to rummage through the contents. Insurance papers, ownership certificate, owner's manual, a couple of unused condoms...

"Will you come down later?" Jane asked cheerily. "Maybe we can set up a board game. Mom bought a Canadian version of Monopoly that's electronic, so you use debit cards instead of paper money. It's actually a lot of fun."

Finding what he was searching for, Elliot shut the glove compartment and got back out of his car. "No, I think I'll pass." He took his Swiss Army knife out of its case. The knife had been a gift from his father on his sixteenth birthday--just two years before his father had died of cancer. Elliot's peripheral vision caught Todd's movement off the veranda and onto the lawn. Time to test the waters.

Jane placed the roses on the ground beside her and slowly backed up a couple of steps. "Elliot?"

Elliot opened the knife, extending one long, sharp blade. "Did I ever show you the knife that my father gave me?" He looked past her as Todd quickened his pace to join them. Their eyes locked briefly. Elliot grinned. Here comes the Calvary, he thought. Jane's own fucking body guard.

Jane swallowed, her eyes never leaving the glimmering steel.

"No, I don't think so. Can I see it?" She held out her hand as if accepting another present. "It looks like a good one."

Elliot closed the gap between them. The thunder in his head pounded brutally, the noise filling every molecule of his existence. He held the knife only inches away from her face. "It's an actual Swiss Army knife. Not a knock off or a cheap version." He turned the blade so she could get a better view. "Very expensive. Very sharp."

Jane continued to stare at the blade but dropped her hand back to her side. "Elliot, please put the knife away." Her voice sounded annoyed now. "Elliot, this isn't funny. Put the knife away before someone gets hurt."

Elliot took one more step and touched the flat side of the honed blade to her perfect cheek. Skin so clear, so young, marred only by a faint scar on her forehead. "Dear, sweet Jane. It's not supposed to be funny, and I'll put it away when you give me one straight answer. I just want the truth, Sweetheart. No more of your freakin' lies. Just how stupid do you think I really am?"

"Jane, don't move!" Todd appeared behind her, his face twisted in rage. "Look you fucking moron, get that fucking thing away from her face before I make you eat it!"

Finally, the answer he was looking for. Elliot laughed irascibly, his head splitting in agony, his heart threatening to tear into pieces. Todd was in love with Jane. No doubt. "Don't worry, friend. I'd never hurt Jane." Elliot pulled back the knife, turned and walked back towards his car. With a quick, agile movement, he jumped in between the cars and drove the steel blade into the back tire of Todd's Chev. With some effort, Elliot pulled the blade back out and closed the knife. He watched as the tire began to slowly deflate, making a small hissing noise.

He turned back towards the two. Todd had placed himself protectively between Elliot and Jane. Whatever Todd was thinking, he wasn't talking, only standing there looking as if he was getting ready for whatever was going to happen next. Jane had sat down on the ground breathing rapidly, her eyes wide.

Mrs. Kirkland ran across the lawn to join Jane and Todd. "Elliot Fallis, just what in blue blazes is going on here?" Her voice was shrill, sending another bolt of lightning zapping through

Elliot's brain.

    Elliot ignored her and turned his full attention to Todd. "But you, friend," he pointed his finger towards Todd's face, "that's another story."

CHAPTER TWENTY-NINE

As she crept through the murky stillness of the upstairs hallway, Jane was greeted by the even breathing of her mother harmonizing with the soft, rhythmic snoring of her father. Both were now in deep sleep. Jane's birthday was officially over.

Without the need for a light (she knew every centimetre of this hallway, every hardwood floorboard that would groan unerringly beneath her weight), Jane made her way stealthily to the guest room. The full moon watched over Todd from its lofty perch extending fingers of illumination undeterred by window or lace curtain. He was lying on his back covered by one crisp, white cotton sheet. She crawled under the cover and snuggled up beside Todd on the spool bed.

Jane needed to feel Todd next to her. Todd. Her Todd. Her light. Her life. Her love. The day had been such a roller coaster of emotions that she welcomed the soothing energy of his calm strength, better than any magical elixir to settle her over-strained nerves. She felt him stir beside her and watched as his peaceful features gained ponderous awareness of her presence.

"Jane?" he whispered groggily.

"Ssh, I'm sorry. I didn't mean to wake you." Jane assiduously caressed his brawny arm then began to work her way downward.

"It's okay. I was dreaming about you. It just took me a moment to realize that you were real." He adjusted his position so that he could put his arm around her. "Aren't you worried that your parents will find us in bed together?"

She snuggled in closer, wishing to entirely meld into his side, to become a part of him.

"Not really. They're pretty sound sleepers. As long as we don't turn the stereo up full blast and invite all the neighbours over for a party, we'll be fine. When I come home after midnight, I always make myself a tea, read the newspaper and bop around the kitchen for a while before going to bed. They never wake up."

"Do you want to fool around?" His voice sounded hopeful.

Jane grinned and shook her head in the darkness. "I think that would be tempting fate a little too much." Every part of her body wanted him, ached for him. Her fingers were working their magic as Todd willingly accepted her gifted caresses, her guided stroking. Her Todd. Her love.

"We could go out to the barn," Todd suggested, "before I come all over these sheets." He turned on his side to face her. His warm lips grazed the side of her long neck then lingered on her earlobe where his tongue and teeth gently teased before settling on her waiting mouth.

Jane's hormones began their usual rampage. She wondered how often a person could have sex in one day and still want more. Five times? Ten times? She made a mental note to find out sometime in the near future…her own personal experiment…with Todd's assistance, of course. She moaned in desire but pulled back breaking the seal between them. "Aren't you tired? You have a four-hour drive ahead of you tomorrow. You need to get some sleep. The last thing I want is for you to fall asleep at the wheel because I kept you up all night."

Todd chuckled softly. "You are an insatiable vixen. That's just one of the things that I love about you. Jane, look at it this way, it could be another month before I see you again, so I'll have lots of time to catch up on my sleep." He caught her hand in his. "If you don't want to fool around that's okay too. Just do me a huge favour."

"What?" she enquired, curious at his stopping her, and felt his erection spasm in mid-motion.

"If we're not going out to the barn, you need to leave Sparky alone or I'm going to have blue balls tomorrow the size of watermelons."

Jane quickly released her grasp and stifled a giggle. "Oh. Right. Sorry." She fluttered her eyelids, cheeks burning into a blush. "Sometimes, I forget….so since we don't want you sitting on a bag of peas while driving home, the barn it is then." Shivers streamed down her back as Todd nibbled a firm nipple through the thin, white sleeveless undershirt Jane used as a pajama top. "Mmmm, not fair." She eased his head back.

"It's all Sparky's fault. You woke him up and now he wants to play." Undaunted, Todd moved to the opposite nipple to provide equal treatment, tongue and teeth, toying relentlessly.

Jane swallowed back her lust, not willing to take any further chances of getting caught. "And play he shall. The game's not over until the camel spits." Jane carefully unlinked herself from her impatient lover and crawled out from the beneath the rumpled sheet. "I'll go to my room and get dressed. You listen for me and after I've gone downstairs, count slowly to 160. Then you get dressed and I'll meet you on the porch. Whatever you do, don't turn a light on." Crazy how much she wanted him right now, wanted to open up, engulf him, feel him deep inside of her. Bonded spiritually, physically, mentally. No longer two people but one perfect entity.

Todd softly groaned as he watched her walk away, passing momentarily through the filtered light then into the shadows of the night. "What if I fall down the stairs and break my neck or something?"

She turned to face him and whispered into the darkness, "Just follow the railings and you'll be fine." She blew him a kiss. "Remember, count to 160."

Jane flung a black, rolled-up sleeping bag and a cloth tote bag decorated with purple pansies over the edge and into the golden straw. The mow was high, covered a loft and spilled over one end onto the wooden floor below. Leftover from many years of grain harvests, the straw--blown in loose instead of baled--dominated the right half side of the large barn. Every winter a portion of the straw was utilized as bedding for the cattle. Regardless, the usage never seemed to even out the intake. The mow just kept getting higher and wider, an issue to be dealt with at a later time.

In the spring and summer, hens had often roamed free range and would sometimes create nests in the hay and straw mows instead of in the chicken coop. As a child, it had been part of Jane's chores to locate these obscure nests and to gather the eggs, always leaving one marked egg behind so that the hens would lay there again.

Occasionally, a nest would go undetected until it was much too late and a treasure-trove of swishy, rotten eggs would be discovered. Excited, she would run to Dylan for assistance. The rancid eggs would be carefully stashed away in the back corner of the straw loft, secure from the eyes of their parents, waiting patiently for a family get-together with all of their cousins. Once everyone arrived, the cousins would divide equally into two teams and split the ammunition amongst them. Since the barn was part of her daily existence, Jane knew exactly where to find the best advantage points over her foes. Not once, had she crawled back to the house in search of a water hose, covered in yellow slime and smelling of putrid sulphur.

"Why the sleeping bag?" Todd asked as he climbed the wooden ladder that led up into the loft.

"You obviously didn't grow up on a farm," Jane teased as she reached down and grabbed his hand to pull him up. A teal blue, battery-operated, camping flashlight lit his way. "This isn't a movie. The straw gets really itchy after a while."

"In all the wrong places," Todd offered as he followed Jane to the back of the loft. Thin lines of moonlight squeezed between the barn boards.

"Exactly!" Jane laughed. "We'll just keep all of our wrong places out of harm's way and then you won't have to spend the whole drive back to Coburg scratching your balls." She smiled as she unrolled, unzipped and spread out the sleeping bag near the wall. Crickets, jumping in annoyance, scrambled to get out of the way of their impending doom. "And no bad jokes allowed about making out with the farmer's daughter."

Todd grinned as he fidgeted with the light. "Okay, no jokes but there actually was a movie called, *The Farmer's Daughter*. I think it was made in the late '40's, but it was kind of based in the city so no haymow or straw mow scenes that I can remember. Loretta Young starred in that one. Then there was *The Farmer's Other Daughter*, made in 1965..." Todd stopped in mid-thought when he glanced up and noticed Jane silently staring at him. "Okay, no bad jokes and no obviously unwanted movie trivia either...changing the subject...this is kinda cool. It can be used as a flashlight or as an area light." The beam spread as Todd adjusted the controls.

Jane sat down on the sleeping bag. "It also has a night light feature which I would suggest or you will attract every mosquito and June Bug in the barn."

Shivering involuntarily, Todd changed the light to night

light and sat down next to Jane. He placed the lamp on the straw beside them then visually inspected his surroundings. "I hate bugs. Did you, by any chance, bring the bug spray?"

"Definitely." Jane rooted through the long-handled tote bag that she normally kept for beach supplies. It had been awkward climbing the inset ladder with the tote slung over her right shoulder and the sleeping bag strapped to her back, but no more so than the loads of absconded treasures and fortification she and Dylan had frequently hauled up to their tree house when they were kids. Jane sprayed herself liberally then handed the plastic bottle to Todd. As Todd began to spray his upper body, Jane felt the same all-encompassing sense of melancholy that had overwhelmed her in Welland just before she had left for the summer. "So what do you think of our little Twilight Zone now?"

"It's okay. Your family's nice and your friend, Gertie, is seriously funny. I'd still like to meet Dylan though. Maybe we can pop over to Toronto some weekend and meet him for lunch." Todd tossed the bottle to the side and began to stroke Jane's hair as his eyes adjusted to the soft glow of the dim light. "And, I'd still like to know what this afternoon was all about? That guy should be doing time somewhere. You said that you'd explain later and this is later."

Jane stretched out on her side on the sleeping bag wondering how to explain. "I am sooo sorry about that. Thanks for not pressing charges. My cousin said he'd send me a bill for the tow to Owen Sound to replace your tire, and I'll make sure that Elliot pays for both. I'll give him a choice--pay or face mischief charges or destruction of property charges or something like that. That should work. Elliot's not stupid. He doesn't want a record. He's just a bit hot-tempered."

"A bit?" Todd looked at Jane as if she'd just described a mountain as a slight rise in the earth's crust. "Jane, the guy pulled a knife and held it to your face. He's more than just a bit hot-tempered. He's out of control and that makes him dangerous."

"I know it sounds crazy, but I've known Elliot forever and he's really not a bad guy. Usually, he's just all huff and steam. Problem is that he decided when I was seventeen that I was his possession, and I guess he was a little jealous of you being here. "

Todd shook his head. "Unbelievable. So, what's going to

happen when I leave, when I'm not here to protect you? Are you safe?" Todd joined her in a reclining position. They were close to the side of the barn, well out of the way from view. The barn was cooler than the house. The gaps between the barn boards allowed a slight breeze to permeate the day's lingering heat.

Jane lied. "Nothing will happen." She tugged on Todd's t-shirt to release the material from his jeans. The iconic, enigmatic face of Jim Morrison crumpled as Jane pulled the material high enough to expose Todd's chest. "Elliot will get over it. He always does." Barely touching Todd's areola, she began to draw circles around his nipple with the tip of her index finger.

Todd smiled dreamily, "I love it when you do that. It kind of tickles." A frown overpowered the smile. Todd placed his tanned hand over hers, signaling her to stop. "If that moron hurts you, I swear I'll fucking kill him." He sat up abruptly and pulled his t-shirt back down into place. "Why don't you leave with me tomorrow? You can bunk in with me for the rest of the summer. I'm sure I could get you a temporary job in the office at the construction site.

You might have to put up with a few cat calls initially, but they're a great bunch of guys once you get to know them. Then we could look for a place together."

Jane's hand drifted back down to her side. She knew better than to try again until Todd had his say. Until his mind was appeased, his body would come second. "I'd love to, but I can't. I made a commitment to the hospital for the summer. Every year, they hire one, full-time, summer student in my department, and I'd hate to leave them stranded part-way through. They've been really good to me. Besides, this is the last year for the microfilming. They didn't want to scan the really old patient files onto the main server as it would take up a lot of space, but legally they can't just destroy them either. After the year I'm doing, everything else is totally computerized so they'll be good to go."

"Okay, I get that, but you do realize that Elliot's crazy, don't you? I've dealt with guys like him before and, trust me, it never ends well. They're narcissistic pricks who think they own the world. If he has his sights set on you, it's a delusion that he won't give up easily." Sighing, Todd lay back down on the sleeping bag cuddling up to Jane. He smoothed errant strands of long hair back from her face. "Promise me that you'll stay away from him."

"Relax, Todd. I've survived this long. A couple more months won't make any difference." Jane bent forward and kissed the side of Todd's neck. July. August. Please God, she prayed. Just two more months. Less than 61 days. Surely, I can survive that. Todd, on the other hand, was another story. This afternoon had been too close. "I think, though, it would be a good idea if we meet in neutral territory next time." With the touch of the blind, she popped the top dome of his jeans and caressed his bare skin.

Todd did not stir. "Have you ever slept with this guy?"

"No." Not a lie. The metal zipper in Todd's blue jeans moved easily beneath her grasp.

"Do you want to?" Todd made no attempt to stop her this time.

"No." Possibly a lie, she had to admit that much to herself.

"Are you sure?" he continued relentlessly.

With a groan of exasperation, Jane heaved herself on top of her young lover and straddled him. "Todd, forget about Elliot." She bent over and held herself up by placing her forearms on either side of Todd's head. Her long hair floated down around his face creating an intimate tent between them, their faces only seconds apart. "I want to be with you. Always you. Only you. I want to fuck like two mad dogs in heat." Definitely not a lie. Her heart was racing. "Just you. I promise." Sitting back up, Jane reached into the back pocket of her denim shorts and pulled out an unopened condom. "I could only fine one condom though so you'd better make this last. It's all that's left from my before stock."

Appeased, Todd grinned. "I'm amazed you had one left. Mine are totally gone. You are seriously the only girlfriend I've ever had who insisted on both of us getting tested for HIV and every sexually transmitted disease known to man before riding bareback."

Jane laughed. "That, my friend, is exactly why I insisted on being tested first."

Kissing him sent fire to her groins, a fire that soon engulfed both of them. As his erection grew beneath her, she prepared herself for their dance.

With clothes hastily removed, Todd played her like a fine instrument, taking her to the edge and then prolonging the pleasure of the song. And, just when she was about to scream in the agony of her desire, he plunged deep and hard, over and over, until they were both drenched in the sweet sweat of their exuberant youth. Meshed together, juices exploding, spirits soaring, the universe expanding, they orgasmed simultaneously. And, as they lay in each other's arms, spent and waiting for reality to stabilize, they whispered soothing words of love.

He held her close. "My Jane." He closed his eyes and began to drift away.

She ran her finger through the film of sweat that glistened on his chest. "Did I ever tell you that you have the ultimately perfect penis?"

Todd opened his eyes in interest and turned his head to face her. "What?"

"You have the perfect penis." Jane felt smug…satisfied… happy. She was so lucky to have Todd. The one man who truly understood her. The one man who truly loved her. Her Todd. Her light. Her love.

"Thank you, I guess…"

Jane continued, unabashed, "it's a fallacy that one size fits all. Some of my friends like guys who are hung like horses. Some of them like guys who are not overly endowed because they claim that the guy doesn't rely as much on his penis and is more imaginative, more focused on the needs of the woman. I have one friend who is really into oral sex and she says that her boyfriend is really small, but that he has the best tongue in town so she's in oral heaven. No problem."

"And where do I fit in?" Todd chuckled at his own unintentional verbal slip. "Not literally speaking, of course. Sparky obviously knows his way around."

"Yes, yes, he does." Jane giggled in spite of herself. "You seriously have the perfect penis though. It's not overly huge, and it's not small. When you're inside of me, it feels so fuckingly, indescribably wonderful that there just aren't any words to do it justice. You send shockwaves to every part of my body imaginable." Jane sat up, cross-legged, to extract a bottle of water from her tote bag. After taking a drink, she handed the bottle to Todd. "It's like the ultimate orgasm. You know?" She wanted one, maybe two cigarettes right now--intravenous nicotine would even be better—but didn't want to take the chance of a random spark setting the straw on fire.

Todd smiled, shook his head, and chuckled. "You're too much." He leaned up on his elbow, took a long swallow then handed the bottle back to Jane.

"And you're just right." Jane tucked the bottle away. "And to top it off, I really didn't like sex that much before I met you. It was okay, but I couldn't figure out what all the fuss was about."

Todd's eyebrows raised in surprise. "Really?"

She sighed. "Un-huh. You were my first really good orgasm."

"Yay me!" Todd beamed, looking like he'd just received an A+ on his final exam. "Jane, I have a confession to make." His warm brown eyes grew serious as he stroked her taunt, smooth skin with his free hand. "The first time I saw you, my gut reaction was that you were definitely out of my league. It absolutely blew me away when you agreed to go out on our first, official date. I was so nervous, I could barely breathe through the whole movie. Then the first time we had sex, I kept wondering if I was man enough to keep you interested so I went online and read every sex how-to website I could find. Just for future reference, Cosmo has published some really excellent articles."

Jane bent forward to kiss Todd's forehead. "I love you," she whispered. "I've loved you from the first moment that I saw you." Her Todd. The man of her dreams. The man of her reality. Her soulmate. "I was so excited when you asked me out, that I texted every single person I could think of right down to my mother, who texted back, and told me to make sure I had cab fare in case the date was a bust. I was so nervous before you picked me up that I changed at least a dozen times and ended up calling Gertie, to reassure me that I wasn't as ugly as I felt, and wouldn't absolutely blow the whole evening by being too tongue tied to speak. I don't have a clue what movie we watched, and when you kissed me goodnight, I almost peed myself."

"Quite the pair." Todd chuckled, a radiant smile crinkling

the corners of his humoured eyes.

Jane pulled away and began to get dressed. The dust from the straw was beginning to irritate her sinuses. "And, the first time we had sex, all I could think of was, wow, this guy's got moves so I went online and probably read the very same *Cosmo* articles that you did." Once she finished dressing, Todd wrestled his way into his own clothing.

"I love you too, you know." Todd's voice was quiet, serious, exhausted. He lay back down on his side and patted the area directly in front of him. "What do you think about marriage?"

Her Todd. Her love. Her soulmate. Her husband? Jane's heart suddenly palpitated, thudding ominously before, once again, catching rhythm. "I really don't think about marriage. I think about getting through the next couple years of school and then trying to find a job. Todd, can we please leave this conversation for another time? We need to get back to the house." Jane motioned for them to leave.

"It's okay. You can relax. The look on your face was absolute terror so I won't ask you to marry me anytime soon." Todd grinned, stretched and yawned. "Can't we just stay here for just a little bit longer? I'm enjoying having you all to myself."

"Okay, but just for a while." She tried unsuccessfully to stifle a yawn. "We seriously have to get back to the house before my parents wake up."

As Jane curled up in Todd's welcoming arms, she tried to envision them together, married with a couple of noisy, happy children, careers, a split-level house with a fenced-in backyard where the children could play, two cars or maybe one car and a van, a poodle, two cats…and soon fell asleep.

In the beginning, she thought it was merely a game. She'd been sent to the barn by her dad to throw down a few square bales of hay for the cattle to supplement the sparse spring grazing. Her sister's fiancé had asked if he could help.

Once in the haymow, he had tripped her. Jane had not been quick enough to regain her footing and sprawled awkwardly facedown. A yelp of surprise escaped from her lips without the comfort of caring ears close by. Within seconds, Doug had flipped her onto her back then straddled her hips. Shoving her slim arms just above her head, elbows out like a lopsided diamond, he cuffed her wrists with his massive hands. Jane, twelve, often wrestled with her brother and, on first impulse, this seemed no different.

She squirmed then forced herself to still. His weight was too great to easily toss him aside. She felt his breath, hot against her ear, as he loomed over her. Sharp, dry stocks of winter-stored hay poked her defenseless back through the light blue sweater she wore, the weather too cool yet for a t-shirt and too warm for the added confines of a jacket.

"You're so pretty," he whispered hoarsely. "I really like you a lot." He placed both of her slender wrists in his one, large, rough hand, and with the other, reached down to fondle her small, developing breasts. "I want to make love to you. You'd like that wouldn't you?" He pulled the sweater from her denim jeans to expose her white lace brassiere and rapidly heaving chest.

Jane grimaced, shuddered at his touch, instinctively knowing this was not a game and yet unable to totally comprehend how it could possibly be happening to her. Doug was going to marry her sister. They were going to have a baby. Reaching past the denial, her mind slowly spun into action. "Get off me. You're hurting me. If you don't get off me, I'll scream."

He laughed. "There's no one around to hear you, Jane. Everyone is at the house planning the wedding." Freeing her right breast, he bent down to encapsulate her flesh with his mouth. His right hand explored, roaming over her gently curving body, her waist, her hip, her inner thigh before readjusting himself so he could spread her legs to massage in between.

Jane gasped, angry and confused by the delicious sensations that were beginning to flow through her. "Please, stop. Let me up," she begged. "I'll get in trouble if I don't get the cattle fed."

With a quick, soft bite, he released her nipple and laughed. "Are you still a virgin, Jane? Still playing with boys? Soon you'll feel how hard the cock of a real man gets. Not to worry though. It'll only hurt for a moment, and I promise I'll be as gentle as I can be the first time. Then we'll feed the cattle together. Just you and me, Jane."

She lay very still for a moment, waiting, trying desperately not to cry. Show no fear, she told herself sternly and swallowed hard. This was all Dylan's fault. It was his turn to feed hay. If he hadn't gone to his friend's house, this wouldn't be happening. She felt Doug's weight shift as he slid his sitting position further down onto her legs. She shut her eyes *tightly and tried to control her breathing. His grip on her wrists relaxed as his attention turned towards opening the top dome of her pants and pulling down the zipper.*

With a quick movement, she managed to pull one of her wrists free, twisted her lithe body and knocked him off balance. She scrambled from under him and flew down the mow.

"Jane! Wait!" he called from behind her.

Adrenaline pumping, Jane headed for the stairwell to the lower part of the barn where she could hide. She knew all of the nooks and crannies. He didn't. She knew all of the exits. He didn't. She hid behind a wooden cattle stall, peaking around only enough in the dimness of the barn so that she could see if he was following her.

"Jane," he called as he began to search for her. "If you tell your sister, she won't love you anymore. Is that what you want, Jane? Do you understand? It's all your fault, Jane! If you weren't so pretty, it wouldn't drive me nuts wanting to have sex with you. It's all your fault, Jane! Tell Pam and she won't want you to be her sister anymore. She won't believe you. She'll think you're making it up to be a brat. Is that what you want? Is it Jane?"

"Jane! Jane! Wake up! Wake up! You're having a bad dream."

Jane abruptly sat up. Tears trickled in rivulets down her sodden cheeks. A dream. Bad dream. Just a dream. Todd. Todd was here. Not Doug. Todd. Her Todd. Inhaling deeply to steady herself, the real world phased into focus.

"Are you okay?" He placed an arm around her slumped shoulders, steadying her.

"Yeah, I'm okay. Just a bad dream." She concentrated on Todd, on his eyes, brown and concerned. She ran her tongue over her dry lips and swallowed back the pain.

"Want to talk about it?" he asked as he gently wiped the tears away with the crook of his finger.

"Nothing really. Silly. Zombies were taking over the world, and I couldn't find my cat." Just a dream.

"Which cat? There must be a dozen of them around here." Todd reached past her with his free arm and grabbed the bottle of water.

"Mom won't allow any cats in the house and, most of the barn cats are feral, but a couple are pretty tame. Thisbe is the long-haired calico, and Marlow is a short-haired grey. It was probably one of them. I don't remember exactly."

Another lie to add to the others. How could she possibly tell Todd that her hymen had been torn from her by a predator, a madman when she was only thirteen? The pain had been excruciating, the promised gentleness, non-existent. How could she possibly explain why she hadn't told a soul? How could she make him understand that Doug had totally convinced the child she was that his actions were entirely her fault? How could she admit, even to herself, that she had, initially and in some perverse way, enjoyed his attention, that it made her feel special until the guilt and the self-loathing saturated the very essence of her spirit? How could she adequately describe the angst of weekends spent watching the children while her sister worked, living in immutable fear that Doug would come home early after a long-haul, wired, and looking for trouble? What words could she possibly use to elucidate how she'd finally found the courage to resist only to have him threaten to beat her, to kill her sister, to harm the children if she didn't cooperate, if she told anyone? It was only after she'd mentally imploded in high school that her parents had decided that weekend babysitting on top of schoolwork was obviously too much stress. Their doctor, in his infinite wisdom, had temporarily prescribed anti-depressants and life had carried on.

Removing his arm from her shoulder so he could open the bottle of water, Todd took a long drink then handed the bottle to Jane. "Thirsty?"

"Thanks," she said, accepted the bottle and drank. Just a dream. Awareness dawned on her like a bright light permeating layers of dense fog. Todd. She could see Todd clearly. Too clearly. Daylight clearly. She jumped up, panic-stricken. "Oh my god, Todd, it's morning."

Todd blinked twice, yawned and stretched. "I kinda figured that one out by the way the sun was shining through the barn boards." As usual, he sounded genuinely unconcerned.

Frantic, Jane began to scramble, recapped the bottle and

shoved it, the bug spray, the used and knotted condom (gross but can't just leave it here) into her tote bag. She stood up and headed for the loft's ladder. "Well, don't just sit there. COME ON!"

Todd followed at a slower pace. "I don't see why the big panic. It's only 7 a.m."

After flying down the wooden rungs, Jane watched Todd's descent from the barn floor.

She stood with her hands on her hips looking like an impatient child waiting for her turn at hopscotch. "Yes, and since my dad works all sorts of very strange hours during the week, he makes it a habit to get up early every Sunday morning to make breakfast for everyone."

"No way." Todd jumped down past the last two rungs and landed with a soft thud. "I thought normal people slept in on Sundays."

Jane took Todd by his hand and grinned. "I don't remember saying anything about being normal." Particles of dust floated by her, sailing on streams of filtered light. Ashes to ashes. Dust to dust. If they got caught, they would be Dead on Arrival.

"So, my lady, what do we do now?" Todd started to brush small bits of straw off his clothing. He searched the back of his blue jeans for any unwanted cling-ons.

"First of all, we go outside so that I can have a cigarette." Jane walked towards the gangway door, pulling Todd off balance. He followed awkwardly behind while trying to rid himself of a burr that had made a home on the back of his t-shirt.

"Wait a minute." He let go of Jane's hand and pulled his t-shirt over his head to get a better look at the pesky intruder.

Jane shook her head in exasperation. "I'll meet you outside on the gangway. I won't be able to think right until I get some nicotine into my system, and I have to pee so bad it's about to run down my leg." Without looking back, Jane strode out of the barn and into the bright morning sunlight. She inhaled deeply through her nose, hoping to appease her burning sinuses with the early-morning moisture. Jane searched her pockets for her package of cigarettes. Crunched but still smokeable. She lit one and blew several smoke rings while her mind slowly formulated a plan.

With his t-shirt back on, Todd joined her. "So, why can't we just sneak in?" He ran his fingers through his sun-streaked brown hair and then shoved his hands into his pockets.

"If Dad's not up already, my parents' bedroom is at the top of the stairs. They'll hear us come in." Jane surveyed her own clothing. Clean enough. "I think that I have a better idea."

"Yeah?"

"Yeah. We go inside. I take a quick shower and then you do. We make it look as if we got up early. You know, making the most of what little time we have left to spend together before you leave." She couldn't decide which was worse, her need for nicotine or her punishing need to urinate. Jane decided that she was definitely looking forward to having her own apartment again—a place where she could urinate and smoke at the same time. Although, they had never attempted to keep her from her addiction, both of her parents had made it abundantly clear that smoking was not, under absolutely any circumstances, allowed in the house.

Todd shrugged. "Sure but I still think that you're making too much of this."

"Right and Medusa had a harem." Jane finished her cigarette and stomped the butt out under her running shoe. "Let's go."

As they entered the house, (she'd stuffed the tote bag on the backseat floor of her car until later) the aroma of freshly brewed coffee and frying bacon greeted them. Jane's father, a tall, angular man in his mid-fifties, stood at the stove, making scrambled eggs in a large, cast-iron frying pan. He did not turn around.

"Morning, Dad," Jane ventured brightly. "You're up early."

"Morning, Jane." He glanced around quickly then turned his attention back to the task at hand. "So are you."

Jane swallowed, knowing that she looked like Medusa herself and that bluffing her way through this one would be damned near impossible. "Yup, up at 6:00 a.m. I was just showing Todd the barn. I think that I'll go grab a quick shower and get some of the dust off of me."

Todd interjected, "Is there anything I can do to help you, Mr. Kirkland?"

Mr. Kirkland turned and stared at the twosome. His jaw, set in a frown, relaxed. "Yeah, you can set the table."

CHAPTER THIRTY

Elliot was furious with himself. He knew deep down that he had over-reacted, had totally blown it. He had thought, at one point, of blaming the entire incident on his suffering from an impending migraine; however, a very stubborn part of him still felt that he'd been given just provocation and that his actions were totally within reason. Forcing himself to believe his own lie did not come easily. Regardless, the fact was that he had let his jealousy get the better of him. Again. He had been so close this time and then, out of the blue, a Todd appears to pierce his neatly constructed bubble like a heat-seeking missile. Like any target, Elliot had exploded into a million fragments. He was only human.

Three weeks had passed since Jane's birthday and still no word. Not a sound. For the first week, Elliot had expected a visit from hotshot Constable Jeff with a written warrant for Elliot's arrest. Normally, the boys and girls in blue had a habit of ignoring disputes (short of uttering death threats or murder) between outsiders and the locals hoping the arguments would be settled without unnecessary intervention--especially when the argument was over a woman—but one could never be positive that the century old, unwritten rule would be followed if the outsider insisted on legal recourse. If Todd decided to press charges, the O.P.P. had no choice other than to follow through. After reading him his rights, Jeff would produce a glistening pair of handcuffs, tell Elliot to turn around so he could bind his wrists, guide him into the backseat of the black and white cruiser and then drive him to the red-brick, station house where Jeff would inevitably book Elliot on a mischief or on an assault charge. At this point, Elliot thought, his mother would either have a minor heart attack or cry herself to sleep for a week wondering where she had gone wrong to produce such a violent son. However, Elliot's paranoia, his worst fears, had gone unfulfilled.

In the meanwhile, Elliot had jumped every time the store's doorbells jangled, every time the telephone rang, every time he heard a siren. After losing two nights sleep, he'd even decided to plead guilty and face the punishment--a small humiliation for his impetuousness. Worst-case scenario, first offence, was a night in jail if the charge was assault or willful destruction of property, then probation. Best-case scenario, Elliot would end up with just Community Service if it was only a mischief charge. He'd survive. No Jeff. Nothing. Zilch. Nada.

When no police officer had arrived, Elliot had expected a personal visit from Jane herself, brimming over with anger, her eyes throwing spears and her tongue lashing with words of hatred. She'd come storming in at the very moment when he was least prepared. She'd demand an audience-filled confrontation so that every customer, every potential future customer, and, definitely his boss, would know that they were dealing with the lowest scum of the earth. When she let the spears fly, she would aim straight for his heart, to kill, not just to wound. No visit. Nothing. Zilch. Nada.

No sound. No whispers behind his back. No local gossip relayed by Nick. The silence was ominous. Omnipresent. Unbearable.

Three weeks and Elliot hadn't seen Jane hanging out after work in Donnybrooke or in Owen Sound. Everyone was on high alert but nothing. Elliot had even gone so far as checking out Buck's Hot Spot every night for the past week. He would stay until closing time, watching the door and expecting her to make a grand entrance wearing faded, low-riding blue jeans and a tight t-shirt.

No Jane. Twice, he had thought he had spotted her in the crowd when he first walked in. His heart had beat like helicopter propellers gaining rapid speed for take-off. Then the woman would turn around. Not Jane. She was definitely making herself scarce.

Elliot had come close several times to calling to apologize. He would pick up the telephone and start to dial. Panic would set in. He couldn't breathe, couldn't talk, couldn't think. Sweat would trickle down his forehead creating rivulets of salt, sticky in the heat. Instinctively, he would hang up before the ringing began. Only then would his heart stop racing. Only then could he catch his breath.

The worst part had been Nick. Nick, who spouted curiosity like a whale spouted water, had asked him a dozen questions--how Jane had liked the roses, if he and Jane had plans to go out the next weekend on and on and on. Elliot had tried unsuccessfully to avoid the conversations, but Nick knew him too well. A couple of days later, Elliot had confessed. Nick had been very supportive, had given him a slap on the back and told him not to worry about it too much. He had reassured him that there were plenty of other women out there and, hey, even Glenda still asked about him. In fact, she asked about him so much, that Nick had decided to quit seeing her after the second date, because Elliot's name had crept into the conversation twenty times before he decided to stop counting and drive the pathetically smitten woman home to wait by her telephone for Elliot to call or to text her back.

Everything was back to normal. Elliot got up. He went to work. He spent the day at the store. He went home. He hung out with Nick. He watched television, or played softball, or went out for a drink with the guys. The summer was turning out to be just like any other summer after all.

Elliot's mind quieted as he idly watched an elderly lady, Mrs. Rivers, sitting on a wooden bench under a shade tree halfway across the park. Looking very relaxed in her long, flowered skirt and white cotton blouse--at peace with the hot, muggy weather--she was knitting what appeared to be a brown and green scarf. In July. In the heat. A scarf. Occasionally, she reached into a small, brown paper bag on the bench beside her and tossed an unshelled peanut to a foraging chipmunk or to a black squirrel. Once the small creature scampered away with its treasure, she would pick up her needles and yarn and continue knitting.

Mrs. Rivers' only son had been killed five years ago in a car accident leaving his mother, his wife, his three children, and his two grandchildren mourning his loss. Since then, every nice spring, summer, or fall day you could find Mrs. Rivers sitting in the park between 1:00 p.m. and 2:00 p.m. knitting and feeding whatever small animals may venture near her. Elliot had thought her behaviour quite odd until his boss explained that Mrs. Rivers' son had fallen asleep while driving home from a business trip. He had rolled his brand new, shiny Saturn into a ravine at 1:00 a.m. in the morning and had succumbed to his injuries an hour later. "We all grieve in our own way," his boss had said.

After that, whenever Elliot sat in the park enjoying a late lunch, he would nod and wave to Mrs. Rivers or sit down beside her for a quick chat before leaving her in peace. She was no longer a peculiar old woman to him. She was someone's mother, someone's grandmother, someone's great-grandmother. And, last Christmas, much to his surprise, she'd given him a warm, woolen tuque, hand-knitted, brown and green.

July was almost over now. Three more weeks and the annual ball tournament would officially mark the end of summer. After that, the days would begin to cool and the local farmers would concentrate on bringing in their crops of corn and soybeans before the fall rains set in. And, if he was lucky, his softball team would make the play-offs.

"Can I join you?" A soft, friendly voice inquired from beside him. The voice that was presently haunting his dreams.

Elliot turned towards the voice. "Can I stop you?"

Jane joined Elliot on the park bench. WELCOME TO DONNYBROOKE had been painted on the back of the bench in script blue and white letters--a summer student project sponsored by the Community Club in the attempt to symbolize the friendly essence of small town hospitality. She followed the direction of his eyes. "I didn't mean to startle you."

He lied. "You didn't." He prepared himself for battle--his sympathetic nervous system unconsciously taking over. Fight or flight.

"Can we talk?" she asked.

Elliot studied Jane's face. She was neither smiling nor frowning. Her eyes were hidden behind wire-rimmed, aviator-style sunglasses--the kind with the mirrored lenses. All he could see was his own frowning face staring back at him. "What do you want?" His voice sounded harsher than he had intended. Damn, he thought.

"Just to talk."

"About what?" It was times like these that he wished that he smoked. At least then he would have something to do with his hands. "I'm on my lunch break so make it quick. How come you're not at work today?" He leaned back against the bench trying to look unconcerned by the entire proceedings, cool, calm... indifferent. Just another day like any other day.

"I work this weekend so I have the day off," Jane explained.

"Oh." Another weekend when she was supposedly working,

his thoughts twisted darkly. Right. Another Todd, maybe. Or a Tim. Or a John. He glanced down at his wristwatch. "I have fifteen minutes left then I have to get back to the store." With the manager back from holidays, he could not afford to be late.

"Okay, I'll get to the point. First of all, you owe me for a tow into Owen Sound and for a new tire." Jane handed two, white paper invoices to Elliot.

Elliot's stomach clenched as he accepted the bills and noted the amounts. "Just for the tow and for the tire?" Could he possibly be getting off this easy?

"Yup, pay for both and we'll call it even. This time. But, Elly, I'm warning you, you pull another stunt like that, threaten any more of my friends, and I'll have you charged faster than you can say Jeff Thornton. Understand?"

One look at Jane's face, the serious lines, the set of her jaw, the slightly furrowed brow and Elliot knew that she was not bluffing. He nodded, helpless to disagree. "Do you want cash or would a cheque do? I don't have that much cash on me right now, but I could stop at the banking machine later." Not sure why he was getting off easy, he'd take the deal while it was still on the table. Maybe now, he could finally sleep at night.

"Cash would be good considering your stunt cost me the better part of a week's wages."

"I could drop the money off at your mom's after work." Elliot glanced at his watch. He rose to leave. "Right now though, I have to go."

"Are you busy tonight?" Jane looked up at him.

"Why?"

"I was thinking that maybe we could grab a drink and talk this thing through. Wilson and the Tectonic Plates are playing at Buck's Hot Spot. They rock." Jane grinned. The seriousness had dissipated as fast as a cloud passing over the sun.

Elliot wanted to see her eyes. God, how he hated those glasses. The fact that his heart was beating faster than normal did not help. He obviously wasn't off the hook just yet. "So, how is good old Todd anyway?"

"Fine." Her voice sounded genuine.

No screaming. No yelling. No pathos. No raging

accusations. He breathed deeply and exhaled. He could feel the warp speed of his heartbeat begin to slow down. "Are there any other guys I should know about?"

"Sure, about fifty-four more in my course alone if you want to come down to Welland in September and interrogate all of them. Then there's the rest of the campus...the Refrigeration guys, the Arc Welders, the Journalism students..."

Elliot turned away. "I get the idea." A visual image of the multitudes of male students flashed through his mind--young, eager men with arms full of books, faces full of ready smiles and bodies full of raging hormones. College. Right. Something else he would never be able to afford.

Jane rose from the bench and lit a cigarette. "Well? What do you think?"

With his mind gearing down, Elliot glanced at his watch again. "Nick and I are supposed to shoot a few racks of pool tonight."

"Okay. Some other time then."

Three weeks, he thought. Three weeks of silence, of absolute, unadulterated torture. Now, Jane wanted to `talk things through', whatever that meant. What was he supposed to do? Roll over? Sit up? Beg? Well, he wouldn't. He was a Fallis. He had his pride. He had his mental gun-belt with a notch for every woman he'd ever slept with--twenty-five, maybe thirty by now. He had Nick. He had his job. If she expected him to apologize, she could hold her breath until her lungs exploded for all he cared. He, Elliot Fallis, did not need the hassle. He did not need Jane. He turned around towards her, ready to tell her exactly where she could go and how fast until he saw that Jane had taken off her sunglasses. Her eyes sparkled with friendly warmth. A smile played around her red lips. Lips like cherries--luscious, ripe, and sweet. Oh, so sweet. "I guess Nick can wait. Do you want to meet in Owen Sound or do you want me to pick you up?"

"You decide."

"I'll pick you up around eight."

"Great. See you then. By the way, Buck's back in town." Jane inhaled deeply on the cigarette and blew the smoke out in the opposite direction.

"Buck MacAdangdang?" Elliot asked.

"The one and only. He's claiming that he's the one who discovered the Tectonic Plates and that his club will make them famous." Jane smiled broadly.

Elliot grunted despite his best efforts not to care. "Must be nice to have rich parents. Buck's never worked a day in his life and yet they forked out the cash to buy him a club. Now he walks around like some freakin' big hotshot."

"Aw yes, the MacAdangdangs. I hear they're worth close to a billion so buying Buck 'The Hot Spot' would be like pocket change to them. Besides, Buck's not really that bad once you get past the flash. Sometimes, you have to look past the surface to find the real person." She smiled again and gently touched his arm. "Anyway, I'd better let you get back to work before you get in trouble. I'll see you at 8:00." With a wave, she casually strolled away.

For Elliot, the remainder of the day had gone incredibly slow. The customers talked slowly. They paid for their respective bills slowly. They walked out of the store so slowly that Elliot had to constantly harness the overwhelming desire to push them in the right direction. He had even gone so far as closing the store five minutes early, so that he would not get trapped by the last minute customer who always seemed to forget that the store closed at six sharp and who had nothing better to do than take up another half-hour of his time, asking as many asinine questions as humanly possible, without the slightest, noticeable inkling that he did, indeed, have a life outside of those particular cement walls.

He whistled as he walked into his house. He could hear his mother in their small kitchen fixing dinner. He could smell the casserole cooking in the oven--chicken, probably with mushrooms and peas tossed through egg noodles. Her favourite.

"Hi ya, Ma," he greeted her as he sat down at the kitchen table. She looked so small decked out in a pink, floral, summer blouse and colour-coordinated walking shorts.

"Hi, Elliot. Supper will be ready in a minute." She began to set the table. "How was your day?"

"Fine, Ma. Just fine. How was yours?"

"Oh," she said, "can't complain. I went to visit Mrs. Longstaff. You know, the one with the daughter I keep telling you about. She asked how you were, so I said that maybe she and her daughter could come over for a meal sometime."

Elliot shook his head. "Ma, I do fine on my own thank you. Introduce her to Nick instead. Mrs. Longstaff won't know the difference anyway." Elliot decided to help set the table, jumped up from his seat and grabbed a bottle of ketchup and a bottle of apple juice from the refrigerator.

"Hey man, introduce who to me?" Nick enquired as he stood in the doorway of the kitchen.

"Mrs. Longstaff's daughter." Mrs. Fallis surveyed her son. "You'd better go wash up before dinner. "You get awfully dirty at this job of yours."

"Mrs. Longstaff's daughter wants to meet me, man?" With a look of pleased surprise, Nick folded his arms across his chest and leaned against the doorframe.

"No." Elliot threw a loaf of bread onto the centre of the table. "Actually, she wants to meet me. I just figured you needed more help in meeting women than I do." As long as he could remember, Nick was as smooth with women as sandpaper. The guy just had no moves. No game.

"No way, man. I don't need your leftovers. I'm not that desperate, man." Nick frowned.

"Besides which," Elliot continued, ignoring his brother, "I'm seeing someone right now." Well kinda, maybe. Hopefully, everything would get back on track after tonight.

Mrs. Fallis wiped her hands on her apron. "Are you going out with that Glenda girl again? I really liked her. As my mother would have said, she's bubbly."

"No, Ma." Elliot sat down at his usual place at the table and tilted his chair back on two legs. "That's definitely over."

"Who then, man?" Nick challenged, his face determined.

Elliot felt two pairs of eyes watching him. "Jane Kirkland," he spit out before he could help himself. Was he jinxing everything by telling them now? Maybe he should have waited until tomorrow…

Nick's jaw dropped open. "What?"

"Jane Kirkland. Isn't that Stewart Kirkland's youngest daughter? The pretty, blonde one?" Mrs. Fallis paused on her way to the stove to check the casserole.

"Yup." Elliot nodded as he rocked forward. Settling back on four legs, he buttered a piece of white bread.

"Your father used to play softball with Stewart Kirkland years ago." Mrs. Fallis turned towards Nick. "Nick, my lad, pick up your jaw and go have a shower. Supper will be ready in five minutes."

"Yeah, Ma, in a minute." Nick stared at Elliot. "I thought you and Jane weren't speaking, man."

Elliot placed the slice of bread on the edge of his plate. "We had a misunderstanding. No big deal. It's all good now. In fact, we're going out for a drink tonight. I'm picking her up at eight." Too late to turn back now.

"Hey, man, you said we were playing pool tonight!" Nick glared, noticeably unhappy with the change of plans.

"Yeah. Sorry. We'll do it some other time. Do what Ma says and go have a shower. I'm starving."

"Sure, man, whatever." Nick huffed, turned and walked away.

"Isn't Jane Kirkland a bit younger than you, Elliot?" Mrs. Fallis turned off the stove and sat down at the table to wait.

"A bit but not that much."

The voices trailed behind Nick as he climbed the stairs. He placed his clean clothes neatly on top of the toilet seat lid and turned on the shower. The steam swirled around him. Stripped naked, he stared at himself in the mirror of the medicine cabinet until the steam condensed too thickly on the surface to reflect his image. Raising his hand to the mirror, he wrote `Jane' across the surface in large capital letters. Nick stared at the name, his erection achingly hard. With the palm of his hand, he wiped off the mirror to, once again, reveal his own face.

CHAPTER THIRTY-ONE

Mrs. Kirkland sat at her wooden, kitchen table cracking plump green beans into a large glass bowl. "Where are you going this evening looking so young and pretty?" she asked her daughter as Jane came bustling into the room wearing a short, red sundress and a denim jacket.

Kissing her well-loved mother on the cheek, Jane offered, "Elliot and I are going out for a bit."

"Excuse me," Mrs. Kirkland frowned, "I'm sure I must have heard you wrong. Did you say that you and that rough neck of an Elliot Fallis are going out tonight? I thought you had more sense than that."

Glancing at the kitchen wall clock, Jane nodded. Almost eight o'clock. "You heard right, Mom. Elliot and I are going up to Owen Sound for a while. We won't be late. I have to work tomorrow." She could feel a lecture coming and hoped that Elliot would be on time. Walking over to a wall mirror, Jane checked her hair and her makeup for last minute touch-ups.

"Jane, I think that you and I need to have a chat." There was no question in her voice, only motherly discernment.

"Oh, Mom." Jane rolled her eyes dramatically. She had spent a year living on her own, had successfully managed to keep the rent and utilities paid on time, had managed to avoid getting robbed by a late night mugger, had tried Karma Sutra positions from the Tortoise to the Knot of Fame and yet…the mere tone of her mother's voice instantly teleported her back to being twelve-years-old again. Twelve-years-old with two awkward, gangly legs, like a young fawn trying desperately to overcome a bad case of the wobbles in order to keep up with the rest of the herd. Twelve-years-old with a mouthful of silver braces grinning sheepishly, too embarrassed to smile. Twelve-years-old and wishing she was twenty, waiting impatiently for the ugly duckling to finally metamorphose into a graceful swan.

"Don't `Oh, Mom' me. Quit gawking at yourself. You look fine. Come here and sit down for a minute." She motioned for Jane to sit on the wooden chair across the table from her.

With an emphatic sigh, Jane sauntered over to the chair and

sat down. "And just what, Mother dearest, do you want to talk about?" Jane picked a bean from the pile on the table, bit one in half, picked up another and began to help. With any luck, the lecture would be short and her mother could be appeased without major ramifications.

"Why are you doing this? I thought that you liked this Todd fellow."

Todd. Todd. Her Todd. "I do like this Todd fellow." Jane thought for a moment. Beans snapped loudly, pregnant with the summer's warm rains and morning dew. "Problem is that I kind of like this Elliot fellow too."

"Well, I'm not one to give advice but..."

Jane interjected with a smile, "Yes you are." Advice, she was sure, was her mother's middle name.

Mrs. Kirkland smiled in return. "Okay, yes I am, but I'd be wary of that temper of Elliot's if I were you. He's given you a lot of trouble in the past." Her brow knit in thought.

"I know but most of the time he's okay. He's just a bit jealous is all." Jane could see a car slowing down at the end of the laneway and threw one last bean into the bowl. She stood up to prepare to leave. Saved. One last glance in the mirror to make sure she looked presentable. No beans in her teeth. Bonus.

"Mark my words, Jane, a leopard doesn't change its spots. If he's this unpredictable now, he'll always be. I know that you're a woman now, and I can't tell you what to do but be careful. Okay?"

"People do change, Mom. You of all people should know that. Look at Dad. He's nothing like he used to be." Familiar ghosts caressed her subconscious but were quickly obliterated by her youthful enthusiasm.

"Elliot is not your father."

Jane knew the look in her mother's eyes. It was one of sincere concern. She walked around the table and hugged her mother's strong shoulders. Jane kissed her on the cheek and promised, "I'll be careful. I have my cell phone and money for a cab. If worse comes to worse, I'm prepared. If I can survive okay in Welland, I can manage one night in Owen Sound." Wow, Mom, if you only knew what I actually do when I'm not at home, you and Dad would lock me up and throw away the key, Jane thought.

Jane and Elliot drove in silence while listening to the radio. The evening was warm and clear.

Finally finding his voice, Elliot asked, "Do you really want to go to the bar?"

Remembering her promise, Jane shook her head. Better to keep this evening in neutral territory. "I'd rather take a walk along the harbor if it's okay. I've spent most of the summer inside." For once, sobriety seemed like the better option. Mark that one on the calendar, she thought and inwardly smiled. Chalk one up for Mom.

"Sure."

The stretch along the harbour went from a docking area for large boats to a grassy expanse of undeveloped land, to a marina, to a family area known as Kelso Beach. It was here that they walked, watching families take advantage of the weather for an evening swim and frolic, watching bicyclers follow the scenic trails, watching the comforting commotion of summer.

Jane walked with her hands linked behind her back. "We really need to talk this out, Elliot." She could feel her heart beating a little too fast. This was definitely not going to be easy. Seriously, how crazy was this? On one hand, she was constantly texting with Todd who had just put down a deposit on an apartment for them. He sounded as excited as a child counting down the days to Christmas. On the other hand, there was Elliot. Kind of like having the angel and the devil on her shoulders, tempting her in opposite directions.

He walked quietly beside her. "I know."

"I don't understand why you were so mean to Todd. You don't even know the guy." One family caught her attention--a young husband and wife with a small boy. They were building a sand castle and the youngster was giggling in delight as each new tower was erected and sculptured into part of the architecture. They looked so happy--so very, very happy. The smiles and the laughter were real, not just some wonderfully crafted facade to fool the world.

Elliot nodded his head. "I've thought about this a lot over the past few weeks, and I think I can explain. Jane, when we were growing up, you were always this scrawny little kid with an ice cream cone in your hand. Nick and I thought it was great fun to tease you."

"No shit." Jane couldn't help but laugh and turned her focus back to the task at hand.

"Then, somewhere along the line, you grew up. You were pretty, smart, and I came to hope that someday we'd be together. Problem was that I think I always knew that you would be too smart to stick around here. You are college material. Me, I never liked school enough to risk a massive student loan with no guaranteed job at the end. I'll probably never move out of Donnybrooke, and that's okay with me. I like it there. It's home."

Jane stopped walking and sat down on a painted, wooden bench that overlooked the water. She watched seagulls float in and around the beach, picking up picnic leftovers and screaming their whereabouts to their friends. "That still doesn't explain why you can be nice one moment and a total asshole the next."

Elliot joined her on the bench. "That's harsh."

"But true."

He scratched his temple and brushed back a stray hair. "You're not going to make this easy are you?"

"No way." She reached over to smooth the rebellious lock of chestnut brown hair into place.

"Then let me finish. Okay?" It was Elliot's turn to sound nervous.

Jane nodded. "Okay." She fought the desire to reach into her purse and extract a cigarette to calm her nerves. Could this all be real? The braces were now only an unpleasant memory. She no longer tripped over her own feet in the attempt to adjust to the sudden lengthening of her legs. Had the ugly duckling finally and truly metamorphosed? Was she now a swan? Is that how the world saw her?

"I don't know exactly. Whenever I see you with someone else, a part of me just goes crazy. I want to be with you. I want you to want to be with me. That may sound stupid, but it's true. I don't want to leave here, and I don't know how to make you want to stay, so when I saw you with Todd it just made me feel like I was this stupid, small-town hick. He has everything that I don't have, and it made me angry. Okay? I got so angry that I lost control. If you say that he's just a friend, then fine, he's just a friend."

"And if he was more than just a friend?" Jane could feel her heart quickening. Summer wasn't over yet. She couldn't go back to the way things had always been between them. She couldn't face any more animosity. It was exhausting.

Elliot's eyebrows raised in question. "Is he?"

With her focus on the water, Jane continued. The anger in her voice was undeniable. "That's not the issue here. The issue is that you and I really have no commitment to each other, so if he was more than just a friend, it's really none of your business. Regardless of what he is to me, you don't have the right to assault him or to take it out on his car. And even if you and I did have some sort of commitment, it still wouldn't give you the right to tell me who to see or who I call my friend whether that person is male or female." Maybe, she thought, life would have been simpler if I'd just stayed being an ugly duckling.

With an audible sigh, Elliot agreed. "You're right. Do you want me to make some sort of commitment to you? Is that what this is all about?"

"I didn't say that, but you do expect an awful lot. I never did understand that part. You're like a dog marking its territory, and I'm no man's territory. Understand? If I'm with someone it's because I want to be with that person, not because that person owns me. Are we clear?"

"Loud and clear."

The anger began to subside like a wave heading back out into the ocean. "I'm still planning on going back to school in September."

"Good. I'm glad."

"Are you really?" she questioned, not convinced. It couldn't be that easy. Could it?

Elliot touched her arm gently. "Yes, Jane, really. There's no reason that you shouldn't follow your dreams."

"Even if my dreams are different than yours?" She tilted her head briefly to the right and narrowed her eyes, trying to decide just how honest Elliot was being. Did he truly believe what he was saying, or was he just saying what he thought she wanted to hear? No more games.

"Even if they're different than mine. Believe it or not, I do know how to compromise." Elliot reached over and began to play with a loose strand of Jane's hair.

Jane brushed her hair away from his fingers. Elliot dropped his hand back to his side. Jane was not convinced. "Elliot, I still have two more years of school where I'll be surrounded by guys of all shapes and sizes while you live up here. Can you honestly tell me that it won't bother you to know that? We could see each other occasionally, but most of my energy is focused around school projects and that includes a lot of weekend shoots. Besides that, exams are a major bitch. I don't talk to anyone for weeks except to study."

"I'll survive. You'd be up for Thanksgiving and for Christmas. Maybe I could drive down the odd weekend when you're not busy. It's not like you go to school in Alaska. It's only a three-hour drive. Then there's always the telephone in between, e-mails and I hear computer sex can be fun." He looked hopeful.

"You just don't get the big picture, Elliot." Jane shook her head in frustration. "It's not just school. When I'm finished with school, I'll end up God-knows-where to get my first job. What I don't want is to spend my whole life here living in the boonies. There's a whole big world out there, and I want to be a part of it."

Thoughts whirled through Jane's mind. Elliot. Todd. Elliot. Todd. Her heart felt like it was going to split into two pieces; deep down, she knew that it wasn't fair to anyone. Jane desperately looked for a doorway out and when she found nothing, decided to buy some time. "Elliot, I can't make any promises right now, but I can tell you one thing. Even though I care for you a great deal, I can't handle anymore bullshit."

Elliot rose from the bench and squatted down in the sand in front of her. Taking her hands in his, he looked up into her green eyes. "Maybe you can't make me any promises, but I can make one to you. I promise you this, Jane, it'll never happen again. I'm really sorry. You just have to believe me."

CHAPTER THIRTY-TWO

Elliot hummed softly to himself as he prepared for bed. The evening had definitely gone better than he had hoped. He had been preparing for the ultimate brush off. Sorry, Elliot, you really blew it this time. What you did was unforgivable. I never want to see you or to speak to you again.

Instead, Jane was willing to give him one more chance, and he was intent on making it good. He would show her that there was more to him than most people gave him credit for. He could change. He could learn to trust her. Or at least, he would try, and that was surely a good sign. Wasn't it?

A groggy voice interrupted his thoughts, "Hey, man, I'm trying to sleep."

"Sorry." Elliot sat down on his bed and tossed his jeans into the corner of the room. He stretched out onto his back and stared up into the darkness.

"That's it, man? No details?"

Elliot rolled over onto his side. "Nope. No details. What'd you do tonight?"

"Nothing, man. I did nothing."

"Goodnight, Nick," Elliot concluded and shut his eyes. His thoughts drifted into a quiet space where he and Jane walked, hand in hand, smiling and laughing. Jane's long, blonde hair fell over her shoulders in a silky caress.

Nick glared into the darkness, his smile long since abandoned.

CHAPTER THIRTY-THREE

With Elliot at least temporarily appeased, if not her own heart, Jane felt certain that she would survive. Six more weeks, tops. Five, if she finished her work early.

Jane riffled through the stacks of files, making one stack of papers to microfilm and one to shred. Her office was beginning to look like the rooftops of England in *Mary Poppins*. Piles of paper smoke stacks stood in every corner.

At the beginning of the summer, Jane had mailed the films every day for processing, and they returned in about a week. Since the microfilmed papers could not be shredded until the processed film had been returned and checked, it had taken a couple of weeks to get into a steady rhythm of paper in and paper out. Then her boss had decided that Jane should send the films for processing in allotments of ten to save on the cost of postage. Instead of spending the last hour of the day shredding papers, the smoke stacks had become more and more numerous. Jane was, quite literally, running out of room and, since the information was confidential, all of the papers needed to be kept under lock and key. Jane decided that if the last bunch of films did not return soon, she would be scavenging for a handy storage closet.

A soft knock sounded at her office door. "Come in," she called.

"Jane," one of the other workers peeked around the corner of her door, "there's a gentleman here to see you. Can you spare a moment?"

"I suppose so," Jane walked out into the outer office where four other women worked. "Nick, what brings you down to the coal mines?" Nick. Odd. Not the last person she expected to see at her office but pretty damned close. She walked towards him.

"Is there someplace we could talk in private for a minute?" His eyes glanced around at the other women and then back to Jane.

Jane nodded. "Sure. The cafeteria is just down one floor." Jane turned to a pretty red-head who had sat back down at a nearby desk. "I'm going to take a quick break if that's okay with you. I'll be back in a couple of minutes if anyone needs me."

"Okay." The red-head smiled then returned her attention to

her own collection of papers, the hustle and bustle of her own set of duties.

"Just a sec, Nick." Jane indicated for him to wait as she grabbed her purse from her office. "Okay, follow me." Jane gestured and walked past Nick. He followed. Jane truly liked Nick. He was one of those guys a person could really depend on to be there when you needed him. More than once, in her younger years, he had bailed her out of a tight squeeze when she was too drunk or too stoned to make any rational decisions, let alone find her way home. He had dropped her off at her doorstep, safe and sound. No harm. No foul.

Jane purchased a cup of coffee from the cafeteria's vending machine. "Mind if we go outside to the picnic tables? There's no smoking in the hospital, and I could really use a nicotine boost."

"Yeah man, that's cool," he agreed amiably.

Jane hesitated. "Did you want a coffee or a tea? Maybe something cold to drink?"

"Nope. I'm good. Just need to talk to you for a bit. Lead the way."

"All right." Jane walked through the cafeteria to the outside door that led to the patio, the only approved smoking area for the multitude of hospital employees who were all an integral part of running and of maintaining the excellent service provided in the seven-storey, 200 bed secondary service referral centre. Jane glanced around trying to decide on the best spot for privacy. Another hour, when it was a scheduled break time, and the picnic tables would be full. Obviously, health care providers were just as predisposed to addictions as the general populace.

Jane sat down at the farthest table from the entrance. "How come you're not at work today?" Jane extracted a cigarette from her purse, lit it, and then tilted her head back slightly to bask in the warmth of the sun. The day was going to be gloriously warm and sunny. Jane wished for the hundredth time that she could be lying on a beach instead of stuck inside all day. Almost August and barely tanned. Blasphemy, no doubt. Maybe it was time to try a tanning bed to catch up a bit. Jane was pretty sure there was a tanning salon at the mall and decided to check it out after work. A full body tan would be well worth the money. Very cool. Very sexy.

"Off sick," Nick answered.

Jane focused her attention back on Nick. "You don't look sick."

"No, I'm okay now, man, but when I woke up this morning, I had a serious head-banger."

Jane nodded her sympathies. "Hangovers can be a bitch." She watched as a nurse exited through the hospital patio door. She leaned forward, conspiratorially, so that she could speak to Nick without being heard by the people at the tables next to them. "Do you see that tall, slender brunette nurse carrying the dish of cottage cheese?"

Nick turned around only long enough to get a quick look. He turned back to Jane. "Yeah."

"She's a he." Jane sipped her coffee and tapped the ashes from her cigarette into a metal ashtray, one of several that had been left on the picnic tables in the vain hope that the patio wouldn't end up littered by cigarette butts.

Nick shook his head in confusion. "Excuse me?"

Jane nodded, smiling impishly. "She's really a man. He's in the process of having a sex change. I didn't believe it either when the ladies I work with told me, but it's true. By three o'clock in the afternoon, I swear, if you look really close, he has the start of a five o'clock shadow. Rumour has it that he's gone through with the breast implants, but that he still has a penis." Jane took a long, lazy draw from her cigarette, waiting for Nick's reaction. He didn't disappoint her.

Nick stared back at Jane, his eyes wide open. "I don't remember seeing her...him...her around here before, man." Nick looked seriously perplexed.

"That makes sense." The coffee was bitter, but the caffeine was definitely welcomed. For a second, Jane wondered if she could live without either substance—caffeine or nicotine—or if she'd always remain chronically dependent on the chemicals like millions of others before her. "He's not from here. I've talked to him a couple of times. When I work weekends I'm by myself, and if someone needs a copy of an older medical history that's on microfilm, I have to track that down. Then I have to take it to the ward clerk who has put in the request. He works in one of the surgical units. I'm pretty sure that he said that he was originally from someplace in Saskatchewan.

He moved here so that he could go through the surgery without anyone knowing that he wasn't a she. I can understand that. I mean, it'd be pretty tough to do the transition in your own hometown. Can you imagine?"

"Wild." Nick nodded. "Man, you read about this kind of thing, but you don't expect it to happen here, man. Wow. Unbelievable."

Jane inhaled deeply from her cigarette, blew out the smoke away from Nick and glanced down at her watch. "Speaking of unbelievable, I only have five minutes left before my break is over, and you still haven't told me what's so important that you couldn't have called me at home later." Without grace, Jane sneezed.

"Bless you. You okay?"

Jane nodded. "Thanks. I'm not quite sure if it's allergies or if I'm coming down with something. Anyway, go on." Jane placed her diminishing cigarette in a notch of the ashtray and rooted through her purse in search of a tissue.

"I just wondered if everything was okay between you and Elliot." Nick's eyes followed the brunette nurse as she/he sat chatting with a female co-worker.

Jane blew her nose and sniffed. "Great. Couldn't be better." Jane smiled. She understood the bond between twins. As far back as she could remember, the two had done almost everything together, including teasing her years ago when she was just a kid. When Jane was very young, seven or eight, she loved to visit her grandmother who lived in Donnybrooke. Grams always gave Jane money for a treat at the variety store and would tell her that Jane could walk the half block by herself, but that she had to come straight back. On her way back with her goodies in tow, the twins would inevitably appear out of nowhere. It was like they had built in radar. They would ride on their bikes towards her at full speed, then swerve, just missing her. She'd be fuming. They would be laughing. It was like playing double indemnity, only Nick was basically harmless. He just seemed to follow whatever Elliot did.

"Are you and Elliot going out tonight after the game?" Nick

enquired.

Jane shook her head. "Between this stupid allergy thing and my period starting this morning, I'm good for a hot bath and a warm bed." Jane glanced down at her watch again. "Nick, I hate to cut this short, but my time is almost up." She stubbed out her cigarette and left the butt in the ashtray. "If I don't get back, I'll have to make up the time after four o'clock and, believe me, I'd rather not." She stood up, finished drinking her coffee and walked back into the hospital cafeteria. As they walked towards the blue cardboard recycling bin, Jane heard a familiar voice come up from behind her. Jane tossed the crumpled cup into the proper bin and turned around.

"Hi, Jane." Samantha smiled wistfully at Nick as if Jane wasn't there. "Who's your good-looking friend?" Her eyes roamed up and down Nick's muscular body, appraising him.

"Samantha, this is Nick. Nick, this is Samantha." Jane made the introductions. As they shook hands, Jane noticed the small scrap of paper that Samantha had passed to Nick and smiled, satisfied. The woman was so predictable.

Nick swallowed and found his voice. He nodded to Samantha. "Nice meeting you, but I was just leaving." He turned to Jane. "Jane, I have to get to work." Nick grabbed Jane by the elbow and walked her out of the cafeteria. He shoved the crumpled piece of paper napkin into his pants pocket.

Jane teased. "I think you have an admirer." She fluttered her eyes at Nick in jest. "Did you catch the shadow?"

"Very funny, man." Nick did not look the least amused.

Jane tried on her sincerest face. "Hey, remember that you owe me one. That could have gotten very awkward."

Nick stopped in the hallway. "Yeah, man, no kidding." He retrieved the piece of napkin from his pocket and handed the scrap to Jane. "Dump this somewhere for me, okay, man?" He looked shaken. "And promise me that you won't tell Elliot. If you do, I'll never hear the end of it."

Jane raised her right hand. "Cross my heart and hope you die. Shove an elbow in your eye."

Nick nodded, lost in his own thoughts. "Thanks." He turned and walked quickly towards the nearest elevator.

Jane was still smiling as she returned to her mounds of paper. In fact, she was in better humour now than she'd been all day, allergies or no allergies, cramps or no cramps. Samantha had made it very clear, very early, that any and every man in the hospital was a part of her own personal territory. It didn't matter if he was a doctor or an orderly, married or single, the woman had one of the strongest sexual appetites on earth and every man was her game. Men, she had said, were like fine bottles of wine that needed the right type of woman to `pop' them. The only problem was that Samantha used, abused, and discarded men when their so-called bottles ran dry. Once she was done with the men in the hospital, Jane had no doubt that she would continue to forage forward out into the general populace.

Jane sneezed again. She closed the door to her office and turned on her iPod. Todd had uploaded all his favourite Nirvana and Doors songs which meant that he was secretly hoping to convert her to his taste in music. Jane softly sang along to the lyrics, humming when she didn't know the words and enjoying a peculiar sense of revenge. Samantha may be all woman, all of the time, but Nick didn't know that. It was a small town and rumours spread fast.

CHAPTER THIRTY-FOUR

The ballgame had been close until Nick missed an easy pop fly deep in centerfield that let two runs in. Any other time, he would have aced it. Not tonight. As a result, their team had lost by one run. Considering that they still needed at least two more wins to make the play-offs, Elliot was not impressed.

Elliot glared at his brother as they walked off the field. "What kind of catch do you call that? Ma could have done it with her eyes closed and both hands in her apron pockets."

"Fuck off, man. It's been a rough day." Nick glared back.

"Rough day? Rough day? Ma said that her precious Nick spent most of it lying on the couch with some sort of big, bad headache. Did you tell her that the big, bad headache's name was draft?"

Nick walked around to the back of Elliot's car. He waited for Elliot to open the trunk so that he could throw in his sports equipment. "Look, man, I fucked up one catch all season, and you'd swear I'd just committed armed robbery or something."

Elliot opened the trunk and tossed in his duffel bag. He waited for Nick to do the same, then closed the trunk. "Now is not the time of year to be screwing around out there. You'll end up getting benched."

Without a word, Nick walked around to the passenger side of the car and climbed in.

Cars full of players and fans pulled out of their parking spots and headed off in a trail of tail-lights.

Elliot joined Nick but did not start the car. He rolled down his window and rested his elbow on the edge. The crickets were out in full harmony, still singing the song of summer. The ball field lights clicked off, leaving them in darkness. Maybe he had come down too hard on Nick. One catch was not the end of the world. "Sorry, Nick. I just want to make the play-offs this year. That's all."

"Yeah man, no problem."

"Do you feel up to driving into Owen Sound to grab a beer?" Peace offering.

"Sure."

They drove the ten kilometres to the bar in silence. Nick

played with the stations on the radio, trying to find something that he liked. When he couldn't, he sifted through Elliot's CD collection until he came across a Rolling Stones album that he was fond of. He shoved the disc into the player, leaned back and closed his eyes.

Buck's Hot Spot was crowded by Friday night partiers including some of the guys on both their team and the opposing team, still decked out in their uniforms. Elliot sauntered up to the female bartender and ordered two beers. He felt several good-natured pats on his shoulder with a brief "good game" spoken afterwards. He nodded each time and told the opposing team members that they had just been lucky, that they would slaughter them in the play-offs. This provoked good-natured laughs and "we'll see" responses.

When his order finally arrived, Elliot turned around to discover that Gertie, who was in the process of trying to find room to place an order herself, blocked him. "Hey, Gertie is Jane with you tonight?" he asked.

"Trade you spots," Gertie suggested.

"Sure." Elliot nodded, raised his bottles to shoulder height, tucking them close to his body, turned sideways and edged away from the bar so Gertie could squeeze her way past him. "Is Jane here?" he asked again.

Gertie crawled into the space he had just left behind and hailed the bartender. "Nope. I called her to see if she wanted to come, but she said that she wasn't feeling well."

Elliot smiled. So, Jane really was sick after all. Good. "Catch ya later."

"Sure. Save a dance for me." Gertie turned and placed her order.

Nick had held back, standing just inside the front door. He looked like an assistant bouncer. Elliot handed him one of the beers. "Come on, let's grab a seat."

Nick shook his head. "I'd rather stand, man."

They found a spot at a stand-up table and watched Wilson and the Tectonic Plates perform--guys with long hair and skin-tight pants trying to act sexy. It seemed to be working. Elliot watched as two, young women, both also dressed in skin-tight jeans and trying to get noticed, did everything imaginable to gain the favour of the bass guitarist. They bought him drinks. They preened and strutted as close to the stage as possible. They called him over twice under the guise of special requests. Once within reach, they caressed his bare arms and giggled. What amazed Elliot was how cool the musician was. He smiled and carried on. Tough gig.

Must be absolute hell to have sex-crazed, pheromone-oozing women drooling all over you. Women, who would be more than willing to fulfill any and every fantasy the musician could dream up, and probably a few he would never even think of, just so that the little darlings could text twenty of their closest friends that they had sex with the bass guitarist from the up and coming rock group.

As the band wound its way down towards a ten-minute break, Elliot noticed Buck MacAdangdang's entrance into his establishment. He's okay once you get past the flash, Jane had said. Elliot had another opinion. As far as he could tell, flash was all that man ever had.

Even back in high school, Buck had never tried to fit in. His parents belonged to the exceedingly small, elite club of the seriously rich people in the harbour city and Buck gloated in that fact. They lived in a monstrous house on millionaire's drive, had extravagant, lavishly catered parties and thoroughly enjoyed flaunting their good fortune. Opting for public instead of private school, Buck had worn designer everything from the clothing on his back to the cheerleader on his arm. Buck drove to school every day in his brand new car and pulled into his reserved parking space (made possible by a generous donation from his father). As far as Elliot was concerned, nothing had changed. Buck had gone off to college and had come home the same. Flash. That was Buck. Take it or leave it. Elliot elbowed Nick and nodded towards Buck.

"Must be nice to have that much money," Elliot commented. Buck looked David Bowie cool, but all business, in his beige silk business suit.

Nick grumbled, "Man, did he see you? I can never understand a word he says. Every time I talk to him, it makes me feel dirty, man. Like, go home and have a shower kind of dirty."

Elliot chuckled. "Act cool. He's coming over."

Nick took a long draw from his beer. "You act cool, man. The less I say, the less stupid I'll feel."

Buck greeted the two with a large, open smile. "Well, look who's here! So nice of you to grace my establishment with your presence this evening. Are you enjoying the band?"

Elliot nodded. "Jane recommended them. Said they were great."

"They are irrefragably daedal, I must admit, although the bass guitarist is a bit of a miscreant. Speaking of Jane, how is my favourite denizen, my innocuous angel? I'd trade her in a millisecond for that malevolent harridan I married."

While Nick dove deeper into his bottle, Elliot decided to forage ahead. "Jane's okay, just a bit under the weather tonight. I'll say one thing, Buck, you've really done all right for yourself. You have the hottest club in the area."

Buck nodded and smiled. "I am but a scion wishing for an insouciant existence." He gestured towards his surroundings with his right hand. "This place was given to me by my parents as a bibelot of affection for their oft proclaimed fatuous offspring. How sapient was their decision, only time will tell, but I am not as supercilious as they may believe. No, my friend, I have become a votary to this business, and if I become a wunderkind, it will definitely be due to my obsession and to their complete and utter astonishment. Sadly, I must take my leave now and perambulate. With such an obstreperous crowd, it's a wise owner who aggrandizes his own presence before their good humour metamorphoses into drunken vituperation."

As Buck sauntered away, Nick sighed. "Man, did you understand a word he said?"

Elliot nodded. "About half, which means either Buck's finally too busy to read the dictionary or that he's having an off day."

As the evening progressed, Elliot grew increasingly aware of his brother's quiet mood. Long periods of silence were as much unlike Nick as the lack of thunder was to lightning storms—a rare occurrence at best. Elliot elbowed his brother and pointed to two pretty women headed their way. "Hey, little brother, maybe we can get some action for you tonight. Look at the tits on the brunette. Nice."

Nick chugged the remainder of the beer that he'd been

nursing. He turned, leaned his back against the stand-up table and motioned to a hovering waitress that a refill was required.

"Hi, Handsome. Long time no see." The brunette placed herself directly in front of Nick. Her friend stood off to the side.

"Hi," Nick managed, looking more annoyed than captivated by his good fortune.

Elliot stretched his neck so he could see past the brunette. "Hey, Nick, aren't you going to introduce me to your friend?"

"Samantha, this is my brother, Elliot. Elliot this is Samantha," Nick said placidly. When the waitress returned with his order, Nick dug a twenty dollar bill out of his blue-on-blue uniform pants pocket, paid for both bottles of beer and handed one bottle to Elliot.

Samantha turned around to face Elliot, her eyes tauntingly playful. "Wow, twins. Double the pleasure." She licked her lips seductively. She motioned to the other girl. "This is my friend, Amy."

Amy waved her glass. "Hi." She smiled at Elliot and then at Nick. "Sam, you didn't tell me that he was a twin."

Samantha began to caress Nick's arm. "Didn't know. Makes it more fun this way though don't you think?" Her short, black leather skirt revealed long, slender, muscular legs. Her bodice-laced top exposed a deep cleavage between round, voluptuous breasts. She placed herself close to Nick to make it almost impossible for him to move without touching her. "I just love a man in a uniform. I can think of all kinds of games we can play." She took Nick's beer and casually licked the neck of the bottle.

Elliot grinned. Maybe Nick had missed an easy catch but this would definitely make up for it. "How do you know my little brother?"

Nick grabbed Samantha's hand before she could answer and set his beer bottle down on the table. "Let's dance."

"Sure." She blew a kiss to Elliot before following Nick onto the crowded dance floor.

Elliot watched, amazed by the evening's turn of events. As far as he could remember, Nick hadn't made it past second base in months let alone with six feet of heavenly curves. Elliot could think of at least a dozen guys who would scramble over, if not go directly through, each other for the mere chance of claiming bragging rights on this one. Not that he was all that into locker room gossip, but he knew that there had to be something seriously wrong with any man who didn't at least try to picture Samantha naked. So why, then, hadn't Nick mentioned her to him? Nothing. Not one syllable.

"Do you want to dance too?" Amy enquired shyly without the dramatics.

Elliot put down his beer. "Why not?" He pointed towards Samantha as he watched his brother dance. "Your friend is really something else."

Amy nodded and placed her half-finished drink on the table with the others. "She usually gets what she's after."

"And she's after my little brother?" Elliot's eyebrows raised in quiet puzzlement. He was definitely missing something here and the lack of knowledge irritated him like a clothing tag that itched and scratched until you tore off your shirt to pull the tag out, no longer caring if you couldn't remember whether or not the garment needed to be washed in warm or cold water. He and Nick had an unspoken vow of brotherly disclosure. He and Nick told each other everything.

Always had. Nothing could change that. Or could it?

Amy shrugged. "Looks like it. She's been watching him since you both walked in."

"How come?"

"Probably waiting to see if he had a date."

Elliot nodded, well aware that the art of sexual stalking was a game played by both sexes. "What about you?"

Amy smiled as they made their way onto the dance floor. "To tell you the truth, I'm not here to pick up men, just to dance. My boyfriend is out of town so it was either this or sit at home, watch TV and pout."

"Then you and I will get along just fine. My girlfriend is at home, sick," Elliot confided.

Amy grinned. "Then why are you here?"

"Like the lady said, I'm just here to dance." Elliot watched as the one groupie took off her t-shirt to reveal a skimpy bathing suit top or at least he assumed it was a bathing suit top. She bent over in front of the guitarist to flaunt her breasts--one of which was tattooed with a small, red heart. The guitarist smiled and bounced off, stage left.

As the music slowed down, Elliot moved closer to Nick so that he could see what was happening. Samantha was doing her best to massage every part of Nick's body with every part of her own. She kissed his neck while pressing her hips close to his. Nick, who looked like he wanted to crawl out of his skin, was attempting to put breathing room in between them.

When they were close enough, Elliot tried to finish his previous conversation with Samantha. "So, how did the two of you meet?"

Samantha looked towards Elliot, keeping her cheek pressed against Nick's. "Jane introduced us." She massaged the small of Nick's back with her hands and kissed Nick on the cheek. "Remind me to send her a thank you card." Nick took Samantha's hand and guided her further into the center of the dancers.

Curiosity unappeased, Elliot worked his way around an obviously happy couple to catch up. "You work with Jane?"

"Not exactly. I'm a nurse, but I see her around the hospital and we've talked occasionally." Samantha snuggled closer to Nick, grinding her pelvis into his groin and holding him close with her left-hand firmly planted on his rear.

Nick enclosed Samantha's hand with his larger one, extricated himself from her frontal attack and tried, once again, to get lost in the crowd.

Elliot grunted under his breath as he tried to follow and was waylaid by a couple who moved in between. At this point, Elliot bemoaned, the errant couple would have been better off in one of their bedrooms instead of making out on the dance floor. It was like trying to get out from underneath a bouncing bed. He would move left. So would they. He would move right. So would they. How they managed this exact timing was beyond him, especially since they were both totally engrossed in each other's body parts. Amy finally rescued Elliot by taking him by the hand and ungraciously bumping and excusing their way past.

"Thanks." He winked at Amy.

She smiled. "Sometimes, you just have to take the direct approach."

Elliot caught up to Samantha once more. "So, when did Jane introduce you to Nick?"

"Elliot, would you shut up, man? We're trying to dance and you keep breaking the rhythm." He twirled Samantha around so that he would be on Elliot's side instead of her.

Elliot frowned, exasperated. "Just trying to be friendly." The next song began. Elliot casually maneuvered Amy around so that he was back within talking distance to Samantha who was busy placing small kisses on Nick's very closed mouth. Her hands had worked their way back down to his buttocks where they massaged and caressed.

"Were you guys all at the same party or something?" Elliot continued, unabashed. He noticed the tattooed woman handing the bass guitarist a note. The musician smiled and nodded. The groupie beamed at her friend and did a thumbs up sign. Aw yes, Elliot thought, blow job after this set. Tough gig.

Samantha glared back at him. "If I tell you, will you quit pestering us? We're trying to get acquainted, if you know what I mean. Unless, of course, you want to go somewhere and party together." She ran her perfectly manicured fingernails softly down Elliot's cheek. "I've never fucked twins at the same time. Could be interesting."

Elliot angrily pulled her hand away from his face. "And you're not going to start now. Just answer the question!" Enough was enough.

Before she could, Nick grabbed Samantha's face forcing her head in his direction and kissed her long and deep. After a minute, he pulled back and took Samantha by her hand. "Let's split. We can party somewhere else. Elliot, give me your car keys, man. You can grab a ride home with one of the other guys."

Startled, Elliot dug into his pocket without a second thought and tossed the keys to Nick.

"Here."

The uncharacteristic fierceness of Nick's eyes did not abate. "Did it ever occur to you, man, that the only problem I have with women is you?"

As Elliot watched his brother practically drag Samantha off the dance floor and out of the bar, the shock of Nick's words hit home. Maybe, Nick was right. Maybe, he didn't give Nick enough credit. Elliot couldn't wait to get the details later, once his little brother had settled down some, although he wondered if Nick had just bitten off more than he could chew. He turned towards Amy. "So, are you a friend of Jane's too?"

"No, actually I'm Samantha's neighbour."

"Oh."

"Do you want me to give you a ride home later?"

Elliot nodded. "Thanks."

Nick drove while Samantha fondled his genitals. She had pulled his penis out of his pants, desperately attempting to transform his member from a wet noodle into a solid rock. Nick kept both of his hands on the steering wheel and gritted his teeth. Safely outside of town, on a darkened road, Nick eased off the gas, pulled over and stopped Elliot's car on the gravel shoulder.

Samantha looked up. "Why are we stopping here? I thought we were going back to your place." She cooed, "Can't wait, Sugar?"

"Get out," he told her, his face hard, blank of emotion.

"What?" Samantha hastily let go of Nick's penis and, eyes full of disbelief, sat back in her seat.

"I said, get the fuck out of the car!" Nick reached down, readjusted himself and zippered up his ball pants.

Anger took over as Samantha fought to understand her current situation. "You're serious? You fucking bastard! You can't just leave me out here in the middle of fucking nowhere and fucking drive off! Are you insane?"

"Look...Samantha...Sam... Whoever, whatever you are. Just get the fuck out and leave me alone. Leave me alone. Leave Elliot alone. Leave Jane alone. If you see me again, you don't know me. You tell Elliot or anyone else anything about this and I'll fucking hunt you down and kill you. Do I make myself clear?"

Samantha swallowed and nodded.

"Just use your cell phone and have one of your friends pick you up or call a cab for all I care. Tell them you're at the corner of Grey Road 18 and Grey Road 5. They can punch that into their GPS and find you. Just get the fuck out!" Nick shouted. "Be gone, bitch!"

Dumbfounded and frightened but more angry than

anything else, Samantha opened the car door. "I don't know what your problem is, you impotent fag, but you can all go to fucking hell for all I fucking care!" She slammed the door and stormed off into the dark.

Nick watched in the rear view mirror as Samantha walked away, the car's rear lights temporarily illuminating her way. She...he was walking back to town. Nick spun back out onto the road, gravel spraying in the car's wake, and sped down the road as fast as the car would take him.

Five minutes later, he pulled over onto the shoulder of the road again. This time, he was the one who got out of the car. Stumbling into the ditch, he dropped down to his knees and vomited.

CHAPTER THIRTY-FIVE

Two weeks later, Jane's allergies had transformed from the occasional sneeze and sniffle to a fever and a complex assortment of ailments from aching muscles to an agonizingly tight chest cough. Her doctor had diagnosed bronchitis, prescribed an antibiotic, lots of clear fluids, a humidifier at night and rest. Jane was definitely not impressed.

"Are you still planning on going to the ball tournament dance on Saturday night?" Gertie enquired as the two relaxed in her psychedelic living room, smoking a joint and listening to David Bowie's Scary Monster album, an oldie but a favourite.

The drugs were definitely not helping her cold, but, on the other hand, they were numbing some of the pain. Jane lay back on the blue loveseat, staring at the ceiling. "I'm planning on it if I'm not too sick."

"Are you going with Elliot?" Gertie pulled herself out of her armchair to change the CD and refill her drink.

Jane covered her mouth as a cough racked her body. "Shit." She sat up and sipped on her brandy in the attempt to control the spasms. "Probably not."

"Want a refill?" Gertie offered. "You're the only one who drinks brandy, so you might as well finish the bottle before summer ends."

"Sure." Jane handed her brandy snifter to Gertie to allow her friend to top off her drink.

"Want to smoke another joint?" Gertie asked as she poured the dark amber liquid.

Jane shook her head as another cough took over. "Somehow, I don't think it's helping." She attempted to smile at her friend which was lost to the reality of Jane's physiological distress. She accepted the glass back and sipped at the brandy until the coughing subsided back to its cave of impending horrors.

Gertie, her warm blue eyes full of concern, studied her friend closely as she sat back down in the armchair. "Jane, you look like crap. You should be in bed."

Jane nodded. "No shit." God, how she abhorred being sick; she had neither the time nor the patience for her body betraying her to this extent. "You're probably right, but this is way more fun than sleeping." Jane smiled and took a cigarette out of its package. She lit the cigarette, inhaled deeply and prayed that the smoke wouldn't initiate another coughing spell.

"So, how come you're not going to the dance with Elliot?" Gertie leaned forward and rolled another joint for herself, her tanned, nimble fingers deft at their task.

"It depends on if they win, on what time they would have to play their next game etc. etc. I've seen games go until one a.m., and I'm not missing the dance." Jane tapped her ashes into a shared, cut-glass ashtray. The expectorant that the pharmacist had suggested was finally starting to work. Jane cleared her throat, the phlegm feeling like a hairball waiting patiently to be dislodged and yacked up onto the floor. Once the mucus loosened and started moving, it would be so much better. Gross, but better. "It's the best excuse for a drunk this hick town can offer. Are you taking Ted?"

Gertie shook her blonde head and frowned as she finished rolling and lit the joint.

"Nope. Ted's done." She inhaled deeply, leaned back in her chair and closed her eyes as if savouring the taste, the aroma, the numbness.

Surprised, Jane pushed for more details. "What? When? I thought you said that Ted was God's gift incarnate to women?" Jane continued to sip her brandy. The warmth flowed through her like hot fingers tracing nerve pathways. All she needed now was a pillow, a humidifier and about forty hours of sleep and she would wake up a brand new person. Well, maybe not brand new but at least like someone who didn't feel like she'd been beaten up and tossed into a ditch to die.

Gertie opened her eyes again and corrected, "What I said was that the sex was really good."

"Same thing," Jane concluded. "So, what was it this time—a sixth toe on his right foot, a Gideon bible stashed in his bedside nightstand? I swear you go out of your way to look for faults just so you can have an exit strategy. You do know, on some rational level, that the perfect man is just a myth. Don't you?" Coughing into her sleeve, Jane stubbed out her cigarette in the ashtray. Okay, then maybe she could get by with just a half cigarette occasionally, until the worst of the bronchitis was over. She needed to be healthy again in time for school. Please God, just make it go away and I promise I'll behave. Well, maybe not totally behave, that would be boring, but everything's up for negotiation. Right?

"Of course I do, but you seriously need to wonder about a guy whose all-time, prized possession is a t-shirt that says, 'I got off at Wanker's Corner, Oregon'. Jane, he actually has the t-shirt mounted on the wall in his bedroom." Gertie's look of exasperation contorted her fine facial features.

Jane giggled, "That's actually kind of cute."

"Fine, then you can date him." Gertie deeply inhaled the smoke again and held her breath before exhaling fine filaments.

"I kind of have my hands full enough right now, thank you very much. However, I will keep Ted in mind just in case an opening becomes available in the future." Jane lay back down on the loveseat and faced the ceiling. She fluffed the matching pillow under her head.

Gertie exhaled the remainder of smoke from her lungs. "I'm sure he'd appreciate that. He thinks you're extremely doable, even inquired about the possibility of a threesome a couple of times."

"No way!" Jane exclaimed. It wouldn't be the first time she'd been asked, but she couldn't picture Ted suggesting it.

"Yes, way." Gertie nodded. "Doesn't matter now though. You know who I'd like to take to the dance?" Gertie leaned forward and put the remnants of the joint in the ashtray to burn itself out.

"No, who?"

"Mitchell Whelan." Gertie drew her darkly tanned legs up in front of her, snuggling into the oversized armchair.

A moment passed as the name registered. "Umm…Gertie, I can give you ten very good reasons not to take Mitchell Whelan." Perplexed, Jane gently bent back the thumb of her left hand. "Number one, he's married."

Gertie nodded. "Right, but his wife always introduces him as her present husband so there's a chance that they'll split up."

"About as much chance as you walking through the mall in Owen Sound and randomly bumping into Went Milner," Jane emphasized her point. The last thing she wanted Gertie to do was to get between Mitchell and his wife. That was just asking for trouble.

"Need I remind you," Gertie interjected, smiling, "that we're not staying here and that I'm going to be studying film? There is a very good chance that Went Milner will someday go to Toronto to attend either the Toronto Film Festival or the Indy Film Festival? All I have to do is to keep applying to work or to volunteer at the festivals or to put in a film submission of my own, then there's a very good chance that I could meet Went. All kinds of famous, American actors show up at the meet and greet. Or, I could contact him directly with a fantastic idea and see if he'd be interested in collaborating. Or, he may come to Canada to act in a movie that I just might be working on. I could then, theoretically, bump into him on the set. Or, maybe Dylan will end up working with him, and he could introduce us. "

"Wow, you've obviously been thinking this through. Point to you. If that's your plan then you'd better start working on a screenplay that's either worth submitting to the film festivals or worth collaborating on, or so totally awesome that you can find a Canadian producer to back you who thinks that Went would be perfect for the lead role. You may also want to let Dylan know so he can start auditioning for any parts that may lead to a supporting role in any production that Went has already been signed to act in." Chagrined, Jane released her thumb and pressed the tips of her index fingers together. "Number two, is Mitchell's wife. How well do you actually know Kelly?"

"About as much as I want to. I know she's probably the skankiest bar waitress in Grey and Bruce. When I first moved up here from Kitchener, I'd cover the occasional shift at the tavern if one of the regular waitresses called in sick or needed a night off. I pulled a few shifts with Kelly. Talk was that she's slept with half the men around here just so she can threaten to tell their wives. Comes in handy when Mitchell works in Toronto during the week and Kelly needs something done at home. Need a tap fixed, fuck a plumber."

Jane rolled over onto her side to face Gertie directly. She needed her friend to understand. "Yeah, but not only is she skanky, she's more than slightly psychotic when she's drunk."

"Good to know." Unfazed, Gertie bent forward and

retrieved her drink from the coffee table. She leaned back, drained half and crunched an ice cube between her teeth.

Jane continued. "Number three, they have a child. We have a female honour code here. All married men with small children are off limits as dates to local dances unless their dates happen to be their wives. Check your handbook if you don't believe me."

"But, I love kids," Gertie interrupted, not yet persuaded.

"I thought you hated children."

Gertie shook her head slowly. "I don't hate children. I just don't want any of my own. Mitchell and Kelly's daughter is adorable. Pre-made, toilet trained. Doesn't get any better than that."

"You seriously don't want to meet Mr. Right someday and have a baby?" Jane thought she knew everything about her friend. Guess not. Jane covered her face with her crooked arm to isolate another wayward cough. She wasn't absolutely positive that she was contagious, but good manners dictated proper coughing etiquette regardless. No use Gertie getting sick as well.

Gertie paused briefly, trying to formulate a suitable answer. "It's more like I just shouldn't be around babies, so it's better that I don't have one."

"Meaning what?" Jane retrieved her glass of brandy and took a sip.

Gertie tilted her head forward, lowering her eyes, and ran the tip of her right index finger around the top edge of her drinking glass. "Meaning that my first urge when I hold a baby is to toss it."

"Toss as in literally throw the child?" Jane stared at Gertie, not entirely sure that she had just heard her friend correctly.

Gertie nodded and looked back up again. She finished her drink and placed the glass on the coffee table. "Toss as in I get thinking how easy it would be to physically hurt babies because they're so vulnerable. Then a part of me actually wants to hurt the baby for that very same reason."

"You're not kidding, are you?" Jane loved Gertie like a sister, but she wasn't quite sure how to process this new information. All she did know, by the way Gertie was behaving, was that her normally light-hearted, fun-loving, quick-witted buddy was very close to admitting having homicidal tendencies.

Gertie slowly shook her head, a frown playing the corners of her mouth. "Jane, I would seriously never joke around about something so heinous and so socially unacceptable. The bigger part of me never wants to hurt a child so, only under extreme circumstances where there is absolutely no alternative, will I actually hold one."

"Older children are okay, just not babies?"

"Right."

Jane decided to give her friend the benefit of the doubt. "Gertie, I think we all have times when we struggle between good and evil, just some of us struggle on different levels. I love you, so I would never want to put you into that position. If I ever have a child, I definitely won't ask you to babysit for the first three years."

Gertie's face brightened as she smiled. "Thank you. Look, I know it sounds really horrible and, just so you know, you're the only person I've ever told this, but it's not like I'm a sociopath. I don't go around mutilating kittens and puppies just for fun. I should probably seek counselling to figure out where the urge comes from, but I've just always been like this so I deal with it my own way. I stay away from babies. My Mr. Right would be a man who already has a couple of kids and doesn't want any more."

Jane sat back up on the loveseat and nodded. "Okay, I understand. I'm just thinking that Kelly's not going to just hand over her daughter and her husband to you because you don't want to have a baby and because you've got the hots for Mitchell." Jane reached down to relight the cigarette she'd extinguished just moments before. She made a mental note to pick up a package of nicotine gum to help out with the cravings until she felt better. She inhaled deeply, preparing herself for the coughing to begin again.

Gertie sighed. "Oh, I know that, but if my plan to meet Went Milner doesn't pan out in the next five years, Mitchell's the closest to a Tami Hoag man I've ever met."

"Tami Hoag as in Tami Hoag, the writer?" Jane asked. She was beginning to a worry about her friend's ability to live in reality. Maybe Gertie had inherited the fixation with unattainable men from her mom after all. Or maybe, it was just Gertie's way of grieving the loss of another relationship. Only time would tell.

Gertie rose from her chair. "Want another drink?" she

asked Jane.

Jane shook her head. "No, I'm good."

"Okay." Gertie walked into her kitchenette and talked loudly as she poured herself another round. "The guys in Tami Hoag's books tend to be these tough-guy, teddy-bears who just need to meet the right woman."

"Kind of like the guys in the books by Nora Roberts," Jane offered. Jane hadn't read any books by Ms. Hoag; however, her mother was a huge Nora Roberts fan who was constantly giving her and Pam the books to read after she'd finished.

Gertie walked back into the living room and sat back down in her chair. Her demeanor had completely changed with the change of subject like fresh air blowing through an open window. "Oh, I love Nora Robert's men too. The couples end up having mind-altering sex unlike any experience the woman has ever known before, transcending human consciousness and ultimately discovering the real meaning of existence in itself. Otherwise known as the Big Bang. But Tami's men are no slouches in the sex department either, like the misunderstood cowboy, J.D., in *Dark Paradise* who just needed to be handled gently then ridden hard. At the beginning, he was like just fuck me, use me, and abuse me and she was like, no I don't even like you…so you just know that, eventually, they will get it together, fall deeply in love and ride off into the sunset. It's a given."

Jane laughed. "If I could have my pick of any fictional man, it would definitely be Jack Sawyer from the book, *Black House*, by Stephen King and Peter Straub. I seriously fell in love with this guy. I had to literally keep reminding myself that the book was fiction and that Jack Sawyer only existed on paper. Weird, I know, but that's the bottom line here. There's a huge difference between curl-up-on-a-couch fiction and the men from Donnybrooke. This is real life not just some story made up to entertain the masses. I can't imagine having mind-altering sex with any man from around here or finding anyone even closely resembling J.D. or Jack Sawyer."

"So, you have mind-altering sex with Todd then?" Gertie asked and took a sip of her new drink.

"Todd's not from here. I don't know about mind-altering, but the guy does have some major moves."

Gertie grinned and nodded. "There you go. Mitchell's not from here either. He's originally from Toronto, but we're totally off-track now. I was about to make a point."

Confused and having totally lost track of where their conversation was going, Jane gestured with her hand for Gertie to carry on. "Oh. Okay, then feel free to continue."

"Thanks." Gertie tucked her legs back up onto the chair. "Like I was about to say, I was at a Halloween party a couple of years ago... you know the year that I dressed up as the Angel of Death...and Mitchell and Kelly were there. Mitchell was dressed up like a Vampire. Halfway through the night, he came up to me and told me that if I took off my cross necklace, he and I could be lovers for life. Kelly was busy flirting with every other guy around, so Mitchell and I ended up spending the rest of the party talking. Turns out that he's really intelligent, loves Shakespeare and Robert Frost. Who would have guessed that?"

Jane's heart sank. "Gertie, where's this sudden interest in Mitchell coming from?"

"Mitchell came into the tavern a few days ago while I was there," Gertie admitted, her blue eyes sparkled. "He bought me a drink and we got talking again. The chemistry between us is just so amazing that we kind of exchanged cell phone numbers and e-mail addresses. Toronto is only an hour away from Welland."

Jane's soul froze. She knew where this was going and hoped that, once Gertie was in school, away from the boredom of small town blues, her new-found infatuation with Mitchell would get left behind as well. "Okay then. That explains everything. The fates have decided, in their ultimate wisdom, that the two of you should end up together...but only if you don't meet Went Milner within the next five years...If you don't meet Went, then all you have to do is to make the first move on Mitchell, send him a sex-text and start up an affair on the side."

Gertie frowned. "Now you're being sarcastic."

Totally frustrated now, Jane stubbed out her cigarette once more and stood up to walk around the small living room. "Ya think? Gertie, give your head a shake. Mitchell Whelan has a reputation for being into guns and selling hard-drugs and his wife is a psychotic bitch from hell. Why in the world would you want to get involved in that?"

Gertie was undaunted. "Mitchell's okay. He married Kelly because she was pregnant. Now he's just trying to make the best out of a bad situation. He's not planning on staying with her forever."

Jane sighed, giving up. Nothing she could say would make any difference at this point. Gertie had her mind set and when Gertie set her mind on a man, she was like a heat-seeking missile. "Whatever. If it happens that you actually find yourself about to get involved with Mitchell...like sometime in the future when Kelly has found herself a better meal ticket... just make sure you have all of your ducks in a basket before you jump into the frying pan. That's all I'm saying. Seriously, you'd be better off to buy Ted a new t-shirt and fuck his brains out."

Gertie watched as Jane wound her way around the room. "Jane, Ted dumped me because I'm following you off to college this fall. He said that he didn't want a long distance relationship."

Jane crossed back over to the loveseat and sat back down to face her friend. "Ouch! Sorry. That sucks. Does he have any idea just how hard that course is to get into? It's not like they would take my personal recommendation. You made it in all on your own merit, Gertie."

"Doesn't matter to Ted."

"Okay then. So, forget men. To hell with all of them. We'll go to the dance together and get totally wasted." Jane extended her hand for Gertie to shake. "Deal?"

Gertie bent forward and shook Jane's hand. "Deal." Gertie inhaled and exhaled deeply. "What's new with Todd? Have you heard from him lately?"

"Yup." Jane, restless now, stood up and walked over to study a poster of a marijuana plant growing out of a crack in a city sidewalk. Behind the healthy, green plant was complete, black and white desolation--old warehouses with windows blackened or broken, a half-burned down building, street-dwellers scavenging through refuse and garbage cans in search of some significant treasure. "In fact, he called last night all excited about the new apartment. It's a two-bedroom--top half of a house--about fifteen minutes away from the college." Jane pulled her focus away from the poster. "Have you found a place yet?"

Gertie nodded. "Ted and I went down a couple of weeks ago, and I found a bachelor apartment that wasn't too bad. I think that's when reality set in for him. You know, three and a half hours driving down then three and a half hours driving back again."

"Forget Ted. His loss. At least we're all set housing-wise," Jane stated without enthusiasm. A few more weeks and she would be with Todd. A few more weeks and all of this would be behind her at last.

"You could at least sound happy. I'm the one who just got dumped, not you." Gertie grinned as she sipped her drink and tossed her legs over the side of her chair. "Speaking of being dumped, when are you planning on telling Elliot that it's over?"

The sigh that escaped from her mouth surprised Jane. She had been thinking about that very question ever since her telephone conversation with Todd. For the past two weeks all Elliot could talk about was things that they would do someday. Someday, he would take her to Walt Disney World or to Universal Studios. Someday, they would go for a long hike on the Niagara Escarpment. Someday, they would go to Toronto for dinner and a play. Someday.

Elliot. Todd. Elliot. Todd. Jane felt more torn than she could have possibly imagined. Elliot, the supreme pain in the ass, was becoming a wonderful friend, and a part of her wanted the some days to eventually become a reality. A part of her wanted to make love to him instead of always begging off with a goodnight kiss, saying that the timing wasn't right. A part of her knew that his patience was out of caring, as he never pushed for more. A part of her wanted to stay.

"Earth to Jane," Gertie interrupted Jane's train of thought. "You are going to tell him, right?"

Jane sauntered back to the loveseat. "Yeah, soon. I just have to find the right moment. But, right now, it's time to toddle off home to bed." Jane gathered her belongings and headed towards the door. "I'm exhausted."

Gertie followed. "You, okay?"

"Yup, just tired from spending half of the last night hacking. I didn't sleep much."

"You take care of yourself, do as the doctor orders and call me on Friday with the details for the dance. Okay?" Gertie opened the door to let Jane out.

"Will do."

As Jane drove home, she tried to picture herself telling Elliot that she had just made plans to live with another guy. She didn't like the scenario that played out in her head--Elliot's temper erupting, her fleeing in fear of his anger. She hated the thought of writing a Dear John letter, way too impersonal, but it seemed the lesser evil in a difficult situation. She willed her mind to be still. Scarlett O'Hara had the right idea. She would think about it tomorrow.

CHAPTER THIRTY-SIX

With the Friday night win under their belts, Elliot's team was scheduled to move on to the next round in the tournament. That was, of course, once the rain stopped. If the rain stopped. They had been impatiently waiting for an hour already, with no visible sign of reprieve. He watched the large drops pelt down onto his windshield. Ten more minutes and he was going to the tavern for a beer.

Seeing one of his teammates running towards his own car, Elliot rolled down his window and shouted, "Hey, what's going on out there?"

His teammate stopped, pulled his jacket over his head and veered towards Elliot. "All games have been postponed until three o'clock. They'll make a further decision then. I'm going for a beer. You coming?"

"You bet. Have you seen Nick?"

"Yeah. He's getting a hamburger at the booth."

"Thanks." Elliot waved and rolled up his window before the interior of his car had a chance to become as sodden as the rest of Donnybrooke. Figures. He couldn't remember a tournament yet that at least one game hadn't been rained out. He started the engine of his Camaro and drove over to the concession stand where Nick stood under the shelter of the overhang, eating, and chatting with various other team members. Elliot honked his horn to get his brother's attention. Nick nodded, said his farewells and raced towards Elliot.

He climbed into the car, still munching on a half-eaten burger. "What's up, man?"

"Watch the food." Elliot admonished his brother. "You have enough ketchup on that thing to drown a cow."

"Sorry, man." Nick readjusted his sitting position and shoved the remainder of the burger into his mouth. "Better?" he asked, his cheeks bulging. Small pieces of bun spewed from his mouth as he attempted to talk and chew at the same time.

Elliot glared and decided to ignore his brother's blatant attempt to either be funny or to become the victim of an untimely death. "Games are postponed until three. I'm going to the tavern for a beer. Do you want to come or not?"

Nick nodded in agreement as he tipped back a can of cola to wash down the bulging burger.

As the two began to drive out of the ball park, Elliot spotted Jane's car coming in. He honked his horn for her to stop. Elliot pulled up his vehicle alongside of her car and rolled down his window then waited for her to do the same. "The games are postponed until the rain lets up. We're going to the tavern."

Jane nodded. "Okay. We'll see you there." She rolled up her window and turned her car around to follow.

The local tavern was overflowing with would-be ball players and spectators all waiting to see if the games would eventually continue. Elliot found an empty table near the jukebox and sat down, followed by the rest of his slightly wet entourage. Elliot pulled out a chair for Jane to sit down next to him.

"Hey, Gertie." Nick plopped himself down on a chair beside her. "Are you going to the dance tonight?"

"Going to try my best." Gertie smiled, as she ran her fingers through her damp, blonde hair.

"Can I get you people something from the bar?" Kelly enquired, arriving just as the group began to settle in.

"Two lager." Elliot gestured towards Nick and himself then looked at Jane and Gertie. "And what would you ladies like?"

"You buying?" Gertie asked.

Elliot nodded. "Sure. First rounds on me." Life is good, he thought. Softball. Friends. Beer. Jane.

"Thanks, Elliot." Gertie turned towards the waitress. "Kelly, I'll have a rye and Coke," Gertie ordered, giving Kelly her best warm, friendly smile.

"Make mine a rum and ginger ale, lots of ice," Jane added. "So, Kelly, how's life treating you these days? How are Mitchell and Anna?"

Kelly looked worn and tired. Today would be a good day for tips though so there would be no going home until it was over. "Fine, thanks. Same old. Mitchell's only home long enough to get me knocked up again and then he's off somewhere getting drunk with the boys."

"Another baby. Congrats!" Jane glanced at Elliot. "Better

make sure you give her a good tip. Diapers are expensive." Smiling, Jane turned back to Kelly. "And Anna? She's what, three now? Another year and she'll be in pre-kindergarten. Right?"

Kelly nodded. "Anna's good. She's into everything these days." The conversation was cut short by other patrons vying for her attention. "Gotta run. It's a zoo in here today. I'll be right back with your drinks."

Once Kelly had left, Gertie looked at Jane questioningly. "I thought you were on antibiotics."

Jane nodded. "So?"

"So, you're not supposed to drink while on antibiotics."

"What are you on drugs for?" Elliot rose from the table to prop open the door that led to the covered patio and let some fresh air in.

Jane shrugged. "A slight touch of bronchitis. Nothing major." She grinned at Elliot as he returned. "God, Elliot, you have a short memory. I told you about this days ago."

"Oh yeah. Forgot." Elliot surveyed the room. Half of his team was there now. If the rain didn't stop by five o'clock, they'd be too drunk to play. Stewart Kirkland was a great coach who didn't hassle the players about a lot of things—boys will be boys--but showing up for a game drunk was his limit. He had no sense of humour about that. A couple of beers, okay. Any more than that and expect to sit on the bench until the next game.

Jane continued, "Anyway, a couple of drinks aren't going to hurt me. I was on antibiotics the other night, Gertie, when you were feeding me the brandy, so what's the difference now?"

"True, but you were coughing your head off that night; therefore, the brandy was purely for medicinal purposes."

Jane shook her head. "It's ball tournament weekend for cripe's sake. There's no ball tournament weekend without having a few drinks. It's unheard of."

Gertie shrugged. "Okay, it's your life. At least you sound better than you did a few days ago."

"There you go. If I didn't know what I was doing, I'd be dead by now." Jane summed up her philosophy, "Kill or cure. That's my motto." She turned to Elliot. "Hey, Elly, can I have a quarter for the juke box?"

"Sure." Elliot dug a quarter out of his wallet and handed the coin to Jane. "No country."

"Okay."

Elliot watched as Jane moved her way over to the corner of the room. She smiled and chatted easily with the other patrons as she went. As she bent over to search the listings for a song, Elliot felt the ever-present urge to make love to her. Somehow, his timing was always wrong, but he wasn't about to push the issue. Man, he thought, what an ass she has--the kind that fits neatly on top of legs long enough to wrap around my neck.

He could picture them making love so vividly that it almost hurt--a pain so intense yet so sweet that cold showers were virtually useless. She'd be below him, smooth and creamy skinned, moaning in supreme ecstasy, as he worked his way up her supple body planting kisses from her toes to her forehead. Then he'd wrap those long legs around him and...

"Earth to Elliot," Gertie interrupted.

"What?" he spat out.

"Do you want anything to eat?" She gestured towards Kelly who had reappeared with their drinks.

"Yeah. A burger and fries with gravy," he ordered, plummeting back to reality. "Hey Jane!" Elliot called as he paid Kelly for the drinks, remembering to add a generous tip.

"What?" Jane answered as she walked back towards the table.

The jukebox finally clicked in with John Fogerty's *Put Me In Coach* lyrics filling the room.

Elliot snickered. "Cute."

Jane smiled in return. "I thought it was fitting."

Elliot swatted Jane fondly on her bottom as she walked past his chair. "Are you hungry?"

"A small fry." Jane glanced at Kelly and ordered as she sat back down.

"A burger and large fry for me, please," Nick added to the order then took a long drink of beer.

"You just had a burger," Elliot reminded him.

"Yeah, man, and now I'm having another one." He turned his attention back to the waitress. "And you might as well bring us another round while you're at it. Save yourself a trip. Are you going to the dance tonight, Kelly?"

"Don't know yet," Kelly answered. "Depends on whether or not I can find a babysitter. I wouldn't bet on it though. By the time this day's over, I'll be ready for a warm bath and a cool bed."

"Well if you do go, save a dance for me. Okay?" Nick offered her his best, brilliant smile.

"Will do, Handsome." She winked then headed towards the kitchen to place their food orders.

As the afternoon progressed, Elliot's mood lightened. He made twenty dollars betting on a short, dark-haired ball player from Stratford who said that he could drink an entire mug of draft while standing on his head—a very talented dude indeed. And Nick, who had milled around the tavern searching out various buddies to converse and drink with, seemed to make some headway with Gertie. She was cute, but no match for Samantha who was gorgeous and sizzling hot. Whatever happened with Samantha was still a mystery. Elliot had asked, but Nick refused to say anything more than looks were deceiving. End of conversation.

The best part, by far, was the fact that he and Jane had spent their time drinking, holding hands, and laughing together surrounded by all of their friends. It was now official. Donnybrooke would finally acknowledge them as a couple.

Occasionally, players from other teams would join them at their table. Coming back from a quick trip to the washroom, Elliot found Jane and Gertie immersed in a conversation with two members of a team from Shakespeare.

They were obviously debating on who would win the tournament. The boys from Shakespeare were adamant that this year's trophy would definitely go to them.

"Don't count your chickens until the hens are laid," Jane warned.

"Isn't that until the eggs have hatched? Don't count your chickens until the eggs have hatched," the short-stop corrected.

Jane shook her head. "No, that comes afterwards. First comes the hen that lays the eggs, but if there's no rooster in the barnyard, let's face it, it won't matter how many eggs the hen lays, the eggs won't hatch. So, seriously it's the hen that needs to get laid, not the eggs."

While Gertie laughed, the short-stop remained confused.

"What the hell is she talking about?" he questioned Gertie.

Jane watched quietly as Gertie soothed his ego. "Oh, buddy, if I were you, I wouldn't tax my brain so hard. What you should do is go to Smith Books and get the Coles Notes on Janisms."

"Janisms?"

"Yup," Gertie continued, "adages that went haywire... got stranded somewhere out in the ozone layer of Jane's brain, got twisted and spit out all mixed up and ass backwards."

Elliot sat back down at the table to watch. It always amazed him how easily, how effortlessly, Jane and Gertie slipped into their little routines. Con artists had nothing on these two. Find a mark, bait a mark, play with the mark. One girl was as bad as the other. One girl was as good as the other. Two brains in absolute synchronization.

"There's a book like that? Seriously?" Looking duly impressed, the short-stop had taken the bait. He pointed towards Jane. "And you wrote it?"

Jane shrugged, grinning. "Guilty as charged."

Gertie nodded and sipped her drink. "I wouldn't kid you about that. Honestly. Although, come to think of it, you may need to order the book online because the last time I checked, Smith's Books was sold out. Janisms are becoming quite popular...trendy. There's even a write-up online in Wikipedia. You should check it out sometime."

"Okay, I'll do that."

Gertie leaned over closer, taking on a very confidential tone. "Just don't confuse Jane's Janisms with the religion, Jainism."

"Janism is a religion too?" The ball player narrowed his eyes, on the verge of getting lost again.

"Right, so when you go to Wikipedia, type in J-a-n-i-s-m and not J-a-i-n-i-s-m, otherwise, you'll end up reading about Jainism which is an Indian religion that believes in pacifism... totally different."

"I think maybe I should just stick with the Coles notes version," the ball player decided as he finished his beer.

Gertie nodded her understanding, as if totally

comprehending what a huge predicament lay before him. "Probably a wise decision." She hesitated then added, "You know what would be even better?"

"What?"

Gertie continued, "The easiest thing to do would be to read the Janisms on Jane's blog. She totally explains what the meaning is behind each and every one of her misfit sayings. It really is a life saver as far as I'm concerned. Totally necessary to understand what today's youths are actually saying."

The short-stop's eyes lit up. "Great. How do you find her blog?"

"You can either go online and do a search for Janisms + Jane Kirkwood or I can e-mail you the URL to her website. Either or. Whatever would be easiest for you."

"Cool." The short-stop stood up to leave. "I'll be right back. I just need to find a piece of paper to write my e-mail address on."

As the man left the room, Jane grinned at Gertie, leaned over and spoke softly. "I have a blog? When did that happen?"

Elliot shook his head, wondering what he had gotten himself into. Either these two women would eventually come up with a plan to take over the world, or they might just possibly end up on the wrong side of the law trying to figure out confidence schemes with unsuspecting men as their prime targets. Lord knows, both women were pretty enough to bilk many men happily out of their life savings. The girls were natural born grifters.

By four o'clock, the rain had finally stopped. The afternoon had not been a total waste. The ball diamonds, they were informed, were a drenched mess, but with a bit of hard work, a lot of raking and a load or two of sawdust, the tournament organizers were confident that the games could continue.

"Jane," Elliot finished his drink, "I'm going back to the ball diamond to help out. If everything goes according to schedule, we should get playing around eight. Are you coming to watch?"

Jane turned to Gertie who nodded, then back to Elliot. "Sure. For a while, I guess. But what about the dance? We'll both have to go home and change first?"

"The ballgame should be over by ten. Why don't you and Gertie go and we'll meet you there? That way, you can save us a table." As Elliot stood up to leave, he noticed that the girls hadn't finished their drinks. "Are you staying here?"

"Might as well. We'll catch a bite to eat then head down later to watch our big, wonderful men beat the pants off..." Jane's attempt at being obsequious was overshadowed by her lack of knowledge. "Who are you playing anyway?"

"Guelph."

Jane batted her eyes and tried again. "Okay, we'll catch a bite to eat and then head down later to watch our big, strong men beat the pants off Guelph."

Elliot grinned. He wasn't at all sure whether Jane would even make it to the dance. In fact, he had a hunch that if she drank too much more before going home to change, she would probably end up passing out until Monday. "Gertie, can I talk to you for a minute?"

"Sure."

"Outside." He rose from his chair then nodded towards the front door.

"Okay." Gertie rose to follow Elliot.

"It's not polite to keep secrets," Jane teased as she grabbed Elliot's arm. "What's Gertie's got that I don't?"

"Absolutely nothing, Babe. You are everything that I want. I just need to speak to her for a second." Elliot sat down on the chair next to Jane. Her green eyes were alert, not angry. He leaned in close and whispered in her ear. "Tonight, you and I will dance. Then maybe later, you and I can have our own private party." He was suddenly sure that tonight would be the night. A night that neither of them would ever forget. Jane's wistful smile convinced him it was true. She let go of his arm. "Tonight, I promise you, will be something special."

"What's up, Elliot?" Gertie asked as they walked outside of the tavern. The sun was shining through left-over clouds. The air had cooled.

"I think that Jane's had enough to drink. Can you talk her into slowing down a bit so that she doesn't pass out before the dance?" No matter how high his hormones were, it was time to concentrate on the game. "Maybe take her home for a quick nap or something?"

Gertie shrugged. "Sure thing, Elliot."

"Thanks."

Without Elliot close by, Nick saw his chance. "Hey Jane," Nick plunked himself down in the chair next to hers.

"Hey Nick," Jane responded with a cheerful smile. "Where have you been?"

"Just hanging out." Nick looked around the room. "Where's Elliot?"

"Gertie was just walking him to the front door. He's going down to work on the diamonds. Are you going with him?"

Nick shook his head and indicated the half-finished beer he held in his left hand. "Not yet. Are you going to the dance with Elliot?"

Jane shook her head. "We're going to meet there. He asked us to save a couple of chairs for the two of you." She smiled affectionately. "He really is something else, you know?"

"Yeah, man. Elliot's one of a kind." Nick hesitated for only a second before reaching over and tugging on Jane's arm. "There's a guy outside on the patio who wants to meet you." He nodded towards the propped-open door.

"So?"

"So, I promised to introduce you to him. He plays for Guelph." He motioned for Jane to rise and follow him. "Come on."

"I don't think so, Nick, but thanks anyway." Jane gently shook her arm to break his grasp.

"Aw come on, Jane. He's a really good-looking, and he thinks you're beautiful. All he wants to do is say hi."

"There you are." Elliot had decided to take Nick with him. "I've been looking all over for you."

Startled, Nick released his grasp. He smiled and made a broad gesture with his arms. "Hey, man, and now that you've found me, what can I do for you?"

"You can come and help before you get too drunk to see the ball let alone play." Elliot placed his hand on his brother's shoulder in a non-threatening manner.

Nick rose, left the remainder of his beer on the table and began to follow Elliot. He turned to Jane and saluted. "Later, man."

Jane's face was smiling but not her eyes. "Yeah, man. Later."

CHAPTER THIRTY-SEVEN

"Do you think that it's possible to be in love with two men at the same time?" Jane asked Gertie as they lounged in her apartment smoking a carefully rolled joint. Jane stared at a poster on the wall across the room from her and noticed a small child clinging to the leg of one of the street-dwelling, garbage-rooters. The little girl would be no more than three with the fearful look of third-world hunger marking her pretty but dirty features.

"You're in love with Elliot?"

"I don't know. When I'm with Todd, all I can think about is how good it feels to be with him. We have fabulous sex, talk about everything that we want to do in the future and I just want to hang onto him forever." Jane paused as she inhaled deeply, letting the smoke brutalize her sensitive bronchial passages. She exhaled slowly, blowing fragrant smoke-rings. "Elliot, on the other hand, has been a part of my life, in one way or another, for as long as I can remember."

Gertie leaned forward in her chair and waved her hand in front of Jane's face, breaking her focus. "Hello, Jane? This is the same guy who put a knife up to your face and who slashed Todd's tire."

"Yeah, I know, but Elliot was angry. He's been great ever since."

Concern filled Gertie's voice. "And what happens the next time he loses his temper and he doesn't have a tire to take it out on? What then?"

"He promised me that it would never happen again." Jane handed the joint to Gertie, polished off her drink and stood up to pour another one.

Accepting the spliff, Gertie curled up in her armchair, legs tucked up beside her. She inhaled the smoke and shut her eyes. Taking her time, she exhaled then spoke. "Right. Look, Jane, this all started because you wanted to survive the summer. Don't get sucked into it. Put in your time and then get out. You have all of the talent in the world. Get the hell out of here and make something out of your life."

"I know." With her refilled drink in hand, Jane returned

from the kitchenette and strolled around the living room inspecting each picture, looking for an omen of some sort. She found herself inexplicably drawn to the poster with the sad little girl--a child who did not know how to smile amongst the filth and decay of her existence. "I just wish it was that simple. Elliot has been so super lately. He texts me a dozen times a day just to say hello. He calls me every evening to say goodnight. He sends me flowers for no reason at all. When we're together, he makes me laugh. I've been fighting him for so long that I never really took the time to know him, and now that I do, I wish that I'd gotten to know him sooner, before Todd."

Gertie opened her eyes wide, her brows raised in surprise. "Please don't tell me that you are planning on dumping Todd?"

Jane shook her head. "No. I love Todd or, at least I think I love Todd. He's sexy and he's fun. He's headed in the same direction that I want to go." Jane thought that the child's life must be hell, never enough food to fill an empty belly, never enough blankets to stave off cold winter nights, never enough or, simply, none at all. So why did the child cling so tight, looking so afraid to let go? Her eyes, her eyes, well they looked almost haunted. Could she feel love? Was she loved? What kind of parents could surround their child in poverty and filth and still claim love?

"You can't have it both ways," Gertie admonished and inhaled deeply from the joint.

Jane sighed, her heart torn. "I know."

Gertie exhaled, blowing smoke towards the ceiling. "So what are you going to do?"

Jane broke herself away from the poster, sat down on the wooden coffee table to face her friend. "I don't know. I keep thinking that if I have sex with Elliot once then maybe I'll be able to resolve this somehow."

"How?" Gertie held out the spliff to Jane who shook her head.

"This may sound really weird, but I know what Todd and I are like together. I don't think that he'd be the easiest person to live with on a day-to-day basis, but he's constant, he's stabile and sexually we're compatible. Elliot, on the other hand, is exciting and unpredictable. I never know what's going to happen next. I keep wondering what the sex would be like." Jane swished her drink in the glass, peering into the liquid as if it was a crystal ball that could predict the future.

"Then why don't you just sleep with him once and find out?" Gertie suggested as she leaned forward to place the roach into an ashtray on the coffee table.

"I've thought about that. In fact, I've almost decided that tonight will be the night," Jane admitted. It had been so much easier when she hadn't cared, when this had been nothing more than a game.

"Then do it and get him out of your system, woman. Fuck his brains out. Just do us all a favour." Gertie put her feet back on the floor and took Jane's hands in hers. "If you still choose Todd over Elliot after sleeping with him, leave a will."

CHAPTER THIRTY-EIGHT

The ballgame had been close, but a home run during the bottom of the ninth inning brought in the two runs that they had needed to close the gap and to win. That meant that the team would play again tomorrow, but more importantly, it meant that the entire crew was now in a mood to celebrate.

Elliot was no exception. As he and Nick entered the hall, he surveyed the dark room in search of Jane and Gertie. He poked Nick in the ribs with his elbow and pointed towards the back of the room. "There they are."

Elliot's worst fear vanished. Jane was still mobile. He had seen other tournaments where she'd passed out long before the dance even began. Maybe times were changing for the better. It was common knowledge that Jane was into using mild drugs. He wasn't thrilled about that, especially when she flaunted the use in his face, but he fully anticipated that her using would stop once she was a permanent part of his life. He would help her get past the drug use, even if it meant contacting her parents and doing an intervention. He had to make her see how much she was harming herself. He'd even pay for the rehab if necessary. Cigarettes he could tolerate if he had too, but the rest was just absolute bullshit. She was throwing her life away, and her self-destruction had to stop.

"Hey, Sweetie, I've been saving a chair just for you." Jane smiled and pulled out the chair beside her. "Who won?"

Elliot bent over and kissed the top of Jane's head. "We did. I'll be back in a minute. Do you girls need another drink?"

"Sure," Jane and Gertie chimed in together, looked at each other, and burst into laughter.

"Looks like the two of you didn't stop partying after we left, man." Nick grinned as he sat down beside Gertie. "Did you have fun without us?"

"Is that even possible?" Gertie teased as she regained control.

"Probably not, man, but there's a first time for everything."

The girls broke out into laughter again. What was so funny was beyond Elliot.

Elliot sauntered back to the bar, leaving the trails of giggles behind him. So, okay, Jane was still mobile, but, by the look of her eyes, she was also close to her limit. That meant that Gertie hadn't kept her word after all. That meant that the two of them had been into Gertie's green preserves and, if Jane continued drinking, she'd be passed out before midnight. Jane being passed out before midnight was not a part of his plan. So, okay, what was the plan now? He could feed Gertie doubles to get rid of her faster and buy Jane straight ginger ale, but Jane would probably catch on even if Gertie didn't notice. He could buy Jane a drink and then keep her dancing for the next hour and hope that she would wear off some of the day's alcohol consumption. That sounded better. More feasible. Elliot purchased the drinks and hoped for the best. He also hoped that Nick would take care of Gertie for the evening.

When he got back to the table with the drinks, Gertie and Nick were already dancing. He nodded, satisfied. "So, what did you and Gertie do after we left?" Elliot placed the drinks on the table and sat down.

Jane propped her foot up on Elliot's chair. "Not much. We got bored at the tavern without you so we went back to Gertie's and just hung out. Sorry I missed the game. We sort of lost track of the time. I'm really glad you won though. When do you play again?"

"Not until tomorrow at noon."

"Umm." Jane grinned mischievously, leaned towards him and propped her elbows on top of her knee. Her voice was smooth and slow. "Does that mean you can party ALL night?"

"Is that what you want?" Elliot could feel stirrings below. This was definitely the green light that he'd been patiently waiting for. So many years he'd waited. Waited for her to grow up. Waited for her to come home from college. Waited for her to see him in the same way that he saw her. Waited for her to truly be his. He gently caressed her bare arm, her skin feeling like heaven under his touch.

"I can't think of anything I want more."

"How about we just skip the dance then and go find ourselves a nice, quiet spot right now?" Elliot could feel his heart beating rapidly in his chest, his pulse quickening by mere thought alone. Within his grasp now. So close.

"That sounds like fun, but there's only one problem." Jane smiled brilliantly, her voice light.

"What?" Unconsciously holding his breath, Elliot prepared himself for the worst. Not tonight. Jane, please don't. Not again.

Jane leaned back in her chair and placed her foot back on the floor. "I came here to dance." She stood up and held out her hand.

"Then," Elliot sighed in disappointment, "let's dance." He took her hand in his and let her lead the way.

And as Jane and Elliot danced and laughed, Nick watched. He did not like what he saw. No, not at all. His plan was not working. For the past few years, he'd been able to keep them apart, to secretly keep enough tension between Jane and Elliot that they were foes not friends. A carefully planted word here. A carefully executed conversation there. Keep Elliot jealous, spiteful, and he knew that Elliot's temper would take care of the rest. Keep Jane away from seeing how much Elliot cared. Keep her seeing only his dark side. She wouldn't want him then. She needed a man she could trust to take care of her. A friend she could turn to no matter what happened. Someone who accepted her just as she is with no desire to change her. Someone who truly loved her. Someone like him. "Excuse me, Gertie. I need to go see a man about a horse." Nick needed to take action. He was running out of time.

"Sure." Gertie nodded and watched Nick's abrupt departure as he headed towards the washrooms. "Okay then," she said to no one in general as she headed back to their table.

After relieving himself, Nick strode up to the bar. "Two shots of rum, one with Coke and one straight, man, oh and one shot of straight rye."

The bartender nodded and filled the order.

As Nick walked back to the table, he noticed that Gertie was already dancing with someone else. The short-stop from Shakespeare had found her. Perfect timing. Nick sat down at the table and glanced towards his brother. The song was slow and Elliot and Jane danced close, too wrapped up in each other to notice anyone else. Nick took the single shots and dumped them into the girls' glasses. He picked up each glass and swirled the contents to mix in the additional alcohol the best he could. Nick had a new plan. He smiled.

CHAPTER THIRTY-NINE

The world was becoming a very hazy place. The music echoed somewhere from a distant galaxy and bounced off at least three orbiting satellite dishes before reaching her ears. The feel of Elliot against her felt warm but vague, surreal in the heat of the summer night. He was saying something to her, but the satellite transmissions took precedent.

"What?" she asked, trying to decipher the sound of his voice from the collision of extraneous noises.

"I said there's a party down by the river. Do you want to go?" he repeated. The dance was almost over.

"Sure," she replied and tried desperately to maintain her focus. Jane knew physically that she was well over her limit, that having an in-depth conversation with the toilet was only one more drink away. What she couldn't understand was why. The antibiotics maybe? "I need to go to the washroom first."

"You okay?" Elliot's voice sounded truly concerned.

She smiled and tried closing one eye to obliterate his double. "Yup. All I need is a coffee and I'll be back up to speed," she assured him.

The journey to the washroom seemed endless. People suddenly appeared in front of her wanting to talk, wanting to know if she and Elliot were river-bound, wanting to know if she knew who had any drugs for sale or an extra case of beer at home. She managed the only way she knew how--a smile, a few words, a nod, a stagger.

The washroom smelled like vomit. Jane willed herself to maintain some iota of dignity and to not add to the overpowering stench. She'd been drunk before without any major ramifications. She could do it again. The mirror reflected a rather pale image, supposedly of herself. She squinted her eyes and fluffed her hair. She licked her lips and pinched her cheeks, hoping to bring back some colour.

The next stop was for a cup of coffee, hot and strong. Caffeine was the answer. Massive amounts of caffeine. Better yet, bennies. Maybe Gertie had some with her. Gertie always had a stash. With the cup of scorching liquid in hand, Jane started slowly back to her table. She watched as the liquid waved up at the sides threatening to splash over and burn her. Gertie was her hope. Gertie and about three bennies. Then she'd be back in control, the sick feeling would go away and the sex would be...would be... would be...good, she hoped.

When she finally arrived back at her table the music had stopped. Gertie and Elliot were nowhere in sight. Nick sat, finishing a drink.

"Where did everyone go?" she asked as she maneuvered into a chair on the opposite side of the table.

"Gertie got really sick, man, so Elliot took her home. He told me to give you a ride to the party, man, and he would meet you there."

"Oh." Jane tried to wrap her mind around this new information. She sipped on the coffee. No Gertie. No bennies. Fuck. Coffee then. Two, maybe ten cups. "Okay." She tried to smile.

Nick downed his drink and stood up. "I think that we'd better go. If you're not there when Elliot shows up, man, I'll have hell to pay tomorrow." Nick smiled, rich and friendly.

Jane sighed wondering if it would be possible to take the entire pot of coffee without the caterers noticing. "Okay." She stood up and began to follow Nick. "Nick, be a sweetie and grab a couple of cups of coffee on your way out."

Nick looked back at Jane with curiosity. "I don't drink coffee, man."

"Yeah, I know, but I do and I need massive quantities of caffeine right now or I won't make it to the river." She walked over to the luncheon table and poured a second cup for herself.

"Oh, oh, okay, man." Nick joined her.

Loaded with four lidded paper cups, the two left the hall and walked the short distance to Nick's jeep. "Is Gertie okay?" Jane asked, worried about her friend.

"Should be after a night's sleep. Man, she got tanked." Nick set one cup down on the hood while he opened the door for her. "I don't know what you girls were into this afternoon, man, but you could have at least shared." He shut the door, grabbed the second cup and walked around to the driver's side. "Nice girl that Gertie.

Damn fine dancer too, man."

"Yeah, Gertie's a doll." Jane finished one coffee, scrunched the cup and threw it out of the window. "Here, I have a free hand, give me one of those cups."

Nick did and placed the remaining cup into a cup holder between the front seats. "Man, Jane, at this rate, you'll be floating up to your eyeballs before we get to the party."

Jane just smiled and waited for Nick to start the jeep. Odd that Elliot would have left without her. He could have at least waited long enough to say goodbye. "How come you didn't take Gertie home instead of Elliot?"

"Aw, man, Jane, you know Elliot. He's the original knight-in-shining-armour. Don't worry, he'll be back before you have a chance to miss him, man." He revved the engine into motion and pulled out of the parking lot. "You two seem pretty tight these days."

Jane concentrated on the second cup of coffee. "I suppose."
"You still planning on going back to college this fall?"
"Yup."
"What then, man?"

"Don't know." Jane stared out of the window at the darkness and slunk into silence. Don't know was about as far as she could think right now. She listened to the music that Nick selected, not really noticing who was playing but instead feeling the beat of the bass guitar. She rolled down the window and tossed out the second empty cup. The countryside clicked by with the river only a few kilometres ahead. She could picture the partiers with their bonfires to ward off the darkness and to combat the mosquitoes. Same as any other year. Some partiers would suddenly decide to go skinny-dipping. Others would stay on shore and laugh.

And Elliot would be waiting. He would greet them at the jeep when they arrived and take her by the hand. They would dance to tunes provided by a car stereo or sit by the fire and snuggle. And, after a while, they would bid their farewells and vanish from the midst of the crowd to travel to a quiet, secluded spot where they would finally make love.

The jeep turned right into a long, gravel laneway, startling Jane out of her mental journey. "Where are we going?" She turned to Nick as she crumpled the third cup and placed it neatly on the floor beside her foot.

"Small detour, man. I promised that I'd pick up a case of beer on the way down."

"Whose place is this?" Jane asked as she tried to see something, anything familiar.

"Want the other cup of coffee, man?" Nick took the cup from the holder and offered it to her.

"Thanks." Jane accepted it.

"The farm belongs to the Kopinak's, man."

Jane nodded. "That's right, but I thought that they were away visiting her mother or something."

Nick grinned. "They are, man."

"No way. You're going to go into their house and steal their beer?"

"That's the plan. It's okay, man. I did some work for him last summer so I know where they hide the spare key."

"That's crazy." A brief period of clarity passed over her like a veil lifting. "That's fucking break and enter."

"Man, lighten up. I'll replace the beer before they get back, and no one will know." Nick pulled the jeep up beside the dark house and jumped out. "You comin', man?"

"No way." Jane shook her head emphatically.

"Suit yourself, man." Nick shut the door and disappeared behind the house.

Jane watched and sipped on the final cup of coffee. She waited for the caffeine to click in, amazed by its apparent slowness. If it had been bennies, she would have been dancing by now instead of stuck in this weird limbo land. A light flicked on inside the house. She could see Nick's movements. Jane opened the door and climbed out to stand outside, leaning up against the jeep.

She riffled through her purse to produce her package of cigarettes and lit one, unconsciously swatting at mosquitoes. The limbo land wouldn't be so bad if she was somewhere else, like with Elliot, but here it made her nervous. What was taking Nick so long? His figure was gone from the window. She glanced down at her watch as she sipped the last, bitter coffee. She waited. The cigarette dwindled and was finally stubbed out. The cool night air grew damp. She waited.

A choir of crickets kept her company singing their praises to the star-filled heavens. A night hawk screeched nearby, sending a shiver to course along Jane's arms and to explode between her shoulder blades. All she needed now were a few bats to swoop around from behind the pine trees and she would seriously consider walking the rest of the way to the river.

Her bladder began to send signals of wanting to be released soon from its burden. She waited. She tipped up the cup. Empty. Turning around, she looked inside the jeep, toying with the idea of driving away. The keys were gone. Not wanting to litter the lawn, she crumpled up the final cup and tossed it beside its mate.

She lit another cigarette and crossed her legs as she leaned against the jeep and studied the stars, trying to ignore the slow, achy appeal from below. The Big Dipper, The Little Dipper, Orion and she couldn't remember the names of anymore of the constellations. The appeal grew louder, more insistent. Her bladder wouldn't wait much longer. Okay, she thought, time for action.

"Nick!" she called as she ventured closer to the house. "Nick, hurry up." No response.

Jane followed the general direction that Nick had taken and found herself outside of a back porch. She gingerly opened the screen door. Her bladder began to scream. The thought of peeing down her leg outweighed the thought of entering into a vacationing couple's house. You see, Officer, it was like this. Find a bathroom or mark the territory. The bushes on the right-side are mine, and the closest all-night donut shop is thirty kilometres away.

She stubbed her toe and let out a small yelp before finding the main door to the house. She waited for a dog, but no huge German shepherd arrived to bite off her leg. She opened the main door and made her way into the brightly lit kitchen. "Nick," she called again. "Where the fuck are you?"

Jane searched the bottom floor for a washroom and then climbed the wooden stairs to the second floor. "Nick, this isn't funny," she chastised loudly, hoping that he would hear.

She peered through two more doors before finding the washroom and sighing with relief. She turned on the light and locked the door behind her. Peeing is a wonderful thing, Jane thought as she sat down on the toilet to relieve herself, her bladder stopping its persecution. Yes, always remember that. Peeing is marvelous. Total release. Wonderful--as long as it's not down your leg.

After she had finished, she washed and cupped her hands beneath the faucet to drink from, wanting to cut her coffee-flavoured saliva. Gum would be good, but first she needed to find Nick and get the hell out of this place.

She unlocked the door and opened it. Nick. She jumped, startled by his quiet presence. "You scared the shit out of me. Where have you been?"

Nick grinned. "Just looking around, man. Have you ever been in this house?"

"No," Jane strode past Nick and headed towards the stairwell. "And right now, I'm leaving."

Nick reached out and caught her by her arm. "There's a really beautiful armoire in one of the bedrooms. You've just got to see it, man."

Jane studied Nick. His grasp was tight. "Let go of me Nick. I want to leave."

"In a minute, man. I just want to show you the armoire first." Nick's eyes smiled, reflecting perfect innocence. "It must date back to 1850 at least, man. I was thinking of making a replica for Elliot for Christmas. All I want you to do is take a look to see if you think he'd like it, man."

"I'll look at it if you promise we can leave right afterwards."

"Sure, man." Nick loosened his grip on Jane's arm. "It's over here in this bedroom." He moved her along with him as he walked.

God, this is fucking stupid, Jane thought. Elliot's waiting down at the river and I'm fucking playing Hide-and-Go-Seek with his brother. "Nick, let go of my arm. I'm very capable of walking without your assistance." Jane was abruptly guided into a small bedroom. She looked around as Nick closed the door behind them and turned on the light. There was no armoire. In fact, the bedroom was sparsely furnished at best. A bed. A dresser with a lamp. A guest room, probably.

Nick quickly pulled her towards him and locked her in his

arms. Before the shock could subside, before the neurotransmitters had time to send signals to react in any way at all, he picked her up and placed her on the bed. She felt his weight on top of her, his two hundred pounds paralyzing her small frame.

Jane's limbo land imploded. She swallowed and began to shake. Elliot, she thought. Elliot's waiting. Her mind raced. She watched as the ghosts of the past laughed at her. She saw them dance before her as she felt her t-shirt and bra being ripped from her body. No haymow to escape from this time. No flight of stairs to speed down to safety. No pillow to cover her head to drown out the screams. She felt Nick's lips touch hers and bit back the tears. She turned her head away. "Please, no," she whispered. "Please, Nick. Elliot's waiting."

"Fuck Elliot." Nick laughed as he sat up to straddle her, his weight heavy on her upper legs to impede her mobility. He pinned both of her wrists in his left hand and unbuckled his belt with his right. Nick pulled the belt quickly out of the belt loops, bound her wrists together and strapped them securely to headboard of the wrought-iron bed. "It's about time he learned that he can't always have what he wants. I'm so fucking tired of being the other twin." He leaned forward to kiss her bare, heaving breasts.

Jane tried to squirm free, but his weight was too much. Her wrists screamed in agony as the leather tightened around her soft flesh. If I scream, who would hear? she thought. "Do you really want it to happen this way?" She felt tears slipping out of the corners of her eyes and falling onto the pillow. Slipping and falling. Slipping and falling. "I never thought of you as the other twin. Just Nick...You were...you were...my friend."

"Still am your friend. I love you, Jane. Why can't you see that?" With his hands now free, Nick shifted his weight downward on her legs, coming to rest just below her knees. He pulled down her jeans and her lace underwear.

Jane's mind whirled. She swallowed hard. "I love you too, Nick. Please release my hands. I can't make love to you the way I want to if my hands are bound." Her stomach clenched as she fought back tears.

Nick ignored her. "God, you're so beautiful. But then you know that, don't you? Don't worry, Jane, I'm not going to hurt you.

I love you." Nick lifted himself off of her so he could finish removing her garments then he quickly lay back on top. He spread her legs enough to get his hand in between, spit on two fingers and inserted them into her vagina, moving in and out, gaining momentum, and then slowing again. He bent forward and spoke calmly into her ear. "I'm going to make love to you now. It'll be better than you ever dreamed possible with Elliot. You'll see. You'll enjoy it. I know you will. You'll forget all about my brother. I know you will."

Jane's mind spiraled downwards, trying to find a safe spot, trying to hide. She felt his touch. She felt his mouth biting at her nipple. She closed her eyes tightly, inhaling the pain, not wanting to see as well as feel.

Satisfied, Nick removed his fingers and forced Jane's legs to spread apart farther. He pulled down his pants to expose his erect penis. "Just remember this, Jane. This is Nick's cock. Not Elliot's. Nick's. I may have been the second twin born, but I'll be the first one to come."

Jane bit back a scream as he plunged inside of her. She kicked with her feet and tried to buck away from him. He laughed and drove in deeper, harder with each attempt. "You like it rough, don't you, Jane? I knew you would. I know you, Jane. I love you, Jane." He held her firmly by the hips and moved her to his own quickening rhythm, taking the part of both lovers, making her movements match his own.

Jane spiraled and spiraled downward. Slipping and falling. Slipping and falling. The ghosts laughed louder. The more she fought, the better he seemed to like it, and she wasn't going to give him the satisfaction. And as his rhythm grew faster and faster and he readied for orgasm, Jane's mind fled further and further away, searching for a place of calm with wild, white daisies and bright sunshine. She could hear his moans in the distance, bouncing off at least three satellite dishes before reaching her ears.

"Oh fuck, oh fuck, oh fuck." One final, convulsing thrust, then all grew quiet. She could feel faint caresses, like that of a lover. Then his weight was gone.

She forced her shaking legs to close. They felt like foreign logs of dead lumber. She opened her eyes and the tears slipped out.

Slipped and fell. Slipped and fell.

"Man, I could really use a cigarette right now," Nick decided as he lay beside her on the bed. "Where are yours?"

She swallowed and tried to keep her voice calm. "In the jeep."

Nick frowned. "Too bad. Later." He flopped backwards with his head beside hers on the pillow. "Wow, that was good. You are so fucking tight. It was good for you too. Wasn't it? I know it was. You loved it. Didn't you, Jane?"

Jane did not respond.

Propping himself up on his elbow, he faced her. His eyes were dark with anger. "ANSWER ME!" He pinched her side, twisting the soft flesh. "Tell me that it was good for you too." As he twisted, he pinched harder. "TELL ME!"

Biting back the pain, Jane answered softly, "You were wonderful, Nick. Wonderful."

"Tell me that you love me, Jane."

"I love you, Nick."

"Good. Jane," Nick whispered as let go of his grasp and caressed her side, "I'll untie you and take you home, but you have to promise me something first."

Jane swallowed hard and willed her mouth to work. "What?" Her voice sounded hoarse as if she had spent all night singing bawdry Irish barroom tunes.

"You have to promise me that you'll always remember that I fucked you first, not Elliot. I love you more than he does. Understand?"

Jane nodded.

"And, you have to promise me that you won't tell anyone this happened. Promise me, or I'll just leave you here tied to this bed and the Kopinak's can come home in two weeks to a corpse. The funny thing is," Nick chuckled, "everyone was so drunk at the dance, that I bet I could convince at least half of them that you left with Elliot and that it was me who took Gertie home. Wouldn't that be a hoot? My brother, the hero, doing a twenty-five year stint in jail for murder. Think about it, Jane. And if you ever tell Elliot that you and I made love tonight, I'll tell him that it was your idea, that you were a fucking wild woman. Couldn't get enough. He'd believe me you know. He'd be as angry as all hell, but he'd still believe me 'cause I'm his brother. I know that we'll have to tell him eventually that you want to be with me, instead of him, but not yet. Understand?"

Jane nodded. "I promise."

"Say all of it." Nick pinched her nipple between his fingers sending another round of shooting pain through her breast.

She bit her lip in agony. "I promise. I promise not to tell."

CHAPTER FORTY

Elliot sat by the riverside watching bonfire embers slowly die. Everyone else had left hours ago, but he couldn't bring himself to move. Only one quick message, "I'm on my way," and then silence. Nothing since. Jane wasn't answering her telephone or replying to his text messages. And as the sky grew light, as the sun gently peaked over the horizon, Elliot finally drove home.

CHAPTER FORTY-ONE

Jane woke from her short night's sleep feeling bruised and sore. She had crawled into bed too numb to think and had arrived back into consciousness in pretty much the same condition. When she listened for sounds, the house was quiet. Her parents had probably left already for the tournament.

Jane felt filthy, as if a thousand maggots had crawled over her body during her exhausted slumber. She pushed back the light covers and sat up on the edge of her bed. Somehow, she'd managed to take off her clothing last night, toss her jeans and top on the floor and replace yesterday's garments with a bed-time appropriate t-shirt and striped, cotton pajama bottoms. How did she get home? Jane walked to the window in her parents' bedroom across the hall and looked out. Her beloved Gremlin was parked in the driveway. Okay, she drove. Good. She wouldn't have to go searching for her car.

As Jane walked back to her room, the only coherent thoughts that she would allow to enter her brain were that she needed a cigarette and a coffee, that she needed a bath and that she needed to leave. If she had a hangover, she didn't notice. She stripped the floral, cotton sheets from her bed, gathered her soiled clothing off the carpeted floor and slowly walked downstairs. Every movement hurt.

After putting her sheets into the washing machine and taking a quick pee, Jane poured herself a coffee (thanks Mom for leaving the coffee maker on), grabbed her purse and walked, barefooted, out to the back porch to have a cigarette. As she bent over to pet her favourite calico cat, Thisbe, shooting pains seared Jane's lower back. Fuck. She bit her lower lip as she forced herself to straighten. She dug her package of cigarettes out of her purse then extracted a cigarette out of the package. Jane's fingers quivered as she held the lighter and ignited the tobacco. Okay. She could manage with a few strained muscles. She'd just have to watch how she lifted things for a few days. Pain killers would help. Muscle relaxants. It could have been worse. Thankfully, she was on the pill. Worse yet. She could be dead. Whatever it took, she was leaving today.

Sitting down on a Muskoka chair, Jane absently petted Thisbe who had jumped up onto her lap. Jane stared out at the distance as she sipped her coffee and inhaled the tobacco smoke. Nicotine and caffeine. The lesser of her evils. Absently, Jane noted the dark bruises on her arms, the angry red welts on her slim wrists. Without looking, she was positive that she would find corresponding marks on her torso and on her legs as well. Her inner thighs and her side felt like she'd been mauled by a rabid dog. At least Nick had been too smart to bruise her face. That would have been harder to hide, impossible to just explain away with a casual comment. It could have been worse, she thought. I could be dead. Whatever it takes, I'm leaving today.

Jane placed the cigarette in a ceramic ashtray that sat on a small table beside her, set down her coffee cup and rooted her cell phone out from the bottom of her purse. For a brief second, she thought of calling Jeff then let the moment pass. Better to forget that this had ever happened. Better to just go. Better this way. Just one more secret to permanently lock away in her mental vault of lies and deception. Jane scrolled through her contact list until she came to Todd's name. She swallowed and pressed enter.

The telephone on the other end rang only once. "Hello?" Todd's voice sang through the receiver.

"Hey, Sweetie." She tried desperately to keep her tone light. The rain has passed. The sun was shining. Just another lovely day in Donnybrooke.

"Hey, Beautiful. I was just about to call you."

Todd. Her Todd. Jane's voice was calm as she stroked the purring feline. "Todd, can you please call the landlord and tell him that I'll be coming down today? I need him to meet me at the apartment with a key. Tell him that I'll call him from Vineland when I get down that far, probably shortly after dinner this evening."

Clearly puzzled, Todd responded, "Okay, but I thought that you still had a couple of weeks left to work?"

"I finished early, so I thought I'd go down and get settled in before classes start."

"Great!" Todd hesitated for a moment then added, "I'm off until Tuesday, so why don't I meet you there?"

Jane glanced down at the bruises. Would Todd still love her if he knew? She thought not. How could he? "No. It's okay. You've done so much already. Let me do this part. Okay? You finish your job, and I'll see you in a couple of weeks."

"Jane, are you okay?" Concern had entered his voice.

Jane cringed. It was so unlike her to not want to see Todd. Any other time, she would have jumped at the chance to spend a day with him. Of course, he'd want an explanation.

"Fine, just P.M.S.ing I think, so I'm not in the best of moods. It's a long drive for you when I'd be seriously lousy company." Todd had sisters. He'd understand.

"Okay. Should you be driving then?"

Men, Jane thought and smiled despite herself. "Being moody and having cramps is not the same as being crippled, Todd."

"I know that. I just meant that maybe you should be resting instead of driving."

"If three billion women spent a week resting every time we had our periods, society, as we know it, would fall apart within two months. I'm pretty sure that's why menstrual huts were abolished." Jane picked up her cigarette and inhaled. She could feel a headache beginning and wished that she'd taken a couple of ibuprofen before calling Todd. She needed him to make this easy, and he wasn't cooperating.

"I did read that having sex during your period can greatly reduce the cramping."

Exhaling the smoke, Jane shut her eyes to momentarily block out the world. "Nice try but I'm not actually on my period yet, thus my saying that I think I'm P.M.S.ing, as in Premenstrual Syndrome. You know, the really hormonal, icky, bloated part when a lot of women want to chew the hand off of any man who touches them."

"Right. You did say that, but I was sure that you also mentioned cramps." She could hear his sigh of either confusion or of resignation (she wasn't sure which) over the cell phone. "I'm not going to win today, am I?"

Jane opened her eyes. "Todd, I love you more than I can possibly explain, so you have to trust me on this. All I'm capable of doing, at this exact moment, is making your life miserable. Please do us both a favour and save yourself the trip. I'm more than just one frame out of sync today. All of my channels are seriously pixelating and flickering. And you know what that means."

"Time to turn off the television and do something else?"

"Exactly." Jane tapped the ashes from her cigarette into the ashtray then continued, "I'm going to take down as much as I can shove into the car today. I managed to pick up a few odds and ends at a used furniture store in Owen Sound, including a bedframe that should work with your mattress, but I still need to talk to Dad to see when he can help me move the stuff. By the time you come down, I'll have my crap organized. You won't have to do a thing." Thoughts edged at the corner of her mind. Horrid thoughts. She pushed them away. "Be a sweetie and just humour me on this one. Okay?"

"All right. Let me know when you need help moving the furniture. I can take a day off work to do that."

"You'd end up spending," Jane quickly calculated the time in her head, "like nine hours driving in one day if you drove up here then down to Welland and then back to Coburg. Thanks, Todd, but I can manage on my end. Dad has lots of guys who work for him who owe him a favour or two. We'll manage. Look, I really have to go. Tons of packing to do. I'll call you this evening."

"Okay. You make sure you do that."

"I will. Bye, Todd."

"Jane, I love you."

Jane swallowed back a sob. "I love you too."

The hot bath water encompassed her like a cocoon, close and comforting. She studied her hands, her wrists, her arms, her legs. Gingerly, she traced the red marks that circled her wrists and thought of how to cover them without looking too conspicuous on a hot summer day.

She had seen movies where rape victims scoured their bodies until they bled, trying to rid themselves of the imagined filth. This is what it's like, she thought. It's really real, not just some imagery conjured up by the mind of an overzealous script writer. Jane reached for the bar of soap and began to rub it very systematically over her body. She started with her hands then rubbed the soap suds onto her arms and around her long neck. She pushed the tears as far back into her being as she could humanly manage and concentrated on the tiny bubbles.

By the time her bath was over, the bedding had spun dry of the rinse cycle. Jane threw the cotton sheets into the dryer. Her first instinct had been to throw out her jeans and t-shirt, but she couldn't afford to replace them, so she poured enough laundry soap over the items to kill any germ present, set them to wash and began packing. To the outside world she would look like any normal college student preparing to leave for the next round on her educational agenda. Yup, there goes Jane, starting her second year in Broadcasting she is. Strangers may think it a bit odd that she was wearing on long-sleeve shirt and jogging pants on a hot day, but any random thoughts would quickly pass without making any lasting impressions on their subconscious.

Jane surveyed her room carefully as she packed and made mental notes on what to take and what would have to wait until later. Between her and Todd, they should be able to exist at a fairly tolerable level of upper class poverty. She had her summer wages and a government loan as did he. With any luck, maybe she'd also be able to find a part-time job this year. As long as she had Todd, she would be okay. Todd. Her Todd. He'd hold her through the cold winter nights and keep her safe and warm.

After Jane had packed all that would fit into her small car, including a sleeping bag, and had remade her bed, she wrote her parents a note.

Mom and Dad,

My new landlord called to say that there were a few things that needed to be worked out regarding the apartment, so I'm heading down early. I'll call later and let you know that I arrived safely. I'll call my boss tomorrow and tell her that I'm sorry that I couldn't finish out the summer but would be more than happy to come up on the occasional weekend during the fall if necessary. Still need to figure when we can take the furniture down. Love you both. Talk to you soon.

Hugs,
Jane

Jane placed the note on the refrigerator so that the paper would catch her mom's eyes as soon as she walked into the kitchen. Jane glanced down at her watch. Three o'clock. With light traffic, she would be in Welland well before seven.

Without looking back, Jane left.

CHAPTER FORTY-TWO

Elliot, over-tired and ill-humoured, visually searched the ballpark for Jane. He needed to talk to her. He wanted to find out why she hadn't shown up at the river.

It was three o'clock. His team had won their first game of the day and would be playing again in less than an hour to make up for yesterday's rain delay. Elliot's head hurt from lack of sleep, (he'd be lucky if he didn't end up with a full-blown migraine), but his heart hurt worse from disappointment. Regardless, he was determined not to hang Jane without a trial.

By the time he'd taken Gertie home last night and had returned to the dance, Jane was gone. He had asked a few stragglers, but no one could remember seeing her leave. Elliot had tried calling her cell phone. Jane hadn't answered. Eventually, he had decided to take a chance and head down to the river by himself. Then he'd received her text, so he knew that everything was okay. Why then had she texted him to say that she was on her way if she wasn't planning on going? Obviously, she had still planned to meet him there. And why hadn't she answered her cell phone after sending the text? It just did not make sense. He was almost a hundred percent certain that she didn't stand him up just to just blow him off. She wouldn't do that after all they had been through that summer. Would she?

After keeping an eye on the ditches for a wrecked car on his way back to Donnybrooke, Elliot had driven by the Kirkland farm. Jane's car was in the driveway. He hoped that Jane was there too.

"All I would have had to do was to wait until Jane came back from the washroom before I had taken Gertie home last night," Elliot scolded himself under his breath, "then none of this would have happened. Instead, I told Nick to tell Jane to wait and that I'd be right back." Gertie, beyond inebriated, totally blottoed, had thrown up on the hall floor and then passed out, her face unceremoniously planted on the table. He had literally carried Gertie out of the hall and into her apartment. She had woken up only long enough to give him her door key. He must have been gone ten minutes, no longer. What was so fucking important that Jane couldn't wait ten fucking minutes?

Elliot had asked Nick if he remembered giving Jane the message. Nick had just shrugged non-committedly. "I think so, man, but I was really out of it myself. I'm pretty sure I left just after you took Gertie home, but I can't remember if I saw Jane on my way out or not. Sorry, man. I can barely remember how I got home, man, let alone what happened to Jane. Everything's a bit blurry. Must have been the shrooms that Gertie and I munched on, man. Said she scored them from a friend of Jane's who'd just gotten back from Vancouver. Excellent time until I lost total consciousness, man."

Elliot grimaced. His brother, the fucking idiot. He had asked Nick to do one simple thing. One thing and he couldn't even get that right. "I should have waited," Elliot chastised himself for the hundredth time.

Spying Mrs. Kirkland at the concession stand, Elliot sauntered over to make a few enquiries. "Hi, Mrs. Kirkland," he said as he took a place beside her.

Marie turned towards him with a relish-laden hotdog and a pop in her hands. "Good afternoon, Elliot. Quite the ballgame you guys played. Good luck on the next round."

"Thanks, Mrs. Kirkland." He placed an order for a cheeseburger and a cola. "Have you seen Jane yet today?"

Marie shook her head. "No, can't say as I have. Jane was still sleeping when we left this morning. I figured that she and Gertie would turn up here sooner or later to watch some games, but I haven't seen them yet."

Elliot nodded, biting back a sudden, intense influx of anger. Had she driven herself home? Stupid if she had. Jane had been drinking way too much to drive. The O.P.P. were notorious for hanging out close by, or for setting up ride checks after the dance, just waiting to hand out impaired driving violations and absconding with as many drivers' licenses as humanly possible. All Jane had to do was to wait for him to return from Gertie's, and he would have driven them to the river. Ten fucking minutes. She couldn't wait for ten fucking minutes. Trying to keep track of Jane had always been a difficult task at the best of times. Here one minute, gone the next. The girl was just not one to sit around, idly twiddling her thumbs. Okay, so maybe her intentions had been good at the time, but they were a couple now. She had to start thinking that way. She needed to start behaving that way. Unless she had been dead in a ditch, which he was eternally grateful that she hadn't been, there was absolutely no acceptable excuse for leaving him hanging. No matter what the reason, she could have found a way to let him know.

Marie interrupted his thoughts. "How was the dance?"

Elliot worked to keep his voice even-keeled. He knew it would take a very long time for Mrs. Kirkland to trust him after the last incident, and he was determined to keep it steady. "Good crowd. Lots of fun." Elliot paid for his food and placed the burger on an extra paper serviette.

He opened the bun to dab on more mustard and ketchup.

"Good. Well, I'd better get a decent seat for the next game before they're all gone. I wouldn't worry about Jane. She probably just slept in. I'm sure she'll show up soon."

Elliot nodded in agreement. "If you see her before I do, tell her that I was looking for her. Okay?" Elliot finished dressing his hamburger and placed the bun back on top.

"Will do, Elliot." Mrs. Kirkland nodded, turned and walked towards her husband who was patiently waiting by the bleachers.

Elliot grabbed his cheeseburger and cola and walked to his car to retrieve his cell phone. He opened his car door and sat behind the steering wheel. Elliot took a large bite from the cheeseburger and chewed before setting the burger on the seat beside him and placing the cola in the cup holder. Surely, he thought, Jane would be up by now. If Jane was still sleeping, she might be ticked off at him for calling, but that seemed like a small price to pay. Or maybe, she would be happy that he had called and would thank him for waking her up with an 'Oh shit, you're kidding, it can't possibly be that late' attitude. Either way, they needed to talk. He needed to know what had happened. Nip it in the bud now so it didn't happen again. They obviously needed to set up some relationship guidelines. Why did Jane always have to make everything so fucking complicated?

He reached over, retrieved his cell phone from his glove compartment, swallowed and dialed. No answer on the land-line or on her cell phone. He left a message saying they had won the game and when the next one would be played. Either she wasn't there or she was so dead to the world that she couldn't hear the telephones ringing.

Frustrated, Elliot dialed 411 to locate Gertie's telephone number and let the automated system connect him through.

"Hello?" The voice sounded distant and groggy.

"Gertie?" Elliot asked, not recognizing the voice.

"I think so. Although, right now, I really wish that I wasn't. Who's this?"

"It's Elliot. Do you remember me giving you a ride home last night?" Elliot took a drink from his cola and ignored the remaining cheeseburger. The burger tasted like sawdust. Elliot wasn't sure if the problem was with the burger, or if his taste buds were on strike due to lack of sleep and too many beers during the past couple of days.

Gertie hesitated. "Actually, no, but thanks for bringing me home. The last thing I remember is dancing with Don, the short-stop guy from the Shakespeare team. Cute, but not too bright that one."

Elliot nodded to himself. He surveyed the parking lot, looking for a tall, slender blonde with dark glasses and one killer of a hangover. "Have you heard from Jane yet today?"

"Nope."

"Okay. She hasn't shown up at the tournament yet, and she's not answering the phone so I thought I'd check to see if she was with you." Elliot absently rubbed his temple then dug around his glove compartment looking for a bottle of ibuprofen that he kept there. Finding the plastic bottle, he popped off the top and shook out two pills onto the dash.

"Sorry. I'm pretty sure that there's no one else here. Elliot, sorry, but I have to cut this short. I think I'm going to puke again."

"Feel better soon. Bye, Gertie." Elliot picked up the pills, tossed them into his mouth and washed them down with a swig of cola.

"Thanks, Elliot. Bye."

Elliot glanced down at his watch and decided that he had time to make a quick trip to the farm, but he'd have to hurry. He wouldn't be able to concentrate on the next game unless he knew what was going on with Jane. As Elliot began to shut his car door, a hand stopped him.

"Hey, where are you going, man?" Nick asked. "The game's going to start in 45 minutes and we have to warm up first."

"Warm up?" Elliot glared up at his brother. "We just finished playing a game. Why the fuck would we have to warm up?"

"The pitchers need to warm up, man, and someone has to catch for them."

"Nick, I need to run an errand. If you want to play hind-catch, go ahead. I'll be back in time for the game." Elliot attempted to tug the car door out of his brother's grip. Nick held tight.

"Which leads me back to my first question, man. Where are you headed?"

Exasperated and knowing that he was running short of time, Elliot finally pulled the car door loose from his brother's grasp. "To Jane's house." Elliot was really in no mood to explain everything but knew his twin's tenacity. "She hasn't shown up yet, and she isn't answering her phone so I thought I'd go down and see if she's there."

"Mind if I come along, man?"

"Suit yourself." Elliot shut his door and waited for Nick to walk around the car and climb into the passenger seat.

Nick picked up the cheeseburger before sitting down. "Are you planning on finishing this, man?"

Elliot shook his head. "No. Help yourself."

"Jane could be with Gertie," Nick offered as he took a large bite of the cheeseburger.

Elliot shook his head again as he started his car to leave. "Nope. Tried that already."

They drove in relative quiet, Elliot lost in thought and Nick content to eat free food.

The farm looked still, vacant. There was no sign of activity and no sign of Jane's car. The brothers got out of the Elliot's vehicle, walked up to the back porch of the house and watched as at least six cats zoomed past them, headed for the barn. Elliot knocked on the back door. No answer. He tried the doorknob. Locked. No one was home.

Nick sauntered off of the porch, worked his way carefully through a colourful, three-season flowerbed and peeked in through a kitchen window. "Hey, man, there's a note on the refrigerator. Maybe, it's from Jane."

Elliot joined his twin and cupped his hands beside his face as he peered through the glass. "Or it could have been from Mrs. Kirkland to Jane or it could be a grocery list. That's what Ma does. She writes down everything she's running short of or what we're out of and puts the list on the fridge. Can you read what the note says?"

Nick shook his head. "Only in your dreams, man. It doesn't look like a grocery list though." He turned towards Elliot. "Got your wallet?"

"Yeah. Why?" Elliot tried in vain to see what was written on the note then looked at his twin curiously.

"Maybe I can open the lock on the door with a credit card, man," Nick offered.

"That only works in the movies." Regardless, Elliot dug out his wallet, thinking it was worth a try.

It didn't work.

"How about looking for an open window?" Nick suggested when the credit card failed to produce the desired results.

Nodding, Elliot sent his brother one way around the house while he went in the opposite direction. A part of him knew this was the ultimate example of craziness, breaking and entering into the Kirkland's residence, but most of him just didn't care. If that note was from Jane, it would be worth it. If you'd just answer your fucking cell phone, Elliot thought indignantly, I wouldn't need to do this. Elliot glanced down at his watch and noted the time. They'd have to leave soon to make it for the next game. Stewart would be pissed if they were late.

"Found one, man!" Nick's voice sounded through the air, coming from the south side of the residence.

Without thinking twice, Elliot ran around the building just in time to see his twin climbing through the open bathroom window. "Fuck, I feel like a criminal or something." Elliot groaned.

"Kind of exciting isn't it, man?" Nick grinned broadly as he looked back out through the window. "Go back to the porch and

I'll let you in if it makes you feel better, man. Then you can only be charged for entering instead of breaking and entering."

Elliot glared at his twin. "That's not what I meant. Just move over and get out of the way." After Nick moved, Elliot heaved himself up and into the house. He was careful to shut the window behind them.

The two made their way into the kitchen. Elliot, ahead, walked briskly over to the refrigerator, grabbed the note off of the refrigerator and read the contents.

"Man, by the look on your face, I'd say that it wasn't good news." Nick joined his brother. "What's up, man?"

Mortified, reality annihilating any previous hope, Elliot handed the note to Nick. Elliot then sped past his brother and headed towards the backdoor as if fueled by an atomic rocket pack.

"She's gone," he muttered. "Just like that. She's fucking gone."

Nick read the note and reverently placed the paper back onto the refrigerator with a fake magnetic flower to keep it in place. A smile caressed his lips.

CHAPTER FORTY-THREE

School had begun without incident. Jane's class schedule contained all of the standard second-year courses with one major relief — she had been able to drop radio and sign up for cinematography instead. Although Jane loved to listen to the radio, she had discovered that it really takes a certain type of personality to not go absolutely bonkers in a broadcast booth, speaking to the unknown masses and trying to connect to them strictly on a verbal level. She was far too visual for that.

So much for her fantasy of becoming the sultry, sexy voice that helped long-distance truckers ease through endless midnight hours. "This is Sweet Jane coming at all of you big boys out there. I'll keep you company as the kilometers and the hours roll by…" Reality was such a kill joy.

Gertie had managed to settle in after only getting lost once. The fact that the Broadcasting course had its own wing helped. Except for the occasional general education class in the main section of the college, everything else the students required — the radio labs, the television studios, the film labs, the editing suites, the offices of their instructors, their own common area, a lounge filled with small tables where the students could play cards, eat their lunches or just hang out--was neatly structured and accessible. Go through the common area and walk through the door on the right and you'd find the teachers' offices and the second and third-year television studio. Go through the common area and walk through the door on the left and you'd find the editing suites, the first-year television studio and the radio labs. Go through the door on the left and take the staircase upstairs and you were in the world of film. They were their own community, set apart from the rest of the college's populace, and the students loved it, thrived on it.

And, to top everything off, Jane was thrilled with her new abode. As Todd had promised, the apartment was a quaint, two-bedroom, the top half of a house. Although she wasn't exactly sure what she had expected Todd to find, Jane had to admit that she had been pleasantly surprised. Except for the small kitchenette, the rooms were spacious and airy with hardwood floors. Sometimes, Jane would find herself just sitting and staring out of the living room window at the nearby park and elementary school. She would watch the children play, mesmerized by their innocence and their zest for life. Playing. Laughing. Enjoying life one enthusiastic moment at a time.

Even the landlord suited the area. Flavio Minicucci was in his early seventies, graying but full of life. He had bicycled the two blocks between the apartments and the house where he lived with his wife, Sophia, to meet Jane with the key. Sophia had baked soft, gooey, chocolate-chip cookies for Jane's arrival and had packed them in a pastry box so her husband could store the baked goods safely in the front carrier of his bike. After showing Jane around, Mr. Minicucci had told her to let him know if there was anything else that she needed. He didn't want her to be frightened living by herself until her husband joined her. It had taken Jane a nanosecond to comprehend Todd's deception, but she quickly understood that sometimes slight mistruths were necessary. She had nodded, smiled and thanked him. Mr. Minicucci had even invited Jane to dinner some evening, whatever worked for her. By the time her landlord had left, Jane had felt more like a guest than a tenant.

The bruises had dispersed; the contusions and the strained muscles had healed. The furniture had been moved, including a used, gray sofa and a matching armchair that had been donated by her sister, Pam, after discovering that her and Jeff's combined furniture was too much for the small house that they now rented. A live-in cop boyfriend beat a restraining order any day. Besides which, Jeff was really great with her children, and for the first time in years, Pam felt completely, utterly safe and had hope for the future.

Pam had even offered to support Jane in breaking the news to their parents that Jane was moving in with Todd instead of with Gertie as they had assumed. The reality of having both of their daughters live in sin had been a bitter struggle. In the end, they just wanted their children to be happy. Times were changing. They knew that. New values were replacing the old.

Then Todd had arrived with his vintage movie posters, his double mattress and box spring, his guy stuff and his all-embracing enthusiasm. The second, smaller bedroom had quickly been taken over by a 10-speed bicycle, a free-standing punching bag, boxing gloves, helmets, hockey sticks, knee pads, shoulder pads, and other various pieces of protective gear that Jane didn't quite understand the necessity for, a weight bench and free weights--so much for the thought of renting out the second bedroom to another student to cut down on their monthly rent expenses. When Todd had handed Jane a peace lily in a 10-inch pot, a present from his mom, their apartment officially became their home.

"Jane, have you seen my dark blue t-shirt? The one with Kurt Cobain on the front?" Todd walked into the small kitchen where Jane was situated, still in her pajamas and slippers, at a two-seater table, having a very strong, wake-me-up-please, cup of coffee.

Jane glanced up from her cup. Todd was wearing nothing but boxers. "Nope. Want a coffee?" Yes, life was basically going well. Basically.

"Not yet. I need to grab a shower first. Care to join me?" Todd winked, a mischievous smile illuminating his features.

God, he's so cute, Jane thought as her stomach clenched. Standing up to refresh her coffee, Jane walked over to the counter and replied, "I think I'll take a rain check if you don't mind. My brain's too fuzzy for anything other than coffee right now." Her stomach churned softly. She extracted the carafe from the drip coffee maker and poured herself a refill.

Vexed, Todd's smile disappeared. "You do realize that if I ever decide to cash in all of the rain checks, we're going to have sex non-stop for at least a week, and the only time we'll stop is to take a shower, to sleep, or to call out for a pizza?"

Jane opened the refrigerator door and extracted a carton of milk. "You don't cash in the rain checks, Todd." She poured milk into her coffee, put the carton back into the refrigerator then turned to face Todd. He stood only seconds away from her. The sense of claustrophobia was suddenly overwhelming. Jane took her cup and walked past him into the living room. "I do."

Flustered, he followed. "You know what I mean. It's been a month, and I've heard every excuse possible to not have sex. At first, I thought that you were just too tired from setting up the apartment, which, by the way, you did a terrific job of, and then I thought that maybe it was something to do with starting school again. I know that it can be crazy getting organized, but fuck, a whole month? Before we lived together, you'd come over almost every night to bang, and I could barely keep up to you. Now that we actually live together, you go to bed, curl up on your side and zilch. If I touch you, you cringe. Explain that to me." Todd shrugged his shoulders in exasperation.

     She turned away from him to fend off the bombardment of words. Jane didn't want to see his face, his brown eyes with their mixture of anger and confusion. "Todd, you're over-reacting." She'd been wondering how long he would wait. How could she explain to him that when he chanced too close, she couldn't breathe? How could she explain that the feel of his energy caressing her skin, sent shivers of fear instead of desire coursing through her? How could she possibly explain that it took all of her energy just to have a clear thought these days? How could she explain any of this without explaining all of it? And if she explained all of it, then she'd have to risk losing him. She couldn't do that. Better that Todd be angry with her for now until she could figure things out.

     "Am I?" Todd didn't sound convinced.

     "Look, we can talk about this later. If I'm late for TV lab, I get an automatic zero for the whole day." Jane headed towards their bedroom to get dressed and was abruptly stopped by Todd's hand grabbing her arm. With every ounce of her being, Jane stifled a scream.

     "No," Todd insisted. "I want to talk about this now." He gently turned Jane towards him. "If you've changed your mind about us, if this is something to do with me, something that I'm doing wrong, I need to know."

     Jane studied his eyes, so soft, so brown, so imploring and so full of confusion. Todd.

     This was her Todd. Not some monster from the shadows. Todd. "It's not you. It's all me. I've just been feeling really lousy lately, and I'm not sure why." Part truth, part lie. She could live with that for now.

     Todd's expression turned to one of concern. "Why didn't you say something sooner? Maybe you should see a doctor." Todd released Jane's arm and placed his still-tanned hands on his hips in his typical thought position.

Jane shook her head and shrugged her slim shoulders, as if dismissing her previous stupidity. "I don't know. I thought it would just go away like a flu bug or something. Not worth going to the Emergency Department for."

"The college has a nurse who can refer you to a doctor if necessary," Todd reminded her.

Jane nodded. She'd gone to them for a prescription for the pill during her first year of college. Handy service. "Right. I forgot all about that."

"So, you'll make an appointment?"

Jane took a sip of her coffee and swallowed. "Okay, but I think you're over-reacting. Now go and have your shower before we're both late." She turned to head towards the bedroom once more. Almost there.

"Humour me, Jane." Todd's voice followed her. He followed her.

Jane stopped by the bedroom door. Todd was his usual three steps behind her. She focused on her breathing. When she was nervous or when she felt panic set in, her breathing was the first to lose its rhythm. Then, of course, her ability to speak coherently would diminish. Stuttering came next and then a complete meltdown. Another reason why radio announcing was not up high on her resume. "Okay. I'll go to the nurse's office at lunch time and make an appointment, but she'll just say that it's stress or lack sleep or a forty day virus or something stupid."

"Maybe, but it could also be something more serious like mono. I had a friend who had mono in high school, and it wiped him out for six months. If that's what you have, then we both need to know because it's contagious."

Jane nodded. "Right. You're right. I get it. I'll make the appointment. Now go and have your shower. I need to get dressed."

"Okay, then." Todd nodded in satisfaction, turned and headed back towards the washroom. "If you see my Kurt Cobain t-shirt let me know."

Jane turned, walked into their spacious bedroom, set the coffee cup down on top of her dresser and began searching through several laundry baskets for clean underwear, a pair of socks, her stone-washed jeans and her favourite, grey, lined hoodie. After several attempts, she found what she was looking for as well as locating the misplaced t-shirt. She placed the t-shirt on top of the bed for Todd to find.

Jane discarded her pajamas, sat down on the edge of the bed and began dressing. It was the knowing that frightened her. She had been dragging herself through the days for two weeks now. Every moment of existence had become a severe challenge. Her energy had suddenly been zapped out of her like a balloon popped by a pin. At first, Jane had done well to convince herself that her current fatigue was mental or stress related; however, a part of her did not accept that diagnosis. A part of her, the part of her that obsessed by doing online searches for symptomology, continually checked through her own physiology to establish which systems were still functioning normally. Too many signs now to ignore. Too many symptoms forever and eternally prodding and poking at her shield of denial.

When she had finished her morning preparations, Jane pulled on her running shoes and went outside to wait for Todd. She lit a cigarette, hoping the nicotine would calm her nerves, and gagged.

CHAPTER FORTY-FOUR

Fall had arrived in Donnybrooke with its usual cascade of colours. The surrounding, rolling hills were a plethora of varying shades of yellows, oranges and reds, so brilliant that they inspired busloads of tourists to come with cameras of all shapes and sizes to capture Mother Nature's splendour. Soon the tamaracks would join the party adorned in their best, pale yellow shrouds, standing proudly amongst their evergreen brethren in their distinguished fashion. Energized squirrels and chipmunks skittered and chattered, foraging, collecting, and stashing their winter food supply of nuts, seeds and other edible delicacies. Deer, gentle brown eyes alert, waited, nose to the wind, for the impending sounds of hunters. Coyotes howled, gathered to move to the higher grounds of the escarpment where craggy rocks and crevices provided safe winter shelters. Wild geese honked overhead as their uniform, v-shaped flight patterns caressed the clear blue skies, signaling to all who would listen that it was time to head for a warmer climate and a kinder existence. The air breathed coolly, foreshadowing the long winter months ahead, not quite cold enough for snow yet, but a definite reminder to wear a heavy sweater and warm gloves. The sounds of children laughing, eager to be outside during recesses, wafted through space and time. Elliot noticed none of this.

He noticed that it was time to rotate the stock in the store from leather softball gloves and baseball bats to football cleats and hockey skates. He noticed that the metal shelves needed to be readjusted to accommodate the twenty or thirty different sizes and shapes of hockey sticks this year. He noticed that, after work, one cold beer generally led to at least six and a hangover seemed to be his best buddy. He noticed that, when he had a hangover, it took all of his energy to focus on just making it through the day and this was a good thing. A fine thing. He noticed that, sometimes he forgot to shave, but didn't notice it until he was already at work and, by then, it was too late to care. And not caring was a good thing too. A damned fine thing, in fact.

What he did not care about these days was as long as his ma's never-ending grocery list that hung on the refrigerator door.

He did not care that Jane had blown out of his life one more time without even the courtesy of an explanation or without saying goodbye. Bitch. He did not care that the local gossip mill was busy speculating that Jane had just dumped him out of the blue and left. Stupid bitch. He did not care that Jane's cell phone number had been disconnected and that trying to get a new telephone number for her or her new address from Jane's mother had led to a very short conversation where Mrs. Kirkland had apologized profusely and informed him that Jane had moved in with Todd. Whatever had happened between Jane and Elliot that summer would best be laid to rest. It was over. Done. Let it go. Stupid, fucking bitch.

Yes, it was a good thing, a fine thing that he didn't care. Because if he cared, he might go crazy. And if he went crazy, he just might end up doing something fucking stupid. Bitch.

CHAPTER FORTY-FIVE

Jane, attired only in a light, blue, cotton gown, shivered and wondered why doctors kept their examination rooms so cool when they just had to know that the patients would freeze to death long before they would ever get the chance to be examined. Fresh cadavers, ladies and gents, kept on ice for your convenience. Yup, got 'em by the dozens. Fresh stock every day. Pick the one you want. Fresh and cold. Fresh and cold. Fresh and…

"Ms. Kirkland?"

The voice startled Jane out of her morbid train of thought. Jane sat up and faced the voice. "That would be me," she replied. The doctor, an attractive woman in her forties, was busy scanning through Jane's chart as she approached.

"You are aware that the test came back positive?" There was a look of genuine concern on the doctor's face—a nice face, a pleasant face, the face of a favourite aunt.

Jane grimaced. Yes, she was aware. Painfully aware. She had previously peed on several sticks with the same result. Regardless, there had to be a mistake. "So I was told, but that's impossible." More than impossible, it was unthinkable.

The doctor hovered beside Jane with a look of curiosity. "What makes it impossible?"

Jane patiently explained, "Because I've been on the pill for the past year. There's absolutely no possible way that I could be pregnant. None. It's always worked before. Therefore, there must be another logical explanation for all of this. There just has to be." No test was infallible. Maybe, she'd gotten a bad batch of home tests from the drug store. Maybe, the lab technician had inadvertently switched her specimen with that of another nice lady, a lady who desperately wanted a baby and who was, right now, getting the bad news that she wasn't pregnant after all. Jane began to fidget with her rings, turning them around and around her fingers, trying to shake the vision of cadavers that floated steadily through her mind. Fresh and cold. Fresh and cold.

The doctor nodded in an appreciative manner. "Unfortunately, Jane, as I'm sure you are already aware, the pill is not always a hundred percent effective, especially if taken with other medications, but I suggest that I do an internal exam just to make sure. Okay?" The doctor placed Jane's chart on a nearby desk and closed the door to the hallway. "If you would just lie back and put your feet up into the stirrups, we can begin."

Reluctantly, Jane did as the doctor instructed. The paper crinkled as Jane lay back down on the cool, black vinyl. Fresh cadavers, gift wrapped to your specifications. Bows cost extra. "What do you mean, if it's taken with other medications?" Jane could feel her heart beat steadily like a small drum pounding out the seconds of eternity.

"Antibiotics, even large doses of Vitamin C, can sometimes reduce the effectiveness of the contraceptive." The doctor put on latex gloves then sat down at the end of the examination table. "This is going to be a bit uncomfortable. Trust me, I know."

"Oh fuck." Jane covered her mouth too late. The words had escaped quicker than the Bird Man of Alcatraz.

"Pardon?" The doctor mused as she began.

"Sorry. Nothing. I was just remembering that I had this terrible case of bronchitis and…" Jane squeezed her eyes shut tightly as she felt the penetration of cool metal. Dead meat, ladies and gents. That's what she was. As sure as the sun rose every day in the east. Dead meat.

"And the doctor put you on antibiotics without asking if you were sexually active or what kind of contraceptive you were using," the doctor finished Jane's statement for her.

"That would sum it up, yes." Jane stared at the ceiling. Focus away from the reality of the procedure and count slowly. 99, 98, 97, 96… Focus on the ceiling. 95, 94, 93, 92… Could use a coat of paint. 91, 90, 89, 87… Focus on anything other than the likelihood of her being pregnant. 86, 85, 84, 83… She'd had her period after Todd which meant only one thing. 82, 81, 80, 79… That one thing was just too horrid to even consider. 78, 77, 76, 75… Nick was the father.

"Okay, I'm done. You can sit back up now." The doctor removed her gloves and assisted Jane back into a sitting position. "Your uterus is definitely enlarged with means…"

"Which means," Jane finished for the doctor, "that I'm definitely pregnant."

The doctor nodded and picked the chart back up to make notes. "When was your last menstrual cycle, Jane?"

Jane felt numb. Again. Fresh and cold. Cadavers, get them while supplies last. "The end of July, around the 25th, I think."

"Are you still taking the pill?"

Jane shook her head. "No. When my period didn't show up, I didn't start taking it again. There was no reason to anyway. I'm not having sex with anyone right now." Cadavers. All shapes and sizes. Order online now and receive a second cadaver for free! Only three easy payments of $19.99, plus shipping and handling.

"So, that would make you approximately six or seven weeks pregnant." The doctor finished charting and moved the chair to sit beside Jane. "By your reaction, I would venture that this is an unplanned pregnancy."

Jane nodded. Unplanned. Yes, it was definitely unplanned. At least by her. Why hadn't Nick worn a condom anyway? Even her asshole, ex-brother-in-law had been smart enough to use a condom whenever he had forced himself on her. If it had been the other way around, and she'd been Nick, she would have definitely worn protection, especially with the amount of DNA used in courts...so maybe, Nick didn't consider it that way. Maybe, to him, it was a casual, one night stand? That didn't make sense either. If he truly believed that it was casual sex between two consenting adults, he wouldn't have bound her hands, wouldn't have threatened her. Impossible to rationalize the irrational. A tear escaped down Jane's cheek. I can't do this, Jane thought. I can't. Nick can't be the father of my child. The guy is nuts. She'd known him her whole life, and she'd never once dreamt that he was capable of such cruelty, of such absolute betrayal. She didn't want to find out what else he was capable of.

The doctor handed Jane a tissue. "Would you like to give some thought to your possible options? You are still well within your first trimester."

Options, Jane thought. Options? What options? There were no other options. "I want an abortion." Jane wiped away the tear, hardening herself against any and all other possibilities.

The doctor studied her calmly. "Are you sure?"

Sure. Positive. Absolutely. Undeniably. Jane made herself

sound firm. "Yes. This baby was conceived through sexual assault. I want an abortion."

The doctor, her brow knitted, her eyes serious, reached out and took Jane's hand in hers. "You were raped?"

Jane felt panic rise. Raped. What a horrid word. She wanted to flee but steeled herself and looked directly into the doctor's kind eyes. "Yes."

"Did you report it to the police?"

"No." Jane hung her head and thought her voice sounded very small, like a child after being caught doing something very, very bad.

"May I ask why not?"

Jane raised her heavy head and cleared her throat. Their eyes met then, sharing a common understanding only known by a victim — that sometimes silence was the only absolute protection one has. A silence, so deep, so all encompassing, that you cannot hear the sound of your own thoughts. You have no voice. Jane sputtered, searching for the appropriate explanation. "I knew him...I was drunk...there were no witnesses..."

Doctor Lee nodded and raised her hand. "It's okay. I understand. What I would suggest then is that we take a smear to check for any STDs and a blood sample to check for HIV. You should get retested for HIV in six months and then at a year just to make sure."

"All right," Jane agreed. The idea that Nick could be contagious hadn't even occurred to her.

"If I can get you to lie back one more time, this won't take long."

The abortion was scheduled for the following day. No muss. No fuss. A simple procedure really. Day surgery. Then it would be over. The nightmare would be over. She and Todd could go on as planned, and no one would ever know except she and that nice lady doctor who had been so totally understanding that Jane had ended up crying despite her best efforts at cold-hearted bravery.

Jane spent the rest of the day walking through the noisy city streets trying to not think of the baby that would be spending its day totally concentrating on the dividing and splitting of cells.

After all, it wasn't really a baby yet anyway. It was an embryo. An embryo. It wasn't sucking its thumb or whiling away the hours postulating the cause of relativity. It was an embryo less than a centimetre long. An unwanted embryo at that. If only the baby had been Todd's, but it wasn't. It was Nick's, and it would ruin everything. Everything.

Pale leaves broke free from their parent captors, floated and twirled in the slight breeze until finally landing gracefully onto the cooling earth. Brightly coloured posters, some orange, some green, covered light poles and neighbourhood bulletin boards, announcing upcoming Thanksgiving Celebrations at local churches. Turkey and stuffing, corn, yams, mashed potatoes, fresh baked pie. All Welcome. College students lingered on street corners, laughing as they compared stories to tell the folks back home, or better yet, comparing stories to not tell the folks back home. Small, cherubic children, bundled in warm jackets, slid down aluminum slides in the park with a gleeful, "Watch me, Mommy! Watch me, Daddy!" Black squirrels, tails flagging their presence, skittered and foraged, dreaming of warm attics where they could nest for the winter. Jane noticed none of this.

What Jane did notice was how old she suddenly felt, as if a time machine had transported her heart a hundred years into the future. She noticed how every breath felt like an eternity, how every thought hurt more than she ever dreamed her soul could bear.

By the time Jane found herself back at her apartment, the sun had already set and the streetlights were illuminating a pathway to her future. Yes, Todd. Her future. In her heart, Jane knew that she had made the right decision. There were no other options. None. Absolutely. Undeniably. None.

Todd looked as if he'd been pacing. "Where have you been? Why didn't you answer your cell phone?"

Jane replied simply, "Walking. Thinking." She closed the door behind her and squatted down to take off her running shoes. Once removed, Jane tossed her purse onto a nearby chair and walked towards the kitchen to make herself a tea and a sandwich. She was famished from the fresh, cool air.

Todd followed. "Well? What did the doctor have to say?"

Avoiding Todd's eyes, Jane opened a loaf of bread, took a deep breath and lied. "I have a small, benign tumour attached to the lining of my uterus. Nothing serious really. In fact, she said that it was fairly common. I'm booked in for day surgery tomorrow, and, as long as everything goes smoothly, there shouldn't be any long-term effects. I should still be able to have children someday." Jane opened the refrigerator door and extracted chicken slices, lettuce, a slice of cheese and mayonnaise from the refrigerator to make her sandwich.

Todd let out a whistle of astonishment. His voice edged on anger. "Jesus, Jane. You act as if it's nothing at all. It could have been cancer for fuck's sake. How long have you known there was something wrong? Why didn't you tell me?" Todd absent-mindedly ran his fingers through his long hair, pulling the strands back from his face.

Jane filled a black kettle with water and plugged it into an electrical outlet. She hadn't expected Todd's reaction and was less than prepared to be drilled for details. A nursing student she was not. "A simple 'Hi Jane' would have been nice instead of pouncing on me the moment I walked through the door." After constructing her sandwich, she cut the bread in half, took a bite, chewed and swallowed.

"I've been calling your cell phone and texting you for four hours, Jane. Four hours. I had no idea where you were. You could have at least had the common decency to answer the fucking thing and let me know that you were okay." Todd moved in closer beside her, unplugged the kettle, opened a cupboard door and took out a box of peppermint tea. Taking two mugs from the draining board, Todd placed a teabag in each and filled the cups with boiling hot water.

Jane turned to face him. "I'm sorry. I had my phone turned off. I didn't want to talk to anyone, just think." She stroked his arm to placate him. Jane had always known that Todd had a temper, had seen what he could do when the temper became unleashed, but, instinctively, she also knew that this time, his anger masked his fear. "I've known for a while that there was something wrong. I just didn't know what exactly and since it was a woman's thing, I didn't think that you'd be interested." Not a lie. That made it easier. Jane took a spoon out of a drawer and removed the teabag from her mug.

Todd's voice changed then, the anger gone. "Jane, you have to understand that when something concerns you, it concerns me too. If something happens to you, it happens to me too. You're not alone. I love you." He put his arms around Jane's shoulders and hugged her close to him.

Jane shut her eyes, rested her weary head on Todd's shoulder and allowed herself to smell the tangy scent of his aftershave, to feel the warmth of his body next to hers, to feel his arms around her, to feel his strength, his gentleness, his love. She caressed his back with her fingers, following the curves of his shoulder blades, then tracing the hollow of his back. She smiled as he kissed her hair, feeling the stirrings below pressed into her. Todd. Her Todd. "Make love to me, Todd," she whispered. "Please, make love to me."

His voice was hoarse with wary desire. "Will it hurt you? I can't do it if it'll hurt you. I'd rather wait."

"It won't hurt," she assured him, stroking his hair and kissing his cheek.

"What about the surgery?"

"It'll be okay as long as we use a condom." Jane released her embrace and stood back to look up into Todd's eyes. "It's either tonight or we wait six to eight weeks after the surgery."

Todd searched her eyes for a moment then let go of her waist. "Gotta run," he announced as he jogged to the entranceway, hastily put on his jacket and running shoes then grabbed the keys for his car off a wall hook by the door.

Jane watched for a moment, puzzled, and then asked, "Where are you going?"

He stopped to address her. "Do you have any condoms?"

Jane shook her head and grinned. "No. Good point."

"Right. Neither do I, but the drug store on South Pelham Road is open until 9:00 p.m. so, if I leave now, I can get there before it closes." With that, Todd waved and left.

For the first time in too long, Jane laughed. With Todd out the door, Jane decided that she had time for a quick shower before he returned. The tea was entirely forgotten.

The sex was quick and passionate, then long and gentle. As Jane drifted off to sleep, she felt absolutely, undeniably positive that everything would be okay.

"Mommy?" The little boy wriggled on the restaurant bench as he scooped another spoonful of ice cream into his precious mouth.
"Yes, Sweetie?" Jane studied her young son, so full of life, of love, of mischief. His fine facial features reflected hers, his hair was a light sandy blonde, his eyes, so trusting, so innocent, were hazel.
"When I'm done with this ice cream, can I have two more scoops?" The lad accidentally dropped a small toy truck and disappeared under the arborite table to retrieve his treasure.
"No, Honey. If you have any more, you'll spoil your dinner."
"Maybe," the boy suggested as he reappeared, "maybe, I could have ice cream for dinner."
She laughed and shook her head. That was her boy, always looking for an angle.

Jane woke up in a cold sweat.

CHAPTER FORTY-SIX

Elliot sat in his favourite easy chair, watching his favourite baseball team and drinking his favourite beer. Life could be worse, he decided without true resolve. The score was two to one for the Blue Jays. A great game, all things considered. A few close calls, but the team was maintaining the lead. If they won this game, they'd only need one more to make the play-offs.

He thought of nothing in particular, letting random ponderings trickle past his consciousness largely going unnoticed. Instead, his mind focused on the hind-catcher throwing the other team's runner out at second. Good throw. Elliot wasn't sure of the exact distance between home plate and second base in hard ball, but it looked like one hell of a long way.

The beer was cold. The team was hot. The room was dark except for a dim light shining from one small lamp on a side table and the emanations from the wide-screen television. High Definition was truly amazing. Elliot could see the sweat as the next batter wiped his brow. Easier to focus in the semi-darkness. Easier to not think about anything other than the fact that this was the bottom half of the ninth inning, one out and one runner on first. He'd win fifty bucks in a sports pool if the Blue Jays won the play-offs.

Elliot's being ached for a quiet moment. A moment when Jane did not enter the peripheral of his mind. A moment that was clear, concise and uninfected. Third strike. Batter out. One more out to go and then the game would be over.

He did not initially notice when Nick entered the living room. Elliot definitely did not register the look of supreme triumph that sullied Nick's similar features, the insanity behind the mask.

"Come on, man. You can't mope around here forever," Nick chided his twin as he walked up to Elliot's chair. "No gash is worth that, man. How about going out with me tonight? Maybe Mary has a friend she can set you up with?"

Elliot remained focused on the television screen. "Fuck off, Nick. I'm watching the game." The last thing Elliot wanted was a lecture from his brother regardless of how well-intentioned. The last thing Elliot needed was another pep talk, another speech on how it just wasn't meant to be, another cliché on how there's always another fish in the ocean, another look of empathic sympathy, another pat on the back from anyone, anywhere and especially not from Nick.

"Aw, man, give it a rest. You look like shit. People are talking."

Elliot turned his focus away from the television. The glare in his eyes told all. Don't mess with me, I'm not in the mood. Don't start something we'll both regret later. You don't know. You can't begin to understand. The denial was over, but the whys were left unanswered. The brilliant pain remained. The anger was brimming, threatening to boil over like a kettle full of steam in search of a whistle to sound off its vengeful force. He'd been duped. Played. Conned. Elliot was positive of that fact and he had to live with that. He'd been duped in front of the whole world to see. His world and he had to live in it.

"I don't fucking care what people have to say. Jane is gone. End of story. Good riddance. Hope she and her college butt fuck rot in hell." Elliot rose from his chair. The game had ended. The Blue Jays had won. He was one step closer to being fifty bucks richer. However, his one, uninfected moment lay in ruins because Nick wouldn't shut the fuck up. Elliot, volatile fury barely bridled, took a step, closed the small gap between him and his brother and looked directly into the eyes of his shadow. "Are you happy now? All I wanted to do was watch the fucking game."

Nick let out a long, slow breath. "Ecstatic, man. Just fucking ecstatic."

Elliot bumped past Nick. "I'm going to bed."

As Nick watched Elliot storm away, he grinned. Nick was happier than he'd been in a very long time. Maybe, he'd lost the girl, but that was okay. He had Mary now and she was better than Jane any day. Mary could give as well as she received. The point was that he had won the game. He'd finished the race first. He'd claimed the prize. It was over. It was finally done. He had won.

CHAPTER FORTY-SEVEN

"Jane, are you sure that you don't want me to come with you? I could drive you home after the surgery." Todd, still in bed, watched as Jane dressed.

Jane forced a bright, fake smile. "Absolutely positive. There's no reason for both of us to miss classes this morning. Besides which, the procedure is done with a local anaesthetic so I'll be fine." She walked over to the bed where Todd reclined, his head resting on his hand and propped up by his right elbow. She sat down on the edge and gently kissed his forehead. "I appreciate the offer though." Todd. Her Todd. The love of her life. Her soulmate. She wanted to spend the rest of her life with this man. She was a hundred percent certain of that now. She wanted to marry him, to build a life with him, to have children with him and to grow old with him. In that order. Todd. No more second thoughts. She was all in now, heart and soul, mind and body.

Todd was still not convinced that she should go alone. "I'd feel better if I was with you. All I'll do in class is sit there and worry."

Jane shook her head as she tied her long locks back into a ponytail with a black scrunchy. "I'll be fine. Really. Like I said, it's a simple procedure. Just make sure that you take really good notes in Broadcast Journalism so I can copy them later." Jane loved the way Todd's brow furrowed when he was unhappy. There was no mistaking that look. He wasn't about to be appeased so easily.

Todd grabbed Jane by the arm as she started to rise. She sat back down. His frown deepened. "I don't care about missing a couple of classes this morning, especially when we can download the Powerpoint notes later."

Jane shook her head again. "You know that the Powerpoints only cover the main topics. There's a lot of information that we go over in class that won't be on them but will be on the tests." She traced Todd's frown lines with the tip of her index finger, smoothing away the dark abyss of emotions. "I'll make you a deal. If I don't feel well enough to drive home later, I'll text you. Just make sure you keep your phone on vibrate so it doesn't disturb the rest of the class because I have no idea when I'll be done."

Todd released the grip on her arm and sat up cross-legged on the bed. "I don't like it but okay. Deal. Send me a text either way though so I'm not left hanging again. Okay?"

Jane nodded her consent. "Sure." She glanced at the black, digital alarm clock on their gray painted, wooden nightstand. "Don't you think you should get up soon and get ready for school? There's coffee made in the kitchen." She rose to leave.

Todd's concern vanished from his face, replaced by a broad smile. "It's all your fault, you know." He stretched his muscular arms over his head then grabbed each arm individually behind his back, stretching his neck to the opposite side and causing several audible snaps from his vertebrae.

"What's my fault?" Jane enquired. She loved moments like this, the real life couple moments that emphasized that they were more than just roommates with benefits, that maybe their relationship could endure another two years of school and then the great beyond.

"That I'm not out of bed yet." Todd looked smug, comfortable in his absolute nakedness, the comforter barely camouflaging his usual morning erection.

"And why is it my fault?" Jane's right eyebrow rose quizzically. "I've been up for a couple of hours already."

She loved this man, loved the way that his shoulder-length hair fell naturally, framing his boy-next-door features. She loved the sun-enhanced freckles on his broad shoulders. She loved the fact that, although he could make a superb macaroni and cheese casserole from scratch, he was otherwise lost in the kitchen. She loved the fact that he always made sure he put the toilet seat down. She loved the fact that she never walked into the bathroom greeted at an inopportune moment by an empty roll of toilet paper. She loved the fact that he automatically picked up a dish towel whenever she started doing dishes. She loved the fact that cleaning was not a four-letter word, that he knew dusting meant actually picking up items and dusting underneath, not just around them. She loved the fact that, although he hated sorting his darks from his whites, he would sit in the Laundromat with her for hours, telling stories, while their clothing washed and dried. She loved the fact that, if her car didn't want to start, he was the first to pop the hood to see if he could figure out what was wrong before paying for an expensive mechanic. She loved the fact that he didn't hog all of the covers at night that, instead, he spooned around her to make sure that she was warm and covered. She loved the fact that he would stand up to her one moment, totally ticked off about whatever, and then embrace her the next moment, any argument quickly forgotten. She loved the fact that they could agree to disagree and leave the argument unresolved but with no hard feelings. She loved the fact that, when she walked into a room, he looked at her as if she was the only other person in the universe. She loved the fact that he loved her.

"You were like the bionic woman last night. I'm fucking exhausted," Todd complained good-naturedly without real conviction.

Jane chuckled. "Is that a complaint? If it's a complaint, you're on the wrong floor. Customer Service is two floors down."

Todd ran his fingers through his brown hair and grinned. "Definitely not a complaint."

"Good." Jane tilted her head briefly to the right then straightened. "Do you think last night was enough to hold you for the next eight weeks? Give or take the occasional blow job?"

With a look of great concentration, Todd maneuvered himself to the edge of the bed and dangled his legs over. He hoisted himself up into a standing position, looking stiff but satisfied, like a marathon runner just finishing twenty kilometres. He hugged Jane and kissed her cheek. "Jane, for another night like that, I'd wait ten years if I had to."

Jane hated driving in St. Catharines. Nine times out of ten, she would somehow end up on a one-way street going a totally different direction than her destination required, and then she would get totally lost trying to compensate. This time, Jane wasn't taking any chances. The directions on the MapQuest print-out looked really simple. All she had to do was take the 406 to the appropriate turn off and go from there. Three streets down and then turn left, go down a half a block and she'd be at Doctor Lee's actual practice where the good doctor would perform the abortion-- Manual Vacuum Aspiration also known as MVA. The pamphlet made the abortion sound simple enough. A local anaesthetic was used for the cervix then the contents of the uterus were vacuumed out by a hand-held, plastic aspirator.

"So," Jane spoke softly out loud, "why then does the mere thought of removing this unwanted embryo make my stomach clench?" Nerves maybe… She had so much riding on this. The rest of her life was riding on this one decision.

"Mommy…" a small voice resounded through her mind, an echo from the night before.

Jane rolled down her car window as she drove and, switching hands on the steering wheel, grabbed a cigarette from the ashtray where she'd placed it before starting her journey. Jane had decided to wait for a couple of hours after getting up before having her first cigarette in the hope that she wouldn't gag this time. The second cigarette would be easier, but the first one was brutal.

"Mommy, please," the voice came again, small, distant and insistent.

Jane lit the cigarette and inhaled lightly waiting for the first sign of trouble. On second thought, it probably wasn't such a brilliant idea to wait until she was driving.

"Mommy…"

As her stomach churned, Jane signaled to cross through the lane on her immediate right and pulled over on the side of the road. She shut off the engine and quickly exited her vehicle, kneeling in the ditch just in time to forfeit her peanut butter on toast. I think I'm losing it, Jane thought as she wiped the spittle from her mouth with the back of her hand. After standing up, she walked back to the passenger side of her car. She opened the door and grabbed a bottle of water from the cup holder to rinse out her mouth. Closing the door behind her, Jane leaned up against the warm metal, faced away from traffic, took a gulp of water, swished the welcomed liquid around in her mouth then spat it out onto the ground. Vehicles zoomed past, but Jane did not notice.

What she did notice was that she had miraculously managed to not lose her cigarette. Jane inhaled again, determined that, sooner or later, she would win the battle over her body and exhaled the smoke. A couple more hours and this would all be over. By late afternoon she would be back at her apartment, curled up on her couch with her textbooks surrounding her, drinking tea and trying to decipher Todd's scribble that he passed off for handwriting. He'd sit down beside her to translate and all would be well. All would be as it should be with the only stress in her life being the fact that they had two major assignments due on the same day next week and script outlines to prepare for their Dramatic Script Writing course. Ironic, how she had begged Todd to take the script writing course with her, saying that it would make a brilliant addition to their resumes, and yet, a feasible, original idea still eluded her while Todd had his outline half completed. Jane glanced at her watch and sighed in relief. Lots of time yet. She'd give herself another five minutes to make sure that her body was through recycling and then head out again. She took another drink of water and swallowed.

"Mommy..."

He looks just like me, Jane thought. Her son. No sign of Nick there at all. Just a little boy who looks like his mother. A little boy with sandy blonde hair and hazel eyes. Jane raised the cigarette to her lips and inhaled deeply again, luxuriating in the fact that the gagging had ceased once her stomach contents had fled from her body. Just a smart little boy with a keen sense of logic. Her son. Not Nick's. Hers.

There had only been three weeks between her last rendezvous with Todd at the Lowdown Motel on highway 10 and her night with Nick. Considering that a normal pregnancy lasted between 38 and 40 weeks, three weeks would be easy to explain, especially if the baby arrived early.

"Mommy..."

Jane rubbed her hand over her face. God, what she thinking. This was insane. It had only been a dream. A dream. Nothing more. Just a dream. Maybe her subconscious wasn't totally comfortable with ending the pregnancy, but it was for the best. She didn't have time for baby right now. She had no way of supporting a child while she went to school. She'd have to give up everything and find a job. That was not in her plan. That was not in her carefully drawn out schedule of where she wanted to be and what she wanted to be doing. Children were for later when she was older, like thirty, and established in her career. Children were for later. Not now. She couldn't possibly have a baby right now. Even just considering the idea was insane. There was no way she could have the baby and then put the child up for adoption. She'd never sleep another night in her life wondering where the child was, how the child was doing, what the child had been named and what the child looked like. Was he being abused? Was he loved? Nope. No way. Abortion was the only option. End of the line. No other choice. None. Absolutely none.

Jane walked around to the driver's side and climbed back into her car. She stubbed the cigarette out in the ashtray, put the bottle of water in the cup holder then dug her cell phone out of her purse and dialed.

"Good morning. Chelsea Animal Hospital. Pam speaking," came the voice on the other end.

"Pam. Do you have a second? I really need to talk to someone." Jane glanced at her watch again. Time was ticking by way too fast.

"For you, always. What's up, Jane? Why aren't you in school?"

Jane smiled fondly. Pam, always the mother hen. "I'm pregnant," Jane blurted out and stared out at the cars that whizzed past her, no one stopping to see if she was stranded, no one caring enough even to slow down.

"Oh, Jane," Pam sighed empathetically, as only a sister who has been through an unplanned pregnancy can do. "Have you told Todd yet?"

"No, I thought that I could deal with this on my own." Tell Todd. Tell him what? Tell him that Nick had gotten her pregnant while she was planning on fucking Elliot? That would go over well. Not.

"Oh, Sweetie, you have to tell him. This is Todd's baby, isn't it? Or did you end up sleeping with Elliot over the summer too?"

"I did not have sex with Elliot." Not a lie. Jane's voice sounded harsher than she had intended.

"Okay," Pam backtracked. "Just the two of you were getting so close. Sorry. Never mind me. Forget that I asked. Where are you right now?"

"I'm sitting here in my car on the side of the road on my way to having an abortion which made total sense until about a minute ago, and now I don't know what to do." Jane glanced down at her watch again. If she didn't get back on the road soon, she would be late for her appointment. I can't do this, Jane thought. If I have the abortion, I will kill my son. If I don't have an abortion, I risk losing everything else. How can I possibly make this decision?

"Jane, you have to make the right decision for you. I take it back. Forget about Todd right now. This is your body and your life. You're twenty-years-old and in college. If you decide to go through with the abortion, you can have children later when you're ready. If you decide to have the baby, you know I'll be there for you. I love you. I mean, there are options. You know that. If you decide to not terminate the pregnancy, you can always put the baby up for adoption—there are lots of good people out there who would give anything for a child--or Jeff and I can keep the baby until you're done school. Jeff's on this kick right now where he's decided that he wants six children so having a baby around for a while might just shock him into reality long enough for him to change his mind." Pam's voice was soft and soothing, like a lullaby. "How far along are you?"

"Eight weeks."

"Then you have time. Jane, you don't have to decide today if you're not ready. Take a week if you need to and just think it over."

Jane nodded. "You're right. Thanks. Look, Pam, I have to go." Jane lit another cigarette and started her car.

"Call me later, Pumpkin."

"Will do. Pam, I love you."

"I love you too."

As Jane walked into the doctor's office, she knew, deep down, that she was making the right decision. She couldn't worry about what was right for anyone else but herself. Jane gave her name and her OHIP card to the attendant at the front desk and sat down in the waiting room to bide her time.

As she waited, Jane watched a small boy, four-years-old maybe, play with two small, diecast toy cars, one grey and one red, racing them around on the carpeted floor. The boy's mother was busy attending to another, younger child, but she kept a close eye on the boy's whereabouts. As the boy made his way in Jane's direction she spoke to him, asking him which one was his favourite car. His face beamed as he thought for a second then decided on the red one. The red one was faster, he assured Jane. Jane smiled and said that the red one was a mighty fine car indeed. Then she watched as the lad sped away, this child, this boy, sandy-blonde haired and hazel-eyed.

CHAPTER FORTY-EIGHT

Todd loved the female body. He loved the smooth intricacies of the design, the curves, the crevices, the way that their bodies worked like well-oiled machines. All he had to know was which buttons to push and when, and physically, he could make them happy. Emotionally happy, that was another story entirely.

All women, he decided, should come with their own, unique operating manuals or user guides with clear instructions on what topics were strictly forbidden to mention, what comments would make them fly off the handle or cause them to burst into tears and if he should or should not open a door for them. Each woman was different, that he understood; therefore, a generalized guide would not work. Relationship books were useless. He wanted specifics.

Todd's mother was a kind, gentle woman with a strong spiritual belief system and an even stronger sense of family. She was the shelter in any storm, totally reliable and exuded a great strength that her children all took for granted. His two older sisters were awesome, loved to tease him, but were his steadfast protectors against all evils during his awkward boyhood days. Todd's high school girlfriend, the girl who had shared their mutual loss of virginity, had been sweet and shy. Not one of these experiences had prepared him to meet someone like Jane.

It had taken Todd four months to get Jane to notice that he existed or could potentially exist on another level besides school. Initially, she had treated him like a brother which was definitely not the way he wanted her to see him. Instead of rushing the process, he had used the time wisely and had gotten to know her, had let her get to know him. He had watched her date a couple of their mutual classmates, but nothing seemed to stick. He had watched her get wasted at pub nights, watched her flirt shamelessly and had kept pace himself on occasion, suffering from excruciating hangovers the next day. He had suffered through radio labs with her, both knowing that they sucked royally and both laughing at their obvious lack of talent for announcing. He had helped her study for tests, had curled up on Friday nights with popcorn and a movie, had given her rides to go shopping and had done everything that a good friend would do.

Then, at the college's Christmas party, Todd had asked Jane to dance. Unbelievably nervous, he had waited for a slow song then walked over to her table and extended his hand. When Jane smiled and rose from her chair, his heart had skipped a beat. She was beautiful. He had always thought that she was pretty, but at that moment, seeing her in a form-fitting dark blue dress with her long, blonde hair flowing gently over her shoulders and with her wearing just enough makeup to emphasize her fine facial features, the certain knowledge had struck him dumb. Jane was, simply put, beautiful. Taking Jane's hand, Todd had fought off trembling and had led the way to the center of the dance floor. They had danced, slow and easy, despite his lack of practice. A car he could rip apart and put back together, no problem. Mastering a simple two-step was not as effortless, but he had endured without embarrassing either one of them. It had been at that exact moment, the moment when she had looked up at him and smiled with genuine affection shining through her dark green eyes, that he had decided to officially break off his relationship with the girl back home and focus his attention on Jane. It had been at that exact moment when he had fallen in love.

Falling in love with someone was easy. An emotional barrier lifted and you crossed the line between like and love without even noticing. Like stepping one centimetre to the right only to discover that you're out of ground and falling off of a cliff. It was too late to go back, so you had to hope to grab onto a branch on the way down, or pray for a ledge so you could hold on until a rescue squad arrived. It had taken Todd one semester to fall in love with Jane; it had taken the better part of the second semester to convince Jane to fall in love with him.

In the end, everything had worked out all right. They had slowly transformed from being classmates into a romantic couple, and no one at school had seemed the least bit surprised.

Living together had made total sense. It was the natural progression of their relationship. They loved each other. He trusted her a hundred percent. He trusted that, as long as they worked together as a team, they would make it through whatever life handed them, good or bad. Two more years of school and then off into the big, bad world they'd venture, hand-in-hand, together forever.

    The last year had not prepared him for the past month to be comparable to physical torture. He had been totally confused and anxious by Jane's sudden cold, distant bordering on aloof behaviour. She'd be fine until he touched her, and then it was if an impenetrable wall fell down around her. Thank god that he'd finally found the nerve to confront Jane. He couldn't take much more of her borderline-personality behaviour, happy and normal one minute and then cold as an ice queen the next. No specific pattern. No reasonable explanation.

    As he had predicted, Todd had been unable to concentrate in class. Broadcast Journalism was not his favourite class in the first place. He had no desire to ever be a journalist. He wanted to work on commercials or to help make music videos. Behind the scene stuff, not sticking a microphone in someone's face and asking that person a bunch of mundane questions to enlighten the throngs of viewers. At break time, Todd had ditched the class, headed for the library to do research and had changed his cell phone to ring instead of just to vibrate. He didn't want to chance missing Jane's call or her text.

    He had googled uterine tumours and ended up finding sites on uterine fibroids. That had to be what Jane had been talking about. Todd didn't like what he read. The symptoms included painful periods, prolonged periods, spotting and pelvic pain. Most fibroids were considered harmless; however, the fibroids needed to be watched carefully. Rapid growth can signify a rare cancerous form of fibroid known as a leiomyosarcoma which cannot be differentiated from a benign fibroid by an ultrasound, an MRI or any other imaging study. This type of tumor occurs in less than one percent of uterine fibroids. The site also went on to explain that it is wise to surgically remove any fast growing fibroid before it causes any significant pain and/or permanent damage. If Jane was having the fibroid removed, that had to put her into the rapid growth category, which also put her into the possibility of cancer category. Even a one percent chance of cancer was way too much. Todd felt his stomach clench. The doctors would remove the fibroid then do a biopsy to make sure the growth wasn't cancer. There was a 99 percent chance that Jane would be fine and he had to focus on that.

Fucking hell, Todd thought, I should be with Jane right now. I should be there.

At least now he understood where Jane's head was at. Maybe, she hadn't been totally honest about her symptoms but that was okay. He understood that women could be a bit embarrassed by 'female' problems and that a lot of guys were complete jerks about it. What Jane needed to realize was that he wasn't one of those guys. He didn't blame every bad mood a woman had on being 'that time of the month', and he sure as hell didn't refer to a woman being on her period as 'being on the rag'. His sisters would have cold-cocked him double-time just for thinking that way. Reality was, Todd was always glad when his girlfriend's period arrived. It meant, very bluntly, that no baby had been conceived. The last thing Todd wanted was a child. Ever.

CHAPTER FORTY-NINE

Jane made herself a large mug of chamomile tea, put on her bulkiest, brown, hand-knit cardigan and then paced around the apartment as she waited for Todd to arrive. She'd sent him a text saying that she was okay but that they had to talk. He'd replied that he'd be home soon and that he loved her xoxo.

On the way home from Doctor Lee's office, Jane had practiced what she would say. She had mentally gone over every scenario that she thought possible. If only she could talk to Gertie about this. If only she could talk to anyone at all. It would make it so much easier. She needed a partner in crime but knew that was impossible. Jane couldn't tell anyone that Nick was the baby's father. No one could know. No one. Barring the possibility that the child may one day succumb to cancer, require a bone marrow transplant and she wasn't a match, Jane saw no need for the truth. Truth only made life more complicated than it needed to be. Truth was highly over-rated.

Doctor Lee had been wonderful, gracious, supportive. She had provided Jane with a referral to an obstetrician who was a very trusted colleague of hers and who would see Jane safely through her pregnancy and through the delivery of her child. Doctor Lee had wished Jane the best of luck and had told her that if she changed her mind, to call the office right away. There was still time for an abortion but only for another few more weeks. After the first trimester, the procedure became far more complicated and, depending on the circumstance, was often not approved for medical coverage.

Gertie wouldn't think twice about this, Jane thought. It would be a simple, out you go embryo and Gertie would be on her way. No harm. No foul. Just for once, why couldn't she be like Gertie? It was the dream that had changed Jane's mind. She knew that. In her mind, the baby had transformed from that of a non-being into a small boy overnight. As totally irrational as it may seem to others, it was real to Jane and she couldn't fight that, couldn't change that, and didn't want to change that. This child, who she was carrying inside, was her son. She would have bet her life on that fact and was, in many ways, gambling her future on that fact as well.

The sound of the door opening startled Jane. She wasn't ready for this. Jane had absolutely no idea how Todd would react. She made her way to the living room, placed the mug of tea on the wooden coffee table, curled up on the gray sofa and pulled a multi-coloured, granny-square afghan--a moving away present from her grandmother—up to her waist to make it look like she had just spent her time relaxing instead of walking around aimlessly for the past hour. For some reason, Jane couldn't shake the chill that had embraced her when she'd first walked into the apartment.

More than anything, she just wanted to curl up in a little ball and hide. It would have been so much easier if she and Todd weren't living together. Then she could just drop out of school, change her telephone number and escape during the dark of night. Jane couldn't bear the thought of moving back to Donnybrooke and becoming the focus of a hundred gossiping mouths. Instead, she could go someplace else where no one knew her, find a job and have her baby. Maybe, she could stay with Dylan in Toronto for a while. The masses wouldn't care that she was a single mother. She could get a job as a waitress or work in a call center, blend in. Living in Toronto was about as anonymous as it could get.

"Hey, Beautiful." Todd walked over and sat down on the coffee table to face Jane. "How are you feeling? I've been worried about you all day."

Jane, unable to look directly into Todd's eyes, studied the crocheting, even and concentric, perfectly formed stitches that were her grandmother's claim to fame. "I'm okay, but it's a bit more complicated than the doctor originally thought which is why I said we needed to talk." It's now or never, Jane decided as she pulled the afghan higher over her body and snuggled in underneath.

Todd frowned. "Got that, so let's talk."

Jane glanced up at Todd for a moment and then turned her attention back to the afghan. This was going to be so much tougher than she had originally visualized. Todd loved her. She knew that, but they hadn't been together for very long really….officially, just seven months. She took a deep breath and continued. "Like I said yesterday, the doctor thought that I had a small tumour in my uterus…"

Todd interjected, "Right, I did some research online and the tumours are called fibroids."

Jane nodded, not surprised that Todd, the inquisitive guy he was, would want to know everything that he could about her supposed illness. "Right. So, you probably read that there can be a bit of off and on bleeding involved."

Todd nodded. "I got that."

"So, going by my symptoms," Jane strived to sound logical, "the doctor first assessed me as having a fibroid and suggested the surgery, so we booked that for today. She needed an ultrasound done this morning to confirm her findings, and the ultrasound showed something entirely different."

"What?" Todd's frown had deepened, making him look ten years older than he really was.

"The ultrasound showed that I'm pregnant." A very real tear slipped down Jane's cheek. She brushed the wetness away with the back of her cold hand. "According to the doctor, spotting is common during the first trimester, and it doesn't always mean there's something wrong with the baby. It can be caused by the uterus enlarging."

Todd's face went blank. "What?" As the new information began to sink in, Todd shook his head emphatically. "No way." Looking as if he'd just been hit with a thousand volts of electricity, Todd jumped up from his sitting position. "No fucking way."

Jane blinked and stared at Todd, her heart sinking. This had been her least favourite scenario. She had truly expected Todd to be upset but calm and supportive. "Todd…"

"How the fuck did this happen?" He began to pace around the room looking more bewildered than angry. Todd raked his hair back from his face, turned around and looked at Jane, accusation filling his voice. "You said that you were on the pill? You said you didn't want me to meet you here in August because you were P.M.S.ing. What the fuck, Jane?"

"You can quit making it sound like I planned this. I was on the pill. It's just not always a hundred percent effective. And, obviously, my period never came." Jane watched as he walked out of her view and into the kitchen then back into the living room again. "Todd, can you please sit down for a minute so we can talk about this?"

Todd walked over to the gray armchair, as if keeping his distance, and plopped down. "How far along are you?" He absent-mindedly ran his fingers through his hair again. "No wait, I need a drink. I'll be right back." He jumped up from the chair and went back to the kitchen. After popping open a beer, Todd returned to the living room and sat back down.

"Nine weeks approximately or whatever length of time it was since we met at the Lowdown." Jane watched as Todd drained half the bottle in one long chug.

"Good, so there's still time to abort." He nodded, sighed, shut his eyes and leaned back. "Call and make the appointment. If OHIP doesn't cover it, I'll pay for it. This time, I'm going with you though. There's no way I'm sitting in school and waiting. Fucking doctors don't know what the fuck they're doing half the time. When your period didn't come, why didn't you take a pregnancy test then?"

Stunned, Jane was speechless. There had been no discussion of pros and cons. There had been no hug, no it'll be okay Jane speech. Okay, Todd's just point blankly telling her what to do hadn't been on her list of potential scenarios. The idea had never even occurred to her. Obviously, she didn't know him as well as she thought she did. Jane, more angry than afraid, her pulse rate increasing in preparation for an argument, glared at Todd, but she strived to keep her voice as calm as possible. "Actually, I did, but the pee-on-the-stick test read negative, so I just kept waiting for my period to show up. Then I started spotting and having cramps and feeling like shit. You know the rest. I went to see the doctor and, well, I'm pregnant. It's not the end of the world, Todd. Quit acting like it is."

"Yeah, okay. You're right. There's still time to make this right. We'll just be more careful in the future. Maybe you can get one of those three-month shots instead of depending on the pill." Todd took another long swig of beer. "Fuck, Jane. I spent all day sitting at school, worrying because there was like a one percent chance that you could have cancer." Todd shook his head in disbelief. "This never crossed my mind. Fucking doctors."

"What if I don't want to have an abortion?" Jane chanced,

hoping that Todd's initial shock had passed quickly enough that, at this point, they could have a rational conversation.

Todd's eyes popped open. He sat forward in his chair. "There's no choice here, Jane. We're in school. We can barely afford rent, food and tuition, let alone a kid. There's just no fucking way that we can do this."

"Todd, I know it's a shock. Trust me, I felt exactly the same way at first, but I'm not ready to just kill this child. You have to understand that. There has to be a way. There just has to be."

Todd tipped the bottle back and drained the remainder of the beer. He let out a soft burp. "Jane, children are parasites. First, it will spend nine months feeding off of you, then it'll spend the next twenty years bleeding us both dry. And what about all of the drugs you've taken? Do you honestly expect me to believe that you and Gertie spent the summer clean and sober when I know the shit you were into last year? Jane, I've watched you get so high, it's a fucking miracle that you didn't O.D."

Jane fought to control her temper. The reality of her drug use had crossed her mind on more than one occasion. Thankfully, when Jane had enquired about the risks, Doctor Lee had assured her that, since Jane hadn't used anything stronger than marijuana in August and nothing since then, that the risks were minimal. "We did a bit of pot in July and August, nothing stronger, and I haven't touched anything since I moved back here and that was mid-August. I've already asked Doctor Lee about this and she said the baby should be okay."

"Should be," Todd emphasized.

"Todd, even under the best circumstances, there are no guarantees that any baby will be born perfectly healthy. You just do the best that you can and hope that everything turns out all right."

Todd sat back in his chair, tapping the bottle on the armrest. "Yeah, well, there's still no fucking way that I am doing this. You have to understand that. If you don't want to abort, then put the kid up for adoption. Either way, I don't want this kid, and there's nothing that you can say or do that will change my mind. Either you get rid of it or you can fucking have this kid on your own. That's up to you." Todd placed the empty bottle on the coffee table, stood to leave the room and then hesitated as if a thought had just occurred to him. "Jane, you know that I love you. I'd marry you tomorrow if that's what you want, but you have to get rid of the kid first."

Choking back hot tears, Jane removed the afghan, folded it back and sat on the edge of the couch. She reached forward, retrieved her mug of tea and sipped. Her life was falling apart. Her world was falling apart. How could so much hinge on one small, helpless child? How could Todd ask her to make such a choice? Feeling utterly defeated, Jane stood up, walked out of the room and grabbed her purse from the kitchen table. "Do you honestly think that I would get pregnant to trap you into marriage? Seriously? That's fucking lame even for you, Linwood."

"Jane, I don't know what to think anymore." Todd stood with his hands on his hips.

Jane walked into the living room to face Todd. "Well, let me assure you. This has nothing to do with wanting to get married. And, right now, you're about the last person in the world that I'd even consider marrying." Jane walked back to the sofa, sat down and extracted her package of cigarettes from the bottom of her purse. "Do you ever want children? You know, sometime in the future when your career is established and money isn't so tight?"

"Honestly, Jane, no." Todd's momentum had decreased, his temper settling. "I want to devote my time to my career. I don't want kids. I could never be the type of father that I'd want to be. I'd end up being a part-time dad at best. I don't want to do that. I can't do that."

Jane nodded, her heart breaking in half. "Okay. I get that." She withdrew a cigarette from the package and lit the tobacco, no longer caring about her agreement with Todd that she wouldn't smoke in the apartment, and tossed the cigarette package back into her purse. Jane inhaled deeply, needing the nicotine right now. She'd worry about cutting back or quitting tomorrow. Not today.

"You'll have the abortion then?" Todd looked hopeful.

Jane shook her head sadly as she blew smoke into the room. "No. I've thought about this, and I can't kill this child. I don't want to put the baby up for adoption either. I want to keep him. There's nothing that you can say or do that will make me change my mind either, so if you want to end our relationship, go ahead. If you want to move out or if you want me to move out, then we'll work out the details and move on." Jane tapped the ashes off the end of the cigarette into her cup of half-drunk tea. "You do whatever you need to do. I won't try to stop you. I'll do this on my own."

Todd moved towards her. "Jane, please, you can't be serious. You know it's not that simple."

Jane shook her head and held up her hand to stop Todd's approach. Somehow, deep down inside, she had known that it would come to this. She had wished for a different result. Unfortunately, wishing didn't change the fact that she was not meant to be happy, that she would forever pay for her sins, that she would spend her entire life being punished just for being born. "If you want to know if this is killing me inside, it is. I appreciate your honesty and I'll always love you, but you made it very clear that I have to make a choice between you and the baby so I'm making that choice. I'm choosing the baby. Don't worry, I won't come after you for support, and I can always leave the father blank on the birth certificate." Jane inhaled deeply from the cigarette and brushed away silently falling tears as she exhaled.

"Jane, please…"

Dumping the rest of her cigarette in her mug of tea, Jane suddenly rose, grabbed her purse and started to walk towards the apartment's entrance door. She was about to fall apart and was determined not to do so in front of Todd. She wouldn't give him that satisfaction.

Catching up to her, Todd grabbed Jane's arm. "Where are you going?" His voice was harsh, upset.

Jane stopped abruptly, trapped by his strength. "Let go of me. I need to go for a drive."

"Where are you going? Gertie's? Don't take our business to Gertie. This is between you and me and we're not done talking."

"Let go of my arm, Todd." Jane repeated as the tears continued to fall, unabated. She couldn't look at him. She couldn't look into those brown eyes without wanting to crumble into his arms. All she wanted was for Todd to hold her. She focused her attention on the door and let the tears fall as they may. "There's nothing left to say. There is no you and me anymore. If you can't say it, I will. We're done. We're through. We're over."

Todd blinked and released Jane's arm. His voice harboured on panic. "Are you planning on moving out then?"

Jane shook her head ruefully. "Maybe," Fuck, Jane thought, if it wasn't bad enough that both of their names were on the lease, she'd just given Mr. Minicucci the rent money for October and she couldn't afford to put first and last month down on a new place even if she wanted to leave, "but not until I can find someone to take over my half of the lease, unless, of course, you're willing to buy me out so I can put the money down on a room somewhere else."

Todd shook his head. "Jane, you know that I can't afford to do that." Calmer now, Todd took a step back to give Jane room. "Jane, don't go. We can figure this out. I love you. If you need some space right now, there are two bedrooms. The smaller one is full of my shit anyway, so I can move into it and you can have the bigger bedroom until we work this out."

Jane swallowed and dug a tissue out of her purse to wipe her nose. "That's very large of you, Todd, but I seriously need to get out of here. I don't want to be near you. I don't want to see your face. I don't want to talk to you. I don't want to hear your voice. I just want to be alone." As Jane turned and opened the door to leave, she added, "Todd, whatever you do, do not tell me, ever again, that you love me. Understand? We're done."

"Jane, wait."

Without looking back, Jane left and shut the door behind her.

As Jane drove, hot tears fell. God, how could she have been so stupid to think that there might even be a slight chance that this could work out? Todd didn't even want his own child. What would he do if he found out that the baby wasn't his? Not that it mattered anymore. This baby was her child and she had every intention of having him, keeping him and raising him.

Jane pulled the Gremlin into the visitor's parking spot at Gertie's Southwest Street apartment building. Three storeys high, the building was a well-maintained low-end rental with no luxuries included. Gertie had recently upgraded from her original bachelor apartment to fill a one-bedroom vacancy and liked her new accommodations so much that she was determined to stay there for the next three years. As Gertie had pointed out, it was a roof over her head, the rent was reasonable, the apartment was free of cockroaches and that's all that mattered. That, and the fact, that a seriously cute, single brunette male lived just two doors down. He wasn't the brightest guy in the world but was proving to be a stellar occasional bootie call.

With any luck, Gertie would be alone tonight. Jane couldn't face the idea of trying to make conversation with Mr. Body Beautiful. Jane rooted her cell phone out of her purse, opened her contact list to find Gertie's number and pressed enter. Three rings sounded before Gertie picked up.

"Hey, you," Gertie answered cheerfully. "I looked all over school for you today. I was hoping to get your advice on a research essay I'm working on, and it's due tomorrow."

"Sorry, I wasn't there. It's been a bad day. Are you alone?" Jane's telephone buzzed, announcing that someone was on call waiting. She glanced down at her telephone's display. Todd. Jane's throat constricted. The tears had finally stopped, but there was no way she could talk to him right now without blubbering like a complete idiot. She swallowed away the pain, letting the call go to voice mail.

"Yup, just me and my lap top trying to figure out how to format a Reference page. I really should start paying more attention in class. I remembered how to insert the citations, but I can't remember how to get the Bibliography to populate." The sound of Gertie tapping on keys emanated through.

Jane closed her eyes, trying to visualize her own computer. She'd written so many essays during her first year of school that she generally went into autopilot at this point. "Under the Reference tab, beside where it says Insert Citation, there should be a Bibliography option. If you click on the little arrow beside it, you can choose what format you want to use. Is this for Communications class?"

This time, the sound of the mouse clicking. "I see it! Cool. Thanks. Yup. You'd think the college would just be happy with the fact that we passed high school English instead of putting us through another semester of this crap. Did you get my texts? I tried calling you earlier, but your phone went directly to your voice mail.

You okay?"

"Not really. Can I come up? I'm in your parking lot." Jane's cell phone buzzed again, this time signaling that a text message had just arrived.

"No shit? Absolutely. I was beginning to wonder if Todd would ever give you a night off. Just buzz me when you get to the front door and I'll let you in."

"Thanks. See you in a minute." Jane disconnected the call so she could view the text message. From Todd, a simple 'Where are you'? Jane responded back, 'It's none of your business where I am. Why don't you have another beer, go out, pick up some random chick at a bar, get laid and have fun? You're a free man now. Do what you like. Just leave me alone.'

CHAPTER FIFTY

Todd, his Volkswagen parked across the street at a nearby family restaurant, read Jane's text message response as he watched her walk up to the front door of Gertie's apartment building. As predicted, Jane had gone running directly to her best girlfriend. That made sense, really. The girls were like two peas in a pod. Normally, Todd liked Gertie, she had a wry sense of humour that made him laugh. Tonight, however, was not a normal night. He wanted Jane at home, not sequestered somewhere away from him. Jane needed to come back so they could finish talking this through and come up with a game plan. Their relationship wasn't over. Todd didn't accept that. He and Jane had hit a speed bump, that's all. They'd get over it and get on with their lives. If she wanted some space right now, he'd give her that; but, Jane had left the apartment with nothing, except her purse, so he knew that eventually she had to come home.

Okay, maybe he hadn't handled the situation very well, but fuck, who would under these circumstances? Cancer he could have dealt with. He would have been mortified, but he would have been there for Jane, for every doctor's appointment, for chemotherapy, for radiation, for her hair falling out (he'd even shave his own head in the spirit of solidarity), for every step of the way. But a kid? There was no remission when it came to kids. There was no hoping that it would just go away and never come back again. You were stuck.

Deciding not to push the point any further for now, Todd started his car and pulled out of the parking lot. He'd let Jane have her Gertie time. They could huddle up, as women do, and talk about how awful he is, about what an uncaring, selfish bastard he is. Jane needed to blow off some steam, and he'd let her have that. She was safe, and that's all that mattered.

What Todd needed right now was another beer and someone to talk to. Taking a chance that his friend, Lorne, would be at home, Todd headed towards his classmate's apartment. Lorne, ten-years-older than the majority of the class, had decided to change career paths when the factory that he'd been working in since he left high school had unexpectedly filed bankruptcy and closed its doors the year before. More signs of their unstable economy. With little in the way of a severance package and nothing, but a car, a few R.R.S.Ps and a fairly substantial savings account to show for all of his hard work, Lorne had seen the factory's demise as an opportunity, a promise of better things to come. Working on the line had been tedious, monotonous; however, the bi-weekly paycheque and the benefits had been too comfortable to leave. Now, the future was whatever he wanted it to become and that was just fine by him. At 5′ 6″ tall, sturdily built and Croatian in ancestry, Lorne did not present himself as being an opposing figure. Instead, he had become like a big brother to their little clique and that's exactly what Todd needed. More than anything, he needed a friend.

"Can I get you anything?" Lorne offered as Todd took off his gray, light-weight, snowboard jacket and running shoes. "Beer, water, a coffee? Have you eaten? I just bought some corn beef and was about to make myself a sandwich. Do you want one?"

Todd nodded. "A beer would be good. Food would be good. Thanks." He made his way to Lorne's living room and plunked down into a retro red armchair. It had been less than 24 hours since Todd had experienced the best sex of his life. There was no way that this was over. Jane was just upset. Surely, she didn't mean that their relationship was actually over. It couldn't be. He wouldn't let it be.

Lorne entered the living room, handed Todd an open bottle of cold beer and a cream-coloured porcelain plate containing a very meaty, corn beef sandwich with rippled potato chips and a plump dill pickle on the side. After making a second trip to his kitchen, Lorne returned with his own food and sat down on the matching retro red sofa. "So, what brings you here this time of night?"

Todd, not realizing how famished he was until the smell of the corn beef, took a large bite, chewed and swallowed. "Jane's at Gertie's. I didn't feel like being alone." Todd washed down the food with a swig of beer.

Lorne nodded. "Trouble in paradise?"

"You could say that. Jane's pregnant. She just found out today for sure so she laid the news on me as soon I got home from school." Todd took another bite and chewed. Free food never tasted better.

    Lorne took a drink from his bottle and studied his friend thoughtfully. "Considering that Jane's at Gertie's and that you're here, I take it that you're having a difference of opinion on what to do about your current situation." Lorne picked up his sandwich, took a bite and chewed while he waited for Todd's response.

    "Yeah." A sigh escaped as Todd realized just how serious his current circumstance really was. He placed the food-laden plate on the glass-topped coffee table and leaned back in the armchair. With another mouthful of beer ingested, Todd explained, "I want Jane to have an abortion. Jane wants to keep the baby. She won't listen to reason. A thousand people apply every year for this course, and out of those thousand potential students, the college accepts 65 applicants. That's what, like a seven percent chance of getting accepted in the first place. Then we lost almost half of our class by the end of second semester. Half of our original class either dropped out or flunked out. Half. It took a shitload of hard work, but we managed to make it to second year. Now, she's willing to possibly throw all that away for a kid, and she wants me to risk doing the same. I don't get it."

    Lorne nodded. "Not saying that you don't have a very valid point and I know that the timing is atrocious, but Jane's smart and she's gorgeous. If she was expecting my child, I'd be thrilled. Is she really asking you to risk your own college education or is she asking you to understand that she's willing to risk her own? Did she ask you to drop out of school and support them? Does she want to get married?"

    "Jane didn't say anything about either of us dropping out of school, and she definitely does not want to get married. She told me that I was the last person she'd even consider marrying right now." Todd took another swig of beer. As hungry as he had been a moment ago, for some reason, he had inexplicably lost his appetite.

    "Was this before or after you discussed the possibility of abortion?"

    Unable to meet Lorne's eyes directly, Todd stared at the wallpaper behind the red couch. Like the furniture, the wallpaper was vintage in appearance, black and white interchanging circles and squares reminiscent of a really bad acid trip from the 60's. "We didn't really discuss abortion so much as my saying that she needed to have one," he confessed. "Look, I know that it wasn't my finest hour, but having a kid right now would fuck up everything. I just can't get my head wrapped around it. Not only that, but I don't want kids." Todd desperately wanted to go back to the way his life had been with Jane. Last spring had been so miraculous, so much fun. Work your ass off to get your assignments done then have a few drinks and spend the rest of the weekend having incredible sex. He'd thought he'd found heaven.

Lorne munched thoughtfully on his dill pickle. "You're what, twenty? Of course you don't want kids right now. I didn't want kids when I was your age either. God forbid. Ten years later though, I'm still single with no children and it's a whole different ballgame. My parents died two years ago in a car crash. They drove down to Disney World for a week's vacation and never returned. Their car was demolished by a trucker who ran a red light. Mom died instantly. Dad lived for a few days before the internal injuries got the best of him.

When something like that happens, it makes you take a really good look at your life. You don't know what's going to happen tomorrow let alone five years from now. You look around and start thinking that it would be kind of nice to come home to someone special and maybe have a little you or to a little her running around. It's what gives our life meaning. It's the only part of us that's immortal. It's not like we can wake up one morning and just decide to have a baby. Women, they can walk into a clinic and pick a sperm donor out of a catalogue of choices. They don't even need a man to raise a child. We, on the other hand, have to convince a woman that carrying our offspring is worth nine months of raging hormones, at least twenty pounds of weight gain and god knows how many hours of mind crippling labour to produce a child who will carry on our genetics. What did Jane say when you told her to have an abortion?"

Todd turned his focus towards Lorne. "She basically told me to go fuck myself."

Lorne laughed, good-naturedly. "Sounds like Jane. Look, Todd, you're not going to change her mind on this one if she's already decided. Women produce hormones that make them want to protect the fetus. You can't fight nature. All you can do, at this point, is to figure out how you want to fit into her life. Either you're there for her and for the baby or you're not. I can't decide that for you. If you want to be a dad, then it might mean grabbing a couple of extra evening and weekend shifts at the garage while you're in school to keep your heads above water, or putting school on hold for a few years then going back. If you really don't want to be a dad, then end your relationship. Think of yourself as being a sperm donor. Sign off your rights and walk away. Trust me, there are lots of guys out there who would be more than happy to meet someone like Jane, who would gladly adopt the child and be the father that you don't think you can be. Just don't make a hasty decision that you'll regret later. Take some time and think about this."

Todd's heart sank with stark, crystal realization. "Jane already said that it was over. She said that, since I don't want the baby, we're done."

Lorne sat forward on the sofa and patted Todd's knee affectionately. "She's just upset. Give it some time. In the meanwhile, I do have a spare bedroom if you want to stay with me until the dust settles."

As Todd entered his apartment to gather a few belongings, he ached beyond anything he ever remembered feeling before. His heart was ripping in half. He could barely breathe.

The Gremlin had still been parked at Gertie's apartment building when Todd drove by on his way home from Lorne's. Todd assumed that Jane decided to bunk on her friend's couch for the night. Todd decided that he would text Jane after he was done packing and let her know that it was safe for her to go home. He'd be staying at Lorne's until he could find someone to take over his half of the rent. Maybe, he could convince Gertie to switch apartments with him. That way Jane would have a friend close by. Regrettably, the idea of talking to Gertie right now didn't seem all that feasible either. Gertie was more liable to clobber him with a baseball bat than she would be to open her arms to suggestions.

Like a gentle rain, Todd's tears softly pelted the hardwood floor as he moved from room to room packing his laptop and other basic necessities. Jane had made her choice; he had made his choice. There was no compromise. Lorne was right, there was no going back. Todd had to do what was right for Jane and what was right for the baby, not just what was right for himself. Regardless, Todd knew that time wouldn't change the way that he felt. He loved Jane to the very depths of his soul. He would love her forever.

THE BEGINNING

And as the sun rises before me, my heartbeat quickens in its pace
For there lies ahead everything that should have been,
Every wonderful experience that I should have known,
Every wonderful place that I should have seen.
I begin to run in my excitement, the breeze streams through my hair.
Oh god, it feels so good to finally be here.
And, suddenly, I am lifted…

                        The Future Is In The Sunrise
                        Life in 3-D

CHAPTER FIFTY-ONE

Jane opened her eyes, her vision blurring and wavering as she fought her way back up to consciousness. She tried to turn her head, but, for some reason, she had been immobilized. Jane blinked hard, willing her focus to take hold of a solid object, animate or inanimate. She didn't care which just something to help her figure out what was happening. The last thing she remembered was seeing the coyotes and now this. Everything was extremely bright and the noise, people talking somewhere out of her visual range. It's a ceiling, she thought. The white above me is a ceiling.

Maybe, she was dreaming. Maybe, she had made it safely home and she was now tucked away in her bed, dreaming. She raised her left hand into her field of vision. IV tubes. An excruciating pain seared through her shoulder as she lowered her hand. Fuck, not this again. Not a dream.

Jane swallowed and opened her mouth to speak. Her throat felt dry, parched. She licked her lips. "Hello?" Her voice croaked, just above a whisper. Not good. "Can I please have a drink of water? Anyone?"

A face bobbed before her. "Welcome back." The woman had short, brunette hair, was probably somewhere in her early fifties and wore bright blue scrubs with flying teddy bears. "You're in a hospital. Can you tell me your name?"

Jane swallowed again. Her throat hurt, her head hurt, her neck hurt, her shoulder hurt. The face floated, blurred, threatened to disappear. "Jane. My name is Jane Louisa Kirkland-Fallis. Where am I?"

"Jane, you're in a trauma unit at Harbour View Memorial Hospital, in Toronto. You were in an accident, rolled your car and then brought here by ambulance. You are one very lucky lady to be alive. I'll get you some ice chips then Doctor Rouse will be in shortly to explain your injuries. He insisted that we page him as soon as you woke up. Jane, can you rate your pain for me on a scale from one to ten with ten being the worst?"

"Eleven."

The face smiled in sympathy as she touched Jane's arm. "The doctor has ordered a painkiller for you. I'll be right back."

The face disappeared. Jane struggled to remember, but all she could see were the coyotes. The rest was blank. She reached up with her right hand and felt the restraints around her neck and head. Not a good sign, but at least it explained what was blocking her peripheral vision. She wiggled her toes. Not paralyzed. That was, indeed, a good sign. Brydon. She'd been going home to Brydon. Coyotes, on the road, in the rain.

The face reappeared above her with a white, Styrofoam cup. The nurse dug out a single ice chip and held it to Jane's lips. "This should help."

Jane opened her mouth and accepted the offering. The coldness of the ice felt amazing, the liquid soothed her throat as she swallowed. "How long have I been out? I don't remember crashing." The nurse pulled a cream-coloured privacy curtain around the bed. Jane felt the coolness of the air as the bedding and her gown were moved aside to make room for an injection. A quick, sharp pain in her buttocks then it was over. The covers were replaced, the warmth returned. The curtain was pulled back again.

"There was a gentleman driving on the highway, not too far behind you, who saw the accident and immediately called 911. That was twelve hours ago." The nurse disposed of the needle in a plastic sharp's container then looked up to address someone who had entered the room.

Jane shifted her eyes in the same direction. A man this time. Doctor Rouse probably, tall, slim, short, gray hair, glasses. He grabbed the chart from the foot of her bed.

Jane blinked and tried to focus harder. Twelve hours. She'd been unconscious for twelve hours. Brydon. She'd been going home to Brydon.

Coyotes, on the road, in the rain. Jane's vision doubled as she watched the new face come into view. She blinked and fought to reunite the duplicates into one functional person.

"Hi, Jane," the man spoke. His voice was soft, kind. "I'm Doctor Rouse. It's good to see that you're back with us again. You sustained quite a bad concussion in the accident which caused some swelling of your brain. Do you know what day it is?"

Jane shut her eyes momentarily. So hard to think when everything around her kept shifting, melting, melding. "Yesterday was Sunday so if I've been out for twelve hours, that would make today Monday, August the twelfth." She opened her eyes again.

The doctor smiled and nodded. "Very good. It might take a few days yet before your concentration level is normal, so don't worry if all you want to do is sleep. Your body needs time to heal, and we'll keep a close eye on you. We do need to discuss your other injuries though. They need to be addressed as soon as possible. Can you wiggle your fingers for me, Jane?"

Jane tried to nod and couldn't. She wiggled the fingers first on her right hand and then on her left. "I was on my way home to see my son."

Doctor Rouse glanced at the nurse. The nurse nodded and added, "The police have notified your husband. He's on his way now."

The doctor continued. "Good. I'm going to, very gently, poke the ends of your fingers with a small pin. I need you to tell me if you can feel it."

Jane felt the pin. "Yes. I can feel it."

"Good."

Jane felt the covers being pulled back from her feet. "Can you wiggle your toes for me, Jane?"

Jane wiggled her toes. Such a glorious feeling, wiggling her toes.

"Excellent. Now, I'm going to do the same thing that I did with your fingers. Can you feel that, Jane?"

"Yes."

"Which foot?"

"My left."

"Very good."

Jane shut her eyes again. The lids felt like they had cement blocks weighing them down. Elliot. Elliot was on his way. Would he bring Brydon? She didn't want Brydon seeing her like this.

It'd been dark and the rain was driving her night vision crazy, so difficult to see in the dark in the rain with the headlights only able to cut a minimal path before her. Coyotes, on the road, in the rain. She'd honked her horn, but they didn't move. Odd that. Coyotes, on the road, in the rain.

"Jane. Stay with us, Jane." A woman's voice.

Footsteps running down the hall. Footsteps entering her room in a hurry. Jane felt a hand rub her arm briskly and, with all of the strength she could muster, she re-opened her eyes. Two doctors again, two nurses. Jane blinked several times and mentally willed the people to fuse back together. Strangers in a strange place. Jane wondered about the man who had found her. Maybe the police could give her his name so she could thank him. A Good Samaritan. A complete stranger. "I'm okay." Elliot. Elliot's face coming into view in the background. Unshaved. Upset. No Brydon with him.

"Good." The doctor's voice sounded concerned but professional. "I know it's hard to do right now, Jane, but we need you to stay with us for a bit yet. Then you can rest."

Jane tried to nod again but couldn't. Right, she thought. Restrained. "Okay."

"I'm Jane's husband, Elliot. I got here as fast as I could." Elliot moved forward to stand beside the right-side of the bed, across from the doctor. Elliot bent forward and kissed Jane's forehead. No smile. He had his game face on, masking a million emotions all vying to surface at once. He leaned back again and turned towards the doctor. "How is she? Is she going to be okay?"

The doctor nodded. "She has severe concussion, but she's awake now which is a good sign. We were just about to discuss her other injuries so I'm glad you're here. It'll save me from explaining twice."

"Where's Bry?" Jane interjected.

Elliot turned his face towards her. "He's with your mom. They wouldn't tell us anything on the telephone except that you were unconscious so I told your parents I'd call as soon as I knew what was going on. Your mom was determined to come down, but I couldn't find anyone else to watch Brydon and I didn't want to bring him in case," Elliot swallowed hard, "in case you weren't doing so well. I didn't want to scare him." Jane felt Elliot take her right hand in his and was soothed by the familiarity.

The doctor, who had been watching Elliot, turned his attention back to Jane, talking to her directly. "When your car rolled, you hit a tree. The impact on the driver's side caused the door to concave. As a result, you were knocked sideways which caused a compound fracture of your left clavicle, your collar bone. The roll and the impact also caused a fracture to your neck at the facet joint between C5 and C6. The facet joints are between the little spinal protrusions at the back of the vertebrae that hold the vertebrae together. In other words, right now, there's nothing to stop the two cervical vertebrae from shifting which is why your head and neck are being restrained. From what I can gather by your medical history, you had a previous injury to this area which probably made it more susceptible to breaking. There's no apparent paralysis, and you have feeling in your distal extremities, both of which are very good indications that, once your neck and shoulder have healed, you'll be able to lead a very normal life."

Jane blinked and then swallowed hard. Fuck. A broken neck. At least she wasn't paralyzed. She could be thankful for that.

"So, what happens now?" Elliot asked, turning his attention back to the doctor.

The nurse had disappeared. Jane didn't remember seeing her leave. It was just the doctor and Elliot now. Jane liked Doctor Rouse. She also liked narcotic painkillers. The medication was beginning to take effect. The pain was numbing.

It'd been dark and the rain was driving her night vision crazy, so difficult to see in the dark in the rain with the headlights only able to cut a minimal path before her. Coyotes, on the road, in the rain. She'd honked her horn, but they didn't move. She'd put on her brakes, but had ending up skidding, the tires finding no purchase on the slippery asphalt.

"Jane?" Elliot's voice this time.

His face was staring down at her. He looked tired. She focused on how blue his eyes were. "Yes, I'm here."

The doctor continued, this time talking directly to Elliot. "Jane will need two surgeries. The first one, we'll put a pin in her clavicle to repair the break. Then I would highly recommend fastening a small, titanium plate in the back of her neck to hold C5 and C6 in place. We go in through the front of the neck, past the thyroid gland, to minimize any risks. The floating bone fragments will also be removed at that time to prevent any inadvertent future damage to her spinal cord. After the surgery, Jane will need to wear a halo for anywhere from six weeks to three months depending on how fast she heals. A halo metal ring is secured to the skull with titanium pins, two in the forehead and one behind each ear. Metal rods are then attached to a closely fitted, plastic vest. With this brace, it is possible to obtain absolute fixation and to stop almost all movement of the cervical spine.

After six weeks, an MRI will be scheduled to determine the progress of the repair and if the halo can come off or not. Once the halo has been removed, Jane will transition into a cervical collar that she'll need to wear during the day for another six weeks just to make sure everything is well healed. After that, probably physiotherapy for a while to regain muscle strength. We also need to book some tests to determine if the injury has caused any permanent nerve damage…"

It'd been dark and the rain was driving her night vision crazy, so difficult to see in the dark in the rain with the headlights only able to cut a minimal path before her. Coyotes, on the road, in the rain. She'd honked her horn, but they didn't move. She'd put on her brakes, but had ending up skidding, the tires finding no purchase on the slippery asphalt. She steered to the left hoping that she could just go around the animals instead of taking the ditch, but her car hitched and skidded further than she had expected. The backend began to fishtail.

Drifting again, Jane felt her hand being squeezed. Elliot. Right. Elliot. They'd been talking. Something about surgery. He hovered over her, close to her face. "Jane, do you understand the procedures? I have to sign the papers on your behalf to authorize the surgery."

Jane tried to nod but couldn't. Right. Restrained. "Yes, do what you have to do."

The doctor nodded and gently patted Jane's left arm. "You will be okay, Jane. It's not going to be fun, but you'll get through this. I have an Orthopaedic surgeon on call for your shoulder, then we'll schedule your neck surgery for later in the week. We'll have the forms ready for your husband to sign shortly. Do you have any questions?"

Jane tried to shake her head but couldn't. Fuck. Right. Restrained. "No," she said. Cramps. Even through the painkiller, the abdominal cramps were pulverizing. She slowly drew her knees up, trying to curl in around the new pain. "No. No."

"Jane, what is it?" Elliot's voice sounded panicked as he clung to her hand.

"Elliot, the baby." The devastating pain brought clarity at last. She squeezed Elliot's hand as hard as she could. She had to make them understand. "I think I'm losing the baby."

"You're pregnant?" Elliot's voice, an octave higher than normal, verged on hysteria.

"Eight weeks." Jane grimaced. "I was going to tell you when I got home. I was coming home." She wanted desperately to roll onto her side and to curl up into a fetal position until the contraction passed. Doctor Rouse. Jane looked back towards the doctor. Right, Doctor Rouse was still there. "Please. Do something, please."

The doctor moved quickly. He pressed down on the emergency button to summon a nurse then pulled the privacy curtain back around the bed, cocooning them in. "Jane, listen to me. Unfortunately, it's not all that uncommon for a woman's body to spontaneously abort an early pregnancy after sustaining a severe physical trauma. I'm afraid it's the body's way of choosing a life to save a life."

As the nurse spun through the curtains, the doctor pulled back the covers on Jane's bed. "She's hemorrhaging, a possible spontaneous abortion," Doctor Rouse informed the nurse. "Page Doctor Davis then call up and see if we have an operating room available. Jane may need an emergency D & C. Jane. Jane. Stay with us, Jane."

It'd been dark and the rain was driving her night vision crazy, so difficult to see in the dark in the rain with the headlights only able to cut a minimal path before her. Coyotes, on the road, in the rain. She'd honked her horn, but they didn't move. She'd put on her brakes, but had ending up skidding, the tires finding no purchase on the slippery asphalt. She steered to the left hoping that she could just go around the animals instead of taking the ditch, but her car hitched and skidded further than she had expected. The backend began to fishtail. Car lights popped over a knoll coming straight towards her, beams bearing down on her at warp speed. No choice now but to take the ditch and to hope for the best. Odd that. Coyotes on the road, in the rain.

CHAPTER FIFTY-TWO

Elliot felt frustratingly helpless and severely battered, but not entirely broken as he watched the transporters wheel Jane away on a gurney. She had lost consciousness again so he had signed for the D & C knowing that it was better to get the bleeding under control now before the combined physical assaults on Jane's body weakened her beyond repair. He mourned the loss of a child whom he didn't even know existed until today, still he was eternally grateful that he wasn't mourning the loss of his wife. She'd been coming home to him, to them--to Brydon and to him. He and Jane could have another baby sometime in the future if that's what she wanted. Nevertheless, Elliot shuddered at the thought of how close Jane had come to losing her own life.

That's it, Elliot thought, as soon as Jane's feeling better, I'm pushing to adopt Brydon. This is crazy. In her will, Jane had designated Elliot as part of a joint legal guardianship arrangement with her parents in the event of her early demise. That wasn't good enough anymore. Elliot wanted the assurance that, if something happened to Jane, he would not lose his son as well. Adoption was the only way to leverage himself should Jane's parents file for permanent custody of Brydon. Adoption would provide Elliot with a legal claim. Elliot had willingly taken on the role of Brydon's father; he was the only father that Brydon had ever known. Brydon was his son. End of story.

Elliot walked down the hallway to a deserted waiting room and retrieved a cup of black coffee from a vending machine. He pulled his cell phone out of his pants pocket, sat down in a cushioned wooden chair and placed the full paper cup on a nearby metal end table. After the D & C, Doctor Rouse said they would repair Jane's collar bone. Elliot had no idea how long it would take to perform the procedures, but the doctors had planned on working in tandem as much as possible to avoid Jane spending an exorbitant amount of time under anaesthetic. Doctor Rouse was worried that the swelling of Jane's brain may cause further complications and had assured Elliot that they would monitor her closely for any signs of physiological distress.

Elliot found the telephone number for Jane's mom in his

contact list and pressed enter. The telephone rang only once before being answered.

"Hello?"

"Hi, it's Elliot. I've just seen Jane."

"Thank God. I was so worried. How is she?" Marie Kirkland said then yelled for her husband. "Stewart, quick pick up an extension, Elliot's on the phone!" A second click sounded on the line.

Elliot sighed. "It's pretty serious. Jane has a broken neck and a broken collar bone. She was conscious today and there's no sign of paralysis, which is good news. They've just taken her to surgery to put a pin in her collar bone and then they'll work on her neck in a day or two once they've made sure she's stabile. She had a pretty severe concussion, so they want to wait until the swelling in her brain has gone down before they put her under anaesthetic for very long. I guess the surgery on her neck could take them several hours from start to finish." Elliot paused as he heard Marie start to cry.

"Elliot, this is Stewart. I'm afraid that Marie's a bit overwhelmed by the news. I'll take it from here. This is the second time we've almost lost Jane in a car accident, but she's alive and that's what's important. She's a tough woman. She'll get through this."

Elliot knew that Stewart's assurances were just as much for Marie's benefit as they were for his own. Elliot's heart melted listening to Marie softly crying in the background then Brydon's voice. "Nana. What's wrong, Nana?"

Elliot struggled with his own tears, forcing them back. He couldn't allow himself to break down, not now. Maybe, later when this was all behind him, he'd go out for a really good drunk but not today.

"Stewart, I'm not going to lie to you. It's bad. They want to put a plate in Jane's neck to repair the damage, and she's in a lot of pain. I want to stay down here. I know that Pam is busy with her kids and with the baby, but my mom should be home by two. If you and Marie want to come down, I'm sure my mom would be happy to watch Brydon for a couple of days. I just don't think it would be wise to bring Brydon down here right now. Jane's going to be heavily sedated for the next few days and seeing her like this would probably just traumatize him."

"That makes sense, Elliot. I'll talk it over with Marie and we'll definitely make arrangements for at least one of us to be there. I can't see Marie driving in Toronto by herself. If I need to stay behind to watch Brydon, I'll call Dylan to meet her on the outskirts somewhere and he can make sure that she gets to the hospital safely."

In the background, a soft voice, "Nana. It's okay. Do you need a hug, Nana?"

"Sounds like a plan. I have my cell phone with me so give me a call when you're leaving. I'm going to check out local accommodations while Jane's in surgery. I can book a room for you too if you plan on staying overnight." A part of Elliot wanted to be angry with Jane. If she hadn't left in the first place, none of this would be happening. They'd all be at home right now enjoying the rest of the summer. He and Jane would be at work like any other normal day. Brydon would be at day camp. Marie would pick Brydon up at three o'clock for swimming lessons then the boy would hang out with his nana until Jane picked him up around five o'clock. Elliot would get home shortly after six. They'd have a barbeque, and he'd listen intently to Brydon's constant chatter as the boy retold his day's adventures.

"Thank you. That would be great. We have a few hours before your mom comes home so I'll call around and let everyone know what's going on. Jane's alive, Elliot. She's alive and in good hands. That's all that matters."

"Agreed." Elliot had been struggling with how much information he should give over the telephone, but knowing how emotional Jane could be, Elliot decided that her parents should be prepared. "Stewart, Marie, there's one more thing that I think you should know. Jane was two months pregnant when she crashed the car. She lost the baby. The doctor said that, when we get Jane home, we need to watch for any signs of depression and wanted to know if she has any suicidal tendencies."

Stewart gasped as did Marie who was obviously still listening on the telephone even if she couldn't bring herself to speak. "My god. I'm so sorry, Elliot. This just keeps getting worse and worse. Thanks for letting us know. I understand how difficult this all must be for you as well. Jane's always been a bit high-strung but suicidal tendencies, no. I don't think so. At least, not that I'm aware of. Elliot, are you okay?"

Elliot nodded to himself as he heard Marie hang up the telephone. "I'm okay. I'm just trying to get my head wrapped around all of this. A couple of days ago, I was playing ball in a tournament and the most I had to worry about was not getting thrown out at first base. Can you put Brydon on the phone please?"

"Sure. Hang in there, Elliot."

"Will do."

With his face turned away from the telephone receiver, Stewart summoned his grandson. "Brydon, your dad's on the phone. He wants to talk to you, son."

Elliot listened as the telephone changed hands.

"Daddy?"

"Hey, Bry."

"Daddy, is Mommy okay? Why can't Nana stop crying? After she hung up the telephone, I gave her the biggest hug I could and she just cried more." The boy's voice sounded as if he was on the verge of tears himself.

Elliot clutched his forehead with his left hand, leaned forward and propped his elbow on his knee. "Bry, I need you to listen carefully. Your mom has been in a car accident. She's okay, but she's going to be in the hospital for a while. Your nana is just a bit upset right now, Buddy. Just keep giving her hugs and she'll be all right."

"Okay. Is Mommy in the hospital where she works?"

"No, Bry. She's in a hospital a few hours away from where we live. It's a special hospital where they'll take extra special care of her. Your mommy's sleeping right now, but she told me to tell you that she loves you with all of her heart and that she'll be home just as soon as she can." Elliot blinked back tears as his heart wrenched. He needed a drink. One shot of very strong whiskey. Damn it, Jane, Elliot thought. This is what you get for being so fucking selfish. We have a life together. We have a home together. We have a child together. How could you just walk away like none of that mattered?

"I want to see Mommy when she wakes up? Can Poppa drive me to where you are?" The anxiousness in Brydon's voice was building.

Struggling with the best way to handle the situation, Elliot knew that Brydon wouldn't rest until he saw his mother. The bond between the two was like the threads of a tightly woven cloth. "Look, Bry, it could be very late before your mom wakes up, but let me speak to Poppa again, and we'll see what we can work out. Okay?"

"Okay." Off to the side, Brydon added. "Poppa, Daddy wants to speak to you."

Stewart came on the telephone line. "I'm here."

"I've changed my mind. I think that Brydon needs to see Jane for himself. It'd be different if she could talk to him on the telephone, but I can't see that happening for a day or so. If he can't see his mom, he'll end up so upset that there's a good chance he'll either make himself sick or he'll make the life of whoever is watching him unbearable. If you can bring him down, I can call my mom and then I'll take him back tomorrow if you want to stay here."

"I couldn't agree more. You're right. Brydon's just as bright and as stubborn as his mother. He'll deal better with what he can see than what he can't see. Marie's gone upstairs to pack an overnight bag. I just got the hospital's address off the internet to plug into the GPS. Give us an hour to get organized and then we'll be on our way. I'll give Dylan a call. Chances are I'll get his voice mail this time of day, but if I do, I'll give him your cell phone number. He lives about twenty minutes away from the hospital if he takes the transit."

"Is Marie okay? She sounded pretty upset."

"We're just in shock, Elliot. Marie will be okay. We knew it was bad when the hospital refused to give out any information on the telephone, but it could have been so much worse. Marie just needs to be there for Jane then she'll be okay. Is there anything we can grab for Jane from your house?"

Elliot sat back up in the chair. "Actually, I packed a few things in an overnight bag for Jane and brought them down with me. Jane had been travelling for a couple of days before the accident, so she would have had the basics with her in the car. Her purse arrived with her in the ambulance, but I just haven't had time to track down what happened to her luggage yet. I'm assuming it's still with the car, wherever that is. What you can do is stop at our house and feed the cat before you leave. That would be a big help. Brydon knows what to do."

"Sure thing. You hang tight, Elliot, and we'll see you soon."

"Safe driving." Elliot disconnected the call and took a drink of the bitter brew. Now he remembered why he didn't drink black coffee. Fuck. It had just seemed so much easier, at the time, than trying to figure out all of the lights and the buttons on the unfamiliar vending machine. Coffee black. Simple. Bitter as shit. Fuck.

Elliot put down the cup again, made a quick call to his boss and requested a leave of absence under Compassionate Care. That would give him six week of Employment Insurance so he could be at home to take care of Jane and Brydon. The paperwork would be ready by the end of the week for him to sign. He then called the Human Resources Department at the Health Center where Jane worked only to discover that Jane had booked this week off as vacation time and hadn't actually quit her job. Excellent. Elliot informed the office worker that Jane had been in a car accident and would be requiring an extended recuperation period, perhaps, several months. After the woman's initial shock had abated and words of support were expressed, the very nice lady also guaranteed that she would get Jane's paperwork started. All she needed was for Harbour View Memorial to fax them a copy of Jane's hospital admission and injuries report then she would personally get the ball rolling. In the meantime, Jane had a week of vacation pay then a week of banked sick time. Sick leave would take effect after that. The paperwork would be filed directly online to Service Canada. If Jane wasn't ready to return to work once her sick leave benefits had expired, she could then apply for the hospital's Short-Term Disability benefits and then their Long-Term Disability benefits if necessary. The woman then assured Elliot that they would all keep Jane in their thoughts and in their prayers.

With both he and Jane off work, Elliot knew that it would be tough budget-wise; however, there was no way he could mentally function at work wondering if Jane was doing okay. He had to be with her until he was absolutely positive that she could survive on her own. If that took longer than his six-week allotment, he'd hire a Personal Support Worker to help Jane until he got home from work. They'd just have to dip into their rainy day fund. After all, if this wasn't a rainy day, then he didn't know what was.

What was next? Motel rooms? Toronto was so expensive that the thought of staying for a prolonged period of time made Elliot shudder. It wouldn't take long to use up what little space he did have left on his credit card. He'd noticed some pamphlets on local hospital resources scattered on the end table and started glancing through one for ideas.

"Hey, Elliot. They told me at the Nursing Station that I'd probably find you here. Brought you a coffee. Double double. Right?"

Elliot looked up and truly smiled for the first time that day. Jeff. "Right. Thanks." He accepted the coffee. "I tried getting one from the vending machine, but it was fucking awful. What, no donuts?"

Jeff grinned and shook his head. "Have to watch my waistline or Pam might trade me in for a younger man. Good to see you still have your sense of humour though." He took a seat across from Elliot. "How's Jane doing? Went by her room, but the nurse said that Jane was in surgery."

Elliot took the plastic lid off the paper cup and took a sip of the very hot, very welcomed liquid. "She has a broken neck and a broken collar bone. They're putting a pin in her collar bone right now then they'll work on her neck in a couple of days when they can schedule the surgery. Thanks for finding her for me. I just don't understand what goes through Jane's head sometimes. She'll be fine for a few months and then, out of the blue, she'll just disappear."

Jeff nodded and sighed as he opened his own cup of coffee. "She was on her way home, Elliot, that's the important part. Anything other than that is history. Doesn't matter now. Best to let it go. But, I'll tell you something, when Jane was a kid and Pam was supposed to be watching her, Jane would sometimes take a notion and just take off on foot or on her bike. Pam would call me in a total panic because she couldn't find her, and I'd go over with my dad's old pick-up truck, hoping to hell that I didn't get stopped because I only had my beginners. We'd search the farm and if she wasn't there, we'd head on down the road. Sometimes, Jane would be back at the bush. Sometimes, she'd be a couple of kilometres away. Same damn thing, only Jane has a car now so she can travel farther. God knows why. Don't even think Jane knows. I do know that she wouldn't have meant for this to happen. She would have never crashed her car on purpose. Jane's tough. She'll pull through this. Jane and Pam, they come from good stock.

Managed to track down Jane's car. It's at an impound lot. Total write-off. I'll give you the address so you can contact your insurance company. Tell them where the car is so the adjuster can do an assessment and leave it at that. Trust me, you don't want to see this. It'll give you nightmares for the next five years. Talked to a local cop and he assured me that the accident has been attributed to adverse weather conditions. Hydroplaning on wet asphalt is not that uncommon and the tree, at the speed that the local constables have deduced Jane was travelling at, plus the trajectory of the roll, would have demolished anything short of a Hummer."

Somehow, Elliot did not find the news comforting. He wanted to see the car. He wanted to take a picture of the vehicle to show Jane later. He wanted her to fully understand what her little foray into finding herself cost them or could have potentially cost them. Her life. It could have cost them her life. It could have cost Brydon his mom. It could have cost him his wife. Instead, Elliot took another drink of coffee and swallowed down his irritation. "What about her luggage? Do you know what happened to her luggage?"

Jeff nodded. "Luggage is locked up at the office at the impound lot. Wouldn't let me have it. Jane's belongings can only be released to you or to Jane directly."

"Thanks, Jeff. I don't know how I'll ever repay you."

A brilliant smile encompassed Jeff's features. "We're family. Glad to help. Anything else I can do?"

Elliot sighed. "Can you suggest a cheap motel? I'm lost down here."

Jeff grinned. "Contact the local colleges or universities.

They quite often rent out residence or dorm rooms in the summer when there are no students. Ron and I came down a few summers ago for a training session and that's what we did. Costs like half as much as getting a motel room and a lot of the rooms have small fridges and microwaves."

A short, middle-aged man wearing blue scrubs walked hurriedly into the waiting room. "Mr. Fallis?"

Elliot put down the coffee cup and stood up. "That's me."

The man approached Elliot. "Mr. Fallis. I'm Doctor Davis. There's been a complication."

CHAPTER FIFTY-THREE

Todd was finding it impossible to concentrate. He'd taken a week's vacation as discussed, and now Jane wasn't answering her cell phone or responding to his text messages. She was supposed to contact him as soon as she had arrived safely in New Jersey. That should be today. The original plan was for him to meet her tomorrow, but Jane had asked that he wait for her to contact him first in case she'd run into difficulties and needed to make alternative arrangements. He was packed and ready to go. All he needed was the green light.

Two years, he'd been doing this. Todd raked his fingers back through his layered, shoulder-length brown hair. Two years, he'd been meeting Jane whenever she could manage to sneak away from Elliot. Three times she had promised to leave Elliot and, instead, had always gone back saying that the timing wasn't right. The thought of Elliot making love to Jane drove Todd insane. He also loathed the facts that when he did get to spend time with Brydon, the boy only knew him as his mother's friend, and that they had to meet at Gertie's to keep up the charade. In some ways, Todd had accepted the situation as being his own personal penance. He'd walked away from Jane. He'd walked away from Brydon. Elliot had been there for both of them. That didn't mean that Todd had to like the situation, only that he had to endure the dynamics for now.

When Jane had called Todd about the job in New Jersey, it had been the perfect opportunity for the two of them to start over, especially now that she was expecting his baby. This time, he was determined to be there for both mother and child. He may have irrevocably blown it with Brydon, but this child was his second chance. At first, Todd had been skeptical when Jane mentioned wanting him to father another child. In fact, he had thought it a blatantly horrific idea. Life was complicated enough, and, if it hadn't been for the guise of her visiting Gertie or Dylan, their time together wouldn't have existed, period. In the end, Jane had worn him down, promising to leave Elliot as soon as she found out that she was pregnant. She had promised to keep her sex life with Elliot to a bare minimum and to use a cervical cap when she was with him. She couldn't just quit having sex with Elliot altogether or he'd suspect something. Neither of them needed that right now. Elliot was becoming increasingly possessive of Brydon, and the last thing Jane wanted was to lose her son. Their son. Then, like a universal pardon that Todd's penance was complete, Jane had met him for lunch with the good news. Not only was she pregnant, but she also had the perfect way out, a way in which Elliot wouldn't be able to find her until she had the divorce papers ready.

Three o'clock. With at least a day's drive ahead of him, he should have left this morning. Todd checked his cell phone again. No messages.

His land-line rang, startling Todd. He glanced at the call display. Gertie. Todd grabbed his portable telephone off its dock and answered it. "Hello?"

"Todd, it's Gertie. I'm glad I caught you at home. I was afraid that you'd already left, and I couldn't find your cell phone number. Are you sitting down?"

Todd swiveled the high-backed, black leather office chair away from his personal computer. He wasn't one to get premonitions, but Gertie calling him in the middle of the afternoon instead of Jane, couldn't be good. Had Elliot found out? Maybe, Jane hadn't been able to leave after all. In any event, that didn't make sense. Jane had told him that Elliot was away at a ball tournament for the weekend and everything was going according to schedule. She had just dropped off Brydon at Gertie's and all was well. Was something wrong with Brydon then? Maybe, Gertie couldn't reach Jane either. "Hey, Gertie. What's up? Is Brydon okay? Have you heard from Jane? She was supposed to call me hours ago."

Gertie's voice was soft as if she was trying to keep her emotions under control. "Todd, Brydon's okay. It's Jane. I'm afraid that I have some really bad news."

Todd jumped up from his chair. Sitting down was not an option. "She's okay, right? She's alive, right?" He began to pace.

"She's alive. The rest I'm still trying to piece together myself. From what I can gather, Elliot came home earlier than anticipated and somehow figured out that Jane had really left him this time. He called here looking for information. Brydon had been so upset all day that, when Elliot asked if I knew where Brydon was…I'm sorry. I just couldn't lie to him. I thought if they talked, Brydon would settle down. I didn't expect Elliot to drive all the way down here to get Brydon. I thought that, if he just talked to Brydon, maybe he'd be content to leave it at that."

"Okay, so Elliot has Brydon. Then what happened?" Todd raked his fingers through his hair, trying to remain calm. Fuck. A huge part of the plan had been to get Brydon away from Elliot. Todd admonished himself. He should have taken Brydon. Elliot would have never found him if he'd taken the boy instead of Gertie. Jane didn't want to take Brydon down to New Jersey with her because of the interview and he got that. Gertie's house was on the way to the border. He got that too. He'd been working on a shoot on Saturday that he would have had to cancel. He understood that as well. All of these factors meant nothing when the boy was now with Elliot again. Fucking Gertie. All she had to do was to keep her mouth shut. Fuck.

Gertie continued, "Jane called me to say that she'd turned around to go see you before heading down to New Jersey. She'd had a bad dream or something and needed to make sure you were okay. You know, Jane. She has these like prophetic dreams sometimes, and there was no way she was going anywhere until she saw you in person. Anyway, I told her that Elliot had taken Brydon, so she decided to head home before Elliot could leave the country with her son. I told her that she was over-reacting, that Elliot wouldn't literally kidnap Brydon, but there was no talking any sense into her.

Anyway, to make a long story shorter, Dylan just called me. He'd been talking to his dad and Jane's in Harbour View Memorial Hospital. I'm so sorry, Todd. I should have just not answered the telephone when Elliot called. I had no idea that it would end up this way…I'm so sorry…I'm such an idiot sometimes, but what you and Jane seem to forget is that Brydon loves Elliot. Brydon had spent the whole afternoon upset because he wanted to go home and I just thought…"

Todd could hear tears now as Gertie started to sniffle into the telephone. "Gertie, don't worry about it. What's done is done. I want to know how Jane is. Harbour View Memorial is a trauma center. Did Elliot shoot Jane? What the fuck did Dylan say exactly?" Todd's legs suddenly felt weak, barely able to hold his 190 pounds. He quickly walked back to his chair, sat down and, using his shoulder to hold the telephone receiver to his ear, he began to search online for the address of the trauma center.

The sound of Gertie blowing her nose sounded through the telephone line. "Todd, Elliot didn't shoot her. Jane was in a car accident on the way home. She has a broken neck and a broken collar bone. She's just come out of surgery, but she's still in ICU. Elliot's down with her now. Dylan was heading over as soon as he hung up, and her parents are on their way as well." Gertie ended with an audible sigh.

"I need to see her. I don't care if Elliot's there. I need to see Jane." Todd leaned back in his computer chair and closed his eyes. They had been so close. So fucking close. Jane was wrong. There really was no god. No fucking god. Humans had evolved from protozoa. Darwin was right. Life, as they knew it, was just millions of years of evolution, of natural selection, millions of years that had all led to this moment, at this time. Fuck, Todd thought, if I could just go back and do it over again. If I could go back, none of this would be happening.

Gertie's voice, tears gone now, turned supportive. "Todd, I'd be on my way too, but the only ones who can see Jane right now are immediate family members and that pretty much leaves you and me out of the picture. It's not like you can just show up and announce that you're her boyfriend. As much as Dylan and I would love for you and Jane to get this triangle thing finally resolved, Elliot is still Jane's legal husband. You and I are nothing more than concerned friends."

"Where's Brydon?" Maybe, Gertie was right or, maybe, it was time for full disclosure. Natural selection yes, but what about survival of the fittest? If there was no god, then nothing was preordained. There was no divine destiny, no fate and no guardian angels looking down and gently nudging everyone in the right direction, keeping everyone on some supposed, predetermined pathway. None of it was fucking real. The only things that were real were Jane and Brydon. His Jane. His Brydon.

"According to Dylan, Brydon is with his grandparents."

"Did Dylan say anything about the baby?" My baby, Todd

thought.

"Except for you and me, as far as I know, Jane hadn't told anyone else yet so no, Dylan didn't mention anything about the baby. I'm so sorry, Todd. I know how much you love Jane and how hard this must be for you. This is killing me so it must be a thousand times worse for you. Dylan promised to keep us updated and let me know the moment that Jane's out of Intensive Care."

"I can't just sit here and do nothing." Todd opened his eyes again.

"If you show up at the hospital when Elliot's there, there is a very good possibility that he'll put two and two together. Todd, Elliot's not stupid, and he has a very bad temper when he lets it loose."

"I'm not afraid of him," Todd challenged. He was in excellent physical condition and belonged to a Yonge Street kickboxing gym where he was presently participating in their advanced Competitive Fighters' Training Program twice a week when he wasn't travelling. He could take Elliot down in as little as two moves and that thought was comforting. Survival of the fittest, point blank.

"No doubt, but Jane's in a very vulnerable situation right now. Do you want to put her at risk? Jane's going to need constant care for weeks, if not months, until she's better. According to Dylan, Jane needs a plate in her neck and then a halo. It could be months before that comes off. She's not in any position to leave Elliot right now. You need to be patient. I know this is brutal, but you've waited this long."

Todd sighed. "This is all my fault. Jane moved back home from Toronto because I was being a self-centered jerk. We'd had an argument and I told her it was over, that I couldn't do it anymore. Fuck, Gertie, you know what it was like back then. Jane and I were off and on so often it took a score card to keep track. She was drunk and wanted to piss me off, so she had sex with one of my roommates. It worked. It didn't matter that we were split up at the time, I was so fucking furious when I found out that I didn't speak to Jane for almost a year. I just shut both her and Brydon out and walked away. What kind of a man does that? Brydon's been better off since Elliot took over. They have a house and a backyard, a stabile life. Sometimes, I think I should have just stayed away."

Gertie soothed. "Todd, what happened was a long time ago. You were both really young, and neither of you were ready for the responsibility of a child. Jane has always regretted what she did. She definitely wasn't above using sex for revenge back then, but that doesn't mean she was happy afterwards with her decision. Jane's always been a bit too impetuous for her own good and, this time, there was just no way to take it back. No way to undo what she had done.

And, I agree that Elliot was really good for her and for Brydon in a lot of ways. Jane grew up. She settled down. She seldom drinks anymore, and, except on special occasions, the drugs are mostly a thing of the past. They have a house and a stabile life, yes. The only thing that was missing was you. Jane's never stop loving you. She'd trade her house for you any day of the week. She'd pitch a tent and, as long as she had you and Brydon, she'd be happy. As for Brydon, kids adjust.

I'll tell you what, once Jane is out of ICU, I'll go with you to see her. If Elliot's there, maybe I can drag him down to the cafeteria and buy him lunch so you can sneak in to see Jane."

"Look, Gertie, I appreciate your offer, but I'm not sneaking in anywhere. As far as Elliot is concerned, whatever Jane and I had together ended after college. We've been very careful during the past two years. She has a pay-as-you-go cell phone that she only uses to contact me. She has an e-mail address under a made-up name that she only accesses at work. The only ones who know about us are you and Dylan, and I highly doubt that either of you is going to confess to being co-conspirators in Jane's having an affair.

On the other hand, I can take care of Jane and Brydon or hire someone to stay with them while I'm at work. Maybe, it's time to come clean with Elliot. I seriously doubt that he'd hurt Jane or hurt the baby. Elliot is a lot of things, but I've seen him when he's really angry, and I don't think he's capable of physically hurting Jane. He might try to take me out but not Jane. Even if he wants to, he's not going to do anything to Jane while she's in the hospital, and we can move her to a safe place on her release.

Look, Gertie, I have to go and figure this out. I need to talk to Jane and see how she wants to handle this. I can't just sit here and do nothing." Various scenarios spun their way through Todd's thoughts like a visual collage of possibilities.

"Todd, just don't do anything stupid." The concern in Gertie's voice sounded through loud and clear.

"Too late for that. Stupid was the day I moved out of my apartment and let you move in."

"You do realize that I'm giving up a very convenient man-toy, don't you?" Gertie teased Todd as they met in the hallway of her apartment building just outside of her door. Todd was in the process of moving a large cardboard box packed full of his sports equipment into Gertie's one-bedroom while Gertie was in the process of moving a smaller cardboard box of her personal belongings out of her apartment and into her car. "This would be a whole lot easier if you and Jane would just kiss and make up. Then I wouldn't have to move."

"It's not that simple and you know it." Todd frowned and lowered the heavy box onto the floor. "How come said man-toy's not helping you move?"

"Even man-toys work for a living occasionally." Gertie lowered her cardboard box and set it on top of Todd's.

"Look Gertie, I know this is a bit awkward, but I wanted to thank you for agreeing to switch apartments with me for a while. Lorne said I could stay with him, but I didn't want a stranger moving in with Jane right now." The incipient shock had worn off, still Todd felt lost without Jane.

"Don't thank me. Thank Jane. When you first asked me, I thought you were completely off your meds. When I asked Jane what she thought, it was Jane who insisted that it would be a perfect solution and begged me to give it a try. She also reminded me that it was her idea to end your relationship, not yours, and that I should be nice to you because she was really hoping that we can all stay friends."

"Jane wants to stay friends? Considering she's been avoiding me and hasn't spoken to me in three weeks, I find that a bit hard to believe. Even in class, she sits as far away as possible. Gertie, I love Jane. I just think having a kid right now is a huge mistake. I can't change the way I feel about that."

Gertie nodded. "Todd, I totally agree with you. If it had been me, I wouldn't think twice about having an abortion, but it's not my decision to make so I'm not taking sides. Did it ever occur to you, though, that she's just giving you space? She knows how you feel about the baby. I don't know if, deep down, she's still hoping that you'll eventually change your mind; but, she's calmed down enough on the surface to accept that you may not ever want this child. She's trying to make peace with that.

She's been reading all kinds of self-help, pregnancy books and says that it's bad for the baby if she harbours ill will towards anyone. Or as Jane said and I quote, 'You can lead a bull to water, but you can't make him swim'. She also says that the baby needs to feel peace, love and acceptance around it. Good vibes and all that jazz. Yay for new age shit. I get to spend the next six months doing the daddy vibe instead of getting completely stoned and having sex with random strangers. Good times. Though you know, that's okay. Jane's my best friend, and I'll always have her back."

Todd sauntered around his semi-tidy, two-bedroom apartment, searching for mementos of Jane. Living in a high-rise wasn't his ideal situation, but the Eva Road location was close to a highway 427 access so he could drive quickly across the city, except in rush hour, or catch the 401 to leave town. The building was also secure, clean, close to malls, grocery stores, parks and the side street was tucked away from general traffic. It was a good deal for Toronto and almost affordable on his budget. Todd had upgraded from a one-bedroom the year before in the hope that Jane would agree to bring Brydon down for an occasional overnight visit. Todd wanted the boy to have a space of his own but hadn't gone overboard in the decorating.

The second bedroom, at this point, looked like a general guest room with a simple double bed, a nightstand and a dresser. The room was also occasionally inhabited by a friend who needed a temporary place to stay and who was also willing to chip in on the monthly rent. Overall, the upgrade had paid for itself. Todd had no regrets, even if his desire to have his family under one roof for a weekend had, thus far, gone unheeded.

Various pictures stuffed into an old, wooden cigar box, a flea market treasure found by Jane, sent Todd wandering down nostalgia lane. A class picture taken in third-year, too many faces with unknown journeys. He'd have to make an asserted effort to track down some of his classmates and discover their stories.

Pictures of Jane and Brydon shortly after Brydon was born--a look of unadulterated pride, unconditional love and pure adoration meshed together in her smile. There were pictures from a pot luck dinner at Lorne's apartment when everyone, tired of eating macaroni and cheese, contributed to one decent meal for all. Farther down there were other assorted pictures that included classmates, pictures taken at events vaguely remembered. Todd found, buried on the bottom of the small pile, safely tucked away from unwanted eyes, more recent pictures that he and Jane had taken together during moments stolen from real life. Stolen moments, stolen weekends that should have always been his. The photographs made him smile and made him sad simultaneously. Too little time. He wanted much more. He had at least a hundred pictures downloaded onto his computer, but the printed photos seemed more real somehow, as if the tactile sense made the scenes tangible and still within his touch.

An extra toothbrush stood silently in a ceramic holder on his bathroom vanity because Jane had a habit of forgetting her own. Several plastic containers of face and body cream kept the toothbrush company, waiting for her return.

In his bright, sunny bedroom, framed on top of his wooden chest of drawers was a picture taken the summer before of him, Jane and Brydon playing on the Merry-Go-Round at the park. Gertie had taken the photo and had given it to him, enlarged, as a gift. A framed copy of Brydon's kindergarten graduation picture, the boy looking fiercely proud of his accomplishment, completed Todd's collection of family photos. Every day since Jane had announced her pregnancy, Todd had studied Brydon's photos in wonderment that the child was an absolute male image of his mother. It was if there'd been no father at all with only Jane's genetics being passed along. The only difference was Brydon's eyes were hazel compared to his mother's green. Todd assumed that was due to his own eyes being brown. He couldn't help but hope, a bit narcissistically, that the next child would resemble himself. Unless, of course, the child was a girl and then she'd be better off looking like her mother as well.

Jane's favourite feather pillow, left untouched for the past couple of weeks, hunter green case freshly laundered, lay fluffed and ready on the queen-size bed. She slept only on the left; he preferred to sleep on the right. Perfect symmetry. Todd thought back to the day they had picked out the bedframe. He'd joked about wanting a headboard that he could attach handcuffs to, saying bondage might add some spice to their sex life. There was a store downtown that sold all kinds of cuffs or they could use scarves instead if that was more agreeable. Jane had not welcomed his adventurous suggestion, stating frankly that hell would freeze over before she would ever allow him to bind her wrists; but, if he wanted to be bound, they could definitely arrange that. The fury in Jane's eyes had successfully eradicated the discussion. Instead, they'd ended up choosing a classically styled, paneled, distressed cherry bed with a solid headboard and bun footings. Jane assured him that the bed would last them forever so the exorbitant price was well worth the investment. She then chose a patterned, hunter green comforter and a solid, hunter green sheet set to complete the ensemble. Todd loved that bed. Most of all, he loved the way he felt when he and Jane lay in that bed together, knowing that their child had been conceived there.

  Jane's clothing hung in his closet--a few shirts, a few t-shirts, a couple of pairs of faded jeans, all Kensington Market finds, and a long, black negligee that he only managed to allow her to wear for a minute before he lost any semblance of self-control and tore the silky garment back off again. Her undergarments lay undisturbed in the top drawer of his chest of drawers, lacy bras, bikini underpants and thongs that he vowed to worship one day in her shrine. He ran his fingers along the top of them, feeling the soft material beneath his touch.

  A large, very realistic, but artificial, peace lily inhabited a corner of the room. Jane had laughed when she'd bought it saying that, since they had tortured the original one, it was only fitting to erect a statue in its memory.

  Her white t-shirt nightie he left hanging on a hook on the back of his bedroom door as a daily reminder that, take heart, she would be back again.

  The kitchen held Jane's favourite cup, a large, soaring eagle blue, double-sized porcelain mug that held enough liquid to drown a fish. Beside her mug, sat the white cup she had bought for him as a congratulatory gift. On the front was written "Cameramen Do it With Focus" to celebrate his new job at the production company where he worked. She had almost been more excited than he was by his promotion from being a first assistant or focus puller to that of a bona fide cameraman. Jane's assortment of herbal teas took up the better part of one cupboard shelf.

He was surrounded by Jane. Little things. Big things. Jane things. Items symbolizing stolen moments in time. Moments that should have always been his. There was no god. There was no destiny. There was no fate. There was only Jane and Brydon and him.

A year had passed since Todd had received Jane's e-mail saying that she married Elliot. The initial shock had devastated Todd then the self-deprecating realization that he had brought this on himself had tortured him even more. Wounds not deep enough to be fatal but wounds that refused to bind, refused to heal became his constant companion. He had no one else to blame. Todd couldn't blame Jane. She was just getting on with her life. Without him. Jane was married. Without him.

Todd had tried everything he could think of to get past his grief. Working sixty hours a week hadn't helped. Alcohol hadn't helped. One night stands with women he couldn't name hadn't helped. The occasional joint to survive the worst nights only blurred the lines for a brief while. Reality was still there, stark and naked in the morning light. Jane was married. Without him.

Then came her call. Jane wanted to meet and to discuss Brydon. Todd had felt his gut wrench. Brydon. The child that Todd had walked away from in anger. A child who didn't deserve to be caught in the crossfire. Todd had convinced Jane to meet him at his apartment so they could talk privately. He didn't want strangers to overhear what Jane needed to say; he didn't want strangers to judge him, to see his shame.

Jane arrived on time. Casually dressed in denim shorts and a pink tank top with her long, sun-streaked, blonde hair pulled back into a pony tail, she looked tanned and fit, happy. The summer was hot, but she looked cool and calm after the long drive. If he had expected her to look nervous or love-stricken, lost in the despair that he chronically felt, he would have been disappointed at best. Jane had gotten on with her life. Without him. He truly understood that now.

"Can I get you something to drink? Cola? Fruit juice? Water?"

Todd offered, tough to appear unruffled, friendly when every iota of his being wanted to quake. Two years had changed nothing. He still loved her.

"A glass of water would be good." Jane waited for Todd to retrieve the drink. She held a legal-size, manila envelope in her hand.

Todd handed a plastic bottle of cold water to Jane then led the way into his living room. "So what brings you here? You said it was too important to talk about on the telephone." He sat down on his beige couch and watched as Jane sat down beside him then drew her right leg up so she could face him. She placed the manila envelope beside her. Jane opened the bottle of water, took a drink then placed the bottle on the steamer trunk that served as a coffee table.

"You never were much for small talk." Jane grinned. "No 'so how was the drive?'"

"Jane, you didn't come here to discuss the present congestion issues on the 427. What's up that we couldn't discuss on the telephone?" Todd could feel his heart softly pound against his black t-shirt. He could barely bring himself to look at Jane but turned his body towards her to appear unafraid. So many times they had started out on a couch only to end up on a bed. She's married, Todd reminded himself, chastising the memories for popping into his head.

"Okay. To the point." Jane picked up the manila envelope and handed the package to Todd. "Elliot wants to adopt Brydon. These are the legal papers that you need to sign to give up your parental rights." Her smile had vanished, leaving behind an uncharacteristic seriousness.

Todd felt as if his breath had just been knocked from his chest. He accepted the package without speaking and extracted the long, legal form from within. He scanned through the contents then raked his fingers through his hair. "Jane, I can't sign this." He tossed the form onto the steamer trunk. "Sorry, I just can't do it." Todd stood up, briskly walked to his kitchenette, opened the refrigerator and grabbed a beer. He walked back to the living room, popped the cap and tipped the bottle back.

Jane sat and watched him. "Todd, you haven't seen Brydon in two years. If you sign off, there's no more support payments, no more worries. It's over." The anger rose in Jane's eyes as she struggled to keep her voice calm. "You didn't want Brydon to begin with. Elliot does. If you sign the papers, we can all get on with our lives. I thought you'd jump at the chance."

Todd worked his way back to the couch and sat down. Leaning back, he propped his bare feet on the trunk. "I was actually thinking the other day that I should find a lawyer and file a motion for joint custody. This whole getting on with our lives routine doesn't seem to be working out so well for me."

This time shock registered on Jane's pretty features. "There's no fucking way any judge would give you joint custody when you've made very little effort to see Brydon for the past two years. He doesn't even remember you."

Todd took another drink. With all of his heart he wanted Jane back. He hadn't known just how much until she had walked through the door. If Brydon was the key, then he'd play the hand dealt to him. "I'm not condoning what I did in the past, nor am I going to ask for your forgiveness. I wasn't ready to be a father then. When you moved home, I tried to convince myself it wouldn't be forever, that eventually, you'd move back here and we'd work things out like we've done a million times before. Then you started seeing Elliot, and I tried to convince myself it was too late, that it was for the best, that I had no right asking for anything. One day turned into the next and here we are. You're married to someone else, and I'm still in love with you. So, no, I'm not going to sign the papers, and I would very much like to make arrangements to spend time with my son. Maybe have him every other weekend. If you don't want to do this amicably then I will find a lawyer." Todd turned to face Jane. Until seeing Jane, he'd had no intentions of filing for weekend visitation. Odd, how a moment in time can change everything.

Jane looked dumbfounded. "You're still in love with me?"

Not the response he had expected. He took another drink and set the beer bottle on the steamer trunk. He swallowed back his pride. "Yes."

"You could have told me that before I married Elliot." Jane's features softened, sadness replaced the anger in her eyes.

"You didn't tell me you were marrying Elliot. You told me that you had married Elliot only after the fact," Todd gently reminded Jane. He reached over and lovingly stroked her cheek. "I love you. I've tried everything I can think of to stop loving you, and it hasn't worked. I don't know how to not love you." Todd leaned forward and brushed his lips against Jane's. He pulled her hair loose from the covered elastic and let the length fall down over her shoulders, a gesture he had done hundreds of times before when he wanted to make love to her, when he wanted to feel the golden locks caress his bare skin. He didn't care if she was married. Elliot wasn't real to him. The only thing that was real was the fact that Jane sat before him, her dark green eyes full of desire. Todd knew that look, the one that meant she was all his, physically and emotionally. He pulled himself back. "Tell me that you don't love me anymore, and I'll stop."

Jane whispered, "That's so not fair. Where were you when Brydon and I needed you?"

"Growing up." Todd bent forward again and kissed Jane harder this time, her mouth opening beneath his, letting his tongue slip inside. He could feel the hardness of his erection pressing against his jeans in bound agony. He wanted this woman. The time and the distance had only intensified the feelings. Todd pulled back again. "Tell me that you don't love me, and I'll stop."

Instead, Jane stood up and offered her hand, her face flushed with internal heat. "Which way to your bedroom?"

Todd jumped up before Jane could change her mind and scooped her up into his arms. He nuzzled her neck as he carried her into his room and squatted down to lay her on the mattress that sufficed for a bed.

She smiled up at him as Todd began to hastily undress. "Linwood, what is it that you have against bedframes?"

Todd walked back into his living room and grabbed the cell phone off his desk. He found Dylan's name in his contact list. Choosing options, Todd sent Dylan a message that Gertie had just told him what happened to Jane. He included that Jane was pregnant and to please find out if the baby is okay.

This is crazy, Todd thought. Jane and I are in love. We've been in love since college. Maybe, it had been a rocky road for them, and they had both royally fucked up on occasion, but Todd's name was listed on Brydon's birth certificate as being the boy's father. Brydon was his son. Elliot was Brydon's stepdad, yes, but not the boy's father. There was also a ninety-five percent chance that the baby Jane was carrying was Todd's, and, even if the baby wasn't his biological child, he didn't care. This time, Todd had no intention of just idly standing by and waiting to see what happened. He wasn't a starving college student anymore. It was time to take his family back.

CHAPTER FIFTY-FOUR

Jane reached up and grabbed onto consciousness. She opened her eyes and blinked several times to make sure that she was actually awake. She still couldn't turn her head, and now her left arm seemed to be bound tightly against her bosom by a sling bandage of some sort. The IV line had been moved to the back of her right hand instead of her left. She swallowed, abhorring the medicinal taste in her mouth.

Turning her eyes to the left, Jane saw that Elliot was sitting cross-legged beside her in a padded, black metal chair, glancing through a magazine of some sort. He looked comfortable in his t-shirt, jeans and favourite running shoes, but he definitely could use a shave and his hair looked like he'd forgotten to use a comb when he jumped out of the shower this morning. "Elliot," she managed a whisper.

Elliot looked up, quickly shut the magazine and dropped it on the floor beside the chair. "Jane, you're awake." He rose and stood beside her bed. "How are you feeling?" A genuine look of concern crossed his rugged features.

"I'm not sure yet." Jane ran her tongue along the inside of her mouth. Her teeth felt like they were coated with woolly mittens. "Can you please see if I can have some water?" My kingdom for a coffee, Jane thought. She knew the drill. It would be a while yet before she would receive anything more exciting than clear liquids. The doctors wouldn't take the chance of her becoming nauseated and aspirating on her own vomit while her head was being restrained. "Or maybe a tea?" Black tea was clear, right? Kind of.

"The nurse left a glass of water with ice on your night table. Hang on and I'll get it. She said you should take small sips only." He moved to her left and returned with a Styrofoam cup in his hand with a bendable straw. "Just a second and I'll raise the top of the bed for you." He pressed a button on the bedrail to reposition the top end of the bed.

Jane felt the top half of her body slowly rise and tilt forward as the bed moved into a semi-Fowler position. She grimaced in pain and bit back a groan that threatened to escape. It would be easier to see what was going on if she wasn't lying flat on her back. She didn't want Elliot to panic, thinking he'd hurt her, and lower her back down again. Once Elliot was satisfied, he held the cup in front of her and guided the straw to her mouth. "Thank you," Jane said then took a sip and swallowed. Right, Toronto water. Not the same as their chemical-free well water but a blessing just the same. "Elliot, it's okay. I can hold the cup." Jane reached over with her right hand, careful not to overextend the intravenous lines.

"Okay," he said as he transferred the cup to her grasp.

Jane took another sip. "What time is it?"

Elliot glanced down at his black sports watch. "It's five p.m. You've been out for most of the day. "Do you want me to take the glass back now?"

"Okay." Jane handed the glass to Elliot. He placed it on the overbed table.

"Jane, I'll be right back. I have to let the nurses know that you're awake so they can page Doctor Davis. You were awake in the recovery room, but as soon as they brought you back here, you fell asleep again so he didn't have a chance to talk to you. Will you be okay for a minute?"

Jane tried to nod but couldn't. Right. Fuck. She'd never get used to this. She sighed. "Is he the doctor I was talking to before?" Jane vaguely remembered talking to a doctor.

Elliot shook his head. "No, that was Doctor Rouse. I don't know if you remember, but you started to hemorrhage so they called in an Obstetrician. Doctor Davis is the OBS guy."

Right. Fuck. Memories of the excruciating cramps came flooding back like awakened glimpses of an iniquitous nightmare. "Did I lose the baby?" Jane could feel hot tears sting the backs of her eyes. Todd. I'm so sorry, Todd. She'd wanted so badly to carry his child. She didn't want to hurt Elliot, but she was in love with Todd. No matter how hard she'd tried, that fact hadn't changed. Or maybe, she had really died in the crash and this was her hell, the final judgement for her betrayal.

Elliot frowned, hesitated and then gently stroked Jane's arm through the sling as if he wasn't quite sure if touching her was a wise decision. "That's what he wants to talk to you about, but it would be better if I let the doctor explain. Dylan, your mom and your dad and Brydon are all here. They just went down to the cafeteria to get a bite to eat. Jeff was here too, but he had to leave. He told me to say hi for him. Pam would be here, but she couldn't find anyone to watch the kids on short notice. She'll try to make it down in a couple of days when Jeff has a day off so he can take over."

"I don't want Bry seeing me like this." Jane swallowed fighting back tears, fighting back every emotion that threatened to overwhelm her.

"I get that, but Brydon was really worried. We decided it was better to let him see that you were okay. I'm going to take him home later. Ma said she'd watch him for a few days. Then I'll drive back. Anyway, I'd better let the nurses know that you're awake. I'll be right back."

"Okay." Pam, Jeff and their brood. Four children now. Pam had said that was enough--two boys and two girls. If Jeff wanted more children, he could find himself another wife. Jane's resolve had completely shattered when the last baby was born, a little girl, chubby, tiny and perfect. Ten little fingers. Ten little toes. Jane had previously decided that Brydon would be an only child until she heard this particular baby, with her white-blonde curls and trusting blue eyes, coo and saw her smile. After that, Jane finally had to admit to herself that she wanted another child. She wanted a little brother or a little sister for Brydon, and she wanted said baby soon. She and Dylan were close, but Pam, who was seven years older, had seemed light years away when they were growing up. It was only after they were adults, that she and Pam had found common ground, friendship. Brydon was already six. If Jane didn't have another baby now, she was afraid her children would be the same--bound by blood but not by companionship.

Brydon was her child. Hers alone. The next one had to be Todd's child. She owed him that much at least. She owed herself that much at least.

Jane was almost a hundred percent sure that this baby was Todd's. Along with the cervical cap and the spermicide that she used after her bi-weekly trysts with Elliot, Jane had added a neem oil capsule to his allotted morning vitamins for two months before trying to get pregnant with Todd saying that the herb, which reportedly causes temporary infertility in men, was a new brand of

Vitamin B Complex. Of course, as soon as Jane had found out that she was pregnant, she threw out the rest of the neem oil capsules and went back to their regular brand of Vitamin B Complex. As much as Jane didn't want Elliot's baby, she didn't want to cause him any permanent damage either. The studies she'd read on the internet varied from neem oil being a wonder drug that caused completely reversible, temporary infertility, but did not affect libido or production, to warning that few to no human trials had been performed and that guinea pigs and rabbits had died in the animal trials. Elliot was neither a guinea pig nor a rabbit though so it was an interim risk that Jane was willing to take.

    A tear escaped from Jane's right eye. She'd been so close. She raised her right hand and wiped the tear away. If she'd lost this baby, she'd wait until she was healed and then, hopefully, convince Todd to try again. She'd leave Elliot first this time though so there could be no chance of unwanted parentage.

    Todd. He'd be waiting for her call. Fuck. Did Dylan let Todd know? Jane was eternally grateful that Todd and Dylan were buddies. It had made life so much easier. She loved to watch the two guys interact with absolutely no uneasiness, no unspoken tension between them. They had bonded over a Maple Leaf's home game and had never looked back. Dylan's partner, Paul, had season tickets and since Paul was away at a sales convention, Dylan had taken Jane's advice and called Todd to see if he wanted to go with him instead. Todd had readily agreed. The two men had become fast friends and the rest was history.

    Elliot re-entered the room, followed by a shorter, dark-haired man with glasses. Doctor Davis probably. Elliot moved to the right side of her bed. Doctor Davis stood on her left.

    "Good afternoon, Jane. I'm Doctor Davis. Doctor Rouse called me in to assist with your pregnancy issues." His voice sounded somewhat detached, clinical and professional.

    Jane tried to smile, but her heart hurt far worse than her neck and that was really saying a lot because the pain she was presently feeling was an easy twenty on a scale of one to ten. "Did I lose the baby?" Elliot hadn't given her a direct answer. Maybe, Doctor Davis would. She felt Elliot take her right hand in his.

    "Yes and no which is why I wanted to speak to you directly.

There has been an unexpected complication. Despite the hemorrhaging, the ultrasound showed that you are still pregnant. This can indicate that you were originally carrying twins and that one was spontaneously aborted. At this point, there's no way of knowing for sure, but that's my opinion. Did you have an ultrasound done when you first found out that you were pregnant?"

"No. I have one scheduled, but it's not for a couple of weeks." Jane made a mental note to ask Elliot later to cancel the appointment.

"Okay. Like I said, it's unfortunate, but not all that uncommon for the body to abort one twin. This could have happened for many reasons, but it's probably due to the physical trauma that you've just sustained."

Jane swallowed, wanting to feel happy but instinctively knowing that there was more. "Is the baby that's left okay?" She felt Elliot's hand tighten slightly around hers as if preparing Jane for the worst.

Doctor Davis nodded. "The ultrasound looks promising. The fetus has a strong heartbeat and is size-appropriate for the estimated age. I know this is very good news, Jane, but given your current circumstances, I need to ask if you want a therapeutic abortion."

Jane glanced towards Elliot who was looking down at the bed, refusing to meet her eyes.

She turned her focus back to Doctor Davis. "The baby's at risk right? Is that what you mean?"

Doctor Davis nodded again. "I'm afraid so. As far as the present research states, the pain medications and the MRI present no known risks. Of course, we always suggest that expectant mothers refrain from taking any pain medication unless absolutely necessary. The same goes for MRIs. They should only be done when there is no other choice. That doesn't mean that there are no risks just that the risks have yet to be determined, so I cannot give you an exact answer. However, there is a certain amount of risk with anaesthetic and surgery. Doctor Rouse has determined that the swelling has gone down in your brain sufficiently and has scheduled the surgery on your neck for tomorrow, so if you want the abortion, we should do that as soon as possible."

Jane strived to understand the total implications. They were discussing a life here. Jane did not want to risk the child, but she also knew that she needed to do what was best for everyone involved even if it broke her own heart. "So far, you've told me that I've lost one baby, but the second one has managed to hang on through a car accident and through my shoulder being repaired. What are the risks for tomorrow?"

"There was a recent study done in the United States of ten thousand women. The study concluded that the pregnant women who underwent anesthesia and surgery had a three percent chance of delivering a baby with a birth defect which is comparable to the normal chance of delivering a baby with a birth defect. However, if the surgery was performed during the first trimester, there was a ten percent chance of fetal death or of miscarriage which is substantially higher than if the surgery was performed later in the pregnancy. Unfortunately, your injuries cannot wait until later to be repaired."

Jane could feel her maternal instincts take over and her anger rise. "If my child has a ninety percent chance of survival with little to no risk of being deformed, why would I even contemplate aborting it?"

Doctor Davis raised his hand in the attempt to calm her. "The decision is yours, Jane," he assured her. "If you want to continue your pregnancy, then we will continue to monitor the fetus as long as you're with us and hope for the best. I just want you to be prepared for the fact that you may miscarry after tomorrow, or that your body may decide it cannot cope with your healing process as well as with maintaining the pregnancy and miscarry in a few weeks. Sometimes, women decide it would be better to terminate an early pregnancy until they have fully recuperated from their own injuries and are strong enough to try again." Doctor Davis reached up and adjusted the dark frames of his glasses to sit up higher on the narrow bridge of his nose.

"What if I don't take any pain killers? Will that increase the baby's chances of survival?"

"Jane, after tomorrow's surgery, I'm afraid that the pain will be unbearable for the first while. Again, taking no pain medicine at all is up to you; however, if your body is physiologically stressed past the point of pain endurance for a great length of time, again, this could trigger a miscarriage. I would suggest talking to Doctor Rouse about the best maintenance program and see what he would recommend. Do you want some time to think about this, Jane? Your husband, who is busy being very quiet at this moment, has already told me that the decision is up to you."

Jane contemplated the information for a moment. This child was like her, a survivor. The least she could do was to give the baby a chance. Jane looked up at Doctor Davis and spoke, "I will not abort my baby, not with a ninety percent chance that he or she will survive tomorrow's operation. I'll talk to Doctor Rouse about the pain meds. I can handle a lot of pain. What I can't handle is the thought of purposely killing my child."

CHAPTER FIFTY-FIVE

Elliot wasn't a religious man by any means. When he was a child, his mother would drag him and his siblings, hair combed, freshly scrubbed and appropriately dressed, off to Sunday school once a week, where he and Nick would fidget and count the minutes to freedom. Mrs. Fallis had made sure that all of her children had been properly baptized and confirmed into the church. After that, she had considered her religious duties fulfilled and had let her adult children travel down their own pathways. Nowadays, Elliot's usual pathway included sleeping in on Sunday mornings with an occasional hangover, followed by sex with Jane, if Brydon was still asleep, then a hearty brunch. As a result, Elliot felt like a slight hypocrite sitting in the hospital's empty, quiet chapel waiting for Jane's return from surgery. He'd already tried the busy waiting room and the crowded cafeteria but found no comfort there. He couldn't eat nor could he concentrate long enough to read even a newspaper. Maybe, he could pray.

Elliot closed his eyes and bent his head forward. Dear God, please let Jane be okay and let the baby live. Amen. Elliot opened his eyes and studied the wooden cross before him. Did he actually believe in God? He didn't disbelieve in him. That had to count for something.

If nothing else, the serene atmosphere of the non-denominational chapel helped to soothe Elliot's tattered nerves. The walls were a smooth, warm, cream colour. The mood lighting was set to focus on the large, wooden cross that adorned the wall above the cloth covered wooden altar. A small oak pulpit gave the appearance that sometimes services were conducted here, even though there were only twelve, shortened, wooden pews--six on each side--divided by the middle walkway. Elliot had chosen a seat in a middle pew, a subconscious act dating back to childhood and his not wanting the minister to see that he and his brother were not actually paying attention to the long-winded sermons.

"Elliot," Todd whispered loudly as he slid into the pew beside Elliot. "We need to talk."

"What the fuck are you doing here?" Elliot snarled, not bothering to keep his voice low as there was no one else in the room besides the two of them. He glanced beside him. The man was a little bit older, but Elliot would have known Todd anywhere. He looked just the same as he had seven years ago except that his t-shirt and jeans had been replaced by a large, slightly wrinkled, beige cotton shirt and baggy, khaki shorts. Todd's brown hair was still too long and he still looked as if he thought he lived a step above Elliot.

Todd dropped the whisper and spoke in his normal voice. "I came to see Jane, and I came to talk to you. Dylan said that I'd find you down here. Jane's back from the recovery room. She's still pretty groggy, but she came through the procedure okay."

Elliot began to rise. "I have nothing to say to you so if you'll excuse me, I need to see my wife."

Todd shook his head, reached up and grabbed Elliot by his right arm. "Not before we talk."

With sheer grit and determination not to cause a disturbance in a chapel just in case there was a god out there somewhere after all, Elliot shook loose from Todd's grip and grudgingly sat back down. "Make it quick."

Todd faced the front of the chapel and stared straight ahead towards the presbytery. His voice was calm, matter-of-fact. "There's no easy way to say this, so I'll get to the point. Jane and I have been seeing each other for the past two years, and there's a really good chance that the baby she's carrying is mine."

Elliot turned towards Todd and blinked in disbelief. "You're either crazy, delusional or both. Jane's my wife. She told me that you dropped out of the scene before she moved back to Donnybrooke. Now, you seriously want me to believe that the two of you are having an affair without me knowing?"

Todd glanced towards Elliot as he dug out a batch of recent photographs from his shirt breast pocket and handed them to Elliot. "You don't have to believe me, but you can believe these." Todd then turned his attention back towards the altar as if wanting to give Elliot some emotional space.

Elliot accepted the pictures and, frowning, began to scan through the evidence of Jane's secret life. Todd and Jane looking happy and undeniably in love. Jane and Brydon. Todd, Brydon and Jane. A pit of rage ignited deep down in Elliot's soul, red-hot coals burning through any potential denial. What the fuck? How the fuck? Fucking unbelievable! How could he fucking not know about this? Shit like this just didn't happen in real life. It happened in movies or on television or to other people. It didn't happen to him. Jane loved him. She was his wife. They were supposed to grow old together. All lies? All fucking lies? A few moments ago, Elliot had been here praying for Jane's well-being and now a part of him only wanted her to suffer. Dying under anesthetic was too good for her. She should have been paralyzed. She should have had to spend the rest of her life paying for her betrayal. "All those trips to Toronto were to see you then, not to see Dylan. I never did like that fag." Elliot tore the pictures in half and handed them back to Todd.

    Todd accepted the demolished pictures and nonchalantly tucked them back into his pocket. "They're just copies," he said. He pulled a package of gum out of a side pocket on his shorts and popped a peppermint Chiclet into his hand before popping the gum into his mouth. Todd chewed thoughtfully for a moment before he added, "Dylan's not such a big fan of yours either. If memory serves me correctly, the last hockey game we went to, Dylan referred to you as a homophobic redneck. Anyhow, you can't blame Dylan for this. Using him as a cover story was my idea, not his."

    I'm going to fucking kill you, Elliot thought. "It's bad enough that you're fucking my wife, but the fact that the two of you involved Brydon is unforgivable."

    Todd shoved the package of gum back into his shorts pocket. "Brydon's my son. I wanted to see him. I have a right to see him. When Jane came down a couple of years ago to ask me to give up my parental rights so you could adopt Brydon, it made me realize how much I still loved her, how much I still loved them both. I'm sure you can, at least, understand that much. Jane didn't come looking to have an affair, Elliot. She came down to completely sever all ties with me. I couldn't let that happen. One thing led to another and we started seeing each other again. Elliot, Jane was in the process of leaving you when she was in the car accident."

    Elliot's heart knocked against his ribs unsteadily. Maybe, Jane was having second thoughts and Todd didn't know yet. "She was coming home to me."

Todd shook his head. "To get Brydon. She was coming home to get Brydon because you took her son from Gertie's house, but she didn't plan on staying."

Oh, fuck, Elliot thought. Reality blew past the hot coals with an unstoppable hurricane force. "She's a manipulative, lying bitch. She always has been. The two of you had this planned?"

Todd nodded. "Kind of, but, obviously, Jane wasn't supposed to get hurt in the process. She was on her way to a job interview in New Jersey. We were planning on meeting there then coming back to get Brydon after a couple days. That's why Jane dropped Brydon off at Gertie's.

Elliot, I know this is difficult to hear and you have every right to be angry right now, but, whether or not you like this, Jane is leaving you and we're taking Brydon with us. I just hope that you're man enough to accept that gracefully and let them go. Jane's already been to see a lawyer. She's petitioning for a divorce. She doesn't want anything other than what's hers. She said that, since you bought the house, she's not going to file for half of the matrimonial home. It's all yours. She's grateful for everything that you've done for her and for Brydon, but it's over. All she wants to do is get her and Brydon's belongings out. Oh, and the cat. Jane also wants the cat."

Elliot swallowed hard. He couldn't imagine living in the house without Jane and Brydon. They were his family. His life. Everything he'd done for the past ten years, he'd done for Jane. Everything he'd done for the past four years, he'd done for Jane and for Brydon both. And now? He was just supposed to walk away without a fight? "And if I say no?"

"I've already called Pam who is on her way to your house right now to get Barclay. Jane said you hated the cat anyway, so I'm sure you won't miss him. Otherwise, legally, the house is still half Jane's. She has legal access to the property any time she chooses until the divorce is finalized. If you change the locks, we can get a court order to enter the premises. If you give her any grief at all, we can bring the police with us to oversee the removal of her belongings. Considering that Jane's brother-in-law is a cop, that shouldn't be too difficult to arrange. And, by the way, if any of

Jane's belongings are damaged, you can look forward to destruction of property charges, so I wouldn't get any notions in your head if I were you."

"And Brydon? I'm the only father he's ever known. You abandoned him. You don't deserve to have him. You're nothing but a fucking shadow."

"Actually, Brydon and I have gotten to know each other quite well over the past two years and that's what counts. It's not like he has a lot of memories from the first few years of his life, but I was there the day he was born, and I will continue to be there for him from now on.

In fact, Jane just told Brydon that I'm his real dad, and I'll have to admit, the kid was pretty excited. However, I do realize how much Brydon cares for you, so we want you to maintain visiting rights. It's true that Brydon loves you like a father. That's my fault. I wasn't there for him and you were, so I'll offer you a deal. We are agreeable to supervised visits every other weekend during the transition and, if that goes well, then unsupervised visits and maybe a week over the summer vacation. Since you didn't adopt Brydon, your legal rights are limited here, so I think that's more than fair."

Elliot could feel a migraine beginning at the top of his skull, a pressure pain so great, it threatened to extinguish the scorching coals and the hurricane winds. "And who is going to look after Jane until she's better? She sure as hell can't stay by herself right now or look after Brydon." How could this be happening? How could this fucking asshole, Todd, sit calmly beside him telling him that his life was over?

Todd folded his arms over his chest and leaned back. He turned his head towards Elliot finally facing him. "I've already spoken to her parents. They were a bit shocked by the news, but they are going to move Jane back into their house until she's well enough to get an apartment or to move in with me. I'm hoping Jane will decide to leave Donnybrooke behind for good, but she's pretty adamant that she doesn't want to raise the children in the city, so we'll have a bit of compromising to do. We'll work it out, but that's between us and has nothing to do with you."

Elliot clenched his large hands into fists. He inhaled deeply then let the breath back out again. "I can't fucking believe this."

Todd nodded and faced forward again. "I know how you feel. I had a hard time believing that she married you in the first place. Now we're even."

Trying his best to reign in a temper that was threatening to erupt, Elliot began to lose control. "If we weren't in a chapel, I'd leave you lying in your own blood right now."

Todd shook his head and smiled ruefully. "I don't believe in God, so it wouldn't bother me where we fight. Try if you like, but it won't be me left lying on the floor. I would seriously hate to hurt you, Elliot, and this is a fight you can't possibly win. I'm trained and proficient in several forms of combat, but it's your choice. Take the first swing and end up eating dust or walk away unharmed. Personally, I'd rather shake hands and keep this as civilized as possible."

Right, if memory served him, Todd was into kick boxing or some sort of fucking martial arts or both. Elliot decided he'd have to find another way. "I want a paternity test if the baby survives."

"Understandable, but the best you can hope for is joint custody even if the child is yours. Jane may be a lot of things, but she is also an excellent mother. There's no court that would give you full custody of this baby. Like I said, there's also a very good chance that this baby is mine. I wouldn't get your hopes up too high on this one. I guess we'll deal with that issue once the kid's born. Go home, Elliot. It's over. Jane doesn't want to see you right now. Brydon's staying with me, with Jane's written permission, so he can visit Jane while she's in the hospital. I'm on vacation this week, so I'll make sure he's taken good care of."

The thought of not seeing Brydon was too much, beyond devastating. He should have kept Brydon with him instead of letting Dylan take the boy for lunch and a for matinee movie afterwards, Elliot thought in despair. Fucking Dylan. It'd been a ploy to get Brydon away from him. Had to have been. Away from Elliot and tucked away with Todd. "You could at least let me say goodbye to him."

Todd unfolded his arms, stood up and faced Elliot. "I'll have Brydon call you before he goes to bed."

Elliot stood up to match Todd's height. "You can't do this."

Todd stuck his hands into the front pockets of his shorts. "I just did. It's over, Elliot. Go home. You don't belong here anymore."

	I'm going to fucking kill you, you smug bastard, Elliot thought. Someday, when you least expect it, you will die.

CHAPTER FIFTY-SIX

Todd expelled a deep breath as the elevator doors opened to the fifth floor. He wasn't sure if he had just made the worst mistake or the best decision of his life. He had no doubt that Elliot wasn't about to take the demise of his marriage lightly nor would he make it easy for Jane to liquidate their joint assets. However, none of that mattered right now. What mattered at this exact moment was that Todd had taken action, had made the first step towards the future he intended to claim as his own. His, Jane's and Brydon's future. Together.

Dylan jumped up from his chair as Todd entered the almost abandoned waiting room. "So, how did it go? All of this suspense has been driving me utterly insane!"

Brydon followed Dylan's lead and ran to stand beside Todd. "Todd!" Brydon grabbed three fingers of Todd's much larger hand and started pulling him towards the sitting area where Dylan was standing. "Did you know that Mommy's getting a halo? Dylan said it's not like the halos that angels wear. She won't have wings or have secret angel powers or nothing, but the halo is magical because it'll help Mommy's neck heal. When the halo comes off, Mommy will be good as new!"

Todd focused his attention on Brydon first, bent down and lifted the shorts and t-shirt clad boy into a chair. Todd squatted down in front of Brydon so they could talk, eye to eye. Father to son. "That's great, Brydon, but do you remember how much it hurt when you fell off the slide last summer and broke your arm?"

Brydon nodded and frowned. "It hurt real bad. I couldn't swim or play t-ball for weeks. Worst summer of my whole, entire life."

"Exactly. Well, Champ, that's how your mom is going to feel for the next while. She's going to be very, very sore. She'll be fine, but it's going to take a couple of months for her injuries to heal just like your arm did." Todd kissed Brydon on the forehead. "When she needs to rest, we need to let her sleep. People heal when they're sleeping, so it's important that we don't disturb her just because we want to talk to her. We need to be very patient and wait until she wakes up on her own. She won't be able to do a lot for herself, and you have to be very careful not to run around and bump into her or anything. We need to take extra good care of her right now. Okay?"

Brydon nodded his understanding. "Okay, but when I broke my arm, Mommy made the couch extra comfy with a sleeping bag for the first couple of days and we watched movies and ate chocolate ice cream. Can I do that with her?" The frown disappeared as hope rose.

Todd smiled widely and ruffled Brydon's already unruly hair. "That's an excellent idea, Brydon. I'm sure your mom would love that. For now though, your mom will need to stay in the hospital for a week or so. How would you feel about staying with me for a few days? I'm on vacation this week. You and I can hang out and come visit your mom. There's a swimming pool on the top floor of the building where I live. We can go swimming there every night if you like." The thought of spending quality time alone with his son made Todd's heart lighten. Up until now, their time together had always included Jane. He'd understood that it would take patience to regain Jane's trust, especially where the boy was concerned, but this was the perfect opportunity to take advantage of some much-needed bonding time. Todd would never abandon them again, and this was the perfect chance to prove himself to not only the woman he loved, but to the son he adored.

Brydon hesitated and narrowed his eyes. He tilted his head to the right in the same mannerism of his mother. "Did Mommy and Daddy say it was okay if I stay with you?"

Todd grinned, seeing Jane's reflection before him. "We can ask your mom in a bit, but your dad's not here right now. He had to leave before you and Dylan made it back. He said to say goodbye for him and that he'll see you in a couple of days once he gets everything taken care of at work and has also found someone to look after Barclay." Todd hated lying to the boy, but now was not the time to upset the youngster.

Brydon straightened his head. "Can we call my dad later?"
"Absolutely."

Brydon's expression relaxed. "Okay then, but only if Mommy says it's okay with her. Can we see another movie? They have super huge screens here." Brydon looked towards Dylan who was still standing nearby. "Where did we go to Uncle Dylan?"

"We went to the Imax Theatre, Bry." Dylan said. "The one on Richmond Street," he added for Todd's benefit.

"Right." Brydon nodded then turned back to Todd. "Can we go there again?"

Todd nodded. "Sure, but there's also an Imax theatre at Ontario Place so we can make a day of it and maybe catch a 3-D movie. How does that sound?"

Brydon's face lit up in excitement. "Cool. Can we go to the zoo too? There's this guy there who can get birds to do all kinds of neat tricks. When we went to the zoo last summer, Mommy said we couldn't see everything in one day, so we'd have to see the bird show the next time. I think she was worried that I'd get too tired out because my arm was in a cast. I kept telling her that I was fine, but you know Mommy. She worries a lot."

"Sure."

"How about Wonderland? Can we go to Wonderland? I'm big enough to go on some of the really cool rides now. Not just the kid stuff."

Todd chuckled. "Whoa there, Champ. How about you pick two places that you really want to go to and we'll concentrate on that? After all, we want to spend some time with your mom too, right?" Smart kid, Todd thought. Take advantage of the new guy.

"Okay. I hope Mom says yes."

"Me too, Champ. I need to talk to Dylan for a minute. All right?"

"Yup." Brydon reached out and gave Todd a hug then turned his attention back to a hand-held, baseball videogame that he had tossed on the chair beside him when Todd had entered the room. "I'm on level three. That's my favourite level of all times. Maybe we can do two-player later and I can teach you?" Brydon looked up at Todd with bright eyes masking any fear and sorrow that he may have been feeling.

Todd grinned. "As long as you promise to take it easy on me. Deal?"

"Deal." Brydon turned on his game and immersed himself in the world of make believe. Batter up!

Todd stood back up and turned towards Dylan. "Need a

coffee?"

"Sure." Dylan played along.

The family resemblance never ceased to amaze Todd. Brydon could just as easily pass as Dylan's son as he could for Jane's. Dylan had the same wavy blonde hair, the same finely cut features, the same tall, slim but strong build and the same hazel eyes. Dylan's youthful, boy-next-door good looks had made him a favourite for commercial work and, occasionally, for modeling assignments. As his portfolio had fattened, Dylan was offered small parts on a few locally produced television programs and finally landed a recurring, support role on *Mafia's Blues*, a crime show based on Private Detective/Blues Musician, Mafia Jones, solving a plethora of cases that the local Toronto Police Service was unable to crack. Dylan played Mafia's side-kick and computer-geek counterpart. The program's ratings were excellent and the network had, not only renewed the program for another season, but syndicated the show to several major players in the United States market as well.

The role had been a major breakthrough for Dylan who was finally able to not only pay his share of the rent on time, but to prove to his family that all of his years of waiting and hard work had finally paid off. Undoubtedly, hundreds of hopeful female fans were devastated when Dylan announced that he was in a committed gay relationship-- such was life in the arts. Dylan had made it very clear early on to the network and to his publicist, that he would not play the available bachelor routine just to pad ratings. Thus far, Dylan's overt honesty seemed to be working. He had an ever-growing fan-base, homosexuals and heterosexuals alike.

Hazel. Dylan's eyes were not green like Jane's; they were hazel. Therefore, Brydon had inherited his eye colouring honestly from his mother's side as well. Crap. Maybe, somewhere down the line, Brydon would show a trait that was uniquely his instead of his mother's and then Todd would feel like a small part of the team.

"Has Jane made it back from the recovery room yet?" Todd asked Dylan as the two walked over to a vending machine to put a little talking distance between them and Brydon. Todd dug change out from his shorts pocket, deposited the coins and chose a plastic bottle of orange juice to give to Brydon.

Dylan shook his fair head as he grabbed a coffee from the machine beside. "Not yet. The last time I checked, the nurse said it would be about another half hour or so. Mom and Dad are with Jane, but the nurse said that two people were the limit so I offered to wait here with Brydon. So, come on. I'm dying here. How did it go with Elliot?"

Todd retrieved the bottle from the vending machine dispenser. "Better than I anticipated, but I'm sure he'll cause more than his share of problems once Jane gets home. He's not going to risk causing a scene in public even if he's plenty pissed off right now. I told him that it was over and that Jane had already seen a lawyer about getting a divorce."

Dylan frowned. "Odd that she never mentioned that part to me. Normally, she tells me just about everything."

Todd turned and leaned his back on the vending machine. "Technically speaking, she hasn't, but Elliot doesn't need to know that. I just had to make it very clear that this was the end of the line for him." *Adios Amigo. Ciao Baby. Goodbye. Good riddance.*

Dylan took a tentative sip of the coffee and grimaced slightly at the bitter brew. "I've known Elliot all of my life, and I can guarantee that this isn't over. He'll do everything within his power to make your life and Jane's life miserable. I'm still not sure it was the best idea to handle this here, but I would have given almost anything to see the look on his face when you produced the photographs."

Todd stared at Brydon as the boy sat intensely focused on his game. "Yeah, it was pretty classic. Thanks for the suggestion. I had no choice but to do it now. I couldn't let Jane become totally dependent on Elliot for the next three months. She'd feel too guilty to leave him after that. It was now or never. Did you reach Pam?"

Dylan nodded. "Yup. She has a spare key to their house and said she'd be more than happy to grab Barclay. None of us totally trust Elliot with the cat anyway, so it's better that he's in a safe place. Pam's kids will probably spoil Barclay so badly that he won't want to come home."

"And what did your mom and dad say?"

Dylan sniggered softly. "Before or after Mom fainted and Dad picked his jaw off the floor?"

"After." The last thing Todd wanted to do was to cause waves within the family. He wasn't sure how close Jane's parents were to Elliot, but Todd had to hope that he would eventually be accepted within their ranks as Elliot's replacement. Todd felt a bit like of a jerk having Dylan break the news this way, especially when Jane was so vulnerable, but, again, drastic times called for drastic measures. Jane needed a strong support system right now, and Todd refused to be shut out, hundreds of kilometres away, at the mercy of Dylan or Gertie feeding him occasional updates. From now on, Jane and Brydon would be the center of his universe.

"That Jane and Brydon can stay with them as long as she wants. Personally, I think Mom will be happier with Jane under her watchful eye until the halo comes off. Besides which, Elliot has a lot of respect for my parents. He may be more open to dealing with them when it comes to getting a few of Jane's personal items from the house. Elliot puts up a good front. He'll keep his social face shiny for them, hoping that they'll either take his side or feel sorry for him. And I wouldn't worry about Mom and Dad if I were you. They know how much Jane loved you so the initial shock will pass. They may not agree with their daughter's way of handling things, but, in the end, they both just want to see her happy and healthy."

"Thanks for all of your help, Dylan."

"My pleasure. I always thought that Jane could do better than Elliot. Welcome to the family, Todd."

"Excuse me," a young, petite, black-haired nurse interjected as she walked up to the conversation. "Jane is back in her room now if you want to see her. She's still pretty groggy, so please don't stay too long. She needs to rest."

"Thank you." Dylan nodded at the nurse then turned to Brydon and held out his hand. "Come on, Kiddo. Let's go see your mom."

"Yay!" Brydon smiled, tossed the videogame onto the chair beside him and sped towards them.

"And bring your game with you or someone else will walk off with it," Dylan scolded good-naturedly.

"Right." Brydon spun back and grabbed the game before turning around again and running over to Dylan. He grabbed his uncle's hand. "Are you coming too, Todd?"

"Wouldn't miss it for the world, Champ," Todd assured the boy. Todd longed to tell the boy that he was his father, even though he knew, deep down, that this was not the time. The time would come when he and Jane could sit down together with Brydon and explain the truth. Not today but soon.

As they entered Jane's room, Todd caught his breath. He hadn't been prepared to see Jane looking so fragile. The halo looked ominous, like something straight out of an Inquisition torture chamber, the incision on her neck was covered by a large, white bandage and her right arm was bound tightly overtop her pale blue gown by a beige fabric sling. He exhaled, swallowed hard and put on his brightest smile to conceal his shock. They would get through this. Jane would heal. The halo would come off. They would start over. They would watch their children grow up. They would take each day as it came. Eventually, they would grow old together. Todd vowed never to waste another moment of their time in doubt or in fear. He would take the rainbow by its tail and twist out the pot of gold. He was even willing to consider that maybe, just maybe, there was a god after all.

The head of Jane's bed had been raised so she was basically sitting up at a relaxed angle. She smiled weakly as they neared her. "Hi, guys."

"Hi, Jane." Todd managed to force out. Lame. Crap. Flowers. I should have brought flowers, he thought. Okay. Breathe, Todd told himself. She's still the same woman she was yesterday. Just breathe.

Brydon released Dylan's hand and sped to his mother's side. With all bravery gone now, he began to softly cry. He crawled up onto the bed beside her, snuggling into her and placed his small arm protectively over her stomach. "I love you, Mommy. Please be better soon."

Jane reached down and stroked Brydon's hair. "I love you too, Bry. Please don't cry, Sweetie. It's not as bad as it looks. Just seeing you makes all of the pain go away."

"Hey, Brat," Dylan added. "You gave us quite the scare. How are you feeling? Really?"

Jane continued to stroke her son's hair. "Kind of like I've been walking around all day with a chicken on my head."

Dear Reader,

    First of all, I want to thank you for spending the time to read my book. Personally, I love to read; I love to escape into the other worlds that the stories provide. However, writing this story was not an escape for me. It was a way of looking back on my life and honouring my journey. Although the characters and the situations are fictitious, the common thread of abuse was all too real in my life for far too many years. To be very clear (before I receive a myriad of e-mails complaining that Jane did not report her abusers), I do not advocate silence as far as abuse is concerned. If you are being abused or have suffered abuse in the past, please break the silence and tell someone. I chose group therapy to put the pieces of my life back together. Whatever you choose to do to heal has to be the right step for you. Good luck and know that I am there with you in spirit.

    In reality, I started writing this story over twenty-five years ago, but with being a single parent and working, sometimes seven days a week, finding the time to concentrate on creative writing was not a priority. My children were. As my Grandma Kaufman was fond of saying, "The dust can wait, the children can't."

    After my children grew up and left home, I decided to dust off the manuscript and revisit Jane. So much has changed in the world since I began writing this novel, especially the technology (we didn't have personal computers and cell phones when I was studying broadcasting in college), that it was a necessary task to update and rewrite the entire story. The result was a hundred times better than the original, and as various characters, like Constable Jeff Thornton, popped onto the scene totally out of the blue, I had to trust that there was a reason for their sudden appearance.

    My son, Brandon, was born while I was in college under less traumatic circumstances. During our second year, our class wrote and produced a half-hour program that went out on local cable television once a week. As my pregnancy progressed, I was unable to do many of the physical jobs like climbing up ladders to do lighting, so my teacher, in his ultimate wisdom, assigned me to writing and finally, directing three shows. During my final show as director, I was unknowingly in labour and sat the whole time in the control room switching a hot water bottle from my front to my back trying to alleviate the pains. Brandon was born the next day, five weeks early.

I want to take a moment to thank my college friends for helping me get through that portion of my life. You were my support, my family, my sanity and I don't know what Brandon and I would have done without you. Special mention goes out to: Les Novosel and his mother, Anne, (both deceased now) who took us under their wings and fed us constantly; Tom Lee who, despite our many differences, was always there when I needed a friend; Ralph Richardson who was the technical counterpart to my creative endeavours; Rhonda McCutcheon-Flanagan who looked at our radio announcing teacher, Alan Leith, and assured him that we actually did speak like that where I come from ("Hang on. I'll fallaya back te yer house for a cuppa tea.") and Sheryl Davis, both of whom were constants in my sea of chaos and have remained life-long friends. I'd like to extend an eternal thank you to Penny and Jim Davis for adopting Brandon and me and for treating us like family.

A special note about Alan Leith who passed away in 2013. While I was in school, he was gracious enough to take me into his office at the end of first year and tell me that the only way he wouldn't fail me in radio was if I promised to major in television. Knowing how truly bad I was in radio, I just smiled and took the deal. Thanks again, Al, for the second chance.

And, last but not least, I'm sending a warm hug to Kathleen Roth-Pahl, an amazing friend for many years. I miss you and hope that you are doing well.

As for Jane and Gertie, their stories will continue on…

The Women of Donnybrooke: Gertie's Keeper Of The Hill

(Coming Soon)

CHAPTER ONE

Mitchell knew instinctively that there was something desperately wrong as soon as he turned into his inclined laneway. The century old, two-storey, yellow brick farmhouse he called home sat forebodingly dark. At eight p.m., there should have been lights on in the living room. Even when no one was at home, they always left one light on. Thankful for his four-wheel drive truck, Mitchell carefully plowed through errant snowdrifts as he crept his way up the slippery slope that led to a four-car parking area on the crest directly across from the house. Yes, there was definitely something amiss. The laneway wasn't plowed, Kelly's vehicle was gone and the house looked abandoned. Three very bad signs indeed.

Mitchell loved his fifty acre farm. Tucked away on a side road just outside of Donnybrooke, he had chosen the location when he moved up from Toronto back in his bad old days thinking that living on top of a hill presented the advantage of being able to see any potential police cars speeding down the township road towards him. His mother, a brilliant mechanical engineer and an Olympic calibre markswoman who had given Mitchell his first handgun as a present for his sixteenth birthday, had happily covered the exorbitant tuition costs to pay for her son's Bachelor's Degree in Chemistry. A gifted student who, unfortunately, was not cut out for the tedious confines of a typical lab setting, Mitchell had forgone his Master's Degree and accepted an offer to put his abundant knowledge to use cooking MDMA instead. The promised money had just been too good to refuse.

Then came one chilly Wednesday afternoon when his partner in crime, Bob, had went outside to take a leak. Running back into the house, flustered with his fly still open, he had breathlessly announced that he just seen a line of five, unmarked, black SUVs drive past and turn into their neighbours' laneway. Mitchell quickly sent his then-girlfriend, Wanda, to scout out what was happening.

When she called from her car to warn him that it was a raid, Mitchell and Bob had went to work expediently and efficiently to dismantle their small lab and to destroy or to hide what evidence they could on short notice. As luck would have it, their last batch of MDMA had been picked up two days before, and, deciding that they needed a couple of days off, they hadn't started to make another.

By the time the police had realized the lab's location had been botched and had profusely apologized to the elderly couple next door for almost giving them mutual heart attacks, Mitchell and Bob had loaded up both of their pickup trucks and were heading to the back of the farm towards a still water sink hole that lay just beyond his property line. He'd been warned by his neighbour, when he had first moved in, to stay out of the water. What looked like a normal, small pond was not that at all. His neighbour had tossed a paper cup into the middle to demonstrate, and Mitchell had watched, mesmerized, as the cup began to circle around then had finally disappeared, pulled under by an unseen current.

The two friends unloaded Mitchell's truck first then he went back to the house in the attempt to stall the inevitable. There was no use running. Whoever had tipped off the Drug Enforcement Unit obviously knew what they were doing. His affiliates would be furious by the loss of the ingredients and by the loss of the equipment; however, Mitchell had enough money secretly tucked away now to, hopefully, buy his way back out of this mess if he could just survive the raid.

Parking his truck behind the large, grey barn, Mitchell had worked his way stealthily around the side of the building just in time to watch the same five SUVs drive up his narrow, gravel laneway and come to a halt. He took a deep breath, fastened on a look of bewildered concern and walked out to greet them. When asked if he was Mitchell Whelan, Mitchell had nodded and admitted that he was. When informed of their intentions and handed the warrant to search the house and the property, Mitchell had complied saying that they were welcome to search all they wanted. He had nothing to hide. When he was asked to kneel down on the lawn and to place his hands behind his head while the search was being conducted, Mitchell had also complied. He wasn't fool enough to run thus providing provocation for violence when he was trying to maintain his innocence. Above all, Mitchell hoped that Bob would be smart enough to stay out of sight at the back of the farm until the raid was over and the ten, well-armed officers were no longer a threat.

Two hours later, after scouring the house, the barn and the smaller equipment shed, the team had gathered what evidence they could find which consisted of supposed residue samples and one glass beaker that Mitchell had somehow managed to overlook. Mitchell had calmly waited to see if he would be handcuffed and taken away. Instead, he was informed that formal charges were still pending, and that he was not to leave the province at this time. Mitchell had nodded, politely asked if it was now okay for him to stand up and admitted that his hands were tingling so badly that he could barely feel his fingers. He sighed in gratitude and said thank you when he was told that, yes, he was free to stand. As he rose, Mitchell fought back an urge to smile and diligently worked to keep his face as blank as possible.

Whistling softly, Mitchell strolled into his house as he watched the SUVs leave, walked over to his refrigerator and grabbed a beer. He sat down at his wooden kitchen table and waited awhile before Bob reappeared, still ashen from the experience. Bob quickly grabbed another beer from the refrigerator and joined his friend.

Wanda, who had taken only her purse with her, had left everything else she owned behind and kept on driving. After a couple of weeks, Mitchell gave up waiting for his girlfriend to return and donated her clothing to the Salvation Army. He never heard from her again.

In the end, formal charges were never laid due to the lack of evidence. Almost fifteen years later, Mitchell was still walking the straight and narrow. Much to his mother's chagrin, he had stashed away his degree in chemistry, opted for trade school instead and now proudly displayed his mechanic's diploma and license on his living room wall.

After Wanda had left and Bob had taken off for a new gig, Mitchell had grown lonely on the farm by himself. Kelly had been a pretty little thing back then, small at 5'4" and 115 pounds, she was amazingly strong for her size and had a spitfire personality that made him chuckle. He had known all about her reputation, and she had known all about his. And, to be honest, he wasn't about to take up with some sweet, church-going woman who would undoubtedly drag him off to Sunday services in the attempt to save his soul. Growing up with Irish Catholic parents, Mitchell had all of the religion he could take for one lifetime. Kelly had accepted Mitchell for who he was back then when the local gossip had practically crucified him. So, instead of selling the farm and moving on, Mitchell had married Kelly and put down roots. It had never been about love for him. It had been about his need for personal redemption.

    Today was Valentine's Day. Mitchell wasn't a romantic man by nature; he was pragmatic at best. Normally, he didn't buy his wife long-stemmed, red roses and lavish boxes of chocolates or take her out to a fancy restaurant for candle-lit dinners, but Kelly always insisted on spending the evening of Valentine's Day together regardless even if it just meant opening a cheap bottle of wine and renting a movie to watch. The fact that she hadn't contacted him during the week with a plan had struck him as being rather odd. Not that he cared really, but it did make him more than slightly curious.

    When his curiosity had finally gotten the best of him, he'd tried calling. No answer on the land line and no answer on Kelly's cell phone. If it wasn't for his children, Mitchell would have happily let the anomaly pass without worrying; but, he loved his kids-- Anna and Kieran were the center of his universe — even if, nowadays, he barely tolerated his wife. She was the mother of his babies and he made sure that she had a home, adequate clothing on her back, the basic necessities of life and enough food to eat, but that's where it ended. Still, he couldn't shake the sinking feeling that Kelly had made good on her last weekend's screamed promise. After all, she'd threatened to leave many times before but had never actually followed through. Thus, against his better judgement that driving for over two hours in the midst of a blizzard was probably a serious lapse in sanity, he'd set out to do just that. He had to know for sure one way or another. It wasn't just Kelly he'd be losing, it was his children.

    Mitchell shut off his vehicle, grabbed a small flashlight from an interior storage compartment, zippered up his green parka, put on his black leather gloves and climbed out into shin-deep snow drifts. If this nasty weather continued, he'd be lucky if he wasn't stuck in the morning. At best, he was looking forward to a few hours of shoveling just to turn his truck around.

Pregnant clouds covered the stars and the moon, making visibility through the blowing snow almost nil. Mitchell switched on the light, pulled his parka's hood over his head to protect his ears from the bitter wind and nostril-clenching temperatures as he trudged towards the house. No lights on. No smoke coming out of the chimney. No Anna, no Kieran running out of the side door to greet him. No barking dog. Damn.

Mitchell stopped and let out an eardrum-piercing whistle in case the five-year-old, male shepherd/collie cross was curled up asleep somewhere in the barn and hadn't heard him drive in. They'd adopted Fogerty from the animal shelter after Mitchell had finally given in to Anna's insistent request for a pet. Kelly hadn't wanted the responsibility of cleaning up after a puppy or of training one; therefore, adopting an adult dog had seemed like the perfect compromise. Anna had been over-the-hill excited the day they had driven into Owen Sound to look at potential additions to their family. Kieran, who was only three-years-old at the time, had been really too young to fully understand, but he'd gotten caught up in his sister's excitement nonetheless.

On arrival at the animal shelter, Anna grabbed her brother by his small, pudgy hand, and they ran full speed towards the door before Mitchell could change his mind. Once inside, Anna surveyed the penned creatures carefully while Kieran half hid behind her, suddenly intimidated by the loud barking.

Mitchell watched patiently and discussed the various canines with the attendant. He wanted to know the ages, whether or not they were neutered, house broken and if they liked cats. They had several barn cats that weren't allowed in the house, but he wanted to make sure of their safety just the same.

Anna stopped in front of Fogerty's pen and bent down to talk to the dog that calmly returned her attention and wagged his tail. He was the only animal not barking. When she held her hand to him, palm up as Mitchell had shown her, Fogerty sniffed then gently licked the soft skin. Anna immediately turned to her dad and gave him two thumbs up. "This one, Daddy. Can we have this one?"

Mitchell walked over to greet the dog himself and read the name on the card. "Fogerty. That's a good Irish name. It says that he's a year-old, likes children and cats, is neutered, has his shots and is house-trained." Mitchell turned to the attendant. "Why was he given up?"

"It's a sad story, really." The young, female attendant walked towards them. "The owner ended up with cancer and was too ill to keep him. Fogerty, by the way, means exiled. Ironic, don't you think?" She smiled and turned towards Anna. "So, do you want to take him for a walk and see how that goes before you decide to adopt him?"

"Yes, please!" Anna exclaimed. She turned to hug Mitchell while the attendant went for a lead. "Daddy, Fogerty's perfect! I promise to feed him and to make sure he has water and to play with him and to walk him every day as soon as I get home from school."

Mitchell chuckled, knowing that Anna would do exactly that. He had no doubt whatsoever that it would be Anna, not Kelly, who looked after Fogerty.

Turning towards the barn, Mitchell yelled loudly, his voice getting lost in the wind, "Fogerty!" He whistled again and waited awhile. Nothing. Maybe, he's inside, Mitchell thought.

Mitchell turned back towards the house and continued his journey. No lights, no smoke, no kids, no vehicles, no dog. His stomach clenched as he reached his door and dug his key chain out of his jacket pocket. He kicked the snow from his boots, quickly walked through the closed-in summer porch, unlocked the wooden main door and stepped into his large, empty kitchen. He did a brief scan with his flashlight then flicked on the switch for the overhead. He turned off the flashlight and tucked it into his jacket side pocket. Empty. The room was almost completely empty. He swallowed as reality hit home. No refrigerator, no electric stove, no oak, harvest table, no matching press back chairs, no antique, pine hutch that he'd painstakingly refinished, no pictures on the blue-flower wallpapered walls. They were gone. Everyone, everything was gone.

He could see his breath as he moved around the room. He whistled again just in case Fogerty was somewhere inside. Nothing but the cold to greet him. Kelly had turned off the heat as well. It was a sure way to make the pipes freeze. Mitchell frowned, walked over to the wall thermostat and turned the oil furnace back on. At least she'd left the wood cook stove behind, and he had several cords of wood split in the woodshed. He'd start a fire later. Right now, he just wanted to make sure that the water pipes didn't burst. If he had waited until the weekend to come home, it could have been brutal. Kelly's idea of payback for some imagined wrong no doubt. Her last laugh on him.

Mitchell walked over to the cupboards and began opening the oak doors and pulling open drawers. The dishes were gone. The utensils were gone. The food was gone. The pots and pans were gone. All that was left was a bowl with six eggs that she'd left on the center island. Eggs with no pan to fry them in and no pot to boil them in. Good thing that he'd eaten on his way up from Toronto and had brought beer with him. He'd dig out in the morning and head into town for supplies once the weather settled down.

A whine and a scratch at the outside door caught Mitchell's attention. Fogerty, he thought. Kelly had left him behind after all. Poor mutt. Poor Anna. She'd be heartbroken. He hoped that Kelly had at least enough decency to leave food out for Fogerty in the barn. Otherwise, he could have starved. Mitchell sped towards the door to let the dog into the slowly warming house.

"Fogerty! Hey, Buddy!" Mitchell bent down to greet the confused animal. Fogerty wagged his tail but his eyes looked sad, lost. Mitchell squatted down and brushed the snow off of his friend's sleek fur. "It's okay, Pal. I'm here now. You'll be okay." Fogerty licked Mitchell's face, barked once in response then moved past him into the kitchen. He looked around, sat down and began to whine again.

Mitchell walked over to the island and carefully removed the brown eggs from the large, plastic, white bowl and set them down on the cutting board top. He cracked two eggs open and dumped the contents into the bowl, stirring the slimy gloop around with his index finger. Not sure of the last time Fogerty had eaten anything, he placed the bowl in front of the anxiously waiting canine. "It's not much, but that's the best I can do until tomorrow."

Fogerty sniffed then lapped the eggs up greedily. After licking the bowl clean, he lay down with his head on his paws on the cold tile floor. His tail thumped twice, his eyes closed and he drifted off to sleep.

Geba watched intently as Mitchell worked his way through the rest of the vacant house. She wasn't sorry to see the woman leave. Geba would miss the children, but the woman was an abomination.

ABOUT THE AUTHOR

Avrie Kaufman grew up on a farm in rural Ontario and now lives in a small house a half block from nowhere. She is, according to her daughter, only boring in real life.

Please feel free to send your positive comments and feedback regarding this novel to **AvrieKaufman@gmail.com** or check out her Facebook page online.

Made in the USA
Charleston, SC
12 September 2013